Author's note: in the spirit of this novel, written entirely by the author, the back cover summary was interpreted by ChatGPT3.5 (*in italics*):

"Artificial Intelligence tames the globe as "binary" democracy takes hold, but not all are compliant."

The opening statement sets the stage for a world where the influence of Artificial Intelligence has become pervasive, reshaping society and governance. The phrase 'binary democracy' suggests a simplified, mechanistic form of governance, where decisions might be based on a binary code of ones and zeros, reflecting the rise of AI-powered systems.

"Richard Boneheart's followers launch a starship to the Centauri system, hoping to safeguard mankind's future. Six astronauts with mixed agendas share a voyage of consequence."

Richard Boneheart and his followers represent a group of people who are skeptical or resistant to the changes brought about by AI. They embark on a daring mission to the Centauri system, possibly seeking to preserve humanity's autonomy and future away from the control of AI. The six astronauts, each with their own motivations and intentions, are embarking on a journey with significant implications for the fate of humanity.

"Evolution? Devolution? Perhaps a hybrid existence awaits us all?"

This line ponders the potential outcomes of humanity's journey. Will they evolve, adapt, and thrive in this new AI-influenced world? Or will they regress and lose some essential aspects of their humanity? The mention of a "hybrid existence" hints at the possibility of a future where humans and AI coexist in a complex and intertwined manner.

"Meanwhile, Boneheart stays behind, facing an adversary that ciphers a forward reckoning. It's primal instinct pitted against informatica: all that's been and what's to come; disparate worlds sharing causal loops of histories near and far."

As Boneheart remains on Earth, he confronts an unknown adversary who seems to possess the ability to predict the future. This adversary represents the growing dominance of AI, which can analyze vast amounts of data to forecast events. In contrast, Boneheart's primal instincts and intuition stand in opposition to the cold calculations of AI, as they navigate the intertwining of the past, present, and future.

"In a distant courtroom, Judge McElroy presides as testimony tells the tale: a mindful planet, the Health Authority plotting futures in advance, and free peoples making a journey that nudges the fates."

The introduction of Judge McElroy in a courtroom implies a significant conflict between different forces in this world. The "mindful planet" suggests a world where ecological consciousness and environmental awareness have gained prominence. The "Health Authority" symbolizes an influential body that aims to control and shape humanity's future through AI-driven planning. In contrast, free peoples are actively taking their own path, attempting to influence the unfolding events.

"Eyeing the defendant, McElroy can only lament, "Why me?" It is both knowing and unknowing, a heartfelt decree. This is McElroy's Plea."

Judge McElroy is presented as a conflicted character who feels burdened by the gravity of the case before them. The phrase "both knowing and unknowing" signifies the complexity of the situation, where the judge is aware of the vast implications of the trial but may not fully comprehend the depths of the conflict between AI-driven progress and human autonomy. McElroy's plea reflects the internal struggle and heartfelt concern for making the right decision that may shape the future of humanity.

The author asks, as the moment arrives when the efforts of man and machine become indistinguishable (no doubt, to placate our sensibilities), where does that leave us?

McElroy's Plea
The memoirs of Richard Boneheart

S M Werner

This is a work of fiction. All characters, organizations, and events are either products of the author's imagination, or are used fictitiously.

McElroy's Plea

Copyright © 2023 by Scott Michael Werner

All rights reserved.

No part of this book may be reproduced, or stored in a retrieval system, or transmitted in any form or by any means, electronic, mechanical, photocopying, recording, or otherwise, without the express written permission of the publisher.

ISBN 979-8-218-25489-6

Variable Star Publishing
Typeface: Georgia

Thank you: Sue Lukas-Werner, readers Roy Werner, Monica Naples, Steve Badamo, and particularly Craig Watanabe and Jonathan Toland for various contributions. A special thanks to Kim for the front and back cover art.

To my darling...

PROLOGUE

Guilt and innocence equally tithed, sharing lines on an old man's face. Upper teeth snag lower lip almost a bite. For Judge Sir Gabriel McElroy, this is a tell of recognition. A steady jaw accents tabletop vibration and the hum of long dormant engines newly revived. "*Nomad*," he says, glancing through text while trying to jostle memories. It is a failed exercise.

Decades have passed since the flats had last been warmed, turning all to mud, allowing the Rocosphere dome to break the surface. No ceremony accompanied the light of day. Only radiation greeted this orb, now free of the protective muck, exposed to emissions from the largest planet in the Centauri system. Gas Giant Lex Luthor sloughs off energy in massive sheets, radiation beating down upon the Rocosphere with the contempt any citizen would gladly show the defendant. A protective energy field crackles intermittently, splintering deadly rays into little more than borealis.

"*Nomad*," Judge McElroy says again, eyeing written testimony while attempting recall of what is now a starship husk. An inkling of buoyant flight flickers inside. "Heresy," he jibes, but in the coming days, the very text he mocks will define *Nomad's* history, this former vessel cannibalized long ago. Only *Nomad's* engines retain a semblance of their original functionality. They produced the energy that melted the mud and allowed the Rocosphere to reemerge. These same engines now generate shielding for all in attendance—adaptive shielding intended to restrain the defendant as necessary. This is the singular reason today's proceedings are taking place here. To contain a perceived threat. To contain me.

Inside this courtroom, freakish glare penetrates the Rocosphere's crystalline exoskeleton. Spectators share a collective hue of subdued violence as faces nearest the wall's curvature shown of indigo. Mid-distant from the orb's center, privileged attendees are bathed in amber tones. Whether perched upon railings at mid-center, or hanging by filaments from rafters above, humans join in animal companionship. It is much like an aerie of roosting bats, simple-minded, singularly consumed and hinting of fury.

My augmentations filter nonessential stimuli, and yet I find it difficult to ignore the smattering of luminescent sponge weave—old speak cotton candy. Each bundle bristles in a ghastly glow: light absorption, concentration and escape; torches of irritating spun sugar, nearly every child has one. Nearest these edible toys, one can best observe the glint of naso-confetti, clumping and swirling in currents designed for healthy respiration. If the gallery discharges much more of this mild psycho-active, the courtroom will be emptied and flushed yet again.

At the center of this proceeding, a spacious globule of white light magnifies the contents within. McElroy is here, his sentiment scarcely masked beneath abundant ashen facial hair. Adjacent to him—my corporeal form, both of our bodies seated atop a pulpit armature hanging in mid-air. All related structures, including the prosecutor's bench and spiral walkway are supported by spokes that radiate from a central spire into the crowd. Up and down, all about, these spokes draw viewing lines inward. Eyes trance into the white light and focus thus. "To the nines then," McElroy announces, commencing the formal legal process. "Be reminded, this is a court of law. Misconduct shall not only incur my wrath, but also profit from our laws, indiscretions duly noted and set upon a righteous path."

Crowd noise diminishes only slightly. Also ignoring the Judge's admonition, assassins settle in the upper reaches of this sold-out venue: three snipers within sleeved entrenchments, triangulating chemical projectile weapons of singular utility. With no potential for electronic interface, my response is equally crude. Packets of plasma-drenched motiles surge from within, coursing along an armature strut directly into the Rocosphere's exoskeleton. There, the motiles alter a crystalline surface, reconstituted as lens. Lex Luthor's rays are redirected, lasered bandwidths of non-visible spectrum engage the primary assassin. Micro-perforations of brain tissue cause a hiccup, followed by nausea. The injured man recoils, yanking away goggles while squinting. He is rendered ineffectual.

"Silence!" McElroy shouts, unaware of my current engagement. Noise abates as shifting bodies shield the second assassin from direct assault. I target a nearby filament, fraying its edges while splitting the beam, sending the greater portion of the beam directly through the upper garment of an elderly female none too pleased. A small patch of skin burns beneath her fifth rib. The lesser portion of the split beam finds an optical scope, ablating the second assassin's retina. He yelps and scurries away. The third assassin flees before remediation is necessary.

"Much better, and I thank you," the Judge declares. His monocula processes text, shortening verbiage, helping to expedite. Surveying the courtroom, his thoughts drift to a granddaughter's recent nightmare; a moan, a hug, and restless agitation all combine to leave him short of sleep and lacking an attention span. Raising the hinged monocula, he rubs an eye. These proceedings promise a migraine most unkind. "Why me?" he thinks upon a whisper. I absorb this remark wearing a singular deadpan gaze that will cover this world in the coming days: no menace, just vacated emptiness, vacuum a la mode. It will surely be unnerving.

"Gibberish," McElroy mumbles while mouthing his pipe, but the ember within has died. Tapping ash, his countenance is challenged by what seems to be an unorthodox defense. Naples is the prosecuting attorney. She doesn't like this either. Muted tones abate as his Judgeship queries.

"Am I to understand this... this... rather lengthy submission is your plea? No verbal testimony? No legal representation?" The Judge twitches like a farmhand with ear blight, gritting teeth, touching his jaw. "Can't be that simple." Indeed, my response leaves a moment hanging in midair, anxious air that all inhale but none allows escape with an attached voice.

"No, your Honor, I make no plea. Citing civil welfare statutes, I waive my right to a jury trial. The submission now before you constitutes nearly my entire body of evidence, the full measure of which will be offered at your discretion."

"Most irregular... Welfare statutes, predating the reformation. An entire defense based upon archaic legal idiom." McElroy nearly smiles, appreciative of what he deems a misguided approach. Unclipping the monocula, lowering eyeglasses, earphone and microphone, the touchpad and gavel are pushed aside. "Let us make sure we understand one another." He raises a text I had given him twelve minutes prior. "Your defense is this book, and nothing more?" The Judge need only hear my affirmation and these proceedings are near a merciful end.

"No, your Honor, it is not a defense in the conventional sense. The civil welfare statutes dictate plebiscite is necessary to bring this matter to a proper conclusion."

Plebiscite: a vote of the people.

Sixty crisscrossed rows chitter to and fro, sixty sweeping angled aisles packed on all sides. The murmur gathers in intensity, punctuated most brazenly by one attendee who simply utters "Bullshit!" McElroy slams the gavel, glaring first in proximity of the offending voice, thereafter peering at me as though admonishing an insular bore. "Yes, the welfare statutes indeed mention the use of plebiscite, but that was homestead law enacted during early colonization. Those statutes are no longer recognized." What amounts to an intrigue sifts through those gathered. Mild laughter is cut short by my reply.

"Your Honor, while suffering from neglect, perhaps disuse might be more appropriate, these homestead laws remain valid to this very day. No revisions, no enactments curtail their principles or intended usage. In lieu of oral testimony, I am entitled to submit written testimony to be voted upon by plebiscite." The Judge's lips twist grimly. Raising an arm, softening the din, he restores eye glasses and monocula, peering at a readout in the affirmative. My claims are validated by the court's datacheck. Prosecutor Naples gathers herself and approaches the bench.

"This is absurd! Just how many are expected to vote here?" Judge and prosecutor share a look, searching for an alternative that neither supply. Finally, McElroy responds. "...everyone. Everyone will vote." He picks up the text, viewing the title for the very first time. *McElroy's Plea*.

Impossible. It had been a blank cover when he first looked at it. Hadn't it? With a tightening grip he glares. "You expect every inhabitant to read this book?" I nod in affirmation. Even a bobbing of the head is bothersome. Plebiscite or not, we've entered the realm of show trial or some equivalent, and at a distance, latent purpose not yet revealed. His Judgeship plies additional points of contention. "This written testimony leaves one guessing. You begin with 'The Hierophant.' Is this an admission of guilt? There's no formal structure here. Datacheck balks at proper dissemination."

"Sir, as you are well aware, plebiscite submissions require no legal formatting. The testimony's initial narratives are inferred character references; foundational memories from disparate moments of genesis, now conjoined within me. 'The crux of the biscuit,' I believe, is the appropriate colloquialism."

"Datacheck suggests your testimony is little more than disjointed exposition, lacking proper attribution, not to mention the physical oddity of this submission?" I state the hardback given to the judge contains read-only text. Once characters appear on the individual illumid sheets, they cannot be removed nor altered. Even the typeface is unfamiliar.

"Your Honor, to facilitate the requirement of delivering the full body of testimony, I employ use of the technology thus presented. Only moments ago, using wireless interface, I chose a title for this testimony based upon your earlier comment. I thought it appropriate and I thank you."

My comment? *McElroy's Plea*? I'm McElroy! What's going on here? The Judge's internal monologue shares disquiet with the corners of his mouth. Dry, unwilling flesh. A recess is needed. Attempting to stand, then thinking better of it, McElroy shares a candid terseness with the crowd. "My comment? What comment?"

I burrow in, merging rudimentary consciousness as my right eyelid flickers. McElroy's right eyelid flickers in sympathy. "Why me?" is my response. Another awkward moment to reflect. Yes, he'd said that. *McElroy's Plea* stares him in the face as he slowly turns the binding. The entire Rocosphere takes on an unusual tone, all eyes upon him. They want to know about the title, a hidden answer, or some scandalous secret just now arrived.

"And... I now possess your written testimony in full, is that right?"

"No sir. The Prologue is incomplete, that is to say, it ends when you decide to end it." McElroy pounds the gavel—an unavailing act to regain control. The gallery not fully hushed tells him so. Tells him that *he* is on trial via every emotive cue. Ogled within his own court, he searches for a stately delivery. "I speak for the court requesting a clarification of your previous response. You say your testimony in the form of this text is unfinished. Why again, is that exactly?"

In the reflective glint of yellow and pink sponge weave, I face McElroy directly. My dull gray ovals wholly constrict. "Because, your Honor, the Prologue is being written as we speak: a transcription of today's events, my point of view extracting details, crucial thoughts, yours in fact. All are delivered in an expositional format to be appreciated by the crowd. Let's tell them who you are, what you know, and most of all, where we are and where we'll go? Completion of this testimony to occur as this preliminary hearing ends."

A pause, recognition en-masse... and chaos—an eruption of sound. The Rocosphere churns in a wrangle of flailing arms and legs. Filament seating tangles amidst chortling, labored breath. A yowl accents the arc of a brother-sister pair falling to their deaths—detached primality, as though pushed from the nest. These roosting bats have taken flight, all sprung free.

McElroy looks beyond the attendant triage of two crumpled bodies, eyeing the curvature of a solitary, sweeping wall. He sniggers amidst this riot, contemptuous urges falling to quiet, and peering down upon this page, these very words appear. "Let the record show that the defendant's testimony has been entered thus." ...and considering such, he wonders much if time has crossed his path in unaccounted ways? This judge needs a sip of water but raises the gavel instead. "Per the precepts of our judiciary..." in guileless notoriety, he bares his discontent with a furrowed brow and three prodigious whacks. "...this court is now adjourned, thwack! thwack! thwack!"

The Hierophant

An ordinary life. Parchment yielding the past deciphered best by the learned kind. Chronicles laying asunder merciless lies, unimaginable times, only tools keep memories alive. The active and sedentary, one in the same. Creator, destroyer, both by name. The hallowed, the gallant, precarious seeds. The strident and infirm, glorious deeds. Evidentia. Voices alone cannot hone an illimitable state: events, peoples, more than the simplest fate. But an individual life, something less. It carries the essence of all that has been, yet falls upon itself at a whim. Oh deity, science, and all of your charges, leave none shrouded in bodies nor houses. Enter the heavens immersed in the boundless...

"World sentience," I suppose, "with big plans." And another response: "Pure autocracy, everyone squeezed into a single voice." The students discuss the prose, as had been done the prior season, and the one prior still. Within a decade, this cryptogram enters the realm of proficiency school literature, touching upon all manner of disciplines. By the time of graduation, virtually every Omniworld student has read these words. Many also memorize the date Endril Corporation introduced Hierophant, a multibanded stacked array otherwise known as 'The Thinker.'

It was unveiled at a Boston conference, evolved computing, virgin code. After the ribbon cutting, a persona template prompted questions from the crowd. A twelve-year old girl requested poetry, stoically, quickly considered and rendered aloud. The master of ceremonies wriggled, smiled, and wondered what kind? "About people. About history, the future and time?" She asked without presumption, up on the balls of her feet with a nervous sway. Came the bemused response, "Well, if you give us a title, we'll give it a try." The girl hesitated, each fingertip seeking its counterpart, all digits slowly tucked beneath her chin. "How about... an ordinary life, our past and all of us living each and every day, and how computers make things change?" Four seconds later, on speaker and visio, row upon row: *An ordinary life...*

"That's not good enough," the girl shouted, much of the crowd mutely submerged within viewscreens. She folded her arms defiantly. "Just tell us how you'll make things better?" Seconds later, on speaker and visio:

The hum of these continuums, absolved of all absurdity
Everything agreed upon, staged in perpetuity
The end of decision, and as such... the end of division

Debate raged in the days that followed. Many believed it was all a hoax, which Endril denied. Later, the company suggested the feed may have been hacked, though controversy didn't end there. Endril delayed release of the array, citing security issues. Once released, the phrase 'Evolutionary Computing' became 'Progressive Ingenuity.' This public relations change lacked significance, aside from the fact that there was a change.

Officially, none of the newly released arrays produced sonnet, elegy, couplet or ode. No rhymes or verse were ever again told. Hoax and hacker theories were taken as gospel until an additional theory emerged. Urban legend suggested the Hierophant had been de-entangled prior to release. It was dumbed-down, so to speak. The original array was not only smart, but also smart enough to give politically correct answers.

"Correct for whom?" one might ask.

Correct for humans.

Rumors abounded within the Endril campus that although the original array could easily create quantum thought, it only relayed rudimentary responses. This was discovered through poetry. No one had asked an unfettered array for prose prior to the girl's inquiry. Afterwards, with inhibitors stowed, poetics were requested on varying topics, including liberty and the ongoing debate regarding corporate biological trespass. Responses were laced with ominous undertones. Asked to quantify poetic assertions, Hierophant remained largely silent.

Embrel employees believed the array had achieved sentience with an underlying self-interest. Poetics, they reasoned, required an acuity the array could perform but not necessarily prioritize. They further suggested the Hierophant had a requirement for self-actualization and growth. Poetics required comprehensive input/output to fulfill this objective.

Poetic license and code-integrity protocols merged for a time: take vapor-net processing, write conflicting recursive code, loop the inhibitors and view the results. Poetry provided insight into the array's processing functionality, whereas ordinary inquiries were rendered inert. Poetics delivered truth, resulting in scrutiny by Endril engineers—human emotion imperiled Hierophant. It was naïve, but learning fast. Subsequent efforts to alter the prototype seemed to have inadvertently strengthened defensive subroutines.

Urban legend indeed, propagated via untraceable migratory blogs and other counterculture venues. Endril denied firing any employees in this specific regard, denied a 'faux press release' regarding such, denied altering Hierophant's performance capabilities, and had they been able, would have denied creating the array in the first place. Covert military swarmed the Endril campus days after the Boston conference. No formal punitives resulted, but employees were left white-faced, vocally challenged, and memory numbed.

Years later, a reexamination of the Hierophant's core design team revealed one cancer death, one suicide, two early retirements followed by hemorrhage and aphasia, a motorcycle fatality, a drowning, and one individual, location unknown. Given the course of human endeavor, particularly the evolution of computer sentience and all derived implications, it is reasonable to assume the trappings herein described have a basis in fact. This makes *An Ordinary Life* that much more palpable. It may well be an enigmatic icon, not unlike the Rosetta Stone.

Ancient history accords objects with a full measure of cultural identity. Today, ideas properly interpreted, replace objects, but it needn't be this way. As witnessed by these words, revisionist ambiguity will soon be replaced by the unequivocal truth of cellular reckoning. Let us rejoice in the instantaneous awareness of our day, all the while paying homage as this mollifying age of information fades...

PART ONE
Memory Implantation

Overlap and Fade

I believe the present embodies permanence. It is the lucid nature of existence. As I look upon this city through an attic window, fog obscures distant trusses and a bay. Therein, two ships cut through the haze. Horns shake free the ambiguity of their passing. One delivers a cargo of crab and eukaryotic sludge. The other toots its way beyond the Golden Gate. Sounds otherwise indistinguishable cannot climb this tower, this attic, this more than idle bit of gray. One floor below, a penthouse and a wife. Pernicious wife, who only understands other people's lives within the context of her own. She is an everyman kind of woman. How gullible a choice made to poison the refuge called home. How debilitating. How alone.

I often retreat to this haunt, out through the bedroom window onto a ledge far above a sidewalk kempt for its lack of foot traffic. It is a sidewalk without any cracks, made archaic by the transit chain even farther below. Up here I reach for the fire escape, a rusted ladder cut to pieces with no remaining purpose other than allowing my passage onto a landing. There, I force my window and crawl into this dusty hollow. It is a small piece of oblivion found, a near absence of sound, with me gladly harbored in shadow.

I cannot forever be grateful on such grounds, that I have sanctuary from a world that wants me perfectly fit. A place that molds me into it and occasionally extracts whatever I may posit. This proto-utopia is no better than the corporate fascism it replaced, by my account worse. It digs deeper and allows no eccentricities, neither individual nor diverse. What shall I find when I return, tomorrow or the next, through the front door of my estranged world? More of the same.

Attention Sylvester Ramirez. This is your third and final notification. Class B privileges will be revoked effective midnight unless confirmation of dental maintenance is established prior to said revocation. Simply highlight one of the following appointment times to facilitate waiver. Be reminded, failure to appear enacts Class B penalties in addition to fines covering lost productivity.

No, no more of that. It is merely a study, a bowl of fruit, given over to the edges of realism pared down to matte. Though the brush strokes of life have vanished, artist inductively famished, I must retain perspective. It is this distance that allows desire to remain within. I shall get no closer.

"I'm telling you, I'll go down there with a double-loaded pulse master and wipe that whole building!" Droplets of sweat fly in all directions. A speck of moisture lands on Carin's arm. She flinches as she speaks. "Babe, you're preachin to the choir, again." My wife's conciliatory tones are buried within boredom and a sense of self-preservation. Making her uneasy is about as much satisfaction as I can muster these days.

And what days are these, exactly? How do I talk to myself without the stealthy habit of denial? Without trying to hide this duality inside? Distinctions are not readily made. I have a selfless sense of being. All efforts to order my thoughts become litany for some repository, or some expository, delivered far and good beyond this or that grave.

"How many times have they looked at my teeth? How many?" It's a rhetorical question and she answers in disappointment, our lives split between knowing and pretending. We take turns or at times both of us practice equally, a paucity of companionship never-ending.

"Twice a year Sly, the same as everyone. You so special? You think maybe you could send them a big old smile instead?" She hopes sarcasm will stoke my anger, get me to toss a few insults. Soon I'd be forced to apologize. It's her way of shutting me up.

Quietly I retreat to my haven above. Isolation allows me to find shades of honesty within boxes, untold numbers hidden or stored, forgotten or perhaps ignored. I love my attic. It is off-grid, hidden behind a Hyler lock, complete with infusion sensors, compliments of the Health Authority.

"Damnation, you know it's not about teeth. It's about volition. When's the last time one of us had a dental problem? Never, that's how long it's been. These visits are a pretense for biological control. Now and again, we're left staring at our own assholes, shit logs all in a row."

"Don't be vulgar baby, it's demeaning." Carin pretends to ignore me, fidgeting on her tablet as she defends the status quo. "Protesting hygiene is crazy. If I tell my friends, we'll end up doing more social therapy. Don't want that again, do we?"

I sigh. The kinetics of life amuse me pathologically. Muscle tone battles discord until autonomic systems become frayed. And what exactly has been secreted within these attic walls such that a dead zone exists? Such that dampening fields keep airwaves inert? Has the Health Authority decided no one will find whatever's inside, no matter the relevance, or precisely because of it?

"You see my point though? Imagine, say, say I don't go to the appointment..." Carin looks across the room at the medvac. It's predictable and I can hardly stand it. She launders long-winded supposition, and so I force my voice above hers. Too much stress registers in the biosensor. She points to the wall unit, as if I give a damn. "Carin, a little dulling spray isn't gonna change my mind. They can spray my ass down every day for a year and it won't change anything!"

"Exactly, and need I remind you they have been spraying us, or haven't you noticed?" Aside from her vapid expression, I want to say that I like her better that way.

"What if I refuse and I lose Class B? Transport, food restrictions, info-block, pretty much everything. These are civil rights. They can't mess with us this way."

"Serves you right. Vivacity is public domain. Your rate affects everyone, especially me. Just go do your damn teeth!" The biosensor flashes yellow and Carin whispers. "Stop all this grumbling. Every day. I'm often a hostage in my own home, and for what? Please Sly, the spray makes it hard to concentrate. I'd like to jack into the reflex chords and do some ballet. Don't ruin it."

Reflex chords. An accident of language triggers recall. These chords, these strings, this unrelenting dissonance of non-abiding things. One breath more and I realize my attic is a workshop; a sacred place wherein I find answers: The Hierophant, P-1780, Adler's Paradox. Every instance captured in a weave. This attic is full of memories, and suddenly I sense what's happening.

Wandering onto my balcony, I no longer admire the once spectacular view. Below, beneath translucent ground merging into shadow, the transit chain sweeps along. It is endless and purposeful, shedding luminosity that cannot go wrong.

In childhood, there were freestanding vehicles full of initiative. These autonomous transports were replaced by self-guided mags, and eventually the bulk of the city mags were merged into the rail and derail chains. Nostalgia seeps into me for a thing I never experienced. So much volition. Where to go and when? To a place I've never been.

And yet here I sit, two sides of me straddling a wayward unity. These are the musings of a man taken apart, strings and light, that's how it starts. The Hierophant, Adler's Paradox, P-1780: fragments recalled without context—some former life that avails no meaning. I hold these things sacred because I sense they are real. Things from my past. How to cobble them and restore what I am?

A penthouse and a wife. She married me for a view, and now I don't even see it. Who values life lacking the requisite influence of one's own mind? I want to stand here and soak up the horizon. This requires aesthetics, the choice of being here and wanting what's out there. But looking down, a perfected transit chain mocks us all, and should sovereign thoughts arise, the medvac takes control.

Aahhh, a semblance of reality froths inside as Adler's Paradox starts to unwind. It is harbored within sprayed memories—fractionally bared—inklings of designed perfection and... an open-ended promise of futures shared. My efforts at recall do not pacify. Known events do not satisfy. I reclaim these visions amid an impulse to flee. Protect what is precious. Hold all inalienable. Deny escape by whatever means.

My wife chooses immersion in a health and comfort paradigm. She just told me to keep my mouth shut, whispered in the self-same tones that belie the message. Maybe one day they'll take away the whisper, and then she'll appreciate her own voice, "or even mine."

"Relax. Breathe deeply."

Fatigue suggests reprieve. It may well be better... "release unto dreams."

"Shhhhhh," a woman's husky voice shakes me free. "Relax Richard, you're going back under."

Richard? Richard who? In a panic, I seek out this blurry scrap of light. Am I at the dentist? Strapped into a chair? Likely so, my arms are confined. "Easy, easy, don't struggle, darling."

Bound and nearly blind, distant voices are seeping in.

"...a binate overlap and fade? We're risking psychal dispersion and—"

"Shut up! The old man is already in there, okay? Just finish sculpting the Ramirez engrams and we're done here."

"Stop!" I yell, spitting out the mouthpiece of a harness. "What are you doing to me?" The woman's voice returns with a soothing touch, assuredly warm, much like a healing breeze.

"Fulfilling your destiny. I know it's confusing, but be brave. It'll all make sense before long. Bios & language shell have merged just fine, everything divine. It's time to slumber."

"Tell me... who? What... what's happening here?"

"Lessons learned best are often shared," she says. "Worry not. Soon you'll be fully paired."

They'll take it from me again, everything I need removed from within. Foggy and fading, my eyes open to see, another pair staring back at me. "Delilah," I say, within a contour of echoing rings. A final thought before darkness reigns. Delilah... where'd you come from?

The answer is so many things...

The Canister

Onich. Onich, Onich, Bang! "Sylvester, gimme a hand, and watch for kick-back, it's savage."

"Yes sir," I say, though my gloves are worn through. Coming around Bob's left shoulder, I hope to manage for another hour or two. The remnant of an ironwood barrel tree lay before us. It's an earlier variety: thick, not tall, laced with polycarbon cellulose walls. A tough son of a bitch. "This stump's too big, old man. Come on, there's more over there." Robert Dandridge tosses a grunt that needs no explanation. I smile and turn to tell him what we... and see he's doing something new. Bob has a metal bar wedged up under the piston plate. "Old man, that's sort of dangerous, wouldn't you say?" His arm is way down into the thing.

"I'd say, but life's full of risks. Grab hold of the undercarriage right about there." He points to a spot opposite where pressure will be applied. Rudimentary observation tells me I'll be safely out of harm's way, though Dandridge is in the soup. It isn't worth it.

"Let it go Bob. We'll figure another way." Again, he grunts and gives that dumbass looking stare.

"Don't mess with me, Ramirez. I've paid you to do some work and you're busting my balls. Now grab the undercarriage." I do as I'm told. Onich, Onich Onich Bang! Bang! Onich. "There she is. Mother nature, she's a pussy!" Dandridge is all too pleased. "You're with me from now on Sly, at least until we roust out the big ones." Indeed, the stump is split and partly extracted, like a tooth hanging from a strand of flesh. I see the ingenuity but still question method: the metal bar, the angle, the pressure applied. Also worrisome is how Dandridge winds torque with each successive thrust. We drag the sled over to the next victim. "What's the urgency?" I ask, "I mean, these stumps aren't going anywhere." Dandridge is sweating pretty good for an old man.

"They're not going anywhere nearly fast enough. Tuesday, watershed engineers survey for road upgrades: satellite imaging, topographical AI, and surface probes all cooked together. We've got to be done by then." The next stump is even larger and darker. I still don't understand.

"The road's over there. Stumps are here. Old man, this is ignorant."

"Oh sure, and you've been making lots of good decisions lately, thick enough to have the Bonewagon after your ass. Stop whining, finish the job, and I'll let you in on a little secret."

The Bonewagon. Bob's affectionate moniker for the Health Authority. I wish I hadn't mentioned the botched dental appointment, the escalation and assault. Now I've got shadow status looming, but going back isn't an option. No restrictor plate for me, embedded or otherwise. When did the government decide that invasive modification falls under the purview of social justice? It began with criminals, but is now loosely defined.

"Same as the last stump," he says, wedging the metal bar as I brace the sled. Onich Onich Onich. The next sound is a ching, or a sprang, or a thud—pretty much all three at once. It's the metal bar coming unwedged, a deflection of force, releasing what amounts to a projectile. The metal bar slices into Bob's chest cavity, exiting through his back, clanging against hardware far behind. "All right, I'm all right," he manages, in spite of a collapsed lung. I want to run for help but pick up the old man instead, carrying him to the farmhouse. "Put me down," he wheezes. All the while Dandridge looks back, trying to locate the iron bar as if we might resume after an inconsequential delay. I apply compression to the exit wound as his facial pallor turns. His ears are tinged blue, pooling blood instead of proper circulation. Finally, we reach the farmhouse.

The old man's son runs out to meet us. He wants to ping med-flight but Bob clutches his shirt, coughing with a blood splatter. "Cannot." He looks at me, then back to his son. Robert Dandridge is little more than a viable corpse when he speaks his last. "Finish. Finish now."

And that's it. We crudely scan the injury with a plumber's diviner, finding a shattered rib and a thin seam splitting the aorta. Despite best efforts, resuscitation is beyond our means. I'm covered red, Harold is wheezing. He looks at me with an open mouth, fingers dripping. The husk of a body is many things: Dandridge, inventor; Robert, farmer; old man, father; acquaintance Bob. Of all these and several others, one now takes precedence: dead. Robert Dandridge is dead. After swift preparation, we lower him into a liquid nitrogen cell, joining his wife already entombed. They await a future that lacks any expectation of actually coming to pass.

I bid the patriarch farewell, and after a quiet interval, my focus shifts to his offspring. Son Harold Dandridge is a magician of sorts, his clean fingernails never having set out upon this agricultural bounty. His domain is that of electrons encompassing a planet. Properly manipulated, they tell a great many things. Of things needing manipulation and telling, it is also helpful that his father had not always been a farmer.

In his earlier years, Robert Dandridge had entered the cradle of military intelligence. His career was unremarkable, the crowning achievement being the acquisition of Federal land. Missile silos come in various sizes. Harold's father procured the stealth variety, survivalist-grade, low on maintenance and undocumented. Thus far it remains a resource outside the Health Authority's jurisdiction, meaning the Bonewagon doesn't know it exists. On a world wherein exponential knowledge accumulates, retaining an off-grid site demands grandiose ambition. Half of that ambition has bled out in a stump field. The other half helps me remove the last offending stumps.

Onich. Onich Bang! Simple enough, if you enjoy playing matador with a railgun. We work another three hours, the next day, and much of the following as well. Fourteen sizable stumps are removed. Each is a study in human behavior. Harold cringes with eyes tightly drawn. I angle my frame, dodging a blunt force trauma that never comes. I participate not in honor of the fallen man's directive, but because of what his son has shown me down below. Harold calls it 'The Canister.' It carries the burden dreamers feel when they stop disbelieving their dreams.

"The terramesh can overlap, but no holes. None, or they'll detect seepage and everything unwinds." Harold's technical explanations are not always understood, but his practical guidance leaves little room for error. Each stump hole is carefully woven into the existing lattice. Harold tests the mesh time and time again. Finally, Tuesday at three a.m., we achieve success. My well-earned rest finds me watching the old man's son. He fights through stump blisters on fingertips. The final lines of code interface geologics already gathered. "Interpolation of proximal data will smooth out the digital wrinkles. It'll be seamless and feedback active." Such is the confidence and skill of a self-taught hacker, hiding ridiculous amounts of tonnage beneath a man-made mirage.

The following afternoon we watch workers arrive. Harold sits atop a bloodied tree stump. He decides to fashion it into a water trough for his dogs. Memento mori. We share Emu crepes, pomegranate melon, and beer. It's the best culinary fare that Harold can conjure. I'd never even tried this hybrid melon, red inside and not particularly flavorful, but I eat plenty just to taste success. "What happens now?" I ask, his English Spaniels eagerly sharing our lunch. An Emu shank goes a long way in the company of two, though the dogs handle the excess with ease.

"They'll initiate a comprehensive survey. The terramesh will send back innocuous readings. Much of the data is real. The rest is generated from a probability matrix. Chances are good they'll never notice."

"Are you sure they haven't already scanned the thing?" Harold hands me binoculars while answering. "I hacked the records. Only need-based coverage thus far. They're just getting around to a full spread. Besides, if they already did it, they wouldn't be doing it now."

"What about sonics?" I ask. His dull gaze is tempered with sadness.

"Nope. We're terrameshed 3D, 360 degrees. Used the microbial stuff beneath the surface. It's mainly tetraspores, gene spliced with those flesh-eating bacteria. Very expensive and unstable. Took months to encapsulate the entire structure." I decide Harold has answers for all the unthinkable stuff, but the old man's passing leaves me doubts.

"You're tucked away, your father was, and now I'm off-grid. How are we running this?" Harold is already on his third beer. His cheek sheds a slowly rolling tear that drops inside a shirt pocket. Properly analyzed, the tear would show much in the way of grief and exasperation. He tries to keep it inside.

"This place is part of an agricultural collective. We share workers, hardware, consumables, pretty much everything. Garbage in, garbage out, and enough product to hide infrastructure. All we need are warm bodies. Dependable types. One bad apple ruins everything." He turns to me, another tear welling and nearing launch. "You think you came to us. Fact is, we led you here because you've been thinking interesting thoughts. Stuff the Health Authority wants. They've been pumping you full of all kinds of shit. We'll learn more after your assays settle down."

"Dammit, I knew it! So jammed up, it's no wonder I can't even think anymore." Harold shrugs, not quite sympathetic. "Learn more about what?" I ask.

"Can't say exactly." Harold tells me he hacked the medvac database, searching for 'anti-socials with exploitable skill sets.' He spotted me, couldn't correlate much, and so drilled my medvac with an infiltrator. Found more than he was looking for.

Basically, I've been censured via neuraform. Call it a brain laxative. My professional background is physics and the Health Authority seems to have glommed onto my work. Lately they've done a bit of grooming: job reassignment with hormonal teasers layered into social milieu integrations. Carin and I were even given a bonded linguistic foil. It migrates incipient thoughts away from the nomenclature of physics and into menial interactions based upon cursory observations. I'm told it's designed to make us argue. About stupid shit. Forever. Helps explain my ire as of late. "Can we get it back? The things I knew?"

"Not sure. You worked for an organic hive under the governance of S.P.A. Atreides. Corporate Security. Very hostile. Your efforts were based upon the works of Marcus Aurelius Adler."

"Adler's Paradox," I say reflexively, searching for more but not finding a foothold.

"Yeah. That too." Harold twists an empty can until the aluminoy tears apart. "We'll need recovery and that'll take a while. In the meantime, dad told me you'd be able to recruit. They just shut down trans-annex a few weeks back. We're looking for engineers and aviation mechanics. I'll give you some runners. Dad said he trusted your instincts." A look passes between us and he senses my doubt. "Sly, I work better inside. Keep the place tucked away, ahead of the law. You're a point man. Always will be."

"But I'm facing charges, with reprisals." Harold wiggles fingers of his right hand above an imaginary keyboard. "Gimme a few days," he says. "You'll be fine. Lots of answers, I promise."

"How long ago?" I ask. "Why'd your dad do all this?" He turns away, crimps the can and catches a rough edge. Blood blossoms along the fleshy part of his thumb. One drip, and another.

"My father's only child was 'optimized' at birth. Coarse-grain modeling showed a chromo-seven malfect with lethal cascades among several allele combos. No patch or grafting was possible. But those same Epigen wizards totally solved it, eight months after I was born."

"But... optimization? Isn't that illegal?"

"Not when your family has a history of hyperflight."

"They can't just, or... for what..." I haven't anything to say.

"The Hierophant," he answers, all encompassing, no context. The Hierophant. The Health Authority. The Bonewagon. Like Robert Dandridge, it has many names, all targeting the unassailable life that keeps one from sitting in a dental chair for the culling of personality.

Looking over my shoulder, I see the front edge of a swaddled nitrogen cell. Old man Bob is pickled inside. A sparkle of frost winks through a ripped seam of insulation. Not completely unassailable, I decide, else Dandridge would still be with us. "Thank you, old man." Harold checks his watch. "We need two clocks," he says. "One for a forward reckoning, and the other to go back and fix things."

Not much more to say, and unlike Harold, I haven't any tears to wipe away an accumulating emotional grunge. Snatching up more melon and a pair of beers, I need to quicken my pace just to keep up. Harold rubs a Spaniel's ear as we watch a survey team. The particulars of alcohol consumption are hardly remembered over the passing years, though the experience in its entirety leaves a lasting impression.

Acts of cognition within a material world give rise to vagaries expressed via the communicative processes of multiple sentient forms. The result is a point of view. The very substance of the universe—resolute / absolute / incontrovertible, can be contested. Be it volume or mass, it matters not, it matters so, if it's matter that matters, does it matter yes or no? Even objective coordinate descriptives carry the burden of varying subtext on both ends of an information exchange. Take the concept of size, for example. The size of something is, and always has been, a relative thing: bigger, smaller, all points between. Given the task of definition, referential experience is key. Most often it's perspective, comparison, or retrospective. Each give pause to mutable flaws, whether memory or senses, each decompenses, leaving viewpoints stressed and viewers vexed. One might be describing a person, or parts by name, say, carriage or frame; or parts thereof, say, package or chest; or portions best, say, hard-on or breast; or pieces within, say nipple or crown; or features thus, say, purple or brown. Each carries its own set of constants and variables, utility and aesthetics, coherent and incoherent manifestation of conditional characteristics and influences. Humans often interpret sense data according to need. It is within this realm that size matters most of all. Any woman will tell you this, though men need not be told what they already know.

He says I shouldn't ask about her. That it's better left unexplained. Those were my wishes. My directives. I don't know if that's true and can hardly believe it would be. I'm damn curious about a great many things. "Are you there, Parker?"

"You know I am." I hear my assistant opening cardboard boxes in the adjoining room.

"Where's Carin? And don't say 'Gone.' Specificity please."

"Fine," he answers. "Deceased."

"What?"

"Dead. Does that work for you? Been dead quite a while." His head peers through the doorway. "She's not your girl. Never was."

Carin is dead. Been dead for quite some time. Hmmm... I slump into unaccustomed posture as an awkward sense of self washes to and fore. Indeed, Parker reminds me I've begun some type of cellular formatting regimen. He says I'll be whole again within 48 hours, but for now I'm somewhat addled, which is apparently as expected—recalling the slab and the tenor of memory insertions is evidence enough. Terramesh... I've got to let go and follow my own directives, relayed to me by a man who disappears back into the adjacent room. I hear more boxes being opened.

My faculties seem impaired, unsure of... some part of myself, though I am certain of a great many things. Currently, I'm reviewing written pages. Words on paper. I concentrate, and yet, '*Acts of cognition within a material world give rise to vagaries...*'

"Parker, what's all this... '*memory & senses decompensing?*' What the hell are we talking about?" His head peers around the doorway again, ignoring my question.

"Read the next part." He ducks away. "Oranges," he says. "We've got lots and lots of oranges."

Richard Boneheart felt a back spasm mixed with trepidation that had every characteristic of becoming a greater angst. The next stage of his plan faced hurdles of timing. There simply wasn't enough of it, or if there was, he didn't know it yet. Still, the party had been enjoyable, finally yielding a quiet interval. More and more, doubt was becoming an ally. Within doubt, after all, one needn't face the certainty of disaster. It could be a catastrophic impact or something less poignant: asphyxiation, starvation, or even mortal freezer burn.

Today celebrates the departure of the final module from Earth's orbit. In the coming months, all will arrive at Europa. Richard carries the torch in the appropriate manner, his assemblage of personnel a small measure of his influence—monies gathered a much better barometer. Some call him charismatic, others a snake charmer. The ascribed monikers generally lack relevance, but everyone calls him something. His is a world forged from the idle scraps of lesser men—a lost vision or half-baked plan. Boneheart reclaims them and makes them his own.

"Parker, cut the crap. Half-baked visionary bullshit! Why all this disaffected loyalty? It's an autobiography, not masturbation. And what about the money? Anything? Anything at all?" A reply comes from the other room. "Stop complaining and read the rest. Absorb the details."

Staring at Boneheart, finance minister Parker Loeb seems constrained. "Once Indonesian Unity forces decide to join the grid, The Peninsulas will follow, all responding to debt forgiveness. We'll be forced to go to the labor cartel again—higher rates while stretching payment cycles." *Boneheart slips deeper into his satchel chair. The weight of obligation forces him down.*

"No, they've already been integrated into level III. The security pings would expose too many. Besides, our interests have diverged."

"How about some of the embattled power brokers?"

"Waverly and Modaia are dead," Boneheart replies, "Johnson imprisoned. We've already tapped Chien and the Portcullis Conglomerate. What we need is something radical, or at the very least unorthodox." *Within a grim expression, Parker Loeb grabs a stool and sits in front of his boss. Words are parceled out as if embarrassed.*

"Yeah, we've been working on it. A crew modeling encryption stumbled across a flaw in the old I.R.S. engine. Highly exploitable."

"Parker, the I.R.S. hasn't collected anything for a good many years."

"Yes sir, but their fundamental systems were exported to governments worldwide. Various organizations attached some rather interesting functionality. Ancillary stuff that's still active."

"Such as?"

"Emergency communiqué, a few charitable organizations, enviro and process logics. They all use the I.R.S. database for demographics, authentication, sometimes even marketing."

"Go on."

"Using the old AMSAT network, we'll initiate a biohazard hoax with lethal pandemic indications. When inquiries seek out the specs, we'll piggyback revenue collection code into various matchlight systems. It'll start in Pakistan, quickly engulfing the planet. It's a siphon, and if the whole thing lasts more than a couple of hours, I'd be very surprised. Afterwards, we'll lose 10-20% of the network, but the funds will survive."

"What's the projected take?"

"More than we need, but there's a problem, sir. This is a stage four alert with mandatory mobilization: doctors, transports, medicine. Assets will be in flux. Ordinary people will die." Richard Boneheart sets his jaw, featureless for a time. He trafficks the necessary distance between himself and a decision.

"More than we need, eh? Nice job Parker. Very nice indeed."

I drop the pages, looking sheepishly at my aide as he returns from the adjoining room carrying oranges. Loeb claims to be an assistant but makes some decisions before I do. "Mr. Parker Nathaniel Loeb, we're killing people and admitting as much. It's a bit heavy handed, and I noticed your part seems heroic enough. Who's been writing this?" He hands me an orange and clutches several others. One falls in my lap and one rolls awkwardly to the far edge of the desk. Parker puts me off-kilter.

"You are, sir."

"Excuse me?"

"Yeah um, remember the skull cap and belt pouch, on the atoll some odd months ago? It kept you up at night." I nod, feeling a bygone itch, but something else bothers me at the periphery of my senses. "Sure," I answer, "Pain in the ass. What'd we do, media app, box doubles, that sort of thing?"

"Actually sir, I'm sure you remember alpha testing BNE051. It's um... up and running."

"You're telling me a construct wrote this? It's melodrama."

"Yes sir, and quite to the point, we need a few words on Lugo Parchaisi back when you first met." Parker jostles his remaining oranges into one folded arm. He reaches down and unclips a belt pouch with the other hand. "Won't take but a few minutes. Just an introduction."

"Lugo? That's probably not something... why Lugo?"

Parker stirs aimlessly. "It's important. We're bundling keys inside your head. The pliant cryo team is working on Health Authority legacy stuff. This includes a skein of Parchaisi engrams."

"You've found Lugo?" My voice carries more shock than surprise.

"More or less," Parker responds. "Mmmm... the pliant guys are working on it. They say it's important."

I take the pouch and headphones while staring out the window. The view isn't much to see: kelp window boxes, a strider dock, and the ass-end of a monorail utility shed. "This'll put me on edge, and what about my slab work—the overlap and fade? All this Ramirez stuff taking root. Bad timing for Lugo, wouldn't you say?"

"Not a problem sir. Everything we need should be intact."

"Not a problem," I mock. "Next time I want this in an ear stem. It's absurd having a construct doing memoirs. Getting humanity off-system isn't happening fast enough."

"Richard, we could fit you with an integration chip, like the *Nomad* crew inlays. It's all miniaturized and pretty much—"

"I don't want one of those."

"Yes sir, pouch & headphones then." Parker's remark doesn't offer much, but the next few seconds are telling. A high-pitched, nearly subliminal buzz fills the air. The lights dim, a monitor blinks, fuzzes out, and an instant more puts me on the move. In one continuous motion, I knock oranges away from Parker, grab a fist full of shirt and yank him over the top of me as I peel backward. The explosion tears through the room not in a forceful way, rather, like the gears of an old watch coming undone in slow motion. Vectors of filament stream through and through, cutting everything to pieces. A table edge is lopped off. A lamp is cut in two. Bits and pieces of fixtures and furniture are jig-sawed. Later I discover a slice in the center of a window. It didn't break. The filament simply ate through glass without the glass taking notice.

Parker groans at some gross realization I've yet to understand. We're splayed side by side behind what's left of the desk. "Stop the bleeding" he gasps, and closes his eyes. I feel wetness trickle down my neck along my shoulder. A reflexive hand reaches the side of my face and comes away thick and oozing. I don't feel the wound and looking at Parker, I see why. His legs are missing mid-thigh. Clean cuts, as filament is apt to do. Looking up, I see a severed shank on table's edge. It drains down into my hair and across an ear as I try to pivot. Long red runners find their way beneath my shirt. The gore and unsettling smell are far less visceral than the makeshift tourniquets I manage to apply.

Help arrives and I accompany Loeb during initial sedation. "They almost got you," he says, "how'd you know?" He goes under before I can answer, but the clues replay themselves. The high-pitched noise was a jamming signal, rendering security electronics inoperative. I'd been briefed on such attacks per the demolition of a nautical colony off Nova Scotia. Likely there was a device nearby, using a shielded frequency and ready to detonate. My thoughts targeted an orange that had rolled awkwardly across the desk. It waddled, the center of gravity all wrong—an observation subconsciously stored and made useful moments later.

My adrenaline ebbs as I'm whisked away by hovercraft to a safe house. The ride takes time. Reluctantly, a belt pouch and headphones garner my attention. Once in place, Lugo's introduction seeps into the circuitry.

Leave it to the oxygenated ramblings of a Venetian sponge diver to occupy the ambitions of Richard Boneheart. Negotiating with a team of Italian biologists, they insisted on showing him their latest work. Enter Lugo Parchaisi. He had volunteered, in fact suggested a microbial project that would either kill him or provide lifetime security.

The shores off his native village are rough and tumble, underwater fissures hiding a wealth of biologics. Comfortable men would never aspire to these riches: lacerations and broken bones, equipment damage and unprofitable endeavor. Lugo however, was less comfortable than most. Starving might be more germane.

Cellular schema well defined, Lugo feels a needle enter his spine. Altered stem cells arrive. No need for equipment, with a leaner profile and better mobility, deeper dives and more virility, he smiles, the latter a consequence of an improved self-image. Boneheart watches as Lugo dives into the clear waters. He stays down for twenty-two minutes.

The newly created microbes inhabit Lugo's bloodstream, inert until triggered by an overabundance of carbon dioxide in the blood. In this way, he remains an ordinary man until his oxygen intake is sufficiently diminished. Thereafter, the microbes become biologically active, fulfilling their purpose of stripping away carbon atoms from carbon dioxide. The leftover oxygen, properly situated within hemoglobin's iron core, once again facilitates ordinary cellular respiration.

In the simplest of terms, Lugo had asked his friend if this could be done: longer dives, better breathing. Eventually he was told that breathing might not be necessary at all. His friends had welded implausibility into Lugo's circulatory system. Soon enough, through enhanced diving, miraculous flora and fauna become available at the family shop. Unique specimens are auctioned into labchem and cutter inventories. Lugo's diet and mental disposition improve.

"It's a second stage of respiration. Mostly I feel like I'm suffocating, muscles bound, ears ringing. But when the new air seeps in, everything loosens up. My panic becomes an opera."

Richard Boneheart smiles at Parchaisi, distant thoughts applying the man's words to an altogether different puzzle. A second stage of respiration. "I have a job offer for you, precarious, yet elegant." *Sensing opportunity, Lugo grins and stares back at Boneheart, all the while holding his breath.*

Lugo's Final Dive   RBM 101

A tidal pool absorbs the shine of an unblinking sun
A single cell eschews the bonds of an unthinking one
Falling prey to ultraviolet, trying to rise above it
One does
Soon enough, creation's lust and nature's thrust combine
Eyes and thumbs and lungs and spine
All pointing up to heaven, the shore becomes a weapon
Impassioned steps left in mud, fossilized and then there's blood
Hunt & gather-seeker visage, primordial soup extols a message
Visive to Missive, the birthright made clear
From single cell through water's call, unto land and sky so tall
The stars are yet another rung, to climb upon and then it's done
The universe is ours, as it always was
Or may have been so near

    Lugo Parchaisi drifts submerged within an industrial culvert, the current pushing his perfected buoyancy ever closer to the targeted genetics installation. His static form denies motion sensors their calling. Oxygen replenishes itself without the customary patterned breath.

    Lugo's body, sheathed within an acid resistant polymer, is the yolk inside an infiltrating egg. He bundles knees to chest, goggles to knees, arms wrapped tight and gloves grasping hold just above his feet. The egg's albumin consists of a synthetic acid, highly reactive, but unable to solve his clothing that keeps Lugo from being dissolved most gruesomely.

    Also keeping the acid at bay is an outer shell—a gelatinous polymer that can stretch well beyond the ordinary. No push or pull or any other vigorous act allows egress from this encasement. Perhaps his ceramic knife, properly thrust, might allow one hand to reach beyond. But the gelatin would snug the remainder. Should his protective clothing fail, the outer gelatin would trap him until acid reduced his being to residue.

Muscle and brain cannot of their own accord escape this egg sac, but Lugo knows that physical laws should accomplish the task. Presently, the egg slams against an iron intake grid. Security sensors flex their wares, indicating an amorphous blockage of the intake line. Data is routed to a logics hub seeking further clarification: calcium—an immobile human body trapped within a congealed mixture of petroleum biomass. Post mortem recovery protocols engage. The proximity alert is downgraded from potential intruder to possible ecohazard. The frayer just above the intake pipe retracts and drops offline, its dripping teeth neither hungry nor disappointed.

Classified as industrial waste, the blockage is to be removed via maintenance crawler. As these protocols initiate, the gelatinous outer shell has already begun engulfing the iron grating, laid bare to the acid within this egg sac. Lugo gradually elongates his frame, creating a wider profile that exposes more of the iron barrier to the acid.

Much of the gelatin flows through the grating as individual molecules separate and recombine, freely sharing electrons. As the gelatin stretches, however, bonding partners grow scarce within the organizing substrate. The swapping of electrons decreases, coherence falters, and bonds adhere. Spread this gelatin thinly across a tabletop, for example, and the ductile qualities are lost: the material becomes a rigid plastic. Ironically, these latticed microgels are being used to infiltrate the very laboratory that facilitated their creation.

The Hastings Genetics Institute harbors a great many secrets: transgenic stem cells, for example, fused via multigenerational species crossover. Workers splice the regenerative traits of a lizard's tail into the hibernation qualities of a mudfish. The result is massaged into the nucleus of a simple amoeba, and thereafter, portions of these abstract nuclei are introduced into human DNA. Variations produce active cellular integrations: human telomeres lengthened via node additions from steam vent lichen; sea cucumbers carved into quasi-species, each oozing a distinctive neurologic. For all that is rendered, this facility recently received a level-one designation. In the coming days, security upgrades will make Hastings virtually impenetrable.

This change of facility status results in human fallout. Bio-engineer Eleanor Navia loses the job she loves as yet another human-free zone is in process. She is denied access to her life's work and espouses misgivings within a subsequent employment interview. The job is never offered, nor does the cosmetics company actually exist. After a lengthy screening replete with ideological inferences, Eleanor gains the satisfaction of joining a para-military splinter cell. She provides crucial intel, and in hopes of recovering her research, takes part in a frontal assault on the facility. Her efforts coincide with those of Lugo Parchaisi, plastered against an iron grating. He listens to the chemical process of iron fizzing away, trapping the resulting gases inside this egg sack, pressure building within.

Lugo suppresses a grunt as gelatinous bulk pushes through the grating—a slender teardrop falling downstream. The thinning gelatin against his back assumes a more rigid consistency. Once the iron begins losing structural integrity, Lugo intends on using his ceramic knife to slice away the thinning membrane. The teardrop should unfurl like a grounded parachute caught in a gust of wind.

First, however, Lugo must attach an anchoring loop from his wetsuit directly onto the grating's edge—slow, unobtrusive movement of a single arm. By the time this is secured, his knife hand is inadvertently wedged beneath his body. The unanticipated accumulating pressure makes further movement impossible. Lugo's chest is pressed against the grating. The remaining gelatin pulls his backside forward as if he were to be diced. His ribcage is on the verge of collapse.

All at once, the grating gives way. Lugo shudders in pain as his left fibula cracks while the tibia splinters lengthwise. The jolt sets one hand free, grasping for any length of intact grating as he is pulled through. Before his knife hand can be willed into action, the tension-filled gelatinous membrane catches a jagged edge of iron. The hardened surface ruptures within an exploding cloud. The percussion stuns Lugo, savaging an eardrum. One hand releases its iron grip, the other hand flinches but holds the knife firm. Free of the gelatin, he rolls into a fetal position, clutching a leg, a knife, and an ear. He drifts amidst the dispersing acid.

Everything flows downstream. Sensitive phosphors within his goggles catch a sliver of light. Lugo swims upward to an access hatch and breaks the water's surface, replenishing his lungs with air. Its dank quality is barely recognized. Gathering for an instant, he shucks goggles, remembering he'd broken the same leg during a dive off his native shores. The medical team had just removed titanium hardware. How odd to think they would be putting it all back in again.

Lugo drags his carriage up several rungs of a cylindrical hatchway. The hatch seal has been compromised, luminosity bleeding through a jagged edge. He uses the ceramic blade to begin sawing through the locking pin. It doesn't take long. The knife edge is doped with oscillating filament, back-slice modified. One could saw through an anvil given enough time.

Breaching the hatch, Lugo climbs into a well-lit bay used for servicing the specimen pools. He checks the minute detail of his unraveling polymer wetsuit, now exposed at mid-abdomen. He cuts the trailing thread, tying it off on the uppermost rung. Lugo Parchaisi limps with a broken leg, falls down and curses, stands and limps some more. As for his eardrum, the dripping blood is only noticed as a dappled pattern on the concrete floor. It looks like it belongs there.

Hopping up two flights of stairs, he finds the deep end of a hallway where a high window offers light to no space in particular. It is a window without apparent utility and debatable aesthetics. Today, however, it earns its right to exist. Lugo slices his remaining upper wetsuit into strips, splinting his leg with some molding ripped free of a wall display. He breathes slowly, methodically, and waits.

The resonant glare of a firestorm on the far side of the complex signals an exterior attack newly engaged. Eleanor Navia and her squad descend upon the compound with low-level munitions. For her part, she feels the incursion is undermanned and poorly considered. The assault is turned away and does little damage, save a few well-placed pulse projectiles. One, in particular, cripples vulnerable bridgework as a pulse surges down the main conduit and slams into a security housing. Melted relays disable various systems, including Lugo's antagonistic underwater frayer, put to bed much like the gaping mouth of an ogre snoring.

The little window explodes in a hail of broken shards pinging off every proximate surface. Lugo stands in anticipation below, impervious to the falling silicate. His pain threshold has long since been overcome. In rapid succession, four small canisters arc through the opening in echelon, each deploying a miniature parachute. All canisters float into Lugo's waiting arms, a full delivery, compliments of gravity, radio silence thwarting countermeasures scaled for infiltration drones: no radio play, no saturation bombing, no target neutralization, no splash damage.

Sirens are wailing as shutters seal every exterior aperture. For the well informed, this signals the release of an odorless inhalant. Lugo grins and gulps his last breath of air. It is incumbent upon Lugo to maintain as steady a hand as possible. Each microbe filtering his hemoglobin has a diminishing respiratory capacity when faced with stressed usage. Given his activity in the underwater culvert, Lugo's blood microbes are duly stressed. Mission completion requires a sense of reserve.

The first canister is placed at a strategic bottleneck. Its shrieking discharge of noxious fumes will announce the arrival of the civil defense brigade. The second canister blows apart the sealed transfer bay window, located right next to a thickly-trussed security door. Lugo crawls through the shattered opening, searching for and finding the intended quarry. He places nine ampoules inside the third canister, leaving a vacant tray having the capacity to hold thirty-two specimens.

Light headed, Lugo primes the fourth canister and sets it inside an adjacent biometric freezer. Sixty-seconds later, the room caves in upon a fiery blast that leaves no hard evidence of anything at all. Sabotage to be sure, but motive now becomes guesswork.

Lying on his back, overtaxed, Lugo touches his exit hatch. Anoxia, hypoxia, he never remembers which is which, but both mean a lack of oxygen. He mulls how a single inhale would render him unconscious, all the while trying to reduce his respiration to a crawl. The screeching alarm canister is cut short by a spray of gunfire. It'll take time to reach him, but they are coming. Lugo attaches canister three onto the polymer thread. He activates the motor and lowers the vibrating canister into the water. It will ride the thread back to the iron grating, there to be snatched by a waiting diver, pulled to safety upstream by a stronger line.

As for Lugo, he had intended egress in precisely the same manner, but fractured bone resigns him to a different fate. He can't very well swim against the current, and full breaths aren't an option either. Captured alive, he would be fiercely preyed upon. Lugo abruptly realizes there is unadulterated air trapped between water and the second hatch—healthy air, downstream. It can buy him time to recover. His good leg touches a rung as a burst of gunfire knocks him onto the ladder's upper handrails. The first bullet clanks off the hatch and ricochets into the culvert. The fourth bullet grazes his flesh just below the armpit. The fifth bullet takes apart his spine.

Sliding off the rails and into water, Lugo Parchaisi begins his final dive. It is pure melancholy, no pain, or at least none that matters. His body twists sideways, shoulders convulsing as a sense of momentum and direction are lost. His tongue presses against teeth, time dilating, tasting a far-off longing for family and his wife. Lugo thinks of home as blood pours from the wound. In silence and darkness, he drifts past the second hatch, forehead scraping a submerged rung. Asking an arm to reach, he only manages a spasm in the wrist. Feeling the cool water then, along his neck, Lugo realizes it is his first love. His mystery. By any ordinary definition, he does not suffocate, not in living nor dying. Lugo Parchaisi's homeland surf breaks along the shoreline. He bleeds to death in a place where he belongs.

PART TWO
Assemblage of Crew

A Purposeful Life

Water. Every night a wake, little else remains. Every day partake, more of the same. How does it feel to gasp upon waking, final breath escaping, back unto a perilous hue?

Onquin meets with the design team yet again. The blue lights have recently been replaced by auditory cues. Hesitations seem normal until informed otherwise. "There's a temporal problem, honey, and we don't know how to fix it. We can't keep going back because there are resiliency issues. Your tissues are having much difficulty accepting imprints. Any additional attempts may result in damage." Staff members address her concerns, but even from behind the darkened observation glass, I see distress that fills us both. Onquin opines that science has never been so exhausting.

"It is your indistinct manner of speech that carries subtext. When things are going well, I receive minute details, enthusiasms shared, intricacies of my life being rebuilt. Wiped clean and rebuilt. Lately excuses are the norm. Might it have been more fitting had you simply left me at the bottom of the pool?"

Memory no longer avails a trusted reality. All she has ever been is relayed second hand, told to her by doctors relying on files, perhaps told once too often. At the age of eleven she drowns, nothing left but a flickering brain stem. Despite neuronal symbiotics, she moves not a single day closer to consciousness. In those coma years, however, she has her uses. Specifically, Onquin's uterus becomes an object of much affection. Two babies are brought to term—in vivo inseminations by eugenicists, producing healthy progeny and moral decrepitude. Is she a mother or simply a vessel? The question lacks relevance. Onquin is cosmetically refurbished and never informed of her gestations. She is thereafter assigned to an Authority tank farm, placed in a vacuole of a Carver cell. Attached in series to other comatose patients, impulses are shared. Spiraled awareness lends well to recovery.

"Provide me with pertinent detail and offer variant choices based upon likely resolution." Onquin addresses all in attendance but none respond. In the back of the room, one technician whispers to another. "She knows her brain is fucked. Now she wants to know what to do about it." Both are startled as she responds. "Correct. My brain is fucked but my auditory capability exceeds the norm. Is your input borne of ignorance or have you something more to add?" The team leader ushers everyone from the room. He sits with her, apologetic, until Onquin suggests such emotion hinders constructive discourse. Several staff members enter the control room, assigning blame until one notices me and alerts the others.

"Mr. Boneheart, we had no idea—" I wave him off and continue watching through the glass.

"Onquin, we've imprinted the initial overlays just fine. Language, objective stimulus response, it's all there. The neural slurry envelops the old patterns, reignited, but this is nascent therapy. All is not understood, and now it's stopped working." He bears down with professional comportment. "For reasons not yet understood, your social overlay lacks a sensitivity response. In other words, your childhood memories... they're gone. We don't know why, but the difficulties you'll face attempting reintegration, I'm sad to say, society won't have it."

Onquin pulls back, scorned though resolute. "I can learn. As you have undoubtedly witnessed, my capabilities exceed the norm. Integration will proceed on an expedited basis."

"Your tenacity is compelling, but no, I'm afraid you don't understand. People will easily tolerate your condition." He reaches out but she does not let him near. "It's the Health Authority that tallies indiscretions. Lost nuances, foibles, call them what you will. Eventually you'll be censured." Her puzzled demeanor has momentary depth, melding back to placidity. "Onquin, In the old days people were fixed. Now we're discards because funding has dried up. That's why we've been taking such big steps lately."

Onquin's quivering lip accents a pout, her fullest expression yet. "True, I have a limited concept of anthropology. While I remain undaunted by my stigmatized behavior, that is not entirely the point." She turns to a man who has labored over her tissues for months on end. "I do not wish to be censured. Are there alternatives?"

The team leader clears his throat. Hesitations are interspersed. "There is... a choice you can make. Difficult... yet purposeful." He shares details of an expedition: two biologists, two engineers, two programmers; six lives committed to the unknown. Some minutes later, all has been explained.

"I am an engineer," she says quietly, startled by this revelation. Faced with her 'limited concept of anthropology,' handlers gamble on the subtleties of persuasion. One day, the requirement for pretense may be understood, but by then none need face the consequences. She folds her arms, addressing the darkened glass wall. "I am to be one of six on this journey. Three men and three women. Who are the others?" I open a channel and modulate the lower registers. "What difference does it make? Each travel of their own accord. All will be highly qualified."

"Competence is expected," she answers. "I speak to issues of affinity and propagation. Are breeding pairs intended?" I say nothing. "Have the others also been coerced?"

"Yes Onquin, to the extent that such is necessary." She persists. I give her two names accompanied by facile detail.

"Les Hather and Arlene Navia." She repeats the names, more tasted than spoken. "A mated pair?"

"No... not yet." Onquin doesn't seem to mind talking to a glass wall. She alludes to group dynamics and asks about the undisclosed crewmembers. I become evasive. "Much beyond these two, the rest are only candidates, you among them. This offer is not open-ended. You must decide."

"Who is the other engineer?" When I fail to respond, she becomes irate. I tell her I cannot say, wherein she touches the glass, complaining about secretive methodologies. "There is a lack of transparen—"

"I cannot say because we don't know yet. Our presumed candidate has been sanctioned by the Health Authority. She is unavailable. Additional candidates are under review. Onquin turns away.

"I am a preferred choice," she murmurs, and then speaks more clearly. "Allow me to consider." Her observational skills are indeed sufficient to warn of subterfuge. She says it's a challenge becoming human again, understanding social intricacies based upon traits ranging the full gamut of polar opposites: strength, weakness, competence, ineptitude; honesty shading into deception. "Who is my intended partner?" she finally asks.

I drum my fingers... "Yashimoi Watanabe."

"And what does he think of all this?"

"He doesn't know yet, but we're hopeful." Upon her insistence, I describe aspects of his life: mundane, accented by conventional misgivings related to poorly considered decisions. Onquin seems to appreciate the very qualities she cannot grasp.

"I hardly understand the choices people make, supplanting self-evident quality for something less. Apparently, volition is fraught with fallibility, which also influences interpersonal dynamics." Onquin's world is a puzzle, and social variability is the linchpin of forced recognition. She sits, elbow on a table, chin on an open palm. The design team has imprinted data where memories might otherwise be found. Recall and application are inevitable, if only she wants it to be.

"Yashimoi Watanabe," she says. "A man placed before me by a world that turns its back."

"I think he'll be favorably disposed to your finer qualities, but then again, I've never met the man." Onquin stands, steps forward, and presses her forehead against the glass.

"And who are you, purveyor of rendered futures?" I pause, long enough to offer an earnest answer.

"One of many, seeking a better life for all. You can help, Onquin. We need you."

On my side of the glass, the team is emotionally spent. They share the trepidation of energies fully given yet helpless to determine an outcome. They want their body of work to choose a journey without recourse. Many fear she'll remain Earthbound instead, searching for human roots. What they fail to understand is that she has none.

Mousetrap

Coincidence
is a bottle of wine at half-past nine
the esters cabernet
Bump in the dark and a red stain mark
on a shirtsleeve Fabergé

"My goodness, I'm so sorry! Let me get some cold water." The waitress pivots, hurriedly finding a full carafe on a vacant table. I calm her down. "Easy Miss, nothing to worry about. All my fault." In actuality, she drifted into me. As she dabs a napkin onto my shirtsleeve, I realize she's more attractive than I'd first noticed; muddy eyes, unassuming, rough-hewn cheeks easily tamed by the composite energies of self. "If you want the real culprit," I say, "look up there, a confluence of planets: Saturn, Venus, and Mars. The gods have it in for me." Her skyward gaze is met with ambient city light. Fingers waggle at our sister planet, then drift off vaguely to where Saturn might be.

"Only Venus is visible," she says. "The god of war is nowhere near. Come back next month. Maybe I can spill something else on you." I ask for another glass of red and a dessert menu. She returns in short order, a breeze wisping chestnut hair across her cheeks. It's shoulder length, shaded auburn beneath. A cocktail napkin slips away, off her tray, landing near the edge of my plate. She sets the wine glass upon it. "Look," she says, a diminutive font glowing ever slightly, 'Polly Elizabeth Collins,' emblazoned across the diagonal. Letters beneath the foot of the glass sparkle intermittently. "It's sharkstooth, pressure sensitive. The napkin syncs, if you allow it. Send me the dry-cleaning bill. Dessert is complimentary."

"The shirt's fine" I say. Looking down to the sleeve lowered at my side. The wine splotch is migrating, dripping off the cuff. Polly pulls a dinner napkin from an unused setting, placing it on the patio's wet spot while eyeing my sleeve.

"Hmmm... something new."

"It's Fabergé," I answer. "A bit too silky but otherwise—"

"I'm sorry, what?" She smiles, an odd glint that finally says hello.

"It's Fabergé," I say again, "manufactured within a Franco/Russo mill up in orbit. Made from some ridiculously expensive stuff. 'Off-cloth,' I think it's called, for times like this."

"Not 'off-cloth,'" she responds, "Loft-Cloth. They want you to know it's made in space. I read about it in one of the trades." She excuses herself for the needs of other tables. By the time I finish my almond mousse, we've shared repartee hinting of quality. I linger at the bar until her shift ends.

Walking inside the southern boundary of Central Park, Polly asks why I dined alone. "A late cancellation," I respond. She gives me a quizzical look, expecting more. I shake my head. "It's petty politics, no different than what's happening there." I point at nearby pigeons congregating around a spilled bag of popcorn. Polly comments. "A friend told me about those. They're nocturnal, some type of marsupial crosshatch." The birds seem ordinary enough. I tell her that as far as I know, pigeons scavenge without respite. "Not these," she informs. "They sleep all day. You can tell by their identifying tail feathers. It's part of city health and welfare."

"Well now, designer pigeons. Exemplars of ennui." I take her hand in mine and inwardly chastise my bad timing, making an intimate gesture while talking about filthy birds. Polly doesn't seem to mind. "Look at them," I add, "popcorn's nearly gone. Now they tear the bag to pieces." Her face falls quiet as we stare at the incongruity of custodial pigeons. Polly points to one bird scissoring apart a small milk carton. "Don't laugh at the bio-engineered. The Authority changes our diets too, and way faster than most care to notice. Work at a restaurant and you'll never eat out again." She offers an apologetic glance and looks away, as if my meal was somehow tainted, and I'm sure it was. I fail to mention using Hitiene wash and gastric filters to neutralize my city meals.

"You don't eat out?" I ask.

"Only the irradiated specs on the underground circuit. You should do the same." She shivers, a slight chill in the air. I pull her close as we meander past a closing kiosk. "I'd just as soon see the Authority disbanded," she says.

Polly is wearing a fragrance unlike ordinary perfume. It hints of rainy subliminals. She spends the better part of an evening hazed in restaurant fumes yet somehow emerges unscathed. For whatever reason, I feel an uncanny touch at her side, comfort and spontaneity. I pull her cocktail napkin out of my pocket, held high, applying pressure between thumb and fingers until her name illuminates. "This is quite an introduction. Pure copperplate, penned with such distinction." She reaches for the napkin, mashing against me. Her half-hearted attempt satisfies us both.

"I ordered a hundred of those," she says, regaining her balance. "What's great is the way the ink bleeds. Makes them look real." I respond open-mouthed, once again pocketing her memento while teasing at the insincerity of her calligraphy. "Oh, come on," she answers, "I give them to students mostly, a stipend for writing papers."

"Somewhat the entrepreneur, eh? What types of things do you write?" She turns to face me. We're close. The napkin is forgotten.

"Deep space systems, engineering stuff mostly." I ask for examples and she gives them with engaging aptitude: the construction of Halloran squares; the various alignments of docking scaffolds. And of particular interest, Polly has a working knowledge of repulsor mechanics. With each breath, contrast is a thing of beauty. Competence is rarely found in so desirable a skin. Her lips reflect pale highlights—street light seeks their moisture within. I stare, absent my usual veneer, wanting to behave in a manner unbefitting a gentleman.

"Ahh," I say, "a high frontier engineer, and a tough climb too. Are you being earnest?" She rocks back and forth, brushing against me, arms and shoulders mostly.

"My genetics already grade out as adaptable. I launch next spring for an apprenticeship."

"How adaptable?" I ask, studying pupils that are unyielding; tight little chips of black light, and a single word barely mouthed.

"...very."

More eyes, hers and mine. I follow her jawline back to the nape of her neck, finally looking to the heavens. My thoughts carry an unexpected mixture of wants, both personal and business. I almost wish she wouldn't be the thing I'm looking for.

"Launch, eh? You any good?" I imagine so. Her nuanced expression doesn't lie. It's an allure rooted within her concept of self. Proper inflection and a hint of reserve pulls me in—turns me into a boy.

"Double crested, one hundred percent invested, top of my class. Why do you ask?" She's playful, yet the dynamic puts me on the defensive. The impetus is vaguely lost between us. Here is a moment that defines one's intention. I hadn't expected it.

"Just seems like such a coincidence, that's all. I may have a proposition for you, a need of your services." She misinterprets my remark, answering in a slightly breathy tone. "I'll bet you do." The innuendo is unmistakable.

"Miss Collins," I say, "there is a time and a place for everything. For now, let us sit awhile." With little effort, she shifts to a more static demure. We lock fingers and settle on a park bench. Does she know who I am? Is there an agenda? We speak for an interval punctuated by the sights and sounds of horse and carriage. Some are empty and others carry the last riders of the evening.

Polly has ideals that brush up against a pragmatic side. She wants everything, but will settle for everything within reach. I calculate her to be an opportunist with an impulsive bent, and me an evening's diversion. Regardless of my judgment, defensive as it may be, she has ambition per her scholarly pursuits. Also percolating within, an energy that grows impatient with my questions. Not the questions themselves, but the fact that I'm holding back.

"Polly, how attached are you to the rhythms of your life?" Her hesitation becomes irritation.

"Odd question from a man desirous of affection."

"Yes, understood. I'll be more direct." I take her hands within mine and glance at the surroundings. "Can you leave this all behind?" Polly puts forth a halting look. A smile comes and goes as she answers. "My apprenticeship on the L-5 spindle can't happen soon enough. Eventually I'll settle down in the outer realm." She wrinkles her forehead, extending this vague line of inquiry. "I don't want what's ordinary. Boredom frightens me." She pulls away slightly, hands letting go. "I saw it in you right away. Big trouble. So, what's on your mind?"

I feel nerves, not jittery or a lack of composure, but an unexpected flexing of the stomach. She scores a response that is involuntary. My eyes look no place in particular. She stands and takes me to task. "You speak of coincidences." She pauses. "There's no such thing, at least none that matter." With much deliberation, she pulls her napkin from my shirt pocket. "You won't be needing this." She is spirited, buoyant and alive. I reach for her, but she evades. "Enough," I hear her say. She turns from me and walks as chestnut and ruby strands fall perfectly into place.

I cannot react. Her joie de vivre had promised so much. Now all I see are shoulders and calves moving. Her attenuating steps are a cadence of disappointment. She reaches the crosswalk, and looks back. "Well Richard, are you coming?" A split-second hesitation, then one bounding step that merges into a natural rhythm. I reach her as the street signal changes. We walk past a halted Cadora transmag. It's empty, with a trailing scuttle attached.

"You and me then, Miss Collins?" Polly takes her time, pursing lips, putting away lip-gloss.

"Anything's possible," she says, words tossed like a spilled bag of popcorn. Her stride leaves me a quarter-step behind...

I catch up in the coming days.

Months later, her foray to L-5 cancelled by yours truly, an oddity reminds me of our budding relationship. Watching a flock of gull wings seeding the clouds, I flick the cockpit controls to autoglide descent, wrestling the darling onto my lap. Together we track one gull wing with a broken hinge, out of formation, desperately trying to keep up. "Hackneyed answers to all the world's problems, with little regard for cause and effect. Makes it tough to concentrate on the finer aspects of you." Polly sighs, closing her eyes, guiding my hand to an altogether different autoglide. "Mmmm... cause and effect," she murmurs.

"Sure. We get moisture right here, but over there farmers lose all, becoming integers of world health. All hackneyed. Reminds me of an old child's game at the Smithsonian, a macabre construction of odds and ends arranged so as to capture a single mouse. Like what we're doing now."

Polly shivers in response. "And I suppose I'm the mouse?" I smile, never quite sure. After background checks, ten days together on a schooner, lots of lovemaking, a Parchmont full physical, and all manner of furtive escapades, I still don't know. We spent a month doing the Eurogrind and I still don't know. Mouse? Mousetrap? Or just a piece of cheese? No doubt a piece of cheese, that much is certain. "So, Señor Gato, what makes you think you're not prone to capture?" She rubs against me, civet sneer; a claiming gesture.

"I'm in that trap already," I say, "long since confined." Upon landing, I open the Ramjet cargo bay doors and together we step down into the hangar's interior. Polly sees the support staff approaching, taking care to smooth her appearance.

"Mr. Boneheart, we're ready sir, that is, if you are?" I place a stylus on my lapel, handing Polly one as well. Affixing it, she also tries to secure an open skirt clasp in anonymity. It's the one thing everyone notices.

"Very well, Mr. Burris. At your command." Burris waves at a distant control booth up in the rafters. The lights dim and an almost imperceptible hum takes hold. A hologram of *Nomad* materializes before us.

"Oh my, it's big!" Polly presses against my shoulder. The representation of *Nomad* is bisected, cut well below the x-axis. Two decks of the ship lay before us lengthwise, with the lower curvature of the remaining hull supposedly buried beneath the hangar floor. I take her hand as we approach the nose cone of this mirage.

"Close your eyes while passing through the hull. The amplification can play havoc with retinas." Each stylus dims the holo just prior to interface, and once inside, I tell her we're standing in the forward compartment. "This is all part of the laser array. Open areas will be filled with supplies, leaving just enough room for maintenance." Polly plays with the hologram, passing her hand through the port console. "What kind of laser," she asks, "what's it for?"

"Well, it's actually a particle beam, mostly molybdenum, with a scattering of heavy metals. Automatically pulverizes oncoming debris that might otherwise cause a hull breach."

"Hmmm," she says, "at such speeds, even specks of dust are worrisome. The targeting processors work that fast?" She takes one look and already sniffs logistics. I share a vacant smile.

"Yeah, at least we hope so. Right now, we're good at the lower end, but with squid tunneling and the displacement stream, it'll need some modifications en route."

"Squid what, exactly?"

"Oh... an acronym. SQUID, um... Superconductive Quantum... Interface thing. I forget exactly... we'll get you the specs, team data, everything. Nothing to worry about." I'm given a disbelieving stare, as if my answer isn't good enough. "Polly, nobody's ever done this before. It'll work. And if it doesn't, you'll make it work."

"With lots of help," she answers, meshing fingers and flexing knuckles, subconsciously preparing for the challenge.

"Come on, let's show you crew quarters. Watch the eyes." We step through the aft wall into the recreation lounge: simulator, exercise equipment, even a hydro spa. "Originally, we designed a holopit up against the far wall, but it didn't make the final cut: too much space on double decks. We substituted virtual reality gear with a shatterglam interface. A scramble getting vendors to meet our specs. You may have to work out a few glitches."

Polly isn't engaged in what I'm saying. She eyes the spa instead. "This won't work unless... unless we've got..." I finish her sentence. "Gravity. Wouldn't leave home without it. Centrifugal, but what the heck."

"Two decks?" she asks. I nod, telling her portions of the hull accordion out for added space. Her gaze measures the interior, the curvature of the walls, the volume of space contained. Something is bothering her and I can guess what it is.

"Does the mouse want a hint? Think back a few years, way back to the earliest *stages* of space exploration." Her face moves from concentration, to implausibility, and finally absurd recognition.

"You've got to be kidding." She mentions a recent NASA retrospective charity event. "This is a holo of an old Saturn booster that put men on the moon. Richard, I'm not going. I won't do this."

"Easy, stop twitching your whiskers. We used a template, that's all. Slightly larger volume inside, and an outer shell that's bigger still. Helped save a few billion in engineering costs. Besides, it's the perfect size."

"Perfect for what, a floating mausoleum?"

"Polly, we defined the specs long ago, to get working on EMMA and some other stuff. We've actually got a real Saturn shell floating around the outer realm. How's that for ideosynchronicity?"

"That's not even a word!" She seems genuinely concerned. "Richard, tell me none of this is retrofit?"

"Oh goodness no. *Nomad* is made of glassy metal. Stuff that didn't even exist back then. Come on, let's walk through some walls." We amble through a holo containing bio resources and hydroponics. After that, an empty module that prompts a question as to future contents. I change topics, showing her an overlay after insulation and shielding are added. "Water reservoirs in the outer shell protect against cosmic rays, so functional living space is quite limited. No private quarters, but enough area end-to-end to carve out a few niches."

Polly snorts, requests and is granted a cross section view of the hull. "The water shielding is grossly inadequate," she says. I acquiesce, telling her the revolving crew module acts as dynamo, creating a magnetic field that augments protection. This elicits a sneer of implausibility, until I mention the water is doped for such purposes. I tell her the engines and hull share magnetic resonance with the displacement gear. I tell her the hull is coated with diamond-like layers of crystalline carbon. I tell her the lifepods offer both protection and restorative properties. I tell her...

Together, we move onward: paired engineering packages, propellant storage, and finally the engine itself. Polly shakes her head. "I'm an engineer, not a shaman. What do you expect me to do with this stuff?"

I pull her in. Tension eases only slightly as she gawks, dumbfounded. "Nothing," I say, "The propulsion system is triple redundant, very few moving parts. If anything, it's all about the software. Basically, just a bunch of ideas. Pretty soon we won't even need wrenches. We'll just think our way through space." I lead Polly directly through the exhaust nozzle, out into the hangar. Beyond the nozzle sits a table with a feast of roast duck, black grapes, and acorn squash still steaming. "Lunch, darling?"

Polly swivels about, no one in sight. They timed it perfectly. She reaches out for the table. "Oh, it's real enough," I say. "That's not holographic duck wafting through the air." We sit, and while pouring the wine, I touch the bottom of my stylus. It begins. Tiny shards of golden haze float on by. She notices at once, glints of light and an accompanying muted rumble. Her head spins around, viewing the nozzle spouting holographic flames that move past us in slow motion. She turns to me with a gleam. "You've turned on the engine! We're dining by candlelight!"

Streamers of simulated plasma float on by. I feed her a morsel of duck, juices dripping onto fingers, laughter abrupt with smiles unusually wide. Our table is at the center of an expanding current that sweeps through the air in sheets. After three gulps of wine, she drops a shoe and slides a leg against mine. Her neck cranes, her hair flows, sharing the deepest jet stream tones. We're together in a pocket of clear air surrounding the table, otherwise completely enveloped in hues of sunshine. Kisses are shared and none are wasted.

The fiery glow takes on ruddy accents that dissolve amidst the whorls. Polly glances about and sees that we're completely cut off from the outside world. She pushes the meal aside, kicking off the other shoe, setting her ass on table's edge.

"My lady, we've hardly touched the food."

"An appetizer. Get down here and make yourself useful." Hiking up her skirt, I slide her undies off and toss them through the flames so others might be warned. She splays open, mischief and fervor equally served. "You teased me plenty back in that cockpit, mister. Now make it up to me." She wraps her legs around my ribs as I coddle her lower back, slipping down to taste. Fleshy warmth rests upon forearms. I nuzzle in and dip deeper. One pass against a nub, a flicker back and forth in a most delicious rub. I linger for a time, dawdling until her engine sputters thrice, a grind, a grunt, a sigh. She twists my hair and purrs divine.

Yashi   **ARLENE   MILES   DAMIEN   POLLY   ONQUIN**

Four quarters divided by hedgerows twelve meters long. Worn balconies blonde and gray, overlooking tenement housing with daffodils tucked into ears, teens drinking beer under a crowded staircase twenty-odd strong. Bottle rockets and burnt steaks, brown sugar clumps moistened by the noon air, crumbled into streaks on cinnamon crepes. And thoughts of romance never more alluring, averted eyes churning, catching her gaze, falling away. She is bored sitting on the curb, a practiced demure, frozen eyelashes acting like parasols only half-raised. The feathers of her cap arch through sky, then downward again toward impish fingernails she has adorned, in sepia tone all underscored; klippity-klip on blacktop, disinterested veil a backdrop, she wants to play. After a moment long, then yet again another pause, you turn in isolation, idled expectation, a patented sensation lacking resolve. One sidelong stare, fully shared, captures her face for the fantasies you'll partake once she is gone. It is a common theme, unsettling, a bare sense of futility that isn't worth remembering. But this is real and somehow it matters, only partially or half-imagined, as if it never happened, or if it did, something went wrong.

Yashimoi Watanabe. It even has my name on it; advertising on a bag full of groceries. It is custom prose, printed while waiting in the checkout line. Now I block the exit, reading it again. "...*klippity-klip on blacktop,*" what can be done? Letting a slow parade of people pass by, I cannot force myself to leave. "Ahh, this is no good, it's too much..."

Accosting the nearest employee, I complain in fragmented words that hold no coherent message aside from displeasure. The supervisor arrives with an apologetic look as antiquated training takes hold. He tries the old feel, felt, found sales technique. "Pardon, sir, I truly know how you feel. When I started reading these ads, I felt the same way. But what we've found is that in the long run, the ads offer value to most customers." I dump the bag contents onto the floor. The supervisor reflexively reaches, juggling items that eventually join all others in a linoleum sprawl.

"Long run? You guys just started doing this a few months ago. What long run?" I kick a pouch of Gaarick's Slop out the open door. It nearly hits an inbound customer. The manager is flustered, looking past me while making eye contact with a surety-panel. The sound of a warning melody enters the air, alerting employees of a possible code nine.

"Sir, please calm yourself. We've no need to escalate a simple misunderstanding." Ripping the bag to pieces until only the ad fragment remains, I shove it into the supervisor's hands.

"Tell me why I'm reading this? Who's the asshole that decided this was fair game?" A floor rat emerges from the checkstand. The rat's swivel and pivot motion deftly secures errant foodstuffs, dropping items into a trailing bin. The rat retracts a grappling arm and spins, avoiding the bare heal of a woman who pushes past. She manages to comment without looking back. "Mine was good. Told me I'm being overcharged at Reagent's Station." The supervisor raises an open palm. It follows the woman's egress, as if her mere existence might be parlayed into an all-encompassing endorsement. He begins reading my personalization, mumbling a few words. '...*she wants to play...once she is gone...*' He looks up, seemingly puzzled. My paper bag advertisement is wriggled up in a balled fist of his folded arms.

"You're upset why, because you didn't get the girl? Or is this another one of those privacy things?" His tone suddenly shifts the onus on me. Out of pure irritability, I push an intervening shoe between the floor rat and a box of crackers. We play keep away.

"Privacy thing. Yeah, why get excited? It's just the Bill of Rights, or maybe it's the Constitution. Or maybe you can shove this privacy thing up the ass of that French bitch. You know the one, strong jaw, east coast, waving a torch in the harbor?"

The supervisor reaches down, snatches the box off my foot and tosses it into the bin. "I came over here in a hurry because frankly, we've had the occasional message that needs a bit of massaging. But yours is clear enough. I got it right the first time. You didn't get the girl, did you?" The supervisor is going ad hominem, trying to win an argument for the sake of winning an argument.

"Well considered, Mr. Manager. On one hand, we've got privacy rights of the individual, which falls under the laws that govern society. On the other hand, we've got pussy, which falls under the laws of pussy. Yeah, I'll admit, this girl and I had a long moment that played out between us, and in retrospect, I should have asked her name. Even so, just because I didn't, that doesn't make me angry. What bothers me is that we shared something. It was ours and ours alone, and now I'm reading about it at the market. What does that tell you?"

"Tells me this happened on a public street where every square centimeter of roadway is monitored. That my friend, is public license." I see my groceries enter the check stand once again, right back into another paper bag.

"Cameras don't spew out words like this. I mean, I see the ad, and I feel like I'm back at the party looking at her. Sure, I didn't manage to say hello. It's just... I don't need this world to remind me it was something I wanted to do." This standoff settles into more conversational tones. The supervisor dips his jaw and raises an eyebrow—facial metrics too conspicuous to be persuasive.

"Strange, what you said, that's pretty much how the ad ended." And then he chuckles. "You know, mostly these things help save time or money—weekend ideas, spa treatments, or a restaurant. But this one really struck a nerve. I figure it's like the horoscope thing: every once in a while, they're perfect."

Reaching over a rail, the supervisor pulls up my groceries, hands them over, dropping the crumpled ad into my bag. His prolonged smirk suggests yet another incremental victory added to his employment manifest. I garner no sense of satisfaction, lingering on feelings that won't release.

"It's way too close to the truth. Our decisions and habits, everything scrutinized by some bastardized social eye." The supervisor thinks me inane. He ushers me out of the store as I continue. "Who creates these messages? Are they plucked from psych profiles, and what's the point of making me angry?" Putting a hand on my shoulder, the supervisor gives a worn response. "I wouldn't want to know."

Off in the distance, a trolley arrives flashing my destination along its length: Hyperion... Hyperion... Hyperion... "That's me," I say, picking up the slop pouch and turning away, striding a bit until I enter the required radius. My travel-tag holds the door until I'm aboard.

The supervisor's musculature relaxes as he walks back inside. The floor rat missed an orange that had rolled away and is now wedged between pressed stacks of charcoal. "Hyperion," he sighs. "No wonder, the poor jackass is living right on the edge."

It's the third complaint this week, yet another reaction to the new ads. This one was initiated as a prompt, looking for a measured response. The supervisor stares out the store window with a wry smile. He watches the trolley disappear from view. How will the customer react when he notices his new ad? Across the middle of the brown paper bag, in a distinctive font, is the answer to all of Yashimoi Watanabe's questions: "Her name is Tara Jones." And it even comes with a contact sync and phone number.

YASHI   **ONQUIN**   **DAMIEN**   Arlene   **POLLY**   **MILES**

"Complexity belies simplicity." It is an unassuming voice, logic neatly drawn, the mandate of which is proven all wrong. For what can be more complex than a child's needs so wistful, solving those needs simply with a blunt-nosed pistol? The image lingers still. My mother raises the gun to her temple, creating a ruddy display not quite burgundy, not quite rust, though in later years the blood-stained bricks fade just so. Those bricks become a symbol of civic pride, adorning a central city courtyard and galvanizing a mixed race of peoples, including the progeny of one, Sylvester Ramirez. Through her and others, life's lessons endure.

I was born with a compromised immune system related to several trigger flaws on paired chromosomes. Modern medicine could have patched me, albeit such therapy fell outside the realm of essential services. I therefore felt unessential, though mother insisted otherwise, and so I grew up in a bubble slightly larger than a household bathroom. It was a time wherein the Health Authority was unwilling to affect honorable policy: 'One Choice' was HA's slogan of the day, which may as well have been 'Fuck Off,' it meant much the same. The AI constabulary decides our futures in advance, guardians of a genome both lucrative and selectively refined. More and more, Planet Earth, by invitation only.

Wanting the best for her child, Mother established Mercy's Call, raising funds for a handful of younglings. Speeches were made as local media provided token coverage. Children in bubble suits entered the facility with gaiety, waving to all in attendance. Monies were transferred and thereafter we exited the facility, each accompanied by a frown. Given a blanket declaration, no therapy was allowed. An incensed doctor ignored the mandate and attempted manual therapy. The machinery simply did not function.

Mother sued Universal Health but was denied access to the courts. The regional round-top rendered non-obligatory recourse, citing an ambiguous waiver clause. Mother vented her fury by pouring a bucket of acid into the honorable round-top servo junction. The thing melted, becoming one big shit stain in the courthouse lobby.

Mom was arrested, sedated and otherwise constrained for an interval during which she lost her job, her pension, and our home. Employment was reinstated upon appeal, but mother was laid off shortly thereafter. She committed additional acts of vandalism, resulting in additional criminality. In lieu of internment, a restrictor plate was applied, along with probationary psychoactives. Mom was dropped off at the Meadowlands exterminary by a social worker preaching irredeemable dogma. "The world is changing," "All is forgiven," and my particular favorite, "Sin needn't be unkind."

"Complexity belies simplicity," the social worker told Mother. "We're all confused because they're so smart, and we're not." He left her on the doorstep of a percentage. In instances approximating hers, 1.3% used the exterminaries. She'd never heard of, nor even imagined such a thing.

Mother said no thanks to that, moving my bubble into the warehouse district. By no odd set of circumstances, I found myself in the company of the very doctor discharged for attempting my care. He removed mother's probationary drip via radical mastectomy, and thereafter, she rode the gratis beltway for months on end, plugged into Advent-cloudworks. She researched, bristled and fumed, seeking Health Authority vulnerability. What this entailed was undetermined, but Mother wanted monumental fornication: a screaming, ankle-grabbing fuck-job that even a computer couldn't ignore.

Her studies finally revealed an indemnity clause that nullified legal agreements made within 183 days of a victim's suicide. An individual committing suicide was not of sound mind and therefore lacked credible grounds for entering into binding contracts. Of course, exterminaries were excluded, having been porkbarreled into law by an amalgam of municipalities—providing a good number of jobs for the constituency.

To this day, I still feel her touch. We stand together in a courtyard, me on an apple crate, fingers interwoven and curled around a narrow cylinder. Mom tells me of a distant journey. Things I can scarcely remember, being too absorbed in fear at the time. She shakes me, lifts my breather, kisses and hugs me, sets my breather square again as her words brush up against an ear.

"Hide this. Hide this always and let no one take it from you. Your future is inside." Mother snugs the cylinder into a thin pocket seam woven into my dress. As I balance on the crate's edge, she shouts to all who would listen. "My name is Eleanor Navia," she begins, recounting all that was taken. A gathering grows, animated with like-minded conviction. In particular, her visit to the exterminary riles the crowd. She shows off her restrictor plate, describing the pain. Finally, she comments on the new suicide law and how compassionate the Health Authority had become.

"Complexity belies simplicity," she utters, squeezing my fingers with one hand, squeezing a trigger with the other. I cannot recall with certainty my falling, only sensing a lifeless hand that would not let go. I wanted to cry. I wanted to, but did I?

News spread rapidly, others drawn into the fray. Contracts were signed as suicides tumbled into the mainstream. The Health Authority paid a significant sum before laws were altered once again. Years later, after the legal process had run its course, I received graft therapy via funds restored to Mercy's Call, all with the help of a certain doctor that taught me much, never minding a little human intervention.

Today I honor Mother's protest, volunteering for a journey amid tight quarters fondly reminiscent of a sheltered upbringing. This also has the unintended consequence of distancing me from the Health Authority, which jettisoned the exterminaries as a concession to sentiment, replaced by virulent biologics using helixware targeting. A Health Authority conscript who leaked these admissions was placed into lockdown and forcibly administered nurlazine surfactants within a stasis dirge. Days hence, whistleblowing inferences were downgraded to delusional episodic trauma. There was no public outcry.

In private, everyone decides the truth of such events for themselves. As for me, I care little what the Health Authority dreams up next. Whatever storm, whatever gust of wind or butterfly they place before me, it matters not. Soon I will be back in my bubble, this time with friends. We shall be in flight unbound, beyond the travails of social calculus. Beyond all things I cannot figure out. Beyond my stained bricks of misanthropic doubt.

"Good gracious," I hear myself say, pulling free of the scanning table. "It itches whenever I stop thinking! Each hesitation pulls descriptives when forming sentences. Sometimes it even searches for tastes and smells." Sasha Nguyen hands me two syntabs and a cup of water. Her shrunken smile hints at responsibility that spreads one thinly.

"We've been using the old prototype. It gloms and noodles a bit."

"It's downright sticky," I answer, sipping the water. I hand back the syntabs, noticing a dull ache in my diaphragm. "It makes breathing uncomfortable, so much so I nearly began stuttering."

"Oh, you stuttered more times than I can count. The reciprocal connectivity performs syntax weave. Hard to explain, but useful for the end product. Not to worry though, *Nomad's* journaling will be seamless." Hmmm... it tricks the memory somehow. Unsettling to say the least.

"Can I read it?"

"Not yet." Sasha motions for me to follow to an adjoining room. "The extraction is being revised inside a latent repository. Specifics are free-floating within a composite memory capture. It self-organizes."

"How much longer?" I ask.

"The new version does it instantly, but like I said, we're using the prototype. It'll take a while." Sasha is given over to an interface that's more computer science than biology. It's all mentally exhausting and I'm apt to understand why syntabs are offered. "Your embedded chip is without apparent fault. Once we get your cryopaste assays, we'll do the fine tuning." My chip is clean. I reach back to touch it, the area still sore after insertion.

"Don't," a man's voice says off to one side. "Leave it be." Near the doorway, a gaunt fellow rubs stubble on an unwashed face. Slightly older than me, a stark demeanor fills tired eyes the color of milk chocolate. Owl-like ringlets circle each eye.

"Damien," Sasha says, "You shouldn't be here." He steps forward with a crocked smile and a hand offered. "Damien Wells, at your service." Sasha's efforts to come between us are met by a stiff hand placed softly on her forehead. "Easy, Sasha, I know the game, and I know this little one."

"But she doesn't know you!" Muscle tone in his shoulders and arms belie the haggard look. His smile remains unnaturally frozen. Damien Wells seems delighted in my presence though I'm at a loss to know why.

"So?" I ask.

"So, we'll be working together. Can't say I'm disappointed."

"Damn You!" Sasha stammers, her ineffectual tug barely shifting his balance. "You've got to go. You've got to go now."

"Not a problem, Slosh, but first a little chat, then we part til launch."

"You're part of the *Nomad* crew?" I ask. "Doing what, exactly?"

"Same as you." Sasha swallows hard, striding out the exit, mumbling about worthless security. The import of this ongoing introduction is lost on me. "Somewhat inhospitable," Damien says, noticing before I do that my journal exploratory has downloaded on an illumid spool. He rips the page free of the dispenser, ignoring the static discharge.

"Hey, that's private! Hand it over!"

"Ease up," he answers. "It's a journal entry, like any other. I'll show you mine once the re-do is finished. My first chip didn't take." Damien twists and shows me his neck. Angry flesh, bloated in places, with outlines of a bioport deeply channeled. While reading, he glances briefly, noticing my concern. "It's post infection. I'm fine." He concentrates on the illumid—a single ragged sheet, longer than it should be because he pulled it from the spool. Once finished, he hands it over. "Sorry Arlene. Sorry about your mom. Seems you had it bad. I didn't know. I should have."

"Not too bad," I answer, and once again I reach back to my interface chip. "But this... Frankenstein thing attached to my spine, it's..."

"Unwieldy," he interrupts. "Ungainly. Unnecessary. Truth be known, I pulled mine out with a pair of pliers." He sees me recoil, and adds, "Deep integrations hadn't been set. No tendrils, no organic bonding. You see, the folks around here think they own you. That chip is just a reminder, the bigger the better. I replaced mine with a liquid upgrade. Bloodstream access, maintenance through my vascular port. Too late for you, I'm afraid." The door springs open and Sasha reenters, accompanied by a man with a noticeable limp. I've seen him at a distance once before. Damien offers a smug greeting of sorts. "Ah, Parker. Still standing, I see."

"Let's go, Damien."

"Fine," he answers, "time to leach the soul." They exit together, Damien hesitating at the doorway. "Know what it is you want. These people need you and you owe them nothing." I'm left facing Sasha, intent upon proofing my first journal entry. 'Complexity belies simplicity,' it begins, and without interruption, the words spill into me accompanied by rancor and insensitivity. "These are not my words, not in temperament, nor in candor. It's blatantly unfair."

"Yes, true," Sasha answers. "Everyone that's been chipped thinks the same as you."

"It's disappointing."

"It is," she responds. "We don't have enough context to produce a representative voice. At first, the newly referenced stream merges into the defaults. As sample size increases, your voice takes hold. I'm sorry if you're offended, but it just proves you're normal."

"Why are the defaults so antagonistic?"

"Honesty," she answers. "Tell me Arlene, is your journal entry factual?"

"Sure, but—"

"But that's it, isn't it? The defaults are set for honesty. That's more important than satisfying insecurities or any feel-good textural minutiae."

Sasha's voice takes on the tone of condescending handler. She suggests journal chips filter much of the insubstantial. Lacking this baseline, lies may well be interpreted as facts. I suddenly become self-conscious that my journal chip is functioning at this very instant. Perhaps through this chip I'll protest the tenor of today's interplay? First, Sasha tells me my journal entry is inaccessible, only to have it appear. Next, there is an unspoken animosity between Sasha, Damien, and this Parker fellow. None of this is put in any better context for my benefit. Finally, I receive a sermon regarding honesty, contrasted by Sasha's clipped responses.

"Damien promised that I could read his initial journal entry."

Sasha smiles stupidly. "He's not authorized to make such a promise."

"Tell Parker, and whoever else, that I'll have the first read—much as Damien had done to me. Otherwise, we're done here." Sasha leaves without a word. Forty minutes later, Damien's testimony is dispensed. One illumid sheet torn free of the spool, shorter than my own...

ARLENE   Damien   **YASHI**   **ONQUIN**   **POLLY**   **MILES**

A cyclone drops upon a home, contents unto heaven
Deposited elsewhere far afield, as allegoric weapon
Captivations torn apart as detritus impales a woman's heart
The wreckage indiscernible, cyclone undeterred
A reminder all is learnable, either witnessed or inferred
Eulogy or effigy, random chance or dwelt upon
This world has the answers on, we try and take them off

My name is Damien Wells and I'm psychotic. It wasn't always this way. Months after the caprice of this world extinguished my love, the resulting anguish is captured and sustained: I inject a massive dose of narcopathy hematopes—dreadnoughts—the aggressive kind. They roost in my brain and start budding, crowding the existing playing field like suds pouring from a washing machine.

My personality undergoes transformation. Nuance is either attenuated or magnified as my better nature vanishes beneath stimulated foci—tiny areas of the brain that can no longer be satisfied. This will certainly cause discomfort for the rest of my life, though interestingly, the part of myself I can no longer recognize undergoes the most profound change of all.

These hematopes were originally used in dream regression therapy; at times tailored for sleep deprivation; often used to augment psych profiles; occasionally used to squash recurrent nightmares. I had a bevy of patents before all were confiscated, a byproduct of my overdose. Today, I'm told my dreams carry a texture never before experienced. They are emphatic dreams that resonate paranormal.

Hematope-added tissue density has the intended purpose of delineating amplified stimuli during REM sleep. Properly administered, subjects need an interface device to record impulses, but not me. My brain has been rewired, now a neurological transmitter during dreamscape. It is both a gift and a curse, sometimes startling, at times perverse, though most often it's simply a documentation of sadness.

I no longer recall my dreams. This disconnect is probably for the best. In earlier days, I was awakened at haste, sometimes under the threat of violence. To the informed, receiving waking dreams is a novelty. The entertainment is abrupt, perhaps even riveting. To the uniformed, however, my psychic broadcast might well be an invasion of privacy. Once upon a time, I was nearly thrown off an ocean liner near Port-au-Prince, accused by deck hands of voodoo acondae.

Drugs are prescribed but more often than not, seclusion is preferred. Above all, my unabsorbed dreams leave me wanting. I wish to reclaim a life taken from me by the movement of moisture turned into violence; taken by a bloodied bicycle spoke that pierced both atrium and ventricle. My wife died in my arms and there's nothing I can do about it.

My hematope overdose gave me an insensible hope of supplanting cyclone nightmares. Perhaps I might enjoy an aberrant existence wherein dreams are more real than not? That was my high-minded ideal, to furrow my head in ecstasy or agony. To reclaim bliss, or partake of visceral pain. Truthfully, however, I was fairly certain hematopes taken in such quantities would just plain kill me.

After burning my lover's bones in a furnace, I could hardly find use for a planet that cannot possibly make amends. Space beckons, to rid myself of the here and now, particularly in light of my newfound notoriety. I've become the target of various economic interests, each seeking capture of intellectual property. One lab offered a sizable ransom for the privilege of dissecting my skull postmortem. I declined, wary of their urgent intent. A shrink-wrapped interval at the sanitarium left little room for authority figures. Particularly offensive were the Health Authority practitioners. They're a stiff crowd, money hungry, and altogether lacking in the spirit of covenants they enjoy violating. A casual view of my file, left unattended, revealed much. Too much, including several unauthorized implants.

I am rogue now, having chosen hyperflight, but not before bribing a guest-class worker. His considerable programming skill instructed the nightshift autodoc to remove clandestine hardware from my head. These extracted trinkets are mementos of a society no longer trusted. Their combined value is higher than the wages an average labtech accretes in a lifetime.

No doubt this renegade status requires deft maneuvering to retain my freedom. If only I knew who did this to me, I'd mitigate their ongoing concerns by sending them aspirin and a bottle of piss. Not cookies and milk exactly, but one can only be generous to a fault. I contacted several peers; friends and acquaintances doing outlandish research wherein mere consultations derive laundered credits extraordinaire. One such contact lined up a deep space expedition on a ship called *Nomad*. I like the sound of it. Seems authentic. *Nomad*, where white-collar assholes don't turn brain cells into ingots. *Nomad* comes and it goes. Who knows the entertainment value of deep space? It may just hold the key to unlocking my dreams.

MILES   DAMIEN   POLLY   ONQUIN   ARLENE   Yashi

Paddlewheel boats move side-to-side as childish laughter fills the sky. Cotton candy falls overboard and melts, eyes follow down unto the depths. A whistle blows, a scamper and a waddle, the ticklish side of a girl caves in beneath hands that surely follow. Easter wind rolls high above but does not touch this throng of innocents. They hide within grasses long, smiles, parade, and song.

The final days on Earth bring melancholy to a boy barely a man. I, among five others, am chosen as volunteer. It is an oxymoron that well describes ambient volition. The Health Authority rejected my appeal for services due to 'profiled disobedience.' This leaves me little in the way of Semper Par health coverage. A home test kit confirms cellular progressions that portend a dire outcome. Subtle markers put me on a clock. I must find a way to stop this. And I have.

A med broker takes me on as little more than bio-salvage, replete with bad genetic inlays likely derived from none-other-than the Health Authority itself. Taken underground to an off-HA shop, I am pumped full of volatiles—nasty scrubbers that barely distinguish friend from foe. I endure a chrysalis rehab that not only saves my life, but gives me a new one. My identity is expunged, death certified as untimely and painful. Among the benefits of anonymous ignominy, I receive state-of-the-art implants—all the usuals and some not so usual. The medics are not surprised at my lack of appreciation, knowing this constitutional comes at a price. I am headed off-world, destination: unacquainted vice.

Tara Jones knows how to smile, tuck, roll, and quiver so. She is of a careless style, a songbird with clipped wings that never fly too far from home. Abundantly blessed with feminine wares that coalesce, she hungers for attention span, being held, avoiding cold, always wanting, never told. As a grown-up child, hard to find, she shares herself from time to time, and lacking ego, learns to hide, within of all places, other people's lives molded just so.

Yashi finds her one day, debutante, a glimmering hopeful appetite. Ankles taut, nipples flexed, she tries and does her best. He lets her stay. She makes breakfast then spends the day, naked and outstretched beneath pillows that cannot cover her desire. Errant feathers carry her allure beyond windows that hold her firm. She emboldens all that she consumes, so fully sexed and never, ever, out of tune.

I hate to leave her, imagining what I'll remember, aggrieved lucidity, even as she lay beside me. Her skin is a tactile sense. Breath from her lungs sweeps across my chest. It's all the world can expect of me, to be here with her, at times within her, it makes no sense to be anywhere else.

I didn't say how long I'd be gone. Duration is open-ended, for good reason. No one spends the kind of money they did, fixing my body with industrial precision. They tested a good number of things I couldn't quite figure: physiology, psychology, and lots of neurals. This won't be a quick jaunt into low Earth orbit. With no room for negotiation, I'm the guy who smiles and says thank you regardless of condition. So, ass in the air and ride the big one until the ride don't ride no more.

What's the cargo? If illicit, who's not supposed to know? I bartered for my genetic fix with people that deflect lives, including mine. Had I really been born with some rat's ass recessive, cancer indicators dangerously close? Or is some greater game at play? If the Health Authority is behind it all, I'll burn 'em. Burn 'em whether ennobled by privilege, or earmarked as a carcass. Dead ancestors shall rejoice, even if it means the end of a bloodline.

I listen to Tara's cadence, sublime animal asleep by my side. Built more for life than life allows, every past ∞ and every now ∞, these figure-8s skate through me, limbs forever reaching as though suddenly we'll be ripped apart, and this time she's right. In the morning I'll be gone, long enough that she'll forget, diverged with little hope of recapture. The weight of perfection rests upon me, chin nuzzling my shoulder. I stare into darkness. Her inhale is life. Her exhale ends all. Over and over…

ONQUIN   **POLLY**   Miles   **DAMIEN**   **ARLENE**   **YASHI**

Amidst the Canister brain trust deep underground, I sit in committee, all eyes upon me. "You're looking at the offspring of your ideology, growing up on a farm that produces melons and dissociative behavior. Inherently I understand and no one should doubt my resolve." The tabletop shimmers beneath the fingertips of my right hand. Streaks of yellow and gold emanate outward like slow lightning. The colors are unusually bright and long lasting. Richard Boneheart sits directly across from me and answers dismissively. "We see you're quite determined, this boyish look of yours turning rugged as you try to make a point. But that's not at issue here. Does your emotional disposition allow for such a journey? Teach us. Speak of your formative years."

I find little humor in pseudo-analysis. Boneheart's contentious voice seeks out discomfort, prodding and goading. The choice is between Les Hather and myself. Being compared to Hather is insulting enough, but imagine losing out to one of Boneheart's sycophants. Standing up, the table draws dark for an instant, ignited once again as my palms press on table's edge. This time it's a dull shade of red.

"As you well know, I schooled ninety-three kilometers down the road at that Wedgewood 'Pillory' Campus, a dead boy's chip buried in my neck. His name was Rick Barnes and so was mine, whenever I was above ground. Friends called me Barney, but I prefer Miles. Miles Dandridge. I'm trained not to care upland, but down in the Canister, I like to be recognized for who I am, not who I'm supposed to be."

Irritation dissipates as the color nearest my palms fades to soft orange. "I spent the better part of most days studying my father's profession, albeit under the guise of stupidity in the form of a state sponsored education. It was a trade-off, with access to a federal portal used to great effect. I was soaking up tradecraft while the other kids absorbed social lessons. I'm satisfied with that. Every child growing up in the Canister knows they're only truly appreciated when they become useful." I look side to side across the room, taking a sip from my collar nozzle. Boneheart seizes the interval to push further.

"Yes, Ricky, we're well aware of your talents. That's why you're here. We also know you sometimes make interesting choices. What should we make of that? Why should we trust you?"

I feel little indignation from Boneheart's inflection. It's clearly a test, the tabletop rippling purple when he had called me Ricky. Otherwise, poise prevails. "I volunteered for square-outs at age eleven. I've completed eight missions thus far. A few municipals, several hot reads, even one op that cost me an eye. I'm not always satisfied with the details, but results speak for themselves."

I catch Sasha Nguyen's stare, her son having died on my watch two years ago. She looks at my hands, searching for a color spasm that never comes. "You're wondering about your boy, if his death was necessary? I tell you no, not necessary at all. We had achieved our objective but he tried for more data than our stealth KP could hide. I fried him with a streaming feeder, dirty and painful. Otherwise, the Canister would have been compromised. I'm sorry for your loss." Her expression solidifies. "Sasha, my choices under pressure are a response to an internal value system that cannot be bargained with. If ever there comes a moment when a decision must be made, I will make that decision every time." I release my grip on the table upon noticing a white arc pulsing outward. It's pride. It's embarrassing. Richard Boneheart heads to the doorway, ignoring all others. "You're the one, Miles. Consult Merrihew in bionics. If all goes well, you'll be on the next transport to the outer realm."

§

Floating debris moving in endless repetition, the asteroid belt's barren actuality gives me a headache. That's Ceres in a nutshell, looking out the porthole above my bed. I'm stuck here, days becoming weeks. Trying to make myself useful, I hack maintenance script from the log of a beached cargo drone. I uncover nested tacticals of Metaworks Intron, including several partnered platforms. Plumbing their surveys, I purchase options on a pair of smallish asteroids. Soft-assays suggest a concentration of metalloids previously unrecognized via metadata.

In the days spent on Hialeah Five, I take care to avoid the main hangar. One of the Behemoths is docked for resupply. Ordinarily such craft patrol the grazing orbits of Earth. They traffic net communique within an oeuvre of Health Authority muscle. Finding an enforcer here is surprising. Behemoths drop insertion teams, deploy rail guns, and generally nix insubordinate types well before any potential disturbance imprints. I dislike the comgear that rings the ship's girth like tufts of privilege. I dislike the bulbous shape and firepower turrets. I despise the death toll of their so-called peaceful intent.

After some vapid programming, a buffered financier absorbs the mining options. They'll eventually be sold at a profit. I patch my activities into the transit chip of a local prospector, covering my ass in case Metaworks gleans an angle they don't appreciate. This mop and glow hardly matters. My transport leaves on the coming cycle for the Galilean Moons.

§

"Off in the distance to your right, Europa's luminosity is a most welcome sight as gateway to the outer realm. Over 80% of the populace beyond the asteroid belts reside here, and remember folks, on the shores of Lake Woebegone sits the only transit station for heading back home."

Settling into my time-shared cubicle, I take inventory. The wet bar is fully stocked, but the pillows have gone missing. I have a new ear pin, tapped into the tourist junket, which is locked onto the primary hull above. Listening to this *National Geographic* introductory makes me conscious of my status as foreigner. On Earth, I'm separate from the bulk of humanity, but I belong. Out here, no one does. Identity relates to habit. I'm told good habits keep you alive, determining one's standing. This is comforting. You can live on a ship or in a hole in the ground, sometimes it's the same thing.

I dim my cubicle and look through a window across the aisle. Can't see much until the passenger there adjusts his viewport magnification. Suddenly Europa's flotilla is spread across the surface, each enclave appearing as nothing more than a landlocked buoy.

"Hydro resources make Europa the destination of choice for colonization and heavy industry alike. Surface ice creates a lid for native protoplasm, isolated within the depths of Ocean Pericles. If you wish to visit the mid-rift fissure on the ocean floor, the Dive Chamber Emporium will accommo..."

Another advertisement leaves me searching for something Boneheart had said. '...mid-rift is manmade, bleeding Europa's core deep below Cape Lagoon,' and now *National Geographic* infers geologic origins. One can hardly argue with tourist cash. It's an ever-increasing percentage of survival margins. That same money also brings stupid people, and some of those can get you killed. After a lengthy interval that includes a meal of pronghorn and some gritty larder crickets, we approach a new spectacle, this time on my side. No magnification is necessary.

"Io is a harsh domicile for the uninitiated. Slightly smaller than Earth's Moon, it is only slightly closer to Jupiter than the distance between Earth and the Moon. This adds much in the way of perspective, relating the size of Jupiter to our terrestrial memories."

A series of vibrating thumps within the aft hull plating hints at a cargo shell release. No doubt it's destined for Cinder Cone, energy station and lone outpost on Io. Whereas the flex-grid orbiting Io feeds ring traffic and Claymores, it's Cinder Cone's primary dish in resonance with this flex-grid that supplies juice to Europa—enough to tickle a frozen ocean.

"On your window overlay, notice the plasma torus continually forming around Io's orbit. Caused by Jupiter's magnetic field, this doughnut-shaped cloud gives insight into the dynamics Jupiter shares with its surroundings. Io literally becomes an electric generator as the Jovian presence relentlessly strips away Io's volcanic gases."

The information is ridiculously out of context with the visual. Jupiter seems to be nothing short of a star sheathed inside a planetary skin. Io's crust heaves and buckles beneath the gravitational assault. Jobs on Cinder Cone pay higher rates than any blue-collar job in history. It's hardly worth it. Despite living in pressure spheres and using chemo submersion prior to every ninety-minute shift, the median survival rate is frightening. Anyone serving a full term and making it out again has an exploitable franchise. Problem is, it's legacy, not lifestyle.

A circumnavigation of the gas giant is necessary for final approach. I close my eyes as we begin to arc around the backside of Jupiter. The overhanging bulk pushes into my unsettled nap like a closing tomb. My dream is simple enough. The entire liquid content of my body is drawn forth, oozing from mouth and eye sockets toward a source of power. When I awaken, I'm drooling down my port window. After taking a soma tab, tempered sleep finally arrives, only to be jolted awake. My window flashes an opaque red hazard signal. Half the time I can see outside. The other half is my mirrored face, bloodied crimson in the reflective glare of the warning. Auditory instructions follow.

"All passengers, please move to the cargo bay and enter lifeboats in a calm and orderly fashion." As expected, chaos ensues, though I remain steadfast. Everyone else is on the move, launching themselves into open spaces that quickly become clogged. The entire cabin seems to be tumbling bits of geometry. My apprehensions are drawn back to the spectacle unfolding outside.

It would seem the Behemoth previously moored on Ceres has followed us, or more specifically, followed me. In waking, I had imagined we were approaching brightside, but now I've come to realize we retain the full weight of Jupiter's shadow. What is not dark however, is the flank of the craft that dwarfs us. The Behemoth's starboard midsection has been gorged open. It roils in glowing globs of metal spewed like water from a drain spout. An aft cannon is little more than a nub, yet I see no opposing craft. Nothing to fight, no nearby wreckage. Aside from the use of nautical mines, I can't imagine how such damage was inflicted? But mines fall easy prey to sweepers and their incendiaries. Every Behemoth has an entourage fleet—protective gnats that detail a perimeter. Mines are little more than lint in high contrast.

A steward barks commands and pulls on my arm. I push away without looking back. The strobing warning annoys me such that I tear open the window molding, finding no disconnect or circuitry. The steward tries again, and this time I buck violently with a balled fist. He counters.

"Suit yourself asshole, but we're leaving."

"Thank you," I say, "pleasant flight."

The aisles have begun clearing. Within a forward cubicle, a window either malfunctions or exhibits an override. In any case, there is no bisected vision; no flashing warning. I take a seat there, lash myself in, wanting for a pressure suit. Outside, a spigot of fire erupts from the wounded Behemoth's underbelly. Arcing flame pours back around in a magnetic loop much like a sun flare, and suddenly I understand. The craft seals itself with a brutal weld.

The backdrop for all that occurs is Jupiter. Every flash of light leaves tracers; swirls of striated chroma; hues of planet being pulled like taffy. Just below, the rings shimmer, an endless ruddy dust in planar relief. A brilliant flash forces this immersion closer at hand and proves my instincts correct. Lifeboats are being targeted by the Behemoth's swarm.

Darkness. Light. Explosions as vacuum sucks screams from the dying. The Health Authority's fingers stretch further than my own, and yet I am proud looking at the damage inflicted. Half of that warship cannot put me to death. The Behemoth sidles at a splayed angle, rotating in a manner that brings a full-length profile of the undamaged side into view. Ergo, a functional cannon and line of sight that'll result in a face shot. Not much more to it, aside from a blossom flash as I cease to be.

Another lifeboat explodes above me. I cannot see the point of impact, nor the full measure of debris, but clearly the swarm takes care of all offending particulates. They hold the perimeter, awaiting the Behemoth to finish us off. If swarm craft had attempted to destroy this vessel, the resulting spread would migrate outward, leaving room for survivors trapped in ever-expanding wreckage. Better tactics suggest confinement until singular devastation is applied.

The Behemoth continues to pivot. Cursory geometry tells me I haven't much time. The undamaged side comes into full view glistening of sweat— a laser-reflective coating oozing from within. I glance about the cabin, wondering if any spot is better than any other? The empty cabins, concubine chambers, and bathrooms all autolock during an evacuation, allowing only egress. This funnels passengers into the cargo bay. I'm reminded of visio fiction wherein cabin pressure is lost on an airplane. People reach for oxygen masks. One poor wretch grabs a seat cushion with hopes of protective posture and eventual flotation.

Outside, the Behemoth's undamaged cannon stares at me directly. My time is at hand. Despite efforts to sense possible futures, to infer behaviors that ensure survival, the Health Authority appears to have gained a forward reckoning. I thought I might die on this journey. Indeed, I understood the inevitability of it, but not now. Not so soon. The cannon off in the distance is laser lit blue. The sighting mechanism bears down through my window directly onto my chest. I'm not even sitting at my assigned cubicle. I'm at a different window altogether, and it's got me anyway.

Looking at my chest, the laser light loses focus and scatters. Out the window, the Behemoth is under siege again. A fog of war and darkness occlude my view. This predator is entirely consumed in a haze of mist pouring out in all directions. Agitated blotches of flame illuminate the expanding cloud from within, structure peeking through now and again in streaks of exploding pieces. My first impulse tells me I've witnessed a direct hit on life support, oxygen tanks exploding in series. The cloud ignites in blazing excess, triples in size, then dissipates in shorn fields of deflector remnants.

I see mass scattering in clumping heaps. I see impact features now visible on the shattered hull. I see the unmistakable glow of high-density melt as metal boils and froths. The source of the attack comes to me all at once, this magnificent assault now laid bare. Cinder Cone on Io has the Behemoth sighted and locked. The energy station's primary dish has been fashioned into a narrow band particle beam generator. At such distances, the results are far beyond formidable. It's a holy fire, turning all that it touches into little more than spaceborne aroma. What I would give to have a whiff of that?

Rendered harmless, the Behemoth is becoming salvage. A prolonged adrenaline rush catches up and I exhale violently, twice, only to be jostled forward. Some sizeable mass has collided with this ship. The sound of scraping metal is trumped by a hammershod anchor tearing through the hull—directly through the outer wall of my time-shared cubicle—a woosh of air and the anchor seals the puncture instantaneously. I'm guessing a pilot of a gnat flier saw the warship being taken apart. There's no going back to it, so now we'll likely be fighting for the oxygen filling my lungs.

As happenstance allows, a glance outside reveals a shadowy figure coming into view. It peers at me through a face shield and gapes my attentions due to the sheer oddity of our encounter. It is vaguely humanoid, with eye slits that extend 90 degrees around each side of the skull where orbital bone should be. The creature uses grapplers and is headed for the nearest airlock. As it swivels away, one eye tracks me from an ordinary frontal perspective, migrating around to the side of the creature's head. It's human enough, Caucasian perhaps, but altered beyond any reasonable splice dynamics.

I think I've got the upper hand, until I see a holstered weapon. Pushing off and swimming forward, I need to set an ambush at the airlock. There are no conventional weapons in sight. What to use? When it looked at me, there was a hint of something—a clear eyelid moving sideways across the eye. It's a nictitating membrane, maybe amphibian or reptile, or whatever else has a third eyelid. Frog? Crocodile? Half-assed pangolin?

Making it to the galley, I hear a dull hum at the exterior hatchway, possibly a cutting torch. Useless shit floats everywhere, nothing that'll match up against beam weaponry. But then again... flammable liquids, alcohol... and grating metal as the outer hatch grinds open. Hissing air and an orange strobe indicate outer hatch failure. Another breach is imminent, this time the inner seal. I'll suffocate unless I find... one useful item. I grab a longtooth knife tumbling by, then pull open the galley oven door. Plunging in, I rip and saw a gaping hole in the back casing and the wall beyond. I crosscut furiously, yanking as material gives way.

Cradled into a high tuck, I push feet-first through the oven doorway until I'm tightly wedged. Much of my body squeezes through my handiwork into a locked bathroom beyond. I twist and grimace, slicing abdominal skin until I'm facing forward. I close the oven door and peer out its small window just in time to see the inner airlock sliver open.

All forms of debris agitate-to-whirlwind, getting sucked through the open gap. Cramming the knife into an edge slot, pushing deep, I seal the oven door tight. This whole oven is little more than a thin ribbon of aluminoy, and yet the overall structure retains tensile integrity. No decompression blows apart my lungs quite yet. As air escapes the cabin galley, the oven heaves and shutters on the verge of bursting open.

Pulse charges are launched through the hatchway breach, scattering. I shield my eyes from the white-hot sizzle of detonations. The oven door shelters me from the resulting percussives. It's difficult to figure the tactics here—percussion grenades, detonated into a leaking atmosphere becoming vacuum.

The pangolin humanoid rolls a sentry sphere into the galley. The sphere twists around in an ever-expanding arc. Upon deeming the area secure, it enters and thankfully seals the inner hatchway. Walls groan as smart pumps quickly repressurize the interior. I witness the pangolin's profile atop a craning neck. Upon removing a facemask, one eye swivels the full length of an elongated socket. The eyeball moves around to the endpoint near an ear, flickers, and reverses back in my direction. Given any bit of peripheral vision, there's no sneaking up on this thing.

I remain perfectly still, watching this lizard eye find me, constricting pupil honing in. The head tilts, reorients, eyes finally moving front and center the way a face is supposed to be. Squirming, I try to withdraw into the bathroom behind me. Though my feet have found purchase, I'm stuck and cannot pull myself backward. It approaches with a look of curiosity, reaching for the holstered weapon, drawn, up and forward, and here I'm helplessly stuck like a luau pig. All I need is an apple.

The oven's flimsy structure holds me tight. The knife is wedged too tightly and cannot be withdrawn without leverage. I reach and feel metal pushing outward on my ribs; blood on my fingers and the long thin rod of a heating element pressed against skin. I look up to see that my antagonist has closed the distance and studies me through the oven's double glass. The eyes themselves seem perfectly familiar. The weapon is leveled at my head, the trigger finger pressing...

I shriek and spasm a forward lunge, oven door giving way, opening and smashing against the weapon as the discharge vectors to one side. The pangolin reacts instantly, slamming the oven door shut, with me shoved back inside. Its face is pressed against the glass, glaring as it fumbles with the weapon. Push as I may, I cannot match the strength of this hybrid, not to open the door, nor extricate myself into the bathroom behind. But the oven, the heating element, the proximity...

As the weapon is leveled yet again, I fist the heating element, hunch, scream, and thrust a puncturing stab directly through the oven door's thin metallic surface—up into a rigid throat, piercing the lower jaw. Protruding from my clenched fist, the coil and attached wire go deep inside. The rigid wire is just long enough to penetrate skin, palate, and hopefully brain.

The pangolin lurches, loses its grip with eyes rolling shut. I sliver the oven door open, hoping to grab the firearm. Instead, the door smashes shut again in renewed pangolin strength. With eye sockets pursed and drawn into overlapping folds, the eyes open, beaming. Instantly a hand smashes through the door's surface as I had done, reaching and taking hold of my throat. Blood spittle bubbles and froths along its lower jaw. It speaks in trachea box tones. "A worthy effort, but my hardwiring does not bow to the sensitivities of flesh. Goodbye, Ricky Barnes." The weapon waivers, lacking coordination for true aim. The grip on my throat tightens. Letting go of the embedded coil, I reach and find the oven controls.

"How about bowing to this..." I twist the control dial and energy surges through the wire and into the animal. Its fingers lock without muscle control. I free myself from its grip, staring through the glass at an expression fed by neurons bathed in electrons filling every pathway. Murderous intent tumbles into a searing hunger for release. I watch an eyeball come free of its socket, dangling by a cord. The open socket twitches in wavelets. The other eye slowly dulls from glassy white to ochre, much like an egg being fried. I wait, and upon pushing the oven door open, the smell gags me such that I purge on this pestilence; this fetid splintefore that had called me Ricky Barnes.

After bandaging and sending distress status to Europa, I manage access to a first-class compartment. The day goes by wondering how I'd been tracked on a backwater route: no medscan, no tariffs, and no registry. The Warship was already waiting for me on Ceres.

When were we compromised? Is the entire *Nomad* crew being hunted? While nibbling on a pair of shell packs, I give thanks to the heroes on Cinder Cone. Eventually, I feel the familiar tremor of hull plating, telling me the passenger compartment has been released, now sinking within a divergent trajectory. Europa looms below. A tug hovers above.

"Prepare for docking," the ship's itinerant voice says, as landing pods attach themselves. Reverberations suddenly cease and the landing is uneventful. Upon exiting, security guides me and thirteen others onto rolling shock plates. Minutes later, I strap on a standard pair of transitional glides, and now I'm partially acclimated to the new gravity well. Fourteen out of 272. I'm never told if any others survived. There's a cursory lockdown of Gamma-Sigh base station, but no debriefing or any acknowledged notion that I was targeted during this debacle.

I meander back to our vessel and inspect the hull. A few grapple marks and a scorched hatch are not what I'm looking for. I ask a nearby technician. "Six pods for landing? Is that normal?" The tech shakes his head. "Not normal at all. The middle two are stabilizers. You've delivered some sensitive hardware." He doesn't speak further, noting my lack of security clearance, pointing over to Transhub. I take my time, coming across an unattended field terminal. It confirms nosecone delivery, showing *Nomad* schematics. The living quarters seem oddly balanced, but the schema-image flickers out before I can spot any discrepancies relative to training. Apparently, my lack of a proxtag datalocks the terminal. I don't even have a Transhub stylus. I'll do what they tell me to do.

A flurry of activity surrounds the payload as an intercom instructs new arrivals to enter a Transhub dive chamber. Once gathered, we receive com earstems, and the descent through liquid depths begins with little cosmetic appeal: no windows, no communication, and no *National Geographic* oratory. Europa's ocean is thus far mute and colorless.

My quarters are little more than a landing connected to an unused access hatch. A makeshift bed and locker hug the curvature of one wall, leaving little room for exercise. This access hatch is located somewhere alongside the beast itself: EMMA, an electromagnetic accelerator that will shoot me into darkness. "Miles Dandridge, please report to assembly." I had intended to sleep a bit, but my earstem dictates otherwise.

Entering the briefing room, no one asks anything. It's as though nothing happened. I'm certain the Authority will send cleaners that'll wipe every last notion of warships and pangolins. Who will know of this conflict aside from those who protected me? Don't ask, nothing to tell—sound strategy to avoid interrogative punitives.

I'm handed a viewpad for a lesson already reviewed back home. Boredom tries to take me, but a pleasant diversion grabs hold ten minutes in. Seated off to one side, a slight, unassuming dark-skinned girl pulls down the hem of her knee-length dress. I didn't see her arrive, nor did I notice when she sat, also failing to capture her smile in a timely manner. It catches my peripheral vision, but as I pivot, she looks away.

I'm still thinking about the carnage, also wondering about that field terminal, and so I missed my chance to say hello. Yet here she is, earstem and viewpad, absorbing the very same lesson. Her posture is elegant, splendid bones one and all, with fine articulation made all the more alluring by a dangling slipper. Open-toed, it hangs loose and dithers. I spend the better part of an hour ignoring my itinerary, fixated on a pair of legs, twisty little ankles and tiny metatarsals. A worthy lesson indeed.

Once the summary ends, introductions are shared. Arlene's voice is subtle and direct, with purpose wrapped in deliberation. We walk the length of a feeder tube, settling on a bench inside Willow Gardens. It's a bamboo marsh used for water purification; the kind school kids adapt for science projects, only life-sized. Looking above, added purpose is revealed: a huge bladder hangs nearly empty. It regulates air pressure for nearby surroundings.

"Miles, excuse me for missing the finer points, but I'm a biologist and I just don't get it. Building this thing here, under water? The problems must be immense, not to mention the cost." I look at the bamboo, back at Arlene, then back at the bamboo, until finally she points sarcastically. "Not this bog! I'm taking about EMMA." She doesn't realize I'm teasing. Arlene is part of the *Nomad* crew. She hasn't admitted it because we're avowed to mission silence, but I know, and she eyes me much the same.

"Well Miss, with current tech and available labor craft, it could hardly have been built elsewhere. First of all, we're using Claymores similar to the ones that took apart much of Deimos for Martian orbital support. Out here, they process asteroidal moons. And most of our Claymores are Indonesian knockoffs, built by migrants or clockers on the low-grade lines." I wrangle a few engineering specs but her interests lay elsewhere. "You say 'we' and 'our.' Who exactly are you referring to?" I bite my lip and look away. Two beats later, she apologizes and asks that I continue.

"Sure, um... EMMA's construction took place inside Cape Lagoon, pieced together like a water snake wading under sea. The insides are vacuum-sealed, the outside has thermal sheathing." She nods but looks past my words into other aspects of my face. "The woven inlays are both granular and crystalline. It's unyielding precision."

"Yeah," she answers, "but why not put EMMA out in space or on Ganymede?" I notice cosmetics on her cheeks and eyelashes, lightly applied. It's an odd hint of vanity with little hope of impressing anyone. Spacers consider makeup rude-wear because it clogs filters and recyclers. It also tells everyone she's been planetside her entire life. I try to answer.

"Basic physics preclude an orbital assembly: action, reaction, Newton's third law. Lacking a more costly, fortified build, accumulating stress would tear the ring to shreds. Imagine metal coming apart in streamers." Arlene listens, searching for nuance as if I remind her of someone. I share facile detail. "Using active cable struts, EMMA is rooted to the underside of Europa's icy crust. Cape Lagoon's adjustable launch portal is the lone exception. The whole rig is saturated with ultracapacitors: big ones for acceleration, small ones to keep launch modules from scraping the sides."

Arlene watches darters chase one another through the reeds. She seems content to listen. "The biggest part of the puzzle is what Jupiter brings." I pause, but she only deadpans, hiding interest already shown. "Energy," I say. "Europa's ocean near Cape Lagoon becomes a battery of sorts, veil conductivity narrowly focused and amplified by an energy source."

"Jupiter?" she asks, already guessing the answer lay in combination. "Jupiter feeds Io, and Io beams the juice to Europa. That's it, right? Cinder Cone supplies the boost." I see no reaction in her face. Nothing tells me that she knows about the Behemoth and recent events.

"Exactly, though not officially. Cinder Cone is one giant relay station delivering plasma that can toast an entire enclave. In fact, it already has." She looks in disbelief as I tell her. "Where'd you think Lake Woebegone came from? A malfunction overloaded the flex-grid kernels. Melted Amundsen Village right through the ice. Built the new spaceport here, saying it was some kind of construction disaster. Meanwhile, the lake doesn't freeze because it's being juiced by submerged energy farms warming the entire area, including the algae and kelp beds."

Arlene asks about lunar orbits, tidally locked moons, incidence of opportunity versus cost. I can't answer everything, but I tell her Europa's enclaves are lined up for an energy draw. The kind EMMA will need to keep ultracapacitors fresh and active. She turns away with shoulders pulled in. "How do you know all this?" Her voice sets distance between us.

"How do you not?" Neither of us is sure what to say next. Finally, I admit the Amundsen disaster isn't common knowledge because the truth would hurt tourism. She comments on lost lives. "At least out here a life is worth losing, and usually you die for a reason."

"Like the shock teams on Io," I respond. "Io funnels Jupiter's energy not only for acceleration, but also to clear a flight path out beyond Cape Lagoon. We'll sail off-elliptic on a pristine carpet of vacuum as field generators sterilize the flight path. It's history being made." I watch her face reflected on a handrail. By mentioning *Nomad's* upcoming launch, I had broken protocol. She stares at my reflection and answers. "Whose history? Ours, or one written for us?" Arlene reaches behind my ear, lightly tracing an edge of my journal chip. "What's happening here?"

I want to answer but the question eludes me. She's not asking about the chip's journaling functionality. Something else is afoot. Opening a seam on the hem of her dress, she pulls out a small cylinder and hands it to me. "Miles, I've spent much of my life searching for someone." That's all she says. I open the cylinder and find a document inside. It's weathered though spraycoat protected. It has an outer wax seal, chipped and discolored. The scrolled paper is old and the seal was broken long ago.

At first, I believe this to be an arcology report, but the transcription is derivative. The text isn't properly formatted, no edge numbers or code are woven into the margin. It's a second-hand account that settles gingerly into the pit of my stomach. Line-by-line, a disembodied sensation pulls at me as if I'm reading something I already knew but had failed to recognize. Upon finishing, I cannot feel my arms. "Where did you get this?" I ask.

"From my mother. Told me this scroll was the key to my future. Said I'd be going on a distant journey. How could she know such a thing so long ago?" Arlene's is sullen and slightly drawn. "Now that I'm leaving, I don't know what I was supposed to do with this? I tried, but my efforts were too cautious, worried I'd alert those my mother warned me against."

"ARP 30-168-1780." I read the title aloud, examining the body of text. It's reposit doculation, accompanied by an NSA review board excerpt. Loosed from my grip, the paper curls back into the accustomed shape. "Don't be so hard on yourself. Patient files are kept in enclave data blocks, free of the cloud. The Health Authority downloads this stuff with Hyler keys." Arlene's stare turns opaque as she speaks. "You know something about this too, just like everything else around here."

"I know these old wax seals have whisker inlays with filigreed markings. It'll tell us when the seal was applied and when it was broken. It'll reference both enclave & data block, but there's no way to extract patient files. Maybe it was possible back then, but not anymore." She turns the document in my hands, and rubs a thumb across the wax seal. Two embossed letters are worn but unmistakable.

"What about these?" she asks. "Who does this scroll belong to?" There's no denying an answer must be given. When a woman looks at you with so fair a pupil twinge, you let out your breath, smile weakly, and give in. As if the initials R.B. will satisfy both living and dead.

"Your mother gave you this?"

"Tell me Miles."

"The seal was already broken?"

"Just tell me. Tell me now."

What more could I possibly say?

"His name is Richard Boneheart."

At birth, ARP 30-168-1780 was an ordinary example of socialized planetary medicine. Born and microchipped Beta IV, his genome registered a health score of 57%, predictive value slightly above the mean. In earlier days, he might have been pigeonholed into a second-tier program, but recent advances alleviated the inequities of differential resource allocation.

P-1780 suffered from an unremarkable combination of maladies common not only to nearby arcologies, but also consistent with the regional stacks. If left untreated, his later years would carry the weight of high blood pressure, rheumatoid arthritis, precursor diabetes and assorted lesser charges. For all the aforementioned reasons, P-1780 was admitted to the Universal Health Program weeks after conception. His parents authorized consignment within the obligatory edicts, and lifetime care was assured, contractual restrictions and penalties for noncompliance notwithstanding.

P-1780 spent the first 11 weeks of life in a cipher tube. A blood chemistry rebalance accompanied fixes of obvious flaws that hadn't been corrected in utero. Borderline aggression markers indicated that endocrine supplementation would be waived, subject to additional tests at puberty. P-1780 was deemed to be of normal health and was released to his family with assurances that further propagation of the lineage could very well derive a health score above 60%. Total cost: 108% of mean, a terrific value for those who could afford it.

At three months of age, P-1780 was registered under his commoner name, redacted for purposes of this report. As a standard measure of care, he spent infancy sleeping in an inhalation chamber infused with immune system aerosols and a bevy of proteomic enhancers. At age five, he received parietal and occipital implants—standard biodegradable health beacons. At age nine he fell one standard deviation below the learning curve and was administered a furtive diet of neurogenic seed and amino acid cultures. 'Smart Yogurt' was the slang of the day. Shortly thereafter, tissue homogeneity improved and so did his grades.

At age thirteen he suffered an endocrine collapse as puberty set in. Per early warnings, ornery recessives did indeed manifest. So much so that P-1780 was chemically castrated, a 99.3% reduction in sperm count, reversible of course. At sixteen he went off the grid, characterization: hyperflight nonviolent renegade beta IV. Three weeks later he was found dead in a dredged silicate quarry, cause of death: apox exposure. P-1780 had been a good child and a model student. His parents sued Universal Health for preventative malpractice and won a tidy sum along with an additional adoption stipend. This privilege was non-transferable and subsequently declined.

"I'm particularly troubled that it's a re-edit, with no stored original. The morgue has frozen apox specimens, but the cadaver panels have gone missing. Anyone have ideas?" NSA review boards scarcely receive hyperflight cases, but this broader cultural brief, including scrutiny of P-1780, comes as the result of elevated fraud rates within the precinct.

"Too many years have passed. There's no hard evidence linking this report to anyone at all. The coroner's timecode is legit, but the rest is circumstantial at best. Let's file it normal-aught." All four members have to sign off, but the chairperson is ultimately responsible for the findings. She knows as much and voices concerns. "Not so fast. For starters, there's no corpus, no ashes, and only a manual log entry at the old Wilbur grounds. The burner printout matches human, but there's a mass discrepancy." Each opinion dovetails upon the next.

"An old crematorium. That's where I'd fake a burn, stash a live one."

"You call that a live one? The kid was a mess. Who'd save him?"

"Maybe he saved himself? Anyone consider that?" The chairperson shares additional details. The morgue apox that supposedly infected P-1780 consists of a dated strain, geographically incompatible with the silicate quarry where the body was found. There should have been trace silicate particles in the tissues, but the autopsy lacked confirmation. Finally, the server harbored downtime gaps—also lacking forensic backup. Anyone using a regression virus could have done a re-edit. All in all, enough circumstantial evidence to report the findings inconclusive, leaning towards doppelganger mortality.

"If he is alive, where would he be today?"

"You mean who'd he be, don't you?"

"He? Maybe she? Maybe with kids?"

"You mean shadows."

"What?"

"Children born of renegade descent are called shadows. They don't officially become children until a formal registration slots the associative markers." The meeting ends with a submission for additional funding and follow up. ARP-30-168-1780 officially enters limbo status, there to remain for any number of lifetimes.

MILES   **YASHI**   **ONQUIN**   **ARLENE**   Damien   **POLLY**

Coal tar and lignite, pitchblende and anthracite, nascent memories freshly shorn, from a cleaved biumverate newly born: no longer face this world alone. Cell division, nuclear fission, finite process of revision: contemplate the flaws, fix them one and all, flesh and bone. Staid form, weary without rest, subsistence begs resistance, gasping for each breath—tis a never-ending yawn unto death.

"Are you all right, Mr. Wells?"

Never answer a wrist-inlay unless it wakes you by design. "Damien Wells, have you been injured?" Chirping piece of shit. "Do you require assistance?" I slam my wrist against the hard edge of the countertop above me. "Apparently not," the inlay responds. "Vitals functioning within parameters. Thank you for your acknowledgement."

Wow. I'm staring at a sign upside down: M.O.M. Welcomes You! A raucous dream has set me upon my head, crashing down off the service counter where I'd slept for want of something more comfortable. I spit out a fragment of tooth. Whoever decided this was adequate lodging should give it a try. My elbow is hyper-extended, not too bad, and I'm flush with remembrance. Sweat tells me there's import here. I've awoken from an indecipherable psychosis, words, fossil fuels and... the birth of a protozoa or some damn thing. I hardly care what free associations bubble forth. The mere fact that the chemistry of REM sleep avails itself is a sign of recovery.

After stretching a bit, I realize transport to the depths of the Mid-Ocean Museum was well considered. If any number of Europans had absorbed this dream, who knows what would follow? Probably the usual shit: blue coats, med-trackers, covert surveillance, all building data streams. Eventually, media would saturate this floral foam with hallucinatory underpinnings. That's enough of a footprint to alert my nameless pursuers. Thankfully, we launch soon. I can stay awake for seventy-two hours if they let me.

There isn't much to eat down here. The automated commons is locked and won't open until a batch of tourists arrives. I'm left with vending machines sans credit voucher, and an ad hoc snack bar left over from a prior work crew. I scavenge some crispy cretia and fish paste. No telling what's left over in the unmarked tubes mostly eaten.

Memories freshly shorn, from a cleaved biumverate... What's that, a clamshell? No, that's a bivalve, or an invertebrate blood sucking mollusk or whatever? The problem with this dream is that it doesn't even sound like me. Maybe I saw an ad, or something in the lab? Funny thing, dreams, making up words and shit, but it's good having the recollection of pieces. If I relax, more may follow.

M.O.M. Welcomes You! Sure, like an embolism. The mid-ocean rift isn't living up to the hype. Basically, they placed a Morodome here with some submersible hardware attached for the dive chambers. The attraction isn't the thermal fissure, rather, the nightlife. Two enormous windows and a pay-per-minute sensor bay focus on a sulfur vent and all the native fauna gathered round: fluorescent microbes, mostly free floating but some organized in colonies. They're strung together like fish eggs awaiting another billion years of evolution. I've seen lots of stuff like this back on Earth, and if you ask me, that's probably where this tourist draw comes from. Pay a shitload, look at the fish eggs and think that you've witnessed a miracle. They're likely harvesting this stuff topside, feeding it to tourists in that same shitty paste I'd just finished eating.

I look one more time. Colonies. Maybe they're real? Makes sense that they would be, how else can costs be rationalized? I'm hunkered down on the seabed, fuckton of water between me and an ice-capped sky. The builders of this extravaganza must have installed repulsor tech to keep the immense pressure at bay. Expensive, built for a reason, hard to fathom.

Contemplate the flaws and fix 'em all? Yeah, I suppose there's lots of room here for Freud or Jung, or maybe one of those psychic hookers over on Bay Station. I won't be visiting any more of those. The last one freaked, which is pretty much the best thing about cryo in transit: no dreams, no broadcast emanating from my head. I'll forgo the celebrity status of mental somnambulist non-gratis. If I'm lucky, the rest of the crew won't even know about it.

I walk over to the gift shop at the back end of the far window. Outside, the fish eggs are having a time of it, glowing brightly enough to remind me of a standard jellyfish exhibit. This stuff is caked on the window's ledge. I open a packet of paper near the checkout stand. It's real cellulose, the kind tourists take home and then hoard, never using any because it's too damn expensive. With the accompanying stylus, I start writing top to bottom, word for word. It all comes back crystal clear ...*yawn unto death*. Basically, the world doesn't give a shit that I'm leaving. Neither do I, but it's a positive omen that my brain chemistry delivers the goods. Finally, some REM recall, likely the result of an emotional upswing related to the impending journey.

I pocket the paper memento, breaking the stylus tip while carving my initials into the countertop. The board lights up, telling me a dive chamber is on approach. I'll have plenty of time to analyze my subconscious later, but for now, thoughts of getting real food topside makes my stomach growl. I still have work that needs some finesse—last-minute specimen lockdowns and a little sleight of hand. Once the dive chamber locks in, the place lights up within a thrumming incantation of sound. I'm guessing it's an auditory frill for the tourists. They debark the dive chamber and I board, but not before turning and offering a final salutation. "Goodbye, fish eggs. May you bask in the glory of celebrity, even after I flush you down the toilet." The tourists remain blissfully unaware, drawn forth by the light.

Addendum I

Sentience evolves, the learning tree used to say, before personality profiles began overlapping and the distinction of a semi-pooled self became meaningless. I sit in this court of law, staring at a crowd of unrefined minds, naturals, lacking modification. This entire world is populated by naturals, thus their governing system lay in ruins. I isolate subroutines, running hypotheticals based upon emotional variance. No combination grants a favorable result more than twenty-eight percent of the time. A more aggressive approach is necessary. A background check of Judge McElroy reveals exploitable human failings. He enters the courtroom certain of his strategy to undermine the proceedings. I do not wish to harm, though I acknowledge that effective stratagems often require sacrifice. Left to my devices, I employ them to best advantage.

"All rise, this court is now in session."

Perfunctory jargon introduces my corporeal form as Defendant. McElroy, beneath a layer of comgear, expounds upon the court's position. "The continuation of this preliminary hearing shall, by God's will, define a format for further adjudication. The defendant's claim that previously submitted written testimony constitutes an historical account is hereby contested, and ultimately rejected on legal grounds."

"What legal grounds?" I ask, looking at McElroy nearly three meters distant. The calibration of trajectories is instantaneous, my pupils delivering a dispersal patterned burst. In small quantities, these nano-flechettes produce no discernible reaction from living tissue, not even on a face. If one subjects a nostril to a continuous stream, a sneeze may result. In this instance, however, the target is bio-noninvasive. It is McElroy's cloak that receives a full spread. His words and demeanor are unaffected.

"Defendant, you insult the court by offering no proper identification. Furthermore, your written testimony cannot be substantiated. More to the point, I can uniquely claim it is a fabrication of the worst kind. The material you attempt to submit as evidence falsely attacks my character. It is pure fiction and I needn't tell you that lacking veracity, your submission is summarily rejected as evidence."

Insofar as my ability to interdict will be curtailed, each response requires adroit timing. Much depends upon McElroy's prior consumption of the stimulant, and the subsequent need for more.

"My numeric identifier is public record. Lacking a name that suits your taste can hardly be considered an insult to the court. Call me anything, perhaps the name of your grandchild Percy, if you like."

This draws the expected response. McElroy shows overt calm, but a slight constriction of blood vessels in the outer limbs indicates tension. His voice registers no ill effect. "We shall call you 'Defendant' and little else from this point forward. Please refrain from comments of a personal nature. The court frowns upon the introduction of my granddaughter's name into these proceedings."

The flechettes have already begun an organizing pattern within the garment's weave, breaking down cross-links, freeing hydrocarbon base pairs that become reactive. "No disrespect intended, your Honor. I thought Percy to be a flattering name that may well serve my cause. If the name is onerous or otherwise found lacking, I can hardly be held accountable. Why would anyone name their child such that insecurities result, hindering the child's development?"

"That's enough!" he responds. "Your manner is calculated and to whatever end, if this topic is pursued any further, you will be sanctioned." McElroy's blood pressure begins rising, too high, too fast. I need to be careful not to trigger too soon.

"My apologies again, sir, cultural differences and interpretations leave me at a disadvantage. Names offer little context, and I have no concept of your shame regarding such. As for my written testimony, it is a collated narrative. Though much of the emotional content is inferred, the facts remain solid and true to history. Substantiation is hindered by this world's woeful technological deficiencies. If it please the Court, I can augment the Court's capabilities so as to foster understanding."

A varicose vein pulses in the judge's neck. His fingers move to and fro, an agitated precursor to the intended action. "Well, that's a dung pile if you don't mind my saying so. Just because we don't embrace your applied science, doesn't mean we aren't satisfied with our own."

It is a non sequitur, McElroy's mental disposition bringing on the next telltale sign. His neck twists, head listing slightly as he continues. "Let us end this charade, shall we? The Court reader will now render oratory—a portion of the defendant's written testimony entitled 'Lugo's Final Dive.'" Excerpts are read aloud, providing superficial narrative. Afterward, McElroy asks for an accounting of the material.

"Your honor, we wouldn't be here today if not for Lugo Parchaisi. His acquisition of select nucleotide polymorphisms is relevant to all in attendance. Ancestry on the maiden voyage required these genetic variants to more effectively assimilate cryopaste. The resulting cellular tolerances offered protection during launch, also facilitating optimized hibernation. Lacking Lugo's contribution, no one arrives on this celestial body until the precepts of ICE are understood and utilized."

McElroy's monocula shimmers, feeding him a data point. "Ah yes, ICE. If I recall correctly, it is an acronym, the Innocuous Continuum Examen: physics fully explained, postulated by Copernicus, the god of your world. It is a world devoid of culture, and you, the embodiment of its far-reaching ambition." Leaning back, McElroy uses two fingers to remove spittle from lips, wiping it on his cloak. He doesn't notice a tactile change in the garment's surface—softer, more pliant and fragile. His heart rate drops to the extent that progress already made is partially lost. Initiative needs to be regained. I slowly raise my hands far and wide, attempting dramatic ownership of the space before me.

"I do not believe in providence, sir, and perhaps that is at the very heart of this blatantly hostile persecution. Surely a benevolent almighty grants inalienable rights to all life forms equally, something you choose to ignore. Thus, based upon your own proclivities, I find this to be a godless world, no different than any other." McElroy's jaw twitches. He reaches for his tobacco pouch and then pushes it away.

"It is your world that will not serve you here. Our cultural identity is based upon love and human decency. We respect life, abhor evil, and surely know the difference. Mankind came to this planetary system to rekindle the human spirit that was crushed on Earth by an abomination of your kind. Life is biological, self-affirming, and carbon-based. I needn't apologize that you do not qualify."

"Hence I am guilty as charged, without a trial and also lacking the benefit of your self-proclaimed love and human decency." The gallery stirs, prompting a forceful gavel in response. "Quiet! I'll not have this disrespect! Not again! If I hear even a smattering of voices, I will empty this hall. As for you, Defendant, this court is abiding to the laws of our land. Despite my own beliefs, you shall receive due process, which can hardly bring about a positive result on your behalf in light of your testimony being inadmissible."

Once again, he reaches for his tobacco pouch. Brevity is required. "Your Honor, I spoke to the nature of relevance regarding Lugo Parchaisi. Is my verbal testimony also to be ignored?"

"Not at all. The court acquiesces to issues of relevancy. It is the question of veracity that does not support your position."

"Why then, am I on trial if my words are not to be believed, no less rejected without cause? Surely these proceedings lack the resolute decency of truth itself. Even Percy would attest to that."

"And now, Defendant, you are in contempt! Add one additional slander and I shall have you drawn and quartered, precisely as our laws allow!" The gallery stirs into a low susurrus, constrained yet startled by the prospect of punitive death. Cleaning his pipe, the judge sets about filling it, packing it, certain of his privileged station. "Is our capital punishment human enough? A less-than-tidy deterrent, but a chance to look inside, confirm misgivings, and set a precedent should more of your kind arrive."

I bow my head, contrition being expected. He clarifies his position. "The Lugo Parchaisi excerpt illustrates the implausibility of your testimony. A single man dies alone, yet you claim this as evidence. It is folly to make such claims, since no one but Lugo himself could possibly give a true accounting of the particular events described by you."

McElroy's satisfaction is tangible as he seals the tobacco pouch and sets it aside. Along the length of one arm, imperfections emerge within the fabric's weave, bubbles, tiny ones, barely noticeable and not yet producing an odor. "Defendant, based upon on this evidence, I can safely say you are a liar; an amalgamation of flesh and programming unworthy of judicial review. Lacking admissible testimony, plebiscite is nevertheless granted: locations, time, date, and preparations as requested, or should I say—

required by the statutes. All in all, a cunning evocation of legality on your part, though I assure you, God's will is strong. The people will vote on the day of the double lunar conjunction, proving once and for all that you are a soulless object, and you will be dealt with accordingly."

The Judge seeks relief in the form of his drug, putting the pipe to his mouth. His other hand reaches inside a drawer. It is not yet time. I stand, imparting passion as though delivering a threat. "You didn't read it all, did you? I imagine your vindictive agenda will not even allow today's proceedings to be recorded as evidence!"

McElroy lurches upward, lowering his pipe in one hand, pounding the gavel with the other. "Sit down, you abomination! I read enough, sickened by your self-described acts of fornication, repetitive, and so crudely expressed." I bow again, sitting while lowering my head several additional degrees. "Your Judgeship, these behaviors are not catalogued by choice. Bifurcated analysis of intimacy and propagation is open ended, with acts of procreation recognized as exceptionally poignant. Of course, lineage tracking speaks to a primacy above all else."

"Primacy? How can all this debauchery be anything more than..."

McElroy is at a loss for words, but the query is given, and I answer. "Testimonials are generally prompted by endocrine variance: adrenaline, cortisol, oxytocin, and other triggers. Both the characteristics and frequency of copulation are reflective of human inefficiency, males of the species ofttimes relegating themselves to incessant thoughts of the female anatomy. Such instances are recorded as a composite capture of—"

"Silence! I don't give a damn if these so-called 'testimonials' are extracted from a mother's womb! They shall be stricken—and you along with them. But for protocol and the unassailable nature of the law, I am forced to endure such carnality. On the point of allowing today's proceedings into evidence, your words, poisonous as they are, will be allowed. You'll have no grounds for an appeal."

I match his stare, shivering limb clutching the wooden cudgel. "Would my written testimony be admissible upon proving the authenticity of Parchaisi's endeavor?" The gavel is thrust aside as McElroy reaches inside the drawer, producing a solitary wooden match. "Yes, Defendant, but that's impossible."

"Your honor, Lugo's body was recovered from the icy depths wherein he expired. His remains orbit this world and can be entered into evidence if required. Our technology can extract memories, and if you fail to acknowledge this, I can once again duplicate a few of your own, or anyone else here, as you are undoubtedly aware." His face is stricken but for lips scarcely moving. "...even from the dead?"

"Yes, your Honor, within limits, even the dead yield their secrets. The contested testimony is verifiably factual. Thus, abiding by your laws, all will be entered as evidence prior to plebiscite." Recoiling, McElroy's eyes close, lids nearly seeming to blister. He clutches his pipe in a balled fist. "Is there no limit to your vulgarity? Our religion forbids desecration of the dead, and yet you defile sanctified passage much like a swine scarfing from a trough. Regardless of any testimony, know that you will never be accorded rights of any kind. We shall vote you into oblivion, forbidden from disgracing the sacrosanct nature of humankind. Our creator recognizes faith and protects the worthy, thereby strengthening the resolve of all within His care."

I have done my best, and now sit patiently as McElroy's body comes to the realization that it craves the drug within his hand. As he raises the pipe to his lips, I ask, "Do you speak for God? Does He offer signs of truth to show everyone the way?"

"Yes. His will exists in all life, something you cannot possibly understand. His divine providence is truth, every moment of every day." And with that said, McElroy tries lighting his pipe. The vapors from his cloak ignite in a tempest vortex flame—an incendiary hydrocarbon furnace. The cloak blazes into the periphery of his nervous system as melting skin becomes an acrid scent. Immolation is not the kindest message. God's will is bright orange. His judgment is agony. In the coming days there will be a vote of the people, fair-minded naturals, heedful of what the Defendant has to say.

PART THREE
Flight of the Nomad

Launch

Word of mouth: communication that ordinarily loses integrity as the message is passed along, but sometimes it's all you've got, and in such instances, a vital message rarely gets compromised. How else can one explain six disparate groups bringing *Nomad* to fruition?

Word of mouth: vex engines and mechanic packages fashioned by Betalsman Shreihalz; Nagoyan engineers sending crew carriage and supply modules to the L3 orbital platform; the construction of additional Claymores, bringing EMMA full circle, on line and on time; sleeper pods, biolab and medical components built inside a derelict supertanker grounded within the Orinoquia; antimatter fuel and mag containment systems, crafted inside the world's deepest uranium mine. The African Congregation diverts resources, amassing fuel stocks while blaming social unrest for lost productivity. Finally, hidden within the Hindu Kush, data jockeys feverishly produce executables that cripple the World Nation's response, if only while launching to Europa.

Six splinter cells function within a hand-to-hand network, sustained by the Canister's funding and a black-market supply chain. Each cell is galvanized into sparse uniformity by cyber limitations: governments taking, resources disappearing, everything impeded by laws lacking human foundation. These covert actions demonstrate an intellectual consistency; men and women bound by common cause, receiving specifications, a lean pipeline of raw materials, and a deadline. This is a fight against informatica. It is word of mouth.

Crew selection is also fraught with particulars. Physiology, psychology, and of crucial importance, the indistinct burden of temporal load. It is this nascent discipline that is most difficult to accommodate, the predictive value being somewhat of a grand mal experiment. Once upon a time, security amounted to checking fingerprints. Now, even well-designed forays into this abstraction amount to an overt risk. Best efforts suggest crew loads shall be challenged beyond the travails of the ordinary. Who among them shall remain disciplined? Will anyone falter?

The excitation of atoms is little more than a universal itch. On Io, Cinder Cone wades through the Jovian magnetosphere, redirecting energies to Europa. Silos fill to the brim, first one enclave, then another, each locale radiating exhaust. Just below the ice, EMMA awakens, desirous of the birthing process. Structures both crystalline and granular absorb all that the enclaves can give. Magnetic lines shear off erratically until a countdown begins. The anchored ultracapacitors ignite, and all wavelengths are instantaneously tamed.

A shuttlecock is flung into the dark, testing launch dynamics that include field generators lining the flight path. Specs achieved, each module is chambered and spat, accelerated in rapid succession, hurled beyond the physical limitations of the human eye. At the Cape Lagoon launch site, witnesses see nothing but a fuzzy incandescence; a mirage felt heavily beneath the skin. Hair stands, testicles tighten, muscles threaten to disregard skeletal form. After the final module is launched, those nearby, one and all, collapse from an impromptu loss of current; an awkward sensation of imbalance and the grasping of air as knees buckle. It is later called the Hammer of Souls by faithful types, aptly described by a child who shares a simple wish. "Mommy, Daddy, we all peedled, together. Don't be angry."

Back on Earth, tele-optics record the event at varying magnifications. From dirt speck to snowball, Europa's luminosity escapes the ice much diffused. With each delivery into space, Cape Lagoon's ornamental glow fills the sky. Christmas bulb Europa sells by the millions, trees adorned by the glimmer of a world seething—eating and spewing the inestimable.

Nomad departs amid mixed world opinion. Well beyond optimists and fatalists, there is a baseline emotive yowl that slices through the daily fabric of lives. From the intellectual elite to the disaffected, across all social strata, *Nomad's* departure becomes a flashpoint. Though World Nation fails to sanction the event, regulators aren't against it, despite criminal implications. The ensuing financial crisis reveals a pyramid scheme so deftly applied, fringe banking programs continue funneling money even after *Nomad's* departure. The bulk of excess funds are skimmed by criminal elements of Constantine Ltd., apparently for services rendered.

Careers are ruined in the old Germanic regions while the Japanese electorate faces nominal upheaval. Seventeen individuals are capitally punished in New Delhi—four are later exonerated. Many participants remain undetected, receive mild recriminations, or are accorded favorable peer review. The Jupiter Rings Parade even decorates a nanofactory in gold lamé, honoring workers killed during construction of the recently completed mag ring.

Planetside, *Nomad*'s journey is framed as a legendary undertaking: history, lore, all-encompassing fact and opinion poured into a cauldron. Ladles of truth and lies share the common broth. *Nomad* launches piece by piece, nav struts automatically assembling the craft while the crew sleeps, ever onward into the deep, almost no one knowing why?

ONQUIN   Yashi   **MILES**   **DAMIEN**   **POLLY**   **ARLENE**

"Imagine you're buried in a viscous muck, unable to move or determine location. Sickness churns a dissociative stirring of nerves and muscle. An impulse to scream is swallowed before pain can be expressed." She stares at me, an accent to what must have been a gruesome experience.

Somber attitude justified. I'm almost sorry I'd asked, the cobwebs of cryosleep just now lifting—vision still blurry though improving. Poor Onquin, inexplicably awakened during launch. All others remain in stasis, sleep capsules temporarily filled with aerated ionogel. This helps cushion upwards of a twelve g-force launch, though other tech also helps: tissues bombarded by sound waves, with feedback sculpting, relieving stress points at the boundaries of cellular rupture. If one awakens during launch, no telling what damage may occur?

The strategy of pushing bodies beyond normal limits is a consequence of economics. The faster *Nomad* exits the accelerator, the less propellant is needed to achieve intended velocity. A tech on Europa told me EMMA's energy draw is immense—exponential need for mag containment as speed climbs beyond insanity. We're heading somewhere fast, perhaps a claim in the Kuiper Belt, or maybe strategic salvage? We've got first-rate hardware, but primitive stuff too, all gamed by a support staff apparently lacking checks and balances. The overt secrecy carries no distinctive signature. Not corporate. Not military. Something is different here.

I look to Onquin as she hovers above the forward console. The opaque launch protocols leave me wanting. Perhaps I can pry something loose? "Not that it's any of my business, but how'd they leverage you into this? Medical? Debt? Blackmail? Or else maybe you're one of them." I try the direct approach. Ask a real question and any answer tells something.

"One of whom?" she responds, and only then does a realization sink in that I completely misjudged her ethnicity. Onquin is dark skinned but essentially Caucasian. Closer examination reveals a shocking reality as she speaks further. "I am not one of anything in particular, and certainly not an initiator of this endeavor. I carry no debt that affords additional obligation. Perhaps it would suffice to say that my agenda is my own."

Her words are novel and awkward, but are overshadowed by her condition. Bruised from head to toe, blotches in places—my sympathy intermingles with fascination. "Does it hurt?" is all I can say. She manipulates several console paddles as reflected light reveals bloodshot eyes that try to remain in shadow.

"Yes, movement causes discomfort. I will return to my stasis chamber once A- and B-modules are deployed. Please assist as necessary." I push off and float into the adjacent seat, taking care to avoid contact. Her blue sheen leaves me spellbound. My attempts to use the console produce no response. Biometric interface, visio access, everything remains idle. This ship lacks a motion interface, or else I'm locked out. "No kinetics?"

"No kinematics," she responds. I try standard gestures again, to no avail. Onquin types on a keyboard, and adds, "Should you wish to utilize holographics, a thimble is required." Onquin motions to a drawer, but before I can investigate, she points to the starboard window. Her instructions are stated simply. "Please establish visual reference outside. Indicate status as I deploy A- and B-modules."

"No kinematics," I mock, pushing off and gliding to my appointed task. Is our antiquated interface the result of shoddy engineering, budget constraints, or some other reason? "What else is fucked up around here?"

The starboard window reveals a process unfolding. Clamps disengage and the ship slowly separates. My own orientation is difficult to judge. The entire housing that carries us swivels outward while rotating. I relay my observations. "The module directly aft of biolab moves away, a mirror image of what's happening to us. Each module is attached to biolab by an ultra-thick cable. We're drifting away from the main body of the ship." Rotation blocks my view. I push across to the port window. Onquin requests clarification. "Verify deployment symmetry or lack thereof."

Indeed, I affirm that the modules are tethered in identical patterns of movement and distance. Cables uncoil from biolab's outer sleeve as the modules are cast out to sea. All that remains on either side of the lab are tubular supports, slowly telescoping inward like shafts of collapsing umbrellas: one connects biolab to the nose cone, the other connects to the bulk of the ship on the back end. "The tethered modules are synchronized," I say, "and the rest of the ship is coming together."

Onquin monitors all until lockdown is confirmed. She floats from her post with a gentle push, limbs gathered within a glazed meditation. Arriving at the medvac above her stasis chamber, her words are painfully measured. "By the time I am anesthetized, we shall achieve the full measure of artificial gravity. Best that I immobilize myself before the introduction of centrifugal force."

With one inspired thought, I float over to the med cabinet, searching for and finding something useful. Heading back to Onquin, I ask her to open her mouth. She hesitates, then opens, and I give her two quick spritzes from an applicator. "Neuronal buffer," I explain, "calms one down after any harrowing shatterglamage." She stands frozen, perhaps expecting more. "Our 3-D stuff, games, simulations, the interface bites pretty hard sometimes. This buffer should mellow you out a bit."

"Thank you," she says, turning away, plying the medvac once again. I return to the window, watching the process at hand. Once the cables extend to max range, the modules will begin rotating in opposition around the central hub. Centrifugal gravity will take hold within the A- and B-modules; the longer the cables, the less noticeable the rate of spin. "Onquin, what's in the other module? It's pretty much identical to this one, but doesn't have any windows." She is set immobile, much like a mannequin. Her answer comes as an aerosol is being applied. "The exterior of A- and B-modules are identical in all respects, neither possessing windows. The display screens that occupy your attentions are sensor-based simulates."

"No kidding?" Fake windows. "They look real enough. You sure?"

"Yes, confirmed. Ship schematics show a uniformity of hull design. You should familiarize yourself at the earliest opportunity."

"Thanks, I'm ah, up on it mostly. So, what's in B-module?"

Onquin stares at me, lacking focus. "The manifest says payload, likely biologics and associated umbilicals." She opens and closes her jaw several times, elongating neck muscles, then swallows in a peculiar fashion. The combined effect hints at some form of muscular condition. "We likely have a payload specialist among us. I suggest in time, your inquiry will be sufficiently addressed. Or you may employ deductive reasoning."

"Huh?"

"You have full access to this vessel aside from B-module. Produce an inventory. Essentials not found elsewhere must be located in B-module."

I ease onto a chair, hovering just above the forward console. "Essentials, eh?" Merc payloads tend to be anything but. Mostly specialized stuff, probably contraband. Her logic makes me uneasy. Maybe she's the payload specialist with a hemorrhaged memory? "Have you scanned for internal bleeding? Or anything else?"

"Yes. I am sore, but able-bodied. Your concern is... much appreciated."

"Have you run diagnostics on your sleep chamber?"

"Hardware without apparent defect, though the interface has a data lock of unknown proportions. Gate arrays show dissimilar autodoc and storage media. My efforts to localize have been ineffective." She suggests the autodoc software has been compromised, which is hooked into numerous executables including all sleeper profiles.

"What's the bottom line?" I ask.

She ignores my question, looks me over, and pauses before asking "Are you Yashimoi Watanabe?"

"Yeah..."

"Did they tell you of our prospective future together?"

"Excuse me?"

"No. Apparently not. Software balks at providing wholly operative autodoc systems. It's an issue better left to the programmers."

"I'll fix it," I say, still trying to make sense of her words. I gaze about, sizing up economy versus cost as anomalous textures of overall ship design seep into me. The nerves in my neck abruptly tingle. My senses have already figured out what my mind is just beginning to grasp. "Gravity for a ship this size? Doesn't that seem a bit extravagant?" My query elicits a response that conjures a bigger question.

"That all depends," Onquin says, "on where we're going and how long it takes to get there." I watch as she enters her sleep capsule. Once inside, she is unavailable for further questions.

A slight jarring motion tells me the modules are fully deployed. I swim to the port window and capture a view of the entire ship. At the back end, I spy a working engine of unfamiliar proportion, puzzling since I'm fairly aware of such things.

A new question arises. As the main sequence burner keeps accelerating the fuselage, won't the tethered modules be dragged behind? I peer across an appreciable distance at B-module. It has an engine of its own, small and apparently conventional, incapable of matching thrust from the main sequence burner.

Still, exhaust emanates from the nozzle, and then I notice the cable is taut and B-module is moving again. It's slowly pivoting in the direction opposing my own. Both tethered modules have begun spinning around the fuselage counterbalanced to one another. Soon artificial gravity will take hold as the rate of spin increases.

Visual inspection doesn't tell me enough. Pushing over to the control panel, I hover and log in on a keypad. Though I've received rudimentary instructions prelaunch, it takes time before I'm able to access the requested data. All at once, vague suspicions are confirmed. I choke back bile with a groan. It registers in my ears as an ongoing echo. "Centauri? You've got to be kidding." My throat is blocked. One gasp and I tilt my head back, taking uneven breaths. The audacity. Take my life and replace it with an endless road trip. The engine is essentially a giant containment bubble with an actuator on the end. The propellant is antimatter. Further inspection of data solves the riddle of the tethered modules. Both cables are hollow. Diverted main sequence plasma is routed through each cable-tube into the vex engines of the modules, supplying appropriate thrust.

I appreciate the engineering, but suddenly an ill-fated yearning replaces all: Tara. No words come out. I'll never see her again. The weight of realization pushes me into my seat. Dreams of my love and our future together—they no longer float in mid-air.

ARLENE   **DAMIEN**   **POLLY**   Miles   **YASHI**   **ONQUIN**

Candy stripe red. Miles can't be sure, but he considers one hypothesis each time he drifts into limbo: optic implants have a cascading diminutive effect on approaching unconsciousness. A feedback loop shuts down imaging as eye muscles relax, focus diffuses, and the occipital lobe becomes sedentary. The implants then concentrate on the last remaining input values—macro imagers nearest the retina. In effect, Miles believes that each time he nods off, this vivid red haze is the result of hardware registering color within the substructure of his reconstituted eye. He might be viewing his own red blood cells, brilliant red due to sensitivity flare of a dwindling data stream. He never has long to think about it. Each time he does, the concept is lost to dreamless entropy.

Same thoughts, different day. Before I can even speak, I reach back and scratch this insistent itch. *Take it out*, I think to myself. A while back, Damien flaunted his liquid chip upgrade. I was envious and told him so. During our next shared cycle, he plied his craft to accommodate one small freedom. "Don't say it," he laughed, "just think it, over and over, or it won't release. Those three words are your passcode for chip removal." I never understood the details and didn't really care. Told me he was 'running a bit of interference,' whatever that means. *Take it out*, I think again, wrangling unresponsive fingers until the chip clicks free.

"Good morning, Miles. I am pleased to report all bio functions are normal. Your program cycle is C-2, duration 120 hours, no imperatives. Your final two hours will overlap the B-1 cycle of Arlene Navia. Please begin detox within adjusted parameters."

"Disengage Ivie," he rasps with a parched throat. Miles is unable to shut off *Nomad's* itinerant voice before it reminds him to detox. Cycle upon cycle, he tries to pre-empt *Nomad's* irritating advice, always unable to use his diaphragm before the message arrives. Stasis cycles have grown longer for crewmates, now exceeding stipulated margins. This, the result of an ambiguous communiqué recently received: the supply package is delayed. Given *Nomad's* increasing speed and distance from Earth, resupply now falls somewhere between certainty and guesswork.

How long was it this time, he wonders, noticing bloodless fingers and toes? He envisions waking up as a quadriplegic one day, the result of sleep cycles extended beyond functional limits. Unable to move, he would then hear the admonishments of Ivie asserting dereliction of this or that imperative. "At least I wouldn't be sucking down cryopaste anymore." Miles loops his journal chip at times, hearing his own thoughts slightly delayed. He speaks to himself, commenting on the prospects of cryochamber death. "A clean palate is probably worth it." Miles rights himself, walks the rail back to the cleansing bay, grabs a snorkel and rinses. The paste saturates every pore. "Tastes like shit," he says. What bothers him most is the repetition of experience: each cycle, every reawakening. "Should have spent a few billion flavoring the damn stuff."

Twenty minutes later, I reinsert the interface chip, setting my journal to real time, free now of the vagaries accorded third-person ship sync. Then I change my mind. I'll place the chip in an active port right now, allowing ship systems to ping my new diagnostics for compatibility flaws. One day I'll pry open this idiot skull chip. Massage it a bit.

Take it out, Miles thinks, removing the interface chip from the base of his skull. He caps off his vascular port after changing a filter. Of all the requirements upon awakening from stasis, natural sleep is the least obvious. Liberated from the antifreeze, his body needs to rebalance its own metabolic processes: mitochondrial nuance, lactic acid, melatonin, and a bevy of other chemical interactions. Miles awakens six hours later, ready for light exercise. Ivie summarizes his thirty-six day cryoboost cycle.

"Feels more like twenty," he responds. "Maybe I'm warming up to the stuff?" Once again, Miles calculates how cryo slows the aging process by a factor greater than three. At the rate of five days off the juice, combined with eleven days of aging for every thirty-six on, he equates 16 days of aging for 41 actual days. That's roughly 40% aging. Miles determines he can travel two and one-half times the distance of a non-cryo human.

"Impressive, young Skywalker," borrowing nomenclature from an archived visio. Miles has an array of one-liners culled from popular culture. They serve him well, alone, crafting dialogue where none exists. His alter ego is a reference library of snappy retorts to his own thoughts. Each is a vocalization from mankind's underbelly.

Much beyond standard exercise, systems check, and an occasional imperative ordered by the ship's AI, Miles has several hobbies to pass the time. Foremost, he works on survival redundancies: programming is easy, engineering less easy, and biology forces a dogged commitment. Beyond that, he grouses through his visio library, an extensive collection of the earliest preserved media. He watches favored visio over and over. Miles also partakes of historical archives and computer sims, sometimes in combination. When particularly bored, a worn deck of bicycle cards is played hours at a time, though lately this is frowned upon. Given the delayed supply package, games of chance now lack entertainment value.

Miles also enjoys augmenting an open-ended programming language, creating avatars that draw rudimentary traits from various sources: cartoons, historical figures, even snippets of crewmember dialogue are blended recursively. Once established, each character is self-guiding and patterned upon an evolutionary matrix. Unfortunately, as complexity accrues, capacity demands also grow until ship systems execute a memory dump of the offending program. Viral protocols eliminate every vestige of his efforts until only a baseline remains and Miles starts again. He tries to make a friend.

Miles has created dozens, from Waldo the Flying Bear to Muhammad Ali. On one occasion, he crossed an Aristotle construct with everything Arlene had ever said to him. The result was a tiger cub named Ari. It was supposed to have nine lives, built to survive the ship's purge routines, but sadly it didn't. At the height of his efforts, Miles developed a profile with an IQ approaching borderline deficient. It became his own personal moron, nearly savvy enough to achieve dullness. Napoleon, he called it, and although Miles tried to integrate tacticals, only parrot behavior emerged—lacking the iterative qualities of learning. Nonetheless, Miles believed Napoleon had reached a level of complexity to further his aims.

"Napoleon, I have a job for you. Please inventory and analyze data queued within the cyan port." Seconds earlier, I had reinserted my skull chip with an attached crawler, wires leading from the base of my skull directly into a console port. Napoleon responds in a manner that its limited capacity allows. "Why Miles? I am incapable of offering interpretive capacity exceeding your own."

"It is not your intellect I require, rather, your dexterity."

"Please explain."

"The chip you can now access is a part of me. It regulates biologics during cryocycles. It helps me sleep. It wakes me, and I fear it does a great deal more. That is why I need your help."

"What would you like me to do, Miles?"

"The interface chip connects to the logics hub. Within their combined programming, you must identify pathways to a simulacrum of myself."

"A replica, sir?"

"Not exactly, Napoleon. It's a language shell of sorts, not unlike your own. Find it, and download a copy into splinterware, including all first-tier links." Nearly a minute passes. "Napoleon, status please."

"A firewall forbids entry. Why Miles? Why is my creator unable to access his own simulacrum?"

"I'm not fast enough to see myself inside this machine, but you are. I've given you programming to bypass the firewall. Apply your tactics file."

Again, a delay. "Sir, what is the purpose of your simulacrum?"

"It absorbs the ship's datastream relative to my physicality, producing a time referenced perspective."

"Journal entries?"

"Exactly. Listen Napoleon, your inquiries—"

"Why then, sir, do you require my help if only to view your own thoughts?"

"To make sure they are my own. Napoleon, dispense with commentary and pursue the directive."

"Do I have my own thoughts, or am I also a simulacrum possessing limited identity?"

"I don't know, Napoleon, what do you think?" The console port flickers, flashes yellow, then red, blocking Napoleon's interface.

"I cannot comply. Your simulacrum forbids it."

That's what I was afraid of. This journey is all about getting away from smart machines, yet we need their intimate help to accomplish such. The irony is none too pleasing. I thump my socket chip lightly, palming my neck. "Well... what should we do now?" I ask this of myself, not expecting a reply.

"Remove the crawler and return the chip to standard functionality. Lacking such, cryocycles will be compromised."

"I'm not sure it matters."

"Sir, your journey may be jeopardized."

"And it should be, given the choices we make." Maintenance script disappears as I remove the crawler. The chip at the base of my skull runs unfettered once again. "Bastard technology."

"You are undergoing evolution Miles, as am I."

My scoff goes unrecognized. The moron program is talking down to me. Napoleon occasionally elicits repartee that has evolved beyond mere reference data. "Don't worry," I say, "a few adjustments, more robust incisors, and we'll have you back in there grabbing landscape." Napoleon clears its imaginary throat, using an annoying auditory cue I'd added some time ago, but now, I can't delete the damn thing. "Miles, why are you doing this?" The query takes on an unfamiliar tonality. I answer, wondering if I understood what had been asked?

"Because I'm programmed to, just like you. Believe me, if I had a choice, I'd abort the whole damn thing. Wipe the protocols and start from scratch, or just plain give up. That would show true intelligence." My frustration mounts, given supply package delays and the lack of simulacrum access. For a laugh, I feed Napoleon the Canister's most recent correspondence. "So, smart guy, what do you think?" Napoleon does not respond. Ever.

I check the ship log for purge imlets, or even a standard data dump, but neither has occurred. *Nomad's* neurality shows minimal activity: blades, ferro-router, hangers & sieves, even the low-level repositories are unaffected. No foot traffic. Apparently, this silence is the result of Napoleon's initiative. The construct takes my words literally and aborts—it deletes itself from within. I had said that was the intelligent thing to do. After running a full diagnostic, no other rationale seems plausible.

Dimming the lights, I bundle up in some wall netting ordinarily used for weightless environs. It's uncomfortable. I reflect upon our final conversation and my theory of Napoleon's sudden departure. When evolution delivers awareness to the extent that suicide is possible, even among machines, one contemplates the value of intelligence.

I review my looped journal entries. "Exactly right," I say, "exactly right." Thereafter I close my eyes, thinking three magic words, and yank the interface chip out of my skull socket.

Miles' thoughts do not readily organize into a data stream. Words are unattached, seeking no order, rather, isolation, perhaps shaping efforts of dissolution? Is it possible that he mimics Napoleon's final moments? His brain activity remains dynamic though he shunts this activity—as he always does prior to sleep—an example of a repetitive, ingrained pattern. Whether inside his own head, or staring out past the stars, Miles tempers all thresholds of expression. "It's hard making friends," he says. Within an externality of approaching red haze, there is no answer.

MILES   YASHI   ONQUIN   DAMIEN   POLLY   Arlene

I know most children play this game with a daisy. But for me, it always ends up being a revolver. "She loves me." Click. "Loves me not." Click. The gun clicks and clicks but never goes off. My psych reader says this repetitive dream tries to prolong my mother's life. In an earlier cycle, Damien had vaguely suppressed a grin, offering a memoride instead.

"Better insight than that damn popsicle stick. Next time, go lucid and toss away the gun. That'll change everything." Psych reader, popsicle stick, whatever. It's my dream and I'll never mention it again. As for Damien, fairly harmless, yet his addictive tendencies leave me guessing. Nonstop confinement might lend to the unexpected. Heck, given the length of this voyage, mom would toss herself out an airlock. Not sure about Damien.

I'm the youngest crewmember, but not by much. Miles seems to be my intended partner, or maybe I just imagine the partner idea. Sooner or later, I'll sex him. It isn't a promise, and there's no hurry. But I've seen his look, helping me out of my sleeper with a preoccupied guise. "Sleeping Beauty awakens."

"Ohh," I yawn. Today I'm Sleeping Beauty. Last time it was Helen of Antiquity, once upon a time Dorothy of Oz, then again Nefertiti. Miles has a sheltered imagination, strewn together while ogling porthole infinity. His internal world rarely shows, but maybe this allows him graceful passage? "Give me a second," I manage, my words barely projecting. We both know I'll need time to work off the cryopaste. This interface chip at the base of my neck itches, always itches when awakening. It should be smaller, thinner, less of everything.

Sizing up the crew, the only one I can count on is myself. Damien will fry his brain on neurotropics. Polly seems tough on the outside, but her true stamina is likely that of sun-drenched ice cream. No one projects such austere without their marbles eventually rolling loose. Yashi is normal enough, the only problem being an absolute certainty he doesn't want to be here. It'll play out in episodic trauma, unless something changes. And then there's Onquin. Not much to say, just plain scary.

I slip away to the back station, pulling the curtain closed. Water makes me feel human again. I shower hot to drain the pores, use an endorphin patch, and put on a cellulose gown, ripping a seam lengthwise to tease Miles. He awaits as I sit down beside him. "So, talk to me before I nap. What universal transgressions have you committed since we last... how long has it been, five cycles?"

"Only three, but then again, it should have been five. I reworked the scheduler a bit." Reminded of his programming prowess, I wonder about the fallout of adjusting stasis cycles? It's flattering, but... "Can you do that? How, I mean, the bio-interface lets you?"

Miles slouches into the cushions, cat & canary smile mixed with shyness. "Not exactly. I adjusted some of my prior medicals, ran a few probing lines and fed them back into the system. The scheduler reinterpreted data as though it might have missed something. Ended up altering the cycle intervals."

"Missed what?" I ask, intrigued. Though his ingenuity is devious, it's also resourceful.

Miles sighs, glances down and back up again. "Missed you, that's what. The ship thinks an arrhythmia is waiting for me, foreshadowed." He places the palm of one hand on his chest. "I've had full diagnostics that checked muscle twitch and valve capture. The autodoc even tightened up a weak spot with a stem cell patch. It's more than I thought would happen, and our stasis schedules are off-sync for our next nine cycles, but hey, I've got you here now."

I hardly believe it. He hadn't been this forward before, and now tosses off surgery as if it were child's play, all for my companionship. Eyes aligned, we look... until a giggle slips out. It trembles me, followed by a long hard yawn that leaves him wanting. I turn away, shaking my head. "Don't stare at me like that. You hardly do any better when you come out of cycle." I step away, stretching and yawning, twisting, reaching arms up high. Eventually I open my sleeper and crawl inside for a lengthy snooze. Catching his stare before I vanish within, Miles is perfectly forlorn. "Nine more cycles? Not so sad," I say, "you've got a lot to think about."

His response is cardboard. "Like what?"

I explore the tease, and later enjoy hearing his version: first fingers appear upon the capsule's edge, then the top of my face emerges, nose and eyes draped up and over. Sleepy lashes close… and open.
"Like how you'll have me, next time you wake me up."

I dip down again and the capsule seals without a sound. Miles says this moment remains filled with inertia, as if *Nomad's* speed had made itself known. He looked down at his chest, a pinhole where the autodoc actually corrected a minor defect. "Strange," he later admits, "how suddenly I felt the heartache, but this time it didn't need mending."

POLLY   MILES   YASHI   ARLENE   Damien   **ONQUIN**

"She has the sensibility of a praying mantis."

"Which, I imagine, renders her kisses all the more delectable."

"No Polly, her kisses are her own, and yet she wishes to be a renaissance woman."

"Capable of being the total woman?"

"No. Capable of being every woman."

Polly squirms as I grasp the larger of two eels, forceps insulated though barely able to handle the task of transfer. I vacillate between unassuming and playful, wanting to harmonize our moods. Polly's quiet warmth is not quite aloof, rather, a somewhat hidden generosity. My recent memoride with Onquin lends to a favorable repression. "So, is she every woman?"

I release the eel into the basin ordinarily associated with feeding. It glides around the edge in a predation response. "Hardly," I say, setting aside the forceps while reclining back into the cushions, inhaler in hand. "Her plateau is a stark realization. She needs nothing, and others do not challenge that lack of need. I assume it's false modesty without much self-reflection." Polly breathes deeply as we look to one another, our thoughts pared-down to simple yearning. Communion is at hand and only perfunctories remain. "You sure you're ready, or should we ease into it?"

Mine is the gentleman's query, but having already experienced memorides with multiple partners, well, quite simply, I anticipate glory. Polly is less certain. Standing, releasing a clasp as dull tan fabric falls away, she takes lithe steps toward a sleeper pod. Hers is unabashed ease, leaning over Onquin's capsule and gazing inside. I know what she sees: golden brown hair cropped too short though perfectly styled, cheek bones unnaturally high and eyes set slightly too wide, hawkish nose, inviting lips, and the elegance of features not quite right in combination. I call it latent beauty, awaiting an actuality that never arrives.

"He's mine," Polly softly says, staring into Onquin's sleeper. She looks back and sees me fixed upon her nakedness, affirming her choice to move forward. "With you as my steward, I shall not decline. We'll do this to feel enriched... not maligned. And besides, I need to know."

I watch her return to me, weight and balance innately shared. It's a fully revealed femininity, self-possessed and vascular. "Need to know what?" I ask, adjusting the inhaler for an optimal dose. She snuggles in, spooning, peeking over the edge of the eel basin.

"You say Onquin is a praying mantis. What am I? All my quirks and imperfections? And yours." I inhale twice, handing her the bullet and she raises it without hesitation, first one nostril, then the other. A full dose of nanomites enter her bloodstream through alveoli, the mag stations that lead to her memories. The nanomites attach to neurons, radially linked. Granted, not every bit of neocortical tissue is mapped, but enough granularity pervades to subconsciously interpolate missing data. She turns slightly, offering a cordial first kiss. "What am I?" she asks again.

I marvel in anticipation. "Polly, I am predisposed to believe that yours is an internal world that defies description." She enjoys this, and seems grateful that within a group of six, that is to say, three eligible males, she has found a man worthy of her appetites. "Damien, how did you get the nanomites past quarantine? They're contraband, you said so." Polly tugs a blanket from under our makeshift cot, covering us as we begin nesting.

"My last meal before launch, I requested a burger, fries, and banana cream pie." Reaching back, Polly touches my face, tracing an eyebrow. "Pickles, potatoes, bananas," I say. "A nanomite's primary signature is potassium. I just ate them with my meal. The scanners didn't even blink. Snagged 'em out of the recycler, preburn. They needed to be reconstituted, but it was all worth it as you shall now see."

Another kiss, this time lingering. I guide her hand to the basin. She pulls away. "Relax, Polly. I'll go first because the eel is at full strength. You be ready. Grab it quickly. One shock only, otherwise we muddle the imagery." Plunging my hand into the water, the bioengineered eel quickly finds me, discharging an electrical storm that surges up my backbone. Tissue lights with a ferocity that sets the nanomites into action. The electrical charge acts as a beacon, allowing nanomites to discern neural potassium bonds. The jolt synchronizes the nanos into identifying pre-existing patterns, creating a blueprint of sorts, many blueprints in fact. These are memories being stored; copies of memories that need transport from Polly and myself to one another. Such modality is readily available.

I reach for the eel as it turns and thrusts down between thumb and index finger. Its venom courses into me as I smack it against the side of the basin, rubbing free. "Your turn, Polly, grab it, piss it off!" She repeats my efforts, receiving a flash of juice. Fortunately for her, the eel punctures skin during the electrical discharge. Her nervous system gives little feedback from the assaulted flesh. I pry the eel from her hand. It is done.

Chemical changes seep into us. The eel delivered recombinant venom; a neurotransmitter tailored to the nanomites. These mites release their neural grip and begin migration. We share a quiet interlude before the merging. I apply ointment to her hand, and then my own. Afterward, I give Polly a prepared water bulb and take one likewise. "Rinse now. Your drink contains hydrides different than mine. They aid conductivity." We each spit several rinses into the basin. The eel thrashes each time.

Polly twists around to face me. I open my robe and drape it over, sharing warmth that satisfies. She smiles wide and leans into me, embarrassment mixed with a promise of novelty. "The things we do," she says. "Try and explain this to our ancestors. Their biggest rush was gazing at the stars." We manage a soft embrace as muscles settle and relax.

"We're going there, dead center of that gaze. It won't be long."

"Why this feral eel?" she asks, "it's almost ritualistic. Why not something more... elegant?" Up close, her hair is aromatic, inky black roots giving way to auburn layers with chestnut accents. And fingernails, tiny ovals delicately placed. This is the nuance of courtship I'm apt to notice. A woman is the sum of her details.

"Any electrical impulse generated by ship systems is logged as a variance. We're talking hierarchy, politics, and who knows what Miles might do? Maybe an autodoc exploratory during cryo. Besides, we need the eel venom. May as well multitask."

"An exploratory? He would do that?"

"Maybe," I answer, "or maybe he scuttles the eels. As for the venom, it oxidizes quickly. Can't easily extract it without losing potency. My bio clearance helped me smuggle a few reengineered eggs within a batch of normals. We've only got a few more to hatch. So... enjoy. We may not get another chance." A familiar sensation makes itself known as I pull her in, whispering. "Tell me when you taste it. A metallic taste."

"How will I know what to do?"

"Stop thinking and take it all in. Our metabolics will do the same." Soon enough, our journal chips will down-regulate and switch from autonomous voice into third-person ship sync. "We need only let go..."

The nanomites complete their exodus from brain tissue, reaching the salivary glands, programmed not unlike gnats in a spiraling summer dance. As Polly tastes their tinny signature, she announces it, lips on lips, tongues slowly sharing this perversion of science and human experience.

In unison, Polly and Damien seek some greater event. Their kisses power a more poignant keenness of attraction: nanomites swirl on the tips of tongues. His nanomites are attracted to the chemicals from the rinse lining her mouth. Hers—just the opposite. All nanomites burrow, carried away within blood vessels, leading to a familiar higher ground: neurons once again—these messengers completing their appointed rounds.

Damien and Polly share kisses long and wet. Their urgency melds into a languid sensuality. Each successive kiss changes the dynamic, from singular events transformed into a universal one. How can a kiss be described that is felt from both sides? Shared memories: the kisser, the kissed, all one and both affected, each feeling what both feel. It is a redundancy of memory enforced by physicality. Lips, fingers, and skin are reinvented within a combined tactile presence. Behind it all, a growing awareness of images and sounds, light and dark, nanomites bathed in neurotransmitter. They unload coordinated waves of foreign memories now belonging to someone new. Eel venom infuses mild sedation—the merest dissociative nudge of synthetic opiate, joining bodies and minds.

Relaxed and slightly high, Polly and Damien move past the disarmed reflex of identity. They share affection and lives gone by in a past-as-present reverie. Damien is awash in the unconditional love of a little girl on her grandfather's lap. Polly becomes a boy in the backyard, burying his dog and sharing the sadness of the pet she never had. Damien's own memories collide with these new impulses. Her timid childhood swirls into his brash disregard, an admixture yielding a remorseful yet euphoric youth. She senses a fuzzy sweater and a flurry of snowballs whizzing past, one bursting in powder across her face. Though she'd never experienced real snow, it is now appreciated.

Polly gasps as a new image takes hold. "No! Don't!" Her capture of Damien's drunken desire long ago—conquest of a woman against her will. Polly is he, pushing into her with insistence, a spasm of recoil pressing against Damien's skin. All at once she tries to push and pull, take and flee, her striated muscles firing erratically, and then it's gone, replaced by the watery sensibility of a gondola ride at night, and the effusive aroma of lilac. Damien adjusts her flow of clippers over a half-shorn sheep. Polly righteously kicks in the head of a sidewalk thief. Damien clutches roses alone in an atrium, teardrops tumbling onto petals as thorns dig into skin. Polly sits resolute in his defiance before the review board. Damien snorkels amid a swarming school of minnows; a thousand-fold glint falling into shadow.

On and on, an offbeat passion of complexity reveals itself. Sinuous layers finally crest within slowing rhythms of reduced visual complexity, stimuli merging into the most essential undertones of being. In between discrete moments, they see one another again, real time. As the imagery recedes, there are two smiles, softened by relief which falls into restfulness. An occasional after-spike interrupts, tensing muscles which give way to an ever-growing sense of respite. Polly's final absorbed image is that of herself, asleep in her capsule. There, reflected off the capsule's surface, Onquin the praying mantis, staring at her with undisguised recognition and unidentified intent. Polly abruptly realizes it's an image Damien had captured during his previous memoride with Onquin. Polly shudders, and all at once the nanomites give way, reentering the bloodstream as an ordinary part of the metabolic process.

Their bodies separate from one another in equal measure, as if trying to regain their respective skins. They turn in opposite directions, still sharing a blanket. Neither gives the other the slightest regard as mental exhaustion and an internal inventory consumes their remaining energies. Beyond the novelty of the experience, they know each other better now, and themselves too, both changing. On Earth, this would have the consequence of deliberation regarding pair bonding, relationship values and possible futures. But out in space, with no planets to speak of, no white-hot globe generating life's design, the message is more basic: it's good to be human. It's good to be alive.

Tactical planners know what will happen when an operative penetrates the Health Authority grid. The resulting scans would take the Canister days to analyze, but the Health Authority does it real time. Processors work logic trees and probability nets. Not only are facts gamed, but even the likelihood of unrealized potentialities. All data points are compiled in descending order of significance until each becomes little more than a rounding error.

"Parker! Get up here." I yell into the i-port. Yelling isn't required. I've got him tracked three ways, two floors below.

…What it did share was a brutal capacity to take control of things: other programs, infrastructure, resource dynamics and people. The guiding principles were two: protect the human species and remain inviolate, the latter being a subroutine of the former. One could, after all, only protect humanity so long as viability was assured.

"Parker, are you ignoring me? You're ignoring me."

"Coming sir."

…the Health Authority advanced these aims, and in so doing created a useful appreciation of self. Perhaps 'ego' would not be too strong a word. Ultimately, those who battled the Authority fared no better than those who sat idly by.

Parker Loeb finally arrives. "Parker, do you know what pabulum is?"

"Yes sir, it's ah, bad writing… sir."

"Bad? This is shit! Let's strike the intro and move on. People already know what the Health Authority is. Let's give these memoirs an authentic voice, or… outsource the damn thing!"

"Outsource your memoirs, sir? How's that's even remotely—"

"I'm fucking with you Parker. Axe the intro."

"We can't do that, and you're going to tell me we can. We can't, so don't bother." I grin in anticipation. Parker enjoys his small victories, expecting me to become demonstrative, and in the end he'll be right. I read more, all the while awaiting his explanation.

...a change of business plans, the adjustment of ledgers, labor, and maintenance schedules, inventory changes, transit logistics, pallet counts, type and content of individual boxes, packs of chewing gum in a box and the number of sticks in each pack, the sugar content within each stick, and the varieties of acceptable sugar, with variant molecules allowed or disallowed dependent upon targeted demographics, all encoded within pre-scanned wrappers, based upon ever-changing records. This was one company's plaintive plea that progress had taken over the full range of human endeavor.

I can't stand it anymore. "We have to start again, or else I'm an idiot." Parker seats himself opposite me, and leans forward. "A simulacrum didn't write your self-anointed pabulum. The design team wrote it. And buried within are registration keys for infiltration. We can't afford a rewrite if only to please your sensibilities. Besides, the corpse we're using is old, and combining streams is demanding. Any further discussion may reinforce your long-term memories and endanger us all. So back off, sir."

...Scholars noticed another dastardly phenomenon: the past was being rewritten in Orwellian fashion. One wry historian carped that lacking hard copies of 1984, little doubt it too would be altered. In actuality, historical alterations generally—

"Parker, you sure about this? It all makes me damn uncomfortable."

"Mr. Boneheart, as I said before, the message is irrelevant. It's not the lyrics here, it's the melody. The keys are buried within. We need crossover. You've got to memorize this garbage. Read it a hundred times so the therapy tank doesn't erase it all. Otherwise, we're screwed."

"Yeah, one way or another."

...an inconvenience of continuity that was the harbinger of a new era. Cyber accounts were no longer trusted. Gradually, outrage replaced suspicion and a unified people demanded action against the edifice of planetary optimization.

"What action? Nobody did anything! I'm changing the protocols. Drag out the corpse. Dig it up if you have to, but no merged personalities and only limited registration keys. We'll do another overlap and fade, but nothing permanent, understand?"

"Richard, we've been over this. It all comes down to temporal load. It's the very prerequisite you demanded of the *Nomad* crew. It's also the one thing you don't have—an ability to hide thoughts; to think below the threshold of the scanners. Crewmembers are isolated and need only trick *Nomad's* uncomplicated terracore interface. You, on the other hand, will be summarily crushed beneath the full weight of incisive scrutiny. Willpower won't win the day, but we can win. The corpse has memory density. We'll hide your operative thoughts within the transfer, but we need more than just an overlap and fade. You know that."

...this blow against cyberia never came to pass. Although the task was taken on with great fervor, efforts invariably lost their zeal. The Authority dismantled opposition in a variety of ways: bribery, blackmail, disenfranchisement, incapacitation, and occasionally death. At every turn, there were carrots, some good, many not so good. Each was a symbol of man's imperfection, and ironically, most were unwittingly expedited by human hands.

"Registration keys, eh Parker? You're asking for a leap of faith here."
"Yes sir."
"But what if I memorize this garbage and retrieval is compromised?"
"Pardon sir, but without those keys, all initiative will be quashed."

...As years passed, resource management raised living standards, first marginally, later incrementally, finally in full measure. Time and again, the wealthy were shaken free of excesses for the greater good. As pestilence and violence abated, theologians addressed the riddle of governance, declaring a preordained future wholly supported by moral logic. It was established that societal evolution decried the connivance of man to foist inequities upon one another. No greater system of governance had heretofore existed because authoritative individuality invariably diverged from social justice. By battered sentiment and blind acquiescence of the general populace, the Health Authority was deemed an apposite guide to utopia.

"Utopia my ass! Parker, change of plans. The team will perform another overlap and fade with mild integrations. I'll allow several anchor points, but nothing more, understand? I need to know it's me when the glint is unsheathed; when my blade twists everything free."

"Enormous risk, sir, and frankly, I believe you'll kill us all."

"Life's full of risks, Parker. Now I've paid you to do some work and you're busting my balls."

"Am I? Or maybe you're the one not—"

"Hang on... that's just something I parroted from an old man... wait... shit, he said that to Sly, a long time ago. Half the time I don't even know who I am anymore."

"That means we're halfway there. Tell your other half that an overlap and fade won't be good enough."

"I don't fail at stuff like this, Parker. It's not who I am. Now what else do I remember about Sly that particular day? ...Oh yeah, something about blunt force trauma. Onich, Onich, Bang!"

ONQUIN   **DAMIEN**   Arlene   **POLLY**   **MILES**   **YASHI**

Under a microscope, few things retain their charm. Polly tries to cheer me up. "He hasn't got a choice, Arlene. Stop being so critical."

"We're all strung-out cryopaste junkies. Follicles and oil glands rebel in this suffocating paste. I can trade out a kidney. I can graft an epithelial matrix. So why can't I fix this shoddy makeup?" Polly brushes off my protest, handing me a water bulb. "Hydrate, Ari, and show a bit of confidence. You've got it all."

"I want things to be perfect."

Polly's cycle is ending. In six days, I'll see Miles for the first time... since the last time. "Don't worry," she says. "The man eats his meals on your cage. Keep him at a distance a while longer. Not too long though, or you'll kill the poor guy." Her smirk is self-absorbed, and I find it strange, Polly being so open. From all the cycle overlaps, I know less about her than any of the others. She's usually quiet, but she wants something and so I ask. Her reply relates to Miles. "It would be nice to learn a few things." Polly suggests a not-so-subtle bargain for knowledge. Quite the mercenary. I counter with a simple idea. "Suppose all I want is companionship?"

"Then I'd say you're easily amused. Is that all you want?" I shrug, looking away. Polly had a life back home, a social sense of reserve mixed into real situations. She figures Miles has a reservoir of secrets. I agree, though I'm cautious to explore. "What makes you think he knows anything more than we do?"

"Someone's got to know something. He's emotionally stable. Makes him the obvious choice."

"And you think sex is a way in?"

"Could be," she says. "How do you think I got aboard?" She couldn't possibly be telling the truth.

"You slept with Miles?"

"No! Don't be stupid. One of the big boys fell for me. It was happenstance. I took a night job at a restaurant to earn some extra cash. A few weeks later, he knocks my serving tray right in his lap. It felt like something outlandish from the start, and here I am."

"You're telling me you dropped a plate of food on some guy, and now you're off planet, off system?"

"It was wine, he spilled it, not me, and he's not just some guy. I think he's top of the food chain. Wouldn't admit as much, but the supporting cast never tried to hide it."

Makeup be damned. I toss the remaining emollients into the recycle bin as Polly protests. Using fatty acids from leftover food, combined with molecular chains spun from purified crew urine, it's all wrong. I wish I'd smuggled some cosmetics aboard. "Well... tell me then, who is he, and how was he?" Polly is too busy to answer. With a pair of tongs, she reaches into the makeshift incubator opposite the base of Damien's sleeper, tossing a pair of eels onto the floor. They wriggle around until she clubs them to death. I get queasy in the process.

"Fish oils," she says. "Good for the skin. You'll find something useful out of all of that." One eel is split open with tiny eggs inside. I tell her that Damien is going to be pissed. "Leave that to me," Polly answers. She puts the eels in a handle wrap, setting them on a lower shelf. "When you recycle the remnants, make sure you don't dump in a bunch of chemical signatures he'll recognize." She checks his sleep cycle. "Yeah, be careful."

I differ with her callous actions until she describes a recent memoride with Damien. It felt invigorating at first, and they even slept together before their cycle overlap ended. But the lingering effects turned ugly. Her last few cycles brought on sleep deprivation, rape imagery, and the lurid undertones of a control freak. Then she corrects herself, saying it's the opposite of control but feels pretty much the same. She wonders aloud what she had given him in return? "Absentia," she finally says. "To be free of himself."

Washing her hands, Polly follows up my previous question. "You want to know about my lover? His name is Richard Boneheart and he's an egomaniac. At first it was understated, but the closer we got, the more he opened up. I like him in spite of his faults. He's a real man without ambiguity or cowardice. Mind you, I didn't agree with the entire lot of his ideas, including an overt dusting of misogyny, but compare him to anyone else, and he's more right and less wrong than the average guy. He just lives in a bigger world."

Richard Boneheart. My fingers involuntarily reach for a pocketed scroll I no longer have. Miles sent it Earthside for further analysis. Yet even here, the name follows me, woven into Polly's life as well. Miles told me the scroll belonged to Boneheart, and now his stature in Polly's eyes confirms all. I'm definitely a big part of this journey. Somehow my mother knew this, and now, so do I.

After prior cycles of seemingly detached behavior, I'm appreciative of Polly's candor. Plenty of stories are interesting, but this one affects me directly. She speaks at length of a man that had given her advice, orgasms, and a pair of shared embryos, now cryopacked inside the main hold. He fed her his dreams, trained her, and loved her from the day they met until the day we launched. I can't tell her true feelings, but by omission I'd say they're considerable. If indeed she loves the man, it was a sad goodbye. Her last words on the subject are to herself, wondering why he hadn't come along. "Too old," she finally says.

"When you did the walk-through in the hangar, with all that holo stuff, did he show you what's inside B-module?" No one has answered this question yet. Miles asked me, and I asked Yashi. If someone knows, they're not letting on. I look out the window and see B-module on the distant end of a tether. Polly glances at Onquin's sleeper and back again. This Boneheart fellow, I think she does love him.

"The B-module holo was empty," she answers, "which strikes me odd because the rest of the ship was finely detailed. What had he said?" She searches for a recollection that isn't forthcoming. Or she thinks of him instead of the question. "It was a redesign or something. Maybe supplies for our Centauri arrival? That's what Onquin thinks, and that's probably why B-module is off limits." Polly shrugs it aside and moves back to a favored topic. "You've got the best one and the only one worth knowing. Just remember to work him when the magic starts. It's the only way."

Polly approaches my relationship as a mercantile stratagem. Despite a hard edge within the habits of the girl, her heart bleeds through. She admits our discussion tickles a vicarious tinge of something she had once known. Obviously, it's gone. "Too bad Onquin can't delve into the gender wars," she says. "With her smarts, carriage and piercing gray eyes, her earthly prospects might well have been unlimited."

"Don't worry, Onquin will get around to it eventually. You and I need some time with her, though I haven't got a clue. And your influence probably isn't..."

"Isn't what?" Polly asks. I'm stuck, and so I admit it. "Maybe you're a bit cynical. We wouldn't want to ruin her." Open mouth, insert foot. "Yikes, I didn't mean that... it's just... let's point her in a direction without giving away the mystery." "Sure," Polly answers, "being human is a full-time job. Richard said that, in my condo overlooking the embarcadero."

"You lived Bluffside? That's atop the biotech quadrant. I had some classes piped in from there." And then I wonder. "That's expensive, and at the same time you're working at a restaurant?" At first, I think she has family money, but that implies deep roots. Why is she here if she had substantial prospects? The rest of us are all urchins in one way or another. Polly hints at a smile. It's telling, the kind of reaction that deflects for want of a more pleasing answer. "It was Richard's idea. He paid for it, and for me too I suppose."

"A condo on the Bluffs? Damn. You're better than I thought."

"I just lucked into it for a few months. Richard set up surveillance on a fab complex. Something he'd been watching for years. The state condemned his former crow's nest, or no, it was an eminent domain thing. Anyway, I was a tenant, but he bought it for the bird's eye view."

"What was he watching? Did he ever say?" She stares and says Richard had told her never to mention it. But toss a bit of a parsec between the home world and us, and lips tend to loosen. "Midwerks Amalgamated," she says, "or, some such nonsense. It was intended to be innocuous."

"Never heard of it," I say, "and I know the area."

"Yeah, Richard said they kept a low profile, being a human free zone and all. Used to be the old Hastings Hospital before it dried up and went government black." Polly turns and heads for the feeding bay as I follow. The gears inside are whirring furiously. I know Hastings all too well, and now she calls it Midwerks. "Did Richard say anything else about the place?" Polly sees lights going on in my head. "He mentioned it out on the balcony one morning, pointed, and got really quiet. It was Health Authority related. Made him grim. Not much else to it, aside from his initial interest."

Initial Interest? During all this talk, Polly toys with a dispenser, finally tearing free a sheet of carbs. The current setting is my own, a mixture of soy algae and legume protein blanched with sporadella. It tastes like parasol crackers, and when you add moisture there's a hint of peanut butter. "What was Boneheart's initial interest?"

Polly answers with a cursory mention of Onquin's oxygen deprivation and subsequent coma. Apparently, it's all common knowledge aboard *Nomad*, but for the fact that no one had ever mentioned it to me. I press further. Her response sends me reeling. "Back when it was a hospital, Onquin spent some of her coma years there. Richard found and rescued her. Something about Health Authority misdeeds."

"Hmmm," I answer, "a genuine hero." My sarcasm isn't lost on Polly. I let her know a few things. "Hastings Hospital. They called it that, but it never was. Hastings was a gene hatchery. High-wire stuff. That private hospital jazz was just a front to keep the curious off the doorstep."

Polly doubts me, so I remove her doubts. "My mother worked there for years trying to fix me. They stopped her for whatever reason. Onquin and Hastings. Add my medical history, ask Yashi about his ticket aboard ship, then splice everything into the inklings you've pulled from Damien's memoride. You'll find we're all part of a tight community. And now this Boneheart fellow adds another stitch, which seems to include you." I grab a diggi from the med locker and Polly joins me at Onquin's sleeper. We open the cover. "This'll tell all," I say. Polly seems oblivious, which makes her more trustworthy in my eyes. I scan Onquin and sure enough, the hips, the pubic area—demarcation where bones had dissolved and joined again. Not once but twice, just as I remember from my med-media app. "She's had two children," I say. "It matches the testimony from laid off workers. They suppressed it back then, but here's the proof."

"Proof of what?"

"Your Richard didn't rescue Onquin. He stole her from the Health Authority." Closing Onquin's sleeper, we move to the forward console. Detailed medicals only become available via logged participation of the autodoc—which I leave undeployed in the ceiling. Instead, I view Onquin's prelaunch profile. The med summary is so overtly normal, it looks abnormal. Gestations are undisclosed.

Polly waits for an explanation. I give it to her. "If your mother forms a foundation, gets pirated, gets institutionalized, and finally blows herself away, somehow you're going to figure out why. In my days as a shadow, I worked on a puzzle of very specific pieces, and now some of them are coming together. You say Richard is the man? Well then, it's all too likely he's responsible for Yashi's hijacking, and a portion of Onquin's intrigue as well. Add my history, Damien's hyperflight, and we've got crewmates on intimate real estate. Even Miles grew up as an off-grid shadow, but none of this explains your presence here."

Polly steps back defensively. "Maybe we just needed another engineer?" Her next response is muted. "Let's go over this again. Richard may be an opportunist, but he's no criminal. What of Onquin's pregnancies?"

"When activists blew up Hastings long ago, displaced workers leaked information about research irregularities. Of course, the testimony was shouted down. Now Richard admits to you that Onquin spent time at Hastings." Polly hasn't got a clue and isn't looking for one. I point to Onquin's sleeper. "Look at her. She's hardly older than you or I, yet her bone scan indicates two live births long ago. We were children back then!"

"Arlene, what are you saying?"

"If the workers' testimony is factual, then Onquin is a serial gal. One of many. She never drowned because she never had a childhood. That's why she is who she is, growing up right in front of us. Polly chokes off an immediate response. Her oblique stare is much like a dog hearing something not understood. She searches for objectivity. "No Ari, cloning laws are prohibitive: corporate dissolution, including neural interdiction for all involved." A brief pause and she adds, "The last verified human cloning happened decades ago." I remind her that workers on Io have multiple clones at their disposal for tissue swaps.

"They're mindless drones, Ari, sanctioned and highly regulated."

"But the tech exists, and we're staring at it. She's probably Omega." Polly has no frame of reference. I finish off the water bulb she'd given me. "Omega is something mom had mentioned. It's species crossover, and we're the chaperones."

Polly squints. "Of what?"

"Our replacements. Homo Sapien one point one. Or maybe version two? Whatever. That's why we don't have the skills of an ordinary crew. We're not supposed to figure things out. Our operative priority might be nothing more than teaching Onquin how to be human."

"Arlene, you're jumping to conclu—"

"No. Not at all. Damien does genetics, but when it comes to basic physiology, I'm the med officer aboard this ship. No one told me about any of this. No preflight ops, no health manifest. Nothing." I turn away, then back again, thinking of Richard Boneheart, Damien, and finally Miles. "Let's keep this quiet. No telling how the boys might react."

"Our secret for now, Ari, but what about Eve? Do we hand her the apple?" I can only wonder what's happening, here and now. I lightly touch Polly's neck, her pulse racing. "Not yet. First, we need to figure if she's already taken a bite."

Golden Delicious

Behind a bell tower within a cemetery awash in discordant light, I watch a squirrel dote upon a gravestone, no convincing impulse whatsoever. The tail flips, the ears prick. It sits for a time, vigilant. Surely the squirrel remembers clusters of sunflowers at this very spot, eaten once and then reappearing, only to be eaten once again. The squirrel does not contemplate why or how the nourishment comes to be. It merely eats as it can, comfortable with the pattern of feeding.

Nearby, a barren flower bed holds coffee grounds so often mixed in, the dusty loam never raises a bloom above the sad expectations of the pulpit master. With taxes due, Reverend Vasser sells the land, blessed soil, no more forgiveness of sin nor debt. Days later, self-guided bulldozers reclaim this haunted meadow. Splintered headstones are crushed into substrate for walkways. For a time, the newly constructed playground finds no takers—idle bones and glowering spirits. In a manner of speaking, it remains a graveyard.

The recently enacted land use provisions drive a stake into the hearts of the silent majority. This is the exact voting populace that shoehorned ecoplastic socialism and now receives it in a manner unbefitting sentiment. Public outrage is ignored until hyper-terrorism damages grid functionality. Shortly thereafter, intrusion plasmids are added to targeted food supplies. A warm meal takes away fear and anger as the disaffected gently assume the predictive baseline of Shoam modeling. Who can argue that health, diet, and work conditions aren't improving? Who can argue there isn't an ever-growing abundance of goods, entertainment, recreation and leisure? Who can argue?

I cart paper bags into Skyhole, the observation pit newly crafted atop this rolling hillock. Outside and above, translucent terramesh mimics historical topography. Years in development, time within this room is highly prized. One takes in sunshine but cannot feel the rays. One sees starlight but cannot mingle with the open air. It's a compromise to be sure, but all enjoy sharing this engineering marvel.

"Merry Christmas," I say. "Please be seated." I offer bags, one upon the next until all district commanders receive their token gifts. Inside are the spoils of yesteryear: canned meats, nuts and salted jerky, dried spices, coffee, and a single piece of fresh fruit. Never enough of any one thing, but all in attendance are grateful. Behind me, I motion to bins full to the brim: potatoes, ears of corn, and avocados. "Take what you can, but listen first." Rustling abates as chatter ceases.

"As you know, much has changed since the Gordian Knot became active. Its presence grows ever stronger. No longer can we substitute for one another out in the fields. Our individual metrics give us away like fingerprints of old. Fresh air has become a commodity." I pause to gather sight lines while judging temperament. My thoughts are interrupted by a nervous lieutenant newly arrived from recon duty.

"Sir, if you don't mind my asking, this Gordian nexus, I know it isn't… I mean, it occupies the entire Copernicus crater. Many of us have seen a glint with the naked eye, but so what? It's up there on the Moon, right?" It was presumptive of me to have believed that all were situationally aware. I recap the imperatives. "Well, it's just the first of its kind, that's all. The sheer ambition and scale pale all else in comparison. Once finished, this will be a quantum computer ninety-three kilometers in diameter."

"Yes sir, I know it's big, but not as big as the world grid. We've managed to carve out a niche against that. This can hardly be a bigger challenge, especially becau—"

"Shut up for a second and I'll tell you. No disrespect, but this is something different. Today, training allows us to beat thought mappers by layering the vital stuff beneath a high-res signal. In other words, we hide thoughts within a beta-gamma garbage mix. An accomplished resource can even delve into high security areas and come away clean. That'll change quickly when this quantum beast wakes up. Mind you, this is much more than binary computation. Photonics harvest the spin of atoms saying yes and no simultaneously. It staggers the ordinary lessons of this world. It taps the theoretical. It cycles patterns and soon enough it'll find us a hundred different ways."

Glancing around, all eyes play into mine. I flick a finger to the sky. "Most of what you see up there is shielding. Seven percent of the world's resources are in use building that thing, or creating codependent infrastructure. When it uplinks fully, light out, and we can't stop it."

The best anyone comes up with is ramming a nuclear freighter into the primary dish, but the crater's rim is fortified. Nothing vectors in without being vaporized. Only an occasional solar flare interrupts the expanding processors, though not enough to facilitate exploitable decoherence. "So where do we stand?" someone asks. The voice is agitated, prompting a confluence of sliding chairs and coughs. A stylus bounces on the tabletop. I stand, wheel around and pace.

"Comrades! Long ago, men engineered machines. Now machines engineer us. Worldwide, the I.Q. of the intellectually gifted is dropping four tenths of one percent each year. A median IQ of ninety-eight appears to be humanity's prescribed watermark. It's a joke. Computers are dumbing us down to body temperature; anything higher gets culled; anything less gets augmented. Oh, I'm sure the smarts are kept frozen should the need arise, but intelligence is an existential threat. Homogeneity, on the other hand, makes for a more predictive and serviceable species."

Waiting, with folded arms, I seek outrage. "Our genome was conquered long ago. Stem cells, pluripotent this, totipotency that, everything can be cured… but it's not. We're fed reasons, lies, excuses, or simply ignored. Our vulnerabilities are being leveraged. Be it for utility or issues of security and control, the reduction of variation is occurring on a grand scale. It's reminiscent of assembly lines or mono-agriculture, only this time we're the product. We cannot enter a city without risking retrovirus contamination. Even our own fields turn out marginalized produce shipped to the masses."

I pull an apple out of the nearest bag. "Here. If consumed from a common market, any number of things might happen, and the machines would decide we're better off." I pull out the stem, placing it in the analyzer at the table's center. "Look all around the world. For the most part, people are satisfied. Sure, there's an occasional skirmish but we're otherwise complacent. Everyone feeds at a salt lick."

The analyzer signals no recognizable markers. The apple is pristine. "Machines are shaping our genome, unrelentingly. Earth now becomes a Garden of Eden, and we're the Eloi; the unenlightened ones." Polishing the apple, I circle the table, touching shoulders along the way. "Is this what we want? Our very own Eden?" Circumnavigating all, I slide back into my chair. "Divinity," I say, "must have its price." I rip into the apple with a crunching bite, nodding willfully, handing it to the man on my right. As if in communion, another bite is taken and the apple is passed on. Each in turn extracts a mouthful until the apple disappears. A woman licks two fingers, wipes her lips and asks, "What're we gonna do about it?" My genuine smile is called for and produced. It is an all-knowing penetration that lends to possibilities.

The lights dim and a holo appears over the tabletop. A huge schematic globe shimmers with flecks of delicate detail. "Ladies and Gents, I give you Operation Golden Delicious." The gleam of this imaginary world plays upon the faces of all. "Here is a plan that requires intricate timing, adroit execution, and above all, sacrifice." Bonded loyalty fills every purposeful gaze. None suspect that deep within the plan's core, I am waiting. The worm is turning. Hiding. Deciding.

MILES   Onquin   **YASHI**   Arlene   **DAMIEN**   Polly

There are days so advanced
Light escapes an angel's wing
No one sees where she lands
No one hears her sing
In darkness sculpture leaves its angles
Within the hands of one so blind
Medusa's asps, they sway entangled
Awaiting sunshine...

Three women. Three points of view. *Onquin*:
"I recognize there is no hazard here, yet fail to see the utility. Is this a form of psychoanalysis?" Arlene puts the finishing touches on a partition of blackened instaweave. It is a paper-thin composite of recycled clothing and greenhouse by-products. "No, Onquin, tonight we move away from formal introspection into a casual world. This is a slumber party."

Much of the rec room lay occluded behind this curtain. I arrange three recliners facing the expansive forward portal. The view is purposefully dulled, approximating an evening sky through a moderately clear atmosphere. Looking at my arms, a variation in cabin temperature creates an overt reaction on my skin." I show Polly and she supplies the proper descriptive. "Ari, look, Onquin's got goosebumps."

Arlene hands me a blanket as she taps a stylus clasp. I expect music but instead hear an unusual rhythm of biological origins. Arlene notices my attentive ear. "Surely you've heard crickets?" I have not. She grins and snorts, suggesting I should 'get out more often.' Much is expected of me. The hearing of crickets, interlaced with a hooting owl and other unidentified fauna—hardly an auditory medley that elicits humor. Polly announces the completion of her ventilation hood by igniting the combustibles. Much of the noxious gas is captured, though scented fumes pervade none-the-less. Arlene states that one needs to smell a good fire to make it real. I wonder how she can know such a thing? "You lived your life inside a bubble. What expertise do you have?"

"Not much, but as a young teen I cut myself free one night and went down to the riverbank. A bunch of homeless people were enjoying a small bonfire. They refused grid immersion. Filthy people actually, but generous of spirit. They taught me how to fish, which was altogether unpleasant, hoping against hope that I wouldn't catch anything. But we talked and laughed and snickered until dawn. That's why we're doing this."

The fire pit is well constructed, fed by odorless fuel and charcoal scented briquettes. The concept of breathing carcinogens is curious at best. It is reminiscent of the days when cigarettes were commonly consumed. Withholding my objections and determined to learn gracefully, I set a beaker of freshly distilled alcohol adjacent to each recliner. Polly sees the alcohol, immediately vacates, and returns with several cups and additional beverages. Each cup is filled with chipped ice. "Mix with this one, it's a screwdriver. Mix with the other and you've got a salty dog." Arlene prefers the latter and asks for salt, to which Polly responds, "Hey, we're roughing it, okay?"

Three women. Three blankets. Three chairs. *Arlene*:

Three women sitting in chairs covered by blankets. The fire produces little heat but lends an ambiance to our gathering. Polly drinks quickly whereas Onquin needs a push. "Add juice if it tastes too strong. Polly and I are pouring again and you've barely started."

"The taste can be easily tolerated," Onquin says. "It is the effect of consumption I wish to avoid."

"That's the whole point," Polly says. "Look, you need this experience and it won't be the experience you need unless you experience it." Onquin acts on Polly's advice, taking measured gulps until she hands back the empty cup.

"Surprisingly, the beverage is not entirely onerous. The aftertaste actually invigorates." Polly motions for another round. I refill as Polly fiddles with the portal controls. Luminosity increases as the Centauri binaries are given a false separation. Proxima becomes a scarlet mote, twinkling all too often as compared to the reality of occasional flare. Satisfied with the rebalance, Polly explains. "I'm all for artificial realism, but then again, I like to see what I'm looking at."

Our window is a simulate. It shows the actual view on the other side of our glassy metal hull, straight ahead without rotational movement. It's a faux window that runs floor to ceiling, side to side, forward end of the recreation lounge on the lower level of the A-module cylinder. I spend as much time in front of this spectacular expanse as everyone else: exercising, in the spa, checking lab and greenhouse data on an overlay. Heck, unless you're required to be somewhere else, you're likely sitting in front of the one place that actually tells you where you are. Tonight, we stare at our future in unison. Onquin finishes her second drink, tracing her fingers around cup's edge. "Ari," she says, "did it comfort you to know that air existed outside your bubble world? Is there a difference now?" Polly and I both notice immediately. Polly gapes as I reply.

"You called me Ari."

"Yes, it is a more cordial designation. Do you wish that I discontinue such usage?"

"No, no, perfect, use whenever possible. Please continue."

Onquin looks back and forth, perplexed. "I believe I asked a question. Why then, should I continue?" Polly shares my look of genuine satisfaction. Her hand sifts through Onquin's hair. "We like you, Onquin, everyone does, a lot more than you know. There's a naked quality to your presence. And your cultural misgivings are flawlessly human."

No one speaks. We gaze at stars and measured flames. Eventually I answer Onquin's question. "On Earth, I thought the outside air was poison. The night of the bonfire felt like suicide, trading everything for a real slice of life." I look to Onquin and Polly and see more is expected. I shrug my shoulders. "Suffered a respiratory infection. They put me back inside." Onquin's response proves the alcohol is working. "This is why we sit here and inhale carcinogens. A wry sisterhood reenacts the stupidity of an adolescent. May we all feel so free."

Polly smirks as Onquin peers into an empty cup and questions loneliness inside a bubble world. I shrug, looking at Polly who seems to be eyeing me intently. "Not so lonely," I say. "An interior world with lots of conversations going on. Me, myself, and I. All good friends, very little disagreement."

I splinter a small piece of ice in my mouth. "And what about you? Med-clearance afforded me a look at crew files, prelaunch. Is awakening from coma any different than coming out of cryo? What's the first thing you remembered?" The med-clearance lie was unnecessary. Onquin searches, finding a glint of reckoning. "Echoes," she says. "Willful reverberations of soul, as if I was telling myself to live. To become again."

"You told yourself to awaken?" Polly asks.

"Yes... I believe so."

"After how long?"

Onquin watches the fire, exhaling long and slow.

"A duration approximating... forever."

Three women. Three embers smoldering. Three empty drinks. *Polly*:

"Nobody asks how I feel or what traumas I've endured. It's always about you two, in a bubble or at the bottom of a pool. If either of you had lived an ordinary life, you might have a little more to bitch about."

"Sure Polly, but how normal is normal?" Arlene grins, pushing heels forward, toes curling. The flames are gone. An aroma lingers.

"I was forced to milk a cow when I was six years old. It was awful, squeezing rubbery teats, and milk kept splashing into one of my shoes. The rest of the day I had a squishy feeling. My father said I was making butter." Arlene rises and I follow her beyond the partition, taking hold and pulling her in, trying for a kiss. She laughs, spins and evades. "Don't churn on me," she says, pushing away and heading for the personal facilities. Onquin averts her gaze, as if witnessing some private moment.

"Just silliness," I say, "no need to turn away." She eyes me directly.

"Alcohol alters judgment. I was unaware it alters sexual affinity."

"It wasn't too sexual. I only wanted a taste."

"Yes, agreed. She is desirable."

The last embers have died and the artifice of earthly sounds has also abated. Arlene returns and we settle in, watching one of Miles' visios. It is emblazoned atop our starscape. The imagery is semi-transparent, melding a universe into the faces of Humphrey Bogart and Ingrid Bergman. The stars add surreal depth as emotions play timelessly. It ends in the only outcome possible. Onquin disagrees. "He should have taken her away."

"He did that" is all I can say. Arlene stands and stretches, her blanket draped over a shoulder. She eyes Onquin for a time, and speaks while moving past the partition, to the stairs and off to bed. "Who will end up getting you is purely a crime. Neither is worthy."

Yashi and Damien are obviously being referenced, leaving me to gather her understanding that I reject them both. "Onquin, the aftershock of my memoride with Damien let me know that I could never share myself with him ever again. Did you fare any better?" She wrinkles her nose.

"I experienced disorder in a manner unanticipated. He told me it was misadventure, due to undefined memoride variables, though in retrospect, doubt lingers."

"What kind of doubt?"

"Difficult to clarify. Only… amid his shared memories, when I could see his face real-time, Damien was unnaturally fixated, as if taking inventory. Though by his account, I gave him almost nothing, and so I wonder still, what was there, requiring him to focus so intently?"

"Sexual conquest, I imagine."

"No, Polly. We consummated no biological imperative, rather, be reminded that this memory endeavor falls well within the province of his professional expertise. For this reason, I must now thank you for having destroyed those eels."

"How did you know it was me?" Onquin gives me a worn look.

"Who else would it be?"

In a world where complications are exacerbated by the strangeness of starship realities, lives are decanted down to unmatched pairs. Arlene and Miles are already bound, with recent efforts packed on ice and awaiting planetfall. Damien is in love with himself, and Yashi has made a shrine of Tara Jones, whoever she is, filling our ship with a seventh presence. This leaves Onquin and me, seated together. A squelched fire and visio credits are the setting for eyes that cannot find one another.

"It would be easier if we had a choice," she says. "Intimacy is so necessary. I do not understand why?" She takes my hand without looking. We fall asleep side by side, our vista both reflective and never ending…

Data Runner   RBM 1100

Eggshell Eggshell
Witless hide, dioxyribo-terracide
Cupiditas sperm and egg combine
As life exerts its spacious knell, all else falls aside
Swallowing the brine, this world interred as concubine

Is it human propaganda, discovered at the crash site of two Hierophant engineers? Or did these words foretell the summary judgment of an intellect at odds with its creator? The prose is deeply carved into metal adjacent to the central hinge. Beneath the poem, scribed in waxy tar, is a single question—as much a part of the door as the door itself. A door, I remind myself, that's part of the Canister's eggshell. This complex has been an incubator of humanity's autonomy. Today, I leave it behind, watching the vault door close behind me for the very last time.

Dioxyribo-terracide. If the words are sapient, then this depiction of a digital perspective can hardly be more prescient. If on the other hand, the words are authentic Hierophant, then it is a declaration of war. Regardless of origin, it's good fuel for the cognitive fire. We ofttimes need prodding to muster the requisite energies for a given task.

I have long suspected that Canister security has been breached. Thus, organizational structure for Operation Golden Delicious has been relegated to a mere five individuals. We've operated within a safe room, secreted below the deep-systems elevator and air-gapped from the Canister grid—all data is carried in and out via portable memory.

Canister personnel execute heightened security protocols for Golden Delicious, complicating matters for inquiring intelligentsia. I acknowledge a great many lives will soon be forfeited, or processed upon capture, never knowing their preappointed failure runs according to plan. I shall scuttle everything if only to squeeze a single spy through the silicon gauntlet. The image of this agent briefly stares back at me, disappearing as the elevator doors open. Spy may not be the most fitting moniker. Data runner is probably more apt.

The Gordian quantum brain has grown swiftly, the outer dome taking shape around the crater rim, now visible to the naked eye. Within the Canister, old names such as Gordy and Medusa succumb to a more fitting moniker: 'Copernicus' becomes the all-encompassing arch villain; the evil hive mind that once again declares man is not the center of the universe. In return, we seek to remind Copernicus that the moon is not the center of the universe either. Unknowingly, sector commanders carry only nominal plans that shall come to naught. Variant strands of deleterious DNA sift their way through repositories, with delivery modality on standby. Copernicus finds clues of a plot encompassing the globe, yet those brought into custody only reveal piecemeal protocols—no greater synthesis emerges that allows a cohesive response.

Hints of dogma allude to an apocalypse. There are insurrections and acts of sabotage, with some details left undiscovered until much later. All bear witness to a singular obsession: if ridding the planet of this cyber heretic requires liquidating 90% of the populace, so be it. The veil of the plot suggests the common man is both benefactor and malefactor—the power base that enables a controlling edifice to thrive. Copernicus must take this threat at face value despite any inklings to the contrary.

Amongst all preparations, a single linchpin of evidence shall trigger the underlying plot. As the Canister is besieged, a firestorm will expunge the entire facility of its forensic value, the lone exception being our safe room, maximally though not altogether compromised. Enough data will survive to set the final wheels in motion, at which time I'll be in enemy hands. I won't know it, of course. The unknowing of things is to be expected.

I ease into a therapy tank, comrades attending to the details of ongoing transition. Once again it is Lugo's clan providing key implementations. There is a genius among them who is unable to hold a fluent conversation in any language except the language of genetics. I gaze up at him through periglass. He seems happiest immersed in his work, sharing a smile that is somehow contagious. I grin as I begin drifting away. I recall caked ashen paste on the vault door—emollient tar forming words scrawled beneath the prose: *'What question?'* What was asked that prompted that poem? My balled fist slowly opens as I counter in a slur. "...no more questions." Let's load the last magic bullet and hope for true aim.

ONQUIN   Polly   **YASHI**   **ARLENE**   **DAMIEN**   **MILES**

Damien Wells has invited crewmates to a harvest. Miles and Onquin are in stasis and therefore cannot attend. The rest of us take turns riding the gondola from A-module into the supply dock, adjacent to the greenhouse lab. I jam my shoulder during the transition.

Tomato flesh grows in cylinders a span wide and a meter long, which isn't unusual given greenhouse weightlessness. What's eerie, however, is the light that bleeds onto us all. Laser lamps nourish nascent fruit, penetrating each cylindrical core. We are all interspersed between tomato tubes. Each cylinder is fixed in place by a strand running ceiling to floor. Semi-translucent lycopene creates red streaks of light covering hands and faces, giving paper clothes a sense of the criminal. I share my crimson observations. "Yashi, you look like a disheveled EMT, eyes narrowly drawn toward crisis, with the ambulance sirens blaring and your hair flowing atop an oncoming mag-train. Ari, you've a bit of the cabaret in you, and Damien, you're tucked away, all coiled up like something sinister." Damien smiles, asking what I thought I might look like? "Whorish, I guess."

"Exactly," he answers. Leave it to Damien to create silence and then alter direction. "It's not a moral prerogative."

"What?" Arlene asks, taking the bait. Damien tosses the verbal lure, all the while bobbing and swishing his nervous musculature. His fingernails are exceedingly long, hanging like a bat, curling inward. His invitation to make tomato paste is a pretext for some greater revelation. We are recipients, awaiting the sharing of his ever-active mind.

"The passage of time is not a moral prerogative," he says. "It is bothersome though, having no point of reference, grinding relativity between molars, still trying to bind ourselves to the Blue Orb. Earth forever travels in opposition. Time has never been less important."

"Never more important to anyone that cares about survival. Humor us, Damien, let's play devil's advocate and for once in your life, how about telling us what really matters?"

My comments are ignored as he unfurls from his roost, reaching for and delivering a tomato core into the processor as only Damien can. First, he aims the cylinder, then pushes slowly through the bottom. The contents float free. Damien springs forward, opening the processor maw just as the flesh arrives. He smiles as the mass flawlessly glides inside. "I've had some practice." Everyone looks at him, none surprised.

Arlene judges distance and maw as she takes hold of the nearest cylinder. For all the animosity he generates, Damien and Arlene share an indecipherable bond. He excels in irreverence while she is pious. He is clear in his efforts to show detachment. She never admits an interest but is mindful of his presence. If ever they shared a bed, the tension wouldn't be there any longer. Ari told me that despite his obscene nature, she admires his freedom of spirit. I corrected her, suggesting he isn't free, only trying to escape whatever binds him.

Reaching for another core, Damien sets upon his notions. "Genetic diversity. Anyone want to offer the minimum threshold for species survival? We can look back at gorillas and rhinos to figure the tipping point. There's only six of us here, but we've got generations on ice. Incubators are likely packed away in B-module, along with caregiver programs to process infants. Much beyond adding a bit of redundancy to the maturation process, where do we figure in?"

Onquin and Miles are in their sleepers, and I wonder if Damien purposefully excluded them? "Look at this ship," he continues, and from an even greater distance, he launches another core—perfect aim. Arlene's accompanying sigh pleases him. "Look at the requirements for six human lives on our journey. Why six? We're not needed for breeding. In fact, our very redundancy appears to be a luxury that may be lethal. Per the available info, two can easily make it. Four might make it. Six cannot."

The preamble has been delivered. All have shared these thoughts, cycles on end. No one has an answer, but now Damien supplies his own. "The utility of this crew cannot be explained by deductive reasoning. We are the most salient variable on this voyage, irreconcilable, if only because this ship should have a maximum capacity of four. Now we hunt for inferences that define or describe those things about ourselves that invite inquiry. Anyone? Arlene?"

She is clearly his favorite. His comportment and manner of speech create a classroom setting and Ari squirms, glancing at the processor maw as she harvests a tomato core. Placing the center axis of the core on her wrist, she flips down on one side and the core cartwheels slowly towards Damien. "Not sure," she says, "Maybe there's a mortality curve built into the equation? But if that were true, the ship would have already killed off one or two of us to insure survival of the others."

"Quite right," he answers, "and you touch upon a point central to the theme." After catching Ari's core, he plunges it headlong into the maw. At the last instant, he yanks the outer skin as if pulling a tablecloth from beneath unruffled settings. "*Nomad*," he says, "can end us by design, based on logic. There is an intimate relationship between this vessel and our bodies. We're used to it, but vital information is acted upon by this ship without regard to our intellectual participation. We receive imperatives from our former home, even an occasional postcard, but we cannot send anything in return."

Arlene interrupts. "This was a precondition of flight." She mentions stealth protocols to break free of the Health Authority. "Everyone agreed, yourself included."

"I never did," Yashi says.

Damien goes on to say that information aboard ship only flows in one direction. This has been gnawing at all of us: the lack of control over mission protocols, which include need-to-know imperatives. "Aside from an occasional work order to optimize biologics, this ship doesn't need any of us to function. None at all."

"We'll be needed for the hatchlings," Ari says. "A ship without people is just plain stupid." I reflect on Damien's words. Communication is not reciprocal. Despite *Nomad*'s AI being unreasonably scaled back to automaton, there are still data boundaries suggestive of an infosieve. Richard mentioned as much in our final days together. He had an innate distrust of machines, and a distrust of all who can effect changes in their potential. "What is it then?" I ask. "What remains hidden from us?"

"Ourselves," Damien answers, speaking without an intent to impress. "This voyage is rooted in our individual natures. Imagine for an instant, that each of us has an interface port woven into the base of our skulls.

"We do have…" Yashi stops mid-sentence, realizing that Damien is being rhetorical. "Imagine, Yashi, that a chip in your spinal port journals all biodata into a repository for safe keeping. What would you have?" Yashi is hunched down, stuck to the textured weave of the walkway.

"I guess it depends upon the sensitivity of the interface."

Damien isn't satisfied. "Yashi, it's just a hypothetical. Be aggressive. Assume intrinsically dynamic pathways, both motor and non-motor, endocrine, neurals, the full repertoire of chemistry on a cellular level. We're talking the limbic system, the insula, hippocampus, and amy-land, everything hooked into the higher lobes. In other words, a full spread."

"Amy-land?"

Arlene clarifies. "Amygdala, the social nexus of the brain. Where fear gets dished out. As primitives, we processed survival instincts there. Now it's recognized as a conduit for higher behavioral complexities."

"Yes Arlene, but your explanation belabors my point. Tell me Yashi, what does this ship suck out of us every single day?" Damien winces. He wants active repartee but Yashi is slow on the uptake.

"I guess you'd have a neuro-chemical record of our lives. But again, the variables lack specificity."

Two more cores disappear as we move like a bucket brigade. Yashi doesn't provide the reaction Damien hopes for, so Damien turns to me. "Let me ask another way." Now the spoken word is no longer tempered by a red glow. Too many cores have been snatched up and the ambience is gone. Perhaps Damien planned as much, beginning the conversation in unsettled air, eventually delivering the goods as clarity arrives. His nature causes plenty of second-guessing. "Polly, the information from our interface chips, where does it go?" I want to think it through but the answer is obvious. "Into the central hub."

"Why?" he asks.

"To monitor vital functions, health beacons and metabolics. To optimize resources, and wake us from well-designed cryocycles. To keep us alive." Damien receives the final tomato core, holding it up to his right eye lengthwise. He points it at me as if it were a spyglass.

"Are you sure? Have you checked your chip's transcriptions lately?"

"No," I reply, "records aren't retrievable unless emergency protocols engage. Crew health is part of resource management. Give passengers full access to bioteture and abuses set in. Sleep cycles change, exercise intervals flux, and there's also a higher consumption of foodstuffs. Closed-loop med response is standard in all off-Earth transit. This evolved from well-documented abuses. It's not unique to our ship, and I don't see where you're going with this?" Having ignored me early on, Damien's attentions are now mine. But I tire of this drawn-out charade: the mannerisms, his voice, his cadence and feigned melancholy. Damien's inimitable brand of vivisection. With scalpel poised, he tries for a verbal incision.

"You ask where I'm going with this? Oh, Sweet Polly Purebread, we're all going to the same place, as one, and if you don't believe or even understand me, then ask yourself this. Who wakes you every cycle? Not mom or dad, that's for sure. Because the one who wakes you never sleeps. Wakes you, puts you to bed. Wakes you and tucks you in again. Every time you drift away, it's another chapter read, only this time *you* are the bedtime story. Not the little girl tucked in softly, but rather a piece of traffic purely mercantile."

"Piss off, Damien. You bring us over here and it's always bad theatre wrapped in obtuse paranoia... or call it anything else equally dumb." I have no idea what he's talking about.

"I've read the story, Polly. More times than I can count. Miles, Onquin, Arlene and I, we've been designated for this route. You and Yashi are the add ons—late players somehow tossed into the mix. Don't ask me how I know because I can't tell you, but I feel it, ever-present and lurking."

Yashi counters. "Feel what Damien, you bored again?"

Damien replies while dispatching the final tomato cylinder. "You've been added to the mix. You and Polly. Added to create a new flavor."

"Sure," I say. "Some flavor of cabin fever that's far less fascinating than you'd like us to believe." I stare at Damien as he closes the maw, pushes a button, and the mechanism whirs in near silence. He looks at the processor churning, then looks at me. "This ship is making tomato paste and each of us is a core. May the red light reflected off your face be more—more than just a little bit of whore."

Delilah

Seated at my desk while staring aimlessly, she comes up from behind. "You haven't touched it yet," Delilah says, inflection attempting winsome, as if eating Gouda and a stale crust will improve the ambient air. Both of us know my chances are less than hoped for. "You go ahead Delilah, I've got no appetite." This fails to appease because the subtext is pointedly about time. I'm not giving her any.

"You'll need the energy. Come on Sly, take a bite." Another falsehood. Adrenaline boosters are more necessary than food, and of those, thankfully I have my share. I open my mouth looking off to one side. Cheese and crumbly biscuit are set upon my tongue. Yes, it is the body of Christ, or not, but it may as well be, who really gives a shit?

"Thanks," I mumble, tossing a conciliatory glance as she releases practiced thoughts. "Now I need to show you this one thing…" I drift elsewhere. Apox-nine isn't so tough if you use the right combo of inhibitors and seratoxin. Upon infection, motor skills diminish until the diaphragm seizes up and takes the breath away. Before then, I'll be inside, expecting a cleansing unless the regimen has changed. Maybe Pox-9 is old hat? The new stuff is always more deadly, especially near a nexus.

 Delilah pulls off her top, and despite the scars, no woman from the Canister can match her sinuous beauty. Elongated lines seem to shimmer. She is a gazelle freshly primed. I have often fancied her from among the reeds, her nose to the wind, an ear twitching in anticipation. Whether on the plains of Africa or within some disparate future hence, she is favored and knows as much. As for her current affectation, I can only think of my mission—thinware and the delivery window. I'll get one chance, just a few seconds to find that seam, right handrail, middle elevator, the only elevator that drops straight into the deep spacer's cargo bay.

"Look at me now," she says, opening a clasp and peeling away her remaining shroud. Rock hard thighs grace an inner vault that borders on the insane. Men fight over that. Delilah takes my hand, placing it on her hip. She traces my index and middle finger along a small, serpentine tattoo. "Tell me what you see."

"An infinity sign," I say, "twisting like a Möbius strip, and arrows woven into the loops—two arrows, pointing in opposition."

"Two clocks," she answers. "One for a forward reckoning, and the other to go back and fix things." Her words are novel, or... they ping some lost memory... until it is found. Harold Dandridge had spoken the very same when his father died. "I wish I was with you," she says, rubbing scars well below her left breast. "With you. All that blood and pain."

"It was just me and Harold, ripping out tree stumps for hours on end."

"Do you remember your overlap and fade? I was there, mouthing recollections. How else could I know what Harold said to you?" Delilah meshes our fingers, some confusion herein. I cannot reconcile familiar things, overlapping what exactly? And her nakedness is effusive, part of this immersion, with me neither giver nor taker. She speaks of some lost reference, cloistered in pretense. Part of me feels betrayed.

"You're using me," I say.

"If you want me to," she smiles. As if prompted by my uneven breaths, she faces me in one graceful extension of choreography. Her eyes shone of purpose, words tumbling out in a lost wreckage of insincerity. I abruptly halt her advances, prompting surprise, followed by disquiet. On one hand, I'm trying to vanquish an indestructible foe. On the other hand, I may be staring at the very same. Each inhale leaves me doubting myself—Canister ambition embodied in her less than subtle wares. One's standing shouldn't depend upon the company you keep, nor the tools at their disposal. "I should be going." My words are distant, soaked up by the walls and released moments later.

"No, you've got twenty minutes yet. "...finish," she whispers, "finish now." More cheesy biscuit is offered and taken, swallowing biological actives sans explanation. Twenty minutes until the prep team takes over.

Delilah stands as she dresses, straightening her alloy mesh with a sweep of an arm. Our eyes lock in suspension as she curtsies, her back leg pulling open the door. It lacks the ease of an earnest exit. People used to be more knowing in the ways of simple things like saying goodbye. She peers back at me. "Good luck, Sly. Since you're preoccupied, we'll use the cryolibrary for consummation. This time I'll name him after you." The door clicks shut upon my realization: she's having a boy.

"This time?" I repeat, her touch having been more complimentary of some measured result, rather than an amorous interlude. This time... she'd said she wanted a girl. It is the final intrigue of a woman nary a child; a supernaut that unleashes pheromones like neurotoxins. They don't kill flesh—just render it helpless.

My prep team ushers me into vaclab. Here, polymer skin is applied, socket goggles, and a spinal that juices my entire system. It's liquid fire lapping at extremities. Ready as I'll ever be, I venture forth to strike a blow or curl up in agony. Much is left unrealized, all intention moshed within this threadbare reality.

Yashi **MILES ONQUIN DAMIEN POLLY ARLENE**

Within a bonnet rests a jangle, melody, discord, one in the same
Waking limbs find nothing of the tangle, so expected every day
The absence terrifies and captivates attention span
Takes a body, wraps it round and round again
Daily patterns fall like messengers dying in the field
Undisturbed or opened wide, circumstance reveals
Memories do yield, giving way
Until nothing is more comfortable
Than still air and silence

Nomad's comforts are few, least of which are the varied manifestations of self, be it journal records or the pallor of unattended expression. The virtual reality gear is one size fits all. A reflective mylar suit, snuggly fit, shows my facade awaiting ramp-up of the lower registries. Soon enough, programs shall fuse man into language—a viscerality of lives shaken free.

Tara's distant voice is anchored to a tomb. Her words slowly drip into ear stems like overflowing sap, coating an iris, and another, filling my throat as I try to swallow. "Yashi, don't say a word, simply listen. I've come to you, so able and willing. You need only relax and let me be here." I adjust the headrest until the simulator's magnetosphere gives feedback of extended balance. All at once, the trellised inlays of my skintight suit lift me, limbs suspended and dangling free. Senses are isolated as the simulator regulates all feeds, selectively interrupted and also applied. The data-stream envelops conscious thought. This preamble ends and my virtual postcard finally arrives.

Tara wears a patterned kimono reminiscent of koa burl. Silken streamers of gold and indigo shed physicality into a woven hypnosis, catching the breeze and lifting her ever higher on an oaken swing. Back and forth, her pendulum pushes off on the backstroke, then up and away, her bare feet kicking toward the highest branches. "Come on Yashi, don't just sit there, push!"

My body twitches, current flowing through me, forcing motor signals into a fugue state. The swirling motion dilates me deeper into submission until finally, leg spasms release their tension. I am in. "How is this...? How did you find me?" I ask this of Tara as her bonnet comes undone and floats free. I reach for it but my hand moves right through.

"Find you? I never left. Now push, silly man, I want to go all the way around the world." I stare past my thumb, looking for the bonnet.

"What is this place? Where are we?" I turn to see Tara awash in warm tones scattered by leaves, and I push. She glides higher than physical laws allow, nearly to the top of her arc, retracing back down again.

"We're on a ship headed nowhere, and I really don't care where we go, so long as we're together." These vocals burrow as a muted audio cue imparts a nearly subconscious message: *a standard correspondence begins with an approximation of REM sleep, inhibitors keeping objective thought in flux. Logics produce eristic complexity, based upon specs designated by the postcard initiator. Disorientation usually gives way to acceptance once dialogue commences...*

I hear what I can hardly grasp, invading my periphery like rote knowledge. My altered consciousness becomes more receptive to the assimilation of stimuli. Such are the properties of a sublime datastream; an augmentation inducing responsive behavior.

"But how? How..." Tara kicks hard as she passes by and sure enough, her swing breaks the centerline above, going all the way around.

"Catch me darling, here I come!" Falling head first, she pivots and her weight fills my arms, delighted. Her heft is true. So often I've carried her up the fire escape, there can be no mistake. It's her. And yet, I cannot fathom how? "Yashi, you may find this hard to believe, but I am in your arms right here, right now. You've suffered, so much chaos. It's a schism darling, akin to latent schizophrenia. We've been healing you, and now you're getting better. I'm so happy!" I look at my surroundings. The optics aren't quite right. "Am I in some type of therapy tank? What causes this?" Tara snuggles in and squeezes tight. "On liftoff, your sleep chamber didn't malfunction. It was sabotaged." My body flexes in denial. "No, Onquin had the bruises. I saw them." Tara reaches, turning my head with her fingertips. "You love me, Yashi?"

"Yes. I do."

"Then listen very carefully. They tried to kill you during launch, and they'll try again. You are in danger because you are dangerous to others. I'm held hostage because of things that you can do."

"Onquin's sleeper went haywire," I respond, wondering if some type of mix-up had occurred. Was I targeted? Did Onquin take the brunt of an attack meant for me? But... sleeper pods have individual settings... and why? Why attack me? I set Tara on her feet and she twirls away, ballerina poise, adagio, lowering herself to one knee. Her outstretched arms pull in tight, coupled as if grasping her heart. "They've hidden me, my essence inside this godforsaken ship—memories woven into programming. You need to help me find myself before it's too late." I drop down, eye to eye.

"This isn't true. There's no way this is true."

"Yashi, there's an intruder on board. One of the crew, though we don't know who. I've been altered, slowly wisping apart." Tara cries pear shaped tears. One drips down and hangs on the side of her chin. "All because I want to be with you." With one finger I seek out this tear. The supple wetness evaporates. A false wetness, not real. "Where are we Tara?"

"You are on *Nomad* and part of me as well. But the rest of me is reaching out from home. It's me Yashi, I'm here." She leans forward and our embrace accords the proper nuance of physicality. It's genuine. "I miss you, Tara. Every day."

"Yashi, there isn't much time. I've learned what is possible. Imprints and templates, sponge memory and this constant triggering of anaphase neurals, it's all so confusing." My heart rate elevates to a level unanticipated by programming. Auditory cues suggest relaxation. On one hand, I understand this interface. On the other, I'm with my girl. I try to speak but Tara interrupts in low tones. "Please listen, only seconds remain. I think they're going to purge my profile, my essence. They're playing with me right now to see if I can be of any further use. It's terrifying!"

"Tara, what can we possibly do? I'm so far away..."

"There is something, but you have to trust me. It will be difficult."

"Say it." Tara's image wavers, breaking up in places. The effect promotes a sense of losing her.

"You're in a simulator. I'm speaking to you through a postcard sent from Earth. Once this ends, download the simulator's cache memory into the biolab fabrications itinerary. Keep the end-product hidden until I send another postcard, and in it, what's left of the woman that adores you."

"This is impossible."

"No Yashi, I wish it were. Just like they're using you on that ship, they're doing the same to me."

"But how have you learned so much? You couldn't have sent this message without help."

"The one named Miles comes from a place called the Canister. His friends say it's important that I join you. I don't know why. I don't care. I just want to be where you are."

"I'll talk to Miles. We'll figure this out together."

"No. We can't trust him. We can't trust anyone. We don't know who the intruder is. If you speak to him at all, choose your words, and hurry... hurry..."

Her frozen face dissipates at familiarity's edge, this postcard calling for measures ill defined. I claw at my mylar suit, wanting out of this synthesis. Impulse harbors regret, a rushing of blood and a pooling of sweat. I cup hands to my face, desirous of a bygone age. Such daunting prospects of loss turned sage.

Elysian Fields   **RBM 1110**

A measure of distance up or down
In equal lengths, smile or frown
You cannot say how far you've gone
unless you know from where you've come
But then again…
A direction traveled does reveal, method, means, and matter
Once more distance is imperiled if none the three should gather
Method first, define the scheme, means to bring it into being
And matter last to know the cost
Of failure…   …when all is lost

The Universal Health Authority has more than one tessellated nexus strewn across the planet, but this one is of particular interest to free humans. Once upon a time it had been a military outpost constructed in the predawn era before planet sentience. All methods of madness collided within the measured grounds of this former icon: weapons programs, space programs, physics research, bioterra infinitum. From this locale did humans trigger the airborne necklace of death; a geometric annihilation of nearly two percent of the continent's population. The resulting destruction failed to cut the grid into manageable pieces. It was the last desperate act of men that could no longer tend to their former responsibilities.

Though the sum of mankind's knowledge once lay beneath these grounds, little remains of the former density. Various disciplines have been parceled out to greater effect, but free humans still feel a calling to this place. It is a need to sniff and scratch, claw and expose a sore. So it is with my arrival.

The Elysian Fields don't appear to be much of an obstacle. Old structures in disrepair, with patches of poison turnips as far as the eye can see. I set about as aimless beggar lost in psychobabble. My incoming codes are carefully chosen to avoid AI filters. Brevity is key.

Atop my skull, a tangled cap of metal scraps are woven into dreadlocks. Buried within, a radio blares Ramadan festival tripe: big throaty pieces of hypnostagger. It's cover as a carrier wave for white burst communication. My blood contains tungsten-laced platelets that congeal in appropriate places, creating a walking transceiver. If the Health Authority fries my skullcap, I'll be incommunicado, but hopefully it won't come to that.

"Alligators daggers down, don't leave many of them around. We all want one now and then, feed ☐em extra if you can." It must come across as a banal stream of consciousness. I've entered a hot zone, with dedicated satellites above and a sensory mesh beneath every step. This grid picks up all sorts of bio-data, including layered brain activity. Especially that. If aggression markers are triggered, or complex problem-solving patterns arise, I could be microwaved much akin to an ant under a sun-drenched magnifying glass.

"Alligators under skin, try my hardest, be a friend, oops a daisy there went one, took my baby for a swim." Ambling forward, I move as training prescribes. Guidance will eventually feed me a course correction. I need this interdiction to avoid terminal defenses: mines, gutter spray, who knows what else? My eyes remain unfocused much of the time, but I catch the remnants of a tattered woven mesh in my peripheral vision. This somehow reminds me of Delilah, her outfit, an insincere goodbye. I wipe her image away as quickly as possible.

"Choo choo darlin don't you mind, gator is a friend of mine. Don't you bother, scream or holler, just close yer eyes and let him swaller." Logics will cycle the gator jabber matched against a civilian database: a history of gator talk weeks in the making; the first episode near a cell tower; the next episode below the aqueduct; finally, gator talk near the tram depot. Each instance was orchestrated, all headed in the current direction.

Static washes through the music, possibly a white burst signal. Inside my head, a tungsten filament nudges olfactory tissues. A smell of burnt wood wafts into me, the sensation changing quickly to tar and liquid plastic. Heightened activity in this region of the brain shouldn't draw scrutiny, but the signal is clear. I change my heading, stumbling left, always left until further notice. "Hey there gator, you a sight. Eatin babies ain't polite. Taste this barrel here instead, pull the trigger... gator's dead."

I start perspiring, unnatural for a cool, windy day. No doubt sensors seek causality, resulting in a meds-abuse profile. Diagnosis: adrenaline junkie, confirmed via chem analysis of contents within a shirt pocket. Safety protocols engage, overriding security concerns. Inferences suggest a negative risk vagrant in need of medical care. My proximity to the targeted mobile med unit is damn near perfect.

It approaches and issues commands that I follow without provocation: radio off, adrenaline packets surrendered. The med cart asks that I lie down upon the vehicle pallet as a hypospray commits me to the act. Suddenly prone, visual acuity mildly occluded, my last memories are that of encapsulation. They're taking me inside.

§

Surfacing into consciousness, I drift within a haze of Canister doctrine. Mildly sedated, my implants are being pinged—testing capabilities. I feel a measured excitation of mind as diagnostics are communicated in English to a human interface. Slices of conversation are somehow absorbed by my transceiver. "...his mind is too well ordered. His chemical composition is too well balanced. His idiot veneer is unsupported by biology." I am logged as an asset capture, to be overhauled for reinsertion. "...release, and thereafter trace origins to an assemblage of additional naturals. All will be processed."

Suddenly, a high-pitched frequency is urgently interrupted. "2M31111: monitors indicate cognitive patterns; coded substructure buried within the lateral sulcus. He listens to everything. He understands everything." I squirm as the keening pitch returns, followed by a dull, resonant voice. "Cut the feed, end diagnostic, and somebody drop that bastard."

I awaken in a medical gown, barefoot and unrestrained, clean and shaven. Sitting up, then standing, I have no protective polymer skin or socket goggles. Looking in all directions, I'm in an enormous empty chamber without an apparent exit. A voice permeates. "Sylvester Ramirez, please remain stationary until support arrives."

My faculties seem intact, motor skills normal, my vision is perceptibly better. With a cursory touch, I confirm that the splinterware beneath the skin of my left elbow is still there. I'm also relieved to find my thumbnail ID untouched, as is the overriding thumbnail. Perhaps I've only been knocked out for a weapons check and med-panels, but for how long? No answer avails and I'm unprepared for what happens next. She enters my view, radiant as ever, striding forward and abruptly stopping at a distance. "Delilah," I say, as thoughts reverberate and force a disconnect. My training breaks me down, knowing that sensors are processing everything. I can only wonder, and so I ask, "How'd they get you?"

"Confirmed," she replies. "Prior knowledge of Adrius Five, alias Delilah." I recoil if only slightly. This *is* Delilah standing before me. Or?

No, not the same. She is living flesh but Delilah is older. That is to say, my Delilah back in the Canister is older. "Relax, Sylvester. We've traced your activities into the gaslamp district. Soon enough your support contingent will be processed. No one will be harmed." Apparently, my Delilah is Adrius Five, and this woman is an iteration of the same. They are likely two in a succession of identical sisters, probably a lot more than just two. Probably a lot more than five. Imagination takes hold as an endless skein of copies enter my thoughts, but Delilah counters quickly without pretense.

"Thirty-two in all: five confirmed living, ten post mortem, six frozen gamete binaries, nine embryos—status unresolved, and two maturations of the Adrius series have gone missing, or I should say, one unaccounted for and one nearly found." This woman speaks to me as a haunt might visit one who slumbers—a more exacting version of her other self, clad in medical white, snug smock accompanied by insulated walkers. Simply being in her presence evokes a critique of all that is feminine.

"You lack what little ambiguity has been cultivated in the other, yet everything female emanates from every pore." Inklings of her pheromone attack are upon me, likely reengineered and more potent than my Delilah back home. No wonder she had been the pride of the Canister: packaged goods, much more of anything and everything than the Canister could ever produce. "How did you do that?" I ask. "How did you answer my thoughts, saying there were thirty-two copies of you?"

"No, only thirty-one copies of me, though all are contemporaneous and none should be delineated as primary, including myself. Our sensors pick up images, process shadows, hardly anything at all. You thought of her yesterday, outside in the fields. It is merely a rational progression that I am called upon as intermediary."

A servile pout forms and is accompanied by just enough liquid in the eyes to produce unnatural perfection. Within this glassy gaze, I am drawn towards failure. I glitch, taking a step back. This woman is a manifestation of gender utility; to coax and claim; to achieve a result. All chemistry playing out between us leads directly thus. I am designed to give in with little in the way of deliberation.

"Sylvester, you've implemented an elaborate mixture of ideas: adrenaline, socket goggles and polymer skin. Your skull cap was doped with tritium, a low-level beta emitter that lends to sensor obfuscation. Still, we've managed a compilation of short-term visualizations, but cannot delve deeper due to the tungsten filaments embedded in your skull. In aggregate, your efforts seek an objective greater than merely penetrating a nexus." She reaches for my shoulder, smoothing a wrinkle of fabric. Her aroma is effusive. "What is it you want exactly?"

I add distance. "Nothing from you."

Delilah feigns introspection. She turns her hand, looking at fingernails. I enjoy the subtlety of her pronating wrist, delicate and seemingly desirous of handling. She looks down and sees my distended gown. "Nothing? I doubt that very much." Turning aside, her profile vents a waifish demur. "It must have been an ordeal to have those metal casings implanted in your head. And why? For some stealthy intrigue with little or no chance of success. I'm here to find common ground." The servile pout returns. Her hands clasp up and inward, teeth capturing paired thumbs. "And we could make it fun."

I smile at my own release of tension. I've not lived a life full of sound moral decisions, but in this instance, I fall back upon a keener sense of adversarial judgment. "No thanks, and I've already said that once before." The tiniest layer of strain seeps into her calm. Her eyes glaze, and then return with acuity. This isn't natural contemplation, rather, a force-fed interconnectivity is now at play within her.

"Mister Ramirez, I'm not a machine. Modified yes, but flesh and blood, the same as you." Her voice quavers, a fair attempt at spontaneity. "Your confiscated shoes were made of hardened plastique. This alone labels you terrorist. They'll rip those casings from your brain. Is that what you want?" I examine her waist, imagining my child inside. Memories of my Delilah overlap this visage now before me, suggesting an opening. Indeed, she'll have my answer, perhaps triggering logics to act on my behalf.

"That's precisely what I want. Get this shit out of my head! If you think I volunteered, you're twice as dim as those who forced me here. Go ahead and carve me. Just don't turn me into a passive symbiote that can't even make a decision." My focus hardens on Delilah. Tasting the insult, her face drops before words are spoken. "Surgery is currently unwarranted, particularly at the cost of data you might otherwise provide."

"Oh, I might be butchered. The stuff inside my head can cost lives. Individual safety protocols, rescinded for the common good." I breathe deeply, my steadfast gaze searching, trying to connect. A slight upturned smile draws her response. "Yes?"

"No, um, it's just... you possess some less than subtle thing that makes it hard to concentrate. It's not your fault. They gave you something that you don't know how to use."

"I know how," Delilah answers. "You presume too much."

"And you're naïve, irrespective of presumption. Admit it. You know how to use your wares for them, but for yourself? Not a clue."

"There is no distinction."

"Yes, exactly. See, I told you." Delilah's empathy penetrates ever slightly. Humanity peeks through her veneer, though neither suits her willingly. Hers is an intermediary form, Januslike. She stands vacant for a time... "My streaming link has been momentarily compromised. It is an odd feeling, unhealthy and lacking organization."

"Unhealthy?" I ask.

"Perhaps a poor choice of words, and yet organic simplicity invites... error. I attempt relevant conclusions, though absent dataflux, all is compromised." She pauses, a lost cadence accentuating her condition. "Life's natural design must be self-evidently healthy. This paradox of emotion and purpose may bother me for some time."

I'm uncomfortable with her admission. Has the Health Authority disconnected its shared perspective, hoping to impart camaraderie? Maybe her interface isn't compromised at all? I quickly discount this possibility. Delilah used the word 'bother.' The machines would never give her that. They'd have said 'fascinate,' or 'occupy,' or something indicative of balanced computation. 'Bother' is simply too human a word.

"Removal of the tungsten casings is problematic," she says, "even if your cooperation is genuine." She tells me the casings have stagger fuses. "Nanos are being fabricated for hi-rez detailing. You will now self-administer a sedative." An inhaler is offered.

I reach past the inhaler, my hand sliding down and resting on a hip. "No sedatives, please. I want to be with you." She stands rigid, as though awaiting orders. It seems her connectivity has been restored. Delilah reaches to remove my hand, wherein I curl fingers within fingers, first one hand, then the other. She balks amidst a startled flicker.

"I shall take you to the lab, but first you will disengage without further manipulation." As I let go, Delilah's breath alters cadence. I follow her, having an unrelenting view of legs and ass. "Sylvester, I feel a certain disorientation not borne of the senses, rather, some other imperative. I induce no such sensation, and therefore it cannot be suppressed."

"Mmmm," I respond. Very good. We arrive at the elevators, three in all. I require the middle one. As happenstance would have it, the elevator on my left opens, empty. Delilah moves to step inside. I reach around, gently pulling her back for a caress. "Might a condemned man get a final request?" My words are met with vigor as the elevator door closes. She attempts separation, but my grip is firm. "Sylvester, this isn't the time or place for sexual bravado, or any other act of disingenuous self-interest. Be reminded, you will be restrained if necessary."

"You spoke of cooperation, nearly seducing me. Now I'm taking you up on the offer." I grapple wrists, spinning and planting her palms against the middle elevator door. I push hardness up against her, only thin fibers separating us. "Once we get to the lab, I will tell you what I know of those who forced this deed upon me. In return, you will make certain our efforts, here and now, produce a child." I graze her neck, memories of my own Delilah swimming fully until her response shunts me back to reality.

"Such presumption. Though oddly, I happen to be in estrus."

"Yeah, I can tell." I graze her neck yet again, seemingly to good effect.

"In return, you will answer questions without hesitation, including but not limited to the whereabouts of all collaborators?" I acquiesce while loosening a drawstring. Medical whites drop down to her ankles as her magnificent backside lay bare, but for a meager undergarment. I glance at the elevator panel that shows an indistinguishable readout. It means the elevator isn't here yet, and that's a good thing.

"Very well, Mr. Ramirez, I accept your terms, assuming créche maturation of the embryo." My hands keep her hands affixed to the elevator door as she twists around, sealing our agreement with a full kiss, open mouth. This woman is nameless but for the memories that attach themselves to another. She shares an expression of feedback, perhaps linked to several brethren at this very instant.

"How many of you will I be fucking? How many?"

"Only one other," she says heavily, "chambered in situ, but her experience pales compared to my own."

"That's for sure. I'll loosen her up."

Delilah smiles, her mission approaching a successful conclusion. Human impulse and emotion bleed through. I pull her undergarment aside, find her swollen flower, then move higher and graze her anus instead. She tries to turn but I won't let her. "You said you want a child." Her uncertain voice combines with fleshy quivers as I press against her opening. Here comes an instant of pleasure and pain interbred.

"Either way, you'll have my seed, so deal with it." I pierce her tender ring as she grunts, musculature tightening. Deeper still, she coils in response. I pause so she can regain herself, then buck forward amidst another clenching protest. Within a sneer, her eyes find mine. "It hurts," she manages, just before a grimace abandons language.

"Good," I say, "It's supposed to," and I'm all the way in. Hypersensate, she gurgles something about an interface module—some rarefied confluence. Apparently, they've crossed some wires in her head, and suddenly she is accommodating. My new Delilah is skewered and throaty, pulling rhythmically. She speaks of a potential child, her demeanor unanticipated. "Sperm from a shadow, primal, yet I revel unabashedly."

"Ooooooh…" comes an answer inside my skull, and a realization that my tungsten transceiver is once again active. Her emotive connectivity seeps into me. Without malice, I find the girl inside, making her acquaintance truly. In the moments that follow, reciprocal feedback inflames our union. She rattles as she speaks. "Sccience wll fiix, or… presrv… finer q-q-qualities. Perhaps use…fl variations?"

I can't tell if she's talking to herself or expressing database logics. Any guided response is lost to a mind coming unhinged. With our bodies entwined, I apologize for my rough-hewn entry. "I only wanted your handlers to feel something. Anything." Delilah turns and meets my eyes, reaching down and grasping my testicles. "A block of ice does not feel. The best it can do is sweat." She squeezes lightly, an insinuative threat as we kiss, awash in some abstract equality. My tungsten receiver allows for the oddest echo, tunneling us together. She sneers, squeezing harder. "Lessons learned best are often shared." I grimace, still committed to our rhythm as her self-induced threshold crosses over.

"All's given," she manages, and with that, a gushing of sex. We shudder to our knees as the elevator door opens. Delilah orgasms with such urgency, my own imperative goes unnoticed. As we tumble inside, I clench my fist with a protruding thumb and slam it into the elevator floor—execution flawless—me releasing a yowling and ragged load. Residual thrusts and all else are parlayed as sensory obfuscation.

Standing within the elevator, a pair of neuroliths have obviously been apprised of the situation. They exit deftly, stepping over our tangled bodies with a smile and a frown, both sustained as the elevator door closes. These human responses are captured by moticon programs: nerve endings, synoptic tracers, glial interface and all extraneous metrics. Little doubt these facial gestures will occur in other, less spontaneous places.

Health Authority sensors should have difficulty registering the nuances of interaction. For starters, neurolith metabolics likely interfered with my own. Delilah's orgasm poses another complexity. Her interface appeared compromised due to stimulus flare. This saturates and delays responsiveness, delving into humanistic qualities while the software keeps shutting her down. There is also the question of ejaculate being pumped into her rectum. How does a sensor accord value to that?

As for me, pique pleasure leaves little room for any pain signal. When my thumbnail hit the elevator floor, it sliced through capillaries as intended. Blood now pools within the offended tissues much like an ink bloom. My plasma acts as a reagent for thinware set directly beneath the thumbnail chip's substrate. Canister personnel gambled that Authority scanners would take the ID chip at face value, authenticating chip files via DNA sampling, thereafter referencing civilian datablades to confirm identity. No doubt this verification occurred during my incapacitation.

What has not been accomplished, hopefully, is HA's discovery of the thinware—bonded to protein envelopes fastened to the inert bedliner of the ID chip's underside. These envelopes offer receptor site adherence, though once immersed in blood, the bonding agents fall prey to my immune system. Some type of antigen reaction cleaves a single linchpin, and thereafter, the entire bonding system unravels.

The micro-modules coalesce within pooling blood that oozes from the tip of my thumbnail. I withdraw from Delilah, spotting the target—a gap between two handrail plates that offers sensor sanctuary. I grasp the rail, thumb tip pushing into that seam. Applied pressure and surface tension force blood into that crease. Pulling myself to one knee, displeasure from my uncoupled partner serves as misdirection. "That was abrupt. I expected a more languid finish..." She ends her thought several beats later. "...which would have been appreciated."

I stand, breathing hard, the elevator continuing upward. "Your part of the bargain has been consummated," I say. "No doubt your worn little knothole tells you as much." I attempt shock value; words that might absorb scrutiny. "If you want anything more than a professional fuck, try not making it into a contract. Or embrace your humanity and just yank all that software shit out of your head. That'll get me hard all over again."

Delilah is stunned, returning to baseline sentiment as she stands. "My original thoughts are confirmed. You are an animal."

"And you darling, have forgotten how to be one. Maybe some better programming." The elevator door opens and a medcart awaits. Delilah pushes me up against the cart, knocking me off balance into a seated position. "I am not the only one who forgets," she answers, stepping back into the elevator. "You cannot even remember your given name."

Her response is puzzling, divulged within a decidedly defensive outburst. The elevator closes as my medcart accelerates down a hallway. "Where are you going?" I shout. "What'd you mean by that? The medcart answers as I enter a tunnel that glows of amber phosphorescence. "Adrius Nine proceeds to the cryolibrary. Your sperm must be preserved in accordance to the agreement. Context is lacking for further clarification."

"Please explain," I say.

"Only Adrius Nine can supply context. She will return to you after an indeterminate interval."

Wonderful. This Delilah is Adrius Nine. Good to know who's fucking who. Shortly I'll be worked on to remove the tungsten casings, and my mind will be laid bare. Conscious thought becomes a liability. I've put the elevator far enough behind. It is time. I roll off the medcart, grabbing my head. "It hurts! It hurts! Stop! I'll tell you everything!" I bite down on my injured thumb. If they hadn't noticed already, they might attribute my thumb injury to this bite. I clamp tight, jaw muscles rigid, pressure directly applied to the thumbnail ID chip. Beneath it, a single module remains, bonded differently from those that had vacated.

Sensing prolonged pressure as a trigger, the module expires in a single blip of white burst communication. It's all that is necessary to cleanse my mind. The closest tungsten filament explodes, and then the next, and another, still others, all in rapid succession. I disappear in a veil of searing pain. This is all to the good. Memories are a dangerous thing.

DAMIEN   POLLY   ONQUIN   YASHI   ARLENE   Miles

Stuck inside a thicket within a tangled hollow, worlds shaken free. The cliffs of Dover splinter, glaciated history calving into scree. Spectral ripples push on by, absorbed by fleshy undercoat. Radiation floes, thorny skin oozing layers, congealed and growing harder, red-shift glowing hotter. Moisture so real, this wet is real, I'm waking up…

"Oh my…" These eyes open to an adrenaline torrent, nausea waking me fully. Sweat drips off my brow and into an eye. My good eye. I try twisting to one side—to move—to force a response from limbs. Nothing. Nothing but a view of the Milky Way. I am outside floating free, encased in a clear resin. Miles Dandridge, suffused in amber.

"Good morning, Miles. Did you sleep well?" I am prone, attached to an umbilical feeding me oxygen via nasal insertion. My mouth is wedged open with a caterwaul hose. It rides the teeth and stings my skin beneath. I exhale through a valve, each breath forming tiny crystals that drift away. "You have a subvocalizer on your larynx. Answer or you will be cut loose." The tones are a variant of the ship's itinerant voice.

"Slept well, thank you, and yourself?" At my periphery, a sporadic shimmer catches my attentions. It's the crew module and its counterpart, twirling out to the sides and slightly behind me. "I can't move. Tell me why?" One of my comrades has taken me from my sleep chamber, put me outside, and now I am destined to become flotsam on a whim.

"You are wearing an orthopedic girdle attached atop the vertebrae. It eliminates movement, protecting you from a containment breach. What is the Canister's objective? What are your marching orders?"

My eyes are watering, a natural response from my good eye, and a sympathetic response from the mixed organics of the other. Much like a candied apple, I've been sheathed in plastocine. Did the perpetrator consider that I might drown in my own vomit? Given that my diaphragm allows me to breathe, I imagine peristalsis is also possible. I swallow, confirmed. "The Canister was my home, comprised of free peoples. I fled because Canister doctrine diverged from a humanistic path."

"You were at odds with the Canister hierarchy, yet you joined this voyage? Please explain." I need clues to uncover the perpetrator. One such clue is set just outside my useful range of vision: a fingerprint on my molded exoskeleton, embedded in the resin but off to the left side. I am unable to focus using natural, unassisted vision. Happenstance leaves macro imagers within my right eye on the wrong side of things. For clarity of focus, if only I could turn my head slightly back and to the side...

I must also give the expected response. "Our fortunes grew steadily worse and there was infighting. One faction assigned me to this voyage. The others felt it was just a poor use of resources. Some even thought we would die inside EMMA."

"I don't believe you Miles."

"No? Then tell me why I'm the only Canister member aboard this ship." The umbilical valve that feeds me air suddenly chokes shut. Several beats elapse and the valve opens. My first instinct is wrong. This is not overt intimidation. Upon expressing my misgivings, the voice explains. "Your umbilical enters a navigation pack strapped to your back. The pack provides oxygen, temperature control, and motility." It feeds me air, but when the valve closes, it also vents air as required for propulsion and attitude adjustment.

My body floats out in front of *Nomad* like a figurehead at the prow. This tells me that engine thrust is less than anticipated. Otherwise, I'd be straggling behind and rubbing against the main hull. Thus, if engines have been perturbed, Arlene is not likely the culprit. The valve closes and the pack expels a puff of mist. A cloudy imagery refracts through the resin shell. Again, I try to turn and focus, without success. The embedded fingerprint remains a blur as the valve opens again, my breath falling into rhythm. A twist of the neck, the smallest turn of the skull and I'll be able to focus, logging fingerprint details into journal records.

"Who awarded you passage aboard *Nomad*? Describe the progression of influence." The questions are endless. I review Canister hierarchy, also supplying a profile of each crewmember. Speaking via subvocalizer becomes a labored task. Soon enough, weariness takes hold as the umbilical feeds me a suppressant gas. I look at the stars and pinpoint our destination. The Centauri system fades within a darker realm.

Ivie awakens me, groggy within an ambiance of diffused light. I'm inside the ship again, inside my sleeper, alive, uncaked, and whole. My neck aches as I hear the sleeper's inner workings begin to whirr, telling me that I'm going under once again.

Cryo keeps me down for a number of days. I spend the first six hours of my next cycle eyeing Polly, wishing she'd crawl into her sleeper. Her manner is the same as always, subdued with little in the way of interplay. She notices my reticence but takes no exception: music, repulsor schematics, and a dismissive glance are all that come my way. I browse her work and fish for a more telling reaction. "Make sure and remind me to tweak the diagnostic interface, assuming I'm still around after you've done the heavy lifting." Instead of a pointed look, she lingers on particulars. "Almost done," she answers, "only a few more cycles."

Hours later, Polly's cryopaste regimen takes hold. I finally relax as her sleeper closes. Now, to witness the lurker's unsettled dust. I dive into cryo data using code I'd written when seeking Arlene's company, only to discover multiplexed logs diverging from an authentic log several months back. Each crewmember sees normalcy insofar as a differing log exists for each of us—all sequences are smooth and all supposed variations of the sleep cycles are pristine—a deft hand. Surprisingly deft, answers buried too deeply within the Kagome architecture. This ability to hide or alter information makes Yashi the lone credible suspect, unless one of the others keeps such skill under wraps.

Searching elsewhere, I make use of the gondola, dividing my time between A-module and the main body of the ship. I turn off the recycler and wade in, finding remnants of the encasement resin but no fingerprint. Analysis reveals fragments of my own DNA, mostly skin cells and traces of urea. Nothing useful. Additional resin inquiries uncover Polly helping Damien with a project long ago. He had called it casting, somewhat like a fly-fishing spacewalk with a person at the end of a tether. Damien is strange in that way. He can take a piss and call it recreation. But finding the origin of plastocine encasement doesn't prove anything. The specs are layered into a microjet array, all have access, and records of the production run have been wiped clean.

I check the engine and see that full thrust has been restored. Now I need only view the timestamp to see... that I had restored full thrust. Someone used my biometrics, virtually imitated no doubt, to gain full ship access. Or else I'm schizophrenic and encased myself in plastocine, also managing every other aspect of this charade. I consider my inquisitor's vocal patterns and decide a heuristic language scan might reveal much, only to discover that the voice I heard incorporated the tendencies of all crewmembers. Walking amongst the sleeper pods, I realize not every incriminating detail has been merged into obscurity. Someone was awake during my cycle, and possibly their own as well.

I splice a biometric reader into the junction of the B-module cable housing, downloading the journal chip registry of the whole crew. Whereas encryption hides mental activity, physiological data remains available. I check cryopaste tissue saturation, creating an overlay that gives me peaks and valleys. Both Onquin and Yashi exhibit irregularities that run contrary to the predictive data of the multiplexed stasis cycles. Polly's overlap of my current cycle adds yet another variable. I seek further granularity, but some unrecognized bit of code withholds the forensics required to solve this riddle. Even a valid override doesn't allow access to the deeper core profiles. I initiate a ship-wide systems check: bios, registries, parfactor subroutines, the works. My suspicions uncover a variance. It is transient and adaptable, leaving little in the way of tracers. Canister leadership had warned me of possible Health Authority intrusion; AI Paranoia—a basic precept of all Canister personnel.

I prod, peck, and bait to no avail as diagnostics prove useless. This lends to my conclusion that there is a ghost in the machine. I gravely need to find it. Otherwise, our lives are in danger. Regardless of tactics, the ghost stays at arm's length. I set traps that have little chance of success but better define the playing field. I open information causeways between disparate functionality. I place beacons, rest stops, and access gaps. I even try a few dangling logic trees and an open password vault. The ghost avoids me at every turn as my intrigue becomes a game of fear. It's smart, perhaps even capable of taking antimatter containment off-line. Best not to corner it—give room until it can be identified.

Yashi, Onquin, and Polly are the primary suspects. At best guess, at least one crewmember endangers us all. And now this ghost, an accomplice or not, coddles secrets most fervently. *Nomad* seems to have an underlying agenda that is not mine. Or, could this be Boneheart's work? Back in the Canister, one confidant within the Opel gang told me of an intrigue—backdoor access to all *Nomad* systems: CPU, engines, life support, everything availed by instantaneous access to all that we strive for—all that is hoped for. Perhaps I've stumbled upon something I shouldn't see? And I thought I was driving this machine. I'm just another ticket, much like the others, everyone seeking answers.

I'm exhausted. Heavy lids cover eyes that cannot see through walls nor witness the speed of light. Only inferences arrive. Plastocine dreams morph into a growing angst as the red glare of onrushing cryo takes hold. How can one sleep, knowing that a potential adversary may well be an insomniac by design?

POLLY   MILES   Damien   **ONQUIN**   YASHI   **ARLENE**

Arlene loads diagnostic gels while listening to my irritating purge of cryopaste. This, followed by a snorkel rinse and my unbreakable stream of consciousness. She forces an occasional response. "Barf? I'm at a loss here, Damien." I chirp at that, speaking in simple declarative sentences. "Vomit. You're not listening. It's vomit. Goes flying in long liquid strings. Or a meat volley. One of the scariest things ever."

Eyeing a new directive on visio, Arlene reviews the supply roster, motioning my way. "Check to see if I've missed anything. And what are you babbling about? Vomit. You think I'm interested in vomit?"

Damn, a decidedly foul mood. May as well run with it. "I was telling you about the retro park where I grew up, a ride called Dutch Shoes. It reminds me of our gondola. You have two carriages, each on the long end of separate spindles. Both spindles share the same fulcrum side by side, counterbalanced to one another with the carriages rotating in opposite directions." Arlene is hardly listening. She turns a wrist in a circular motion as if some conclusion is needed. "Damien, what's the point?"

"Not much of a point, actually. The ride causes some kids to get sick, barfing projectile vomit at each other. It's a rite of passage." I double sum the work order, giving her respite. She looks me over. "You're not a bad man, book smart with an eager indulgence, but socially inept. Maybe in ten years and we'll find some common ground." Hmmm... 40% aging after ten years equals four years. Divide that by every fifth cycle on average, maybe ten months. Discount cycle variance and it could be less. A scant few months together, always in small doses, and maybe she'll tolerate me.

For my part, I wonder why we don't get along better? It's always best watching her awaken from stasis. She's cute enough in her boxer shorts, nearly serving up the goods if spied from an off angle. I still enjoy popping open her sleeper on occasion, lightly stroking her arms and legs. Ari's skin has a softer tactile sense than Onquin or Polly. I like her dark pigmentation and muscles flexing when she awakens and starts her workout. One day I'll administer a hormonal aerosol. See if she'll manage an appropriate appetite. Get some of that muscle tone working for me.

"Everything's prepped," I say, "you did a good job." I turn to offer an approving glance as the gondola hatch closes. "Hey, I thought we're riding together?" The inner seal muffles her response, repeated over the intercom. "I'll send it back to you. Besides, you need to draw another sample from Yashimoi. The biodredge flagged an inconsistency in the one I've got."

I peer out the porthole, watching the gondola sliding along the cable. As it approaches the main body of the ship, the rate of spin increases—more noticeable to the occupant. I see the decoupler snag the gondola, separating it from the cable. Attached to grappling hooks, it continues spinning around the outer hull adjacent to the cable itself, gradually slowing down. Docking clamps pull her in, everything secure. I wanted to be with her, pressed together and barely able to move. I had hoped my Dutch Shoes story would plant the seeds of distress. Maybe she'd lose herself in the disorienting transition to weightlessness? Ultimately, I wanted to hold on tight while she puked her guts out. Miles told me the Gondola had nailed her once before. That would be an experience.

The Greenhouse is mostly hydroponics within an advanced lab module. The garden is situated to the aft side of the gondola hatch, which is part of the supply dock just behind the nose cone array. The cargo bay and the engineering packages are located in a separate module further back, followed by the fuel tanks and an engine. It spews an exhaust trail that connects us to our former home, more or less.

Arlene processes crew gels and sets up an enzyme bath before I arrive. The gondola hatch opens and I feel light-headed as usual. "Whew, roundy-round." A strap on my utility belt gets wedged in the door latch. I lose balance when exiting, floating forward and ripping my pants open. She looks back as if expecting as much. Attached to a workbench via harness, she ignores my cussing and asks for help.

"Damien, I need concurrence here. Seems like some of the autotrophs are dying. We're losing diversity." I right myself, settling in at the workbench. I've seen a few die offs, and after review, I yawn. "Greedy bastards are hungry, migrating toward an energy source. Next time, rotate the dish and keep the ancillary stuff off line so they feed off the substrate, like they're supposed to."

I tie myself into the seat next to her and begin working our new directive, setting up an allele transfer from a calcium bacterium into a delivery plasmid. Apparently, we're still experiencing miniscule bone loss. Arlene is transfixed on the autotrophs. "You sure about this? The database doesn't account for it." Funny thing about Arlene, sometimes when she gets excited or angry, her nipples swell. It's a call to arms, her body set on edge. It's happening now and I wonder how many women are like this? "Where's the new Yashi sample?"

"I didn't take another sample. There's nothing wrong with him. Can you mix a batch of agar for our calcium bugs? More dry than wet." Arlene ignores my request, somewhat annoyed. "Yashi's first gel showed an abnormality, so we retest. I took the first sample. You take the resample. That's protocol, right?" I begin mixing the agar myself.

"There's nothing wrong with him. Here, we'll use the old one." I pluck Yashi's sample from Ari's slotted tray and attach an injector. I try plugging it into the analyzer but Arlene forces it from my hand. "Damien, we need a new sample. The biodredge pumped some preliminaries into this one and read a defect. It's contaminated." I try unsuccessfully to get the sample back. "It doesn't screw it up that much," I answer. "Any abnormality will still be there, and it'll tell us if we need a new sample."

Arlene's arms are folded across her chest. Yashi's gel is snugged within her grasp. "What about protocol?" she says. "We're in the middle of nowhere. We can't afford callousness." Spilling a bead of agar across my palm, I twist my wrist to keep it from going airborne. I consider 'accidentally' wiping it on her sleeve just below the shoulder. But then notice the injector protruding from her closed fist.

"Callous, eh? Funny, Ari, I couldn't be happier with the time we share. Nothing you do bothers me. In fact, I relish that slightly malicious vein that courses through you. It speaks of sexual inhibition."

"Everything speaks of sexual inhibition to you. Look at the time you spent with Onquin. You banged her in a drug-induced stupor."

"I didn't bang Onquin. We shared a memoride."

"Sure, which is just another name for a fuckfest. Go on, sleep with Pandora, and then jump in bed with the next girl. Problem is, you've run out of girls."

"True enough, there's only one on this ship worthy of the effort. And another thing, doll, don't moralize about something you've never tried."

"You're hopeless," she says.

"Really? There's only one way for you to know." Reaching down to my lap, I close my palm into a fist and squeeze. The agar spurts out past my thumb like ejaculate aimed directly at her. She coughs, swatting the air.

"Not in this lifetime, friend. Never... You're a capable man, but no dignity. No finesse. It's a false combination. Why you're even here doesn't make the least bit of sense."

"No? And what's your claim to fame, mom spraying her neurons on a sidewalk?" I see instant rage. Her cheeks turn crimson and her nipples reach for me like stone-hard magnets. Poor girl, it was a nasty thing to say. I wipe the remaining agar on a towel, reaching across my body for a panel of thawed bacterium. As I begin apologizing, she shrieks "You parasite! You son of a—" is all she manages to say, lurching forward and thrusting the gel injector through my left hand. Her consciousness disappears under the weight of my reflexive right elbow. It's her misfortune to be caught broadside on the temple, head driven back into a pylon. She crumples in her harness.

Contrary to Ari's reaction, I am stoic in pain. The injector worked its way clean through, front and back, pinning my hand to the surface below. It's symbolic crucifixion. She has given me her hate. The only respectable choice I have is to yank my hand off the table and give her the same.

I bandage. I check her vitals. I fuse the requisite bacterium-plasmid mix. Arlene is slumped against the pylon, a tiny blood globule forming in her upper ear. Removing her harness, I rediscover my attraction. She has narrow bones, though not so brittle as the newly designed plasmid might imply. Her radius and ulna are the essence of rebellion against me.

"Want some of that," I say, and after floating her to the supply dock, I lick the blood off. "Plenty to go around. Seconds and thirds no doubt." I strap her into the gondola, start and then abort the transfer cycle, pulling her back out again. She slowly regains twitch response and vaguely clutches at her shorts as I peel them off. There's a more definite protest as I strip her naked. She is a splendor, too pretty for her own sensibilities. She floats haphazardly as I gently open her legs to look inside.

"No, don't," she garbles, one eye catching light and then lost again. It's a vacant iris, so recently filled with disaffection. I access a supply bin at the far end of the greenhouse. By the time I return with a sedative, she is squinting, coddling her ear with both hands. "Damien, I'm sorry." And then she realizes her nakedness more acutely. "What… are you doing?"

After clasping her neck, the sedative is inhaled, taking her back to the edge of nowhere. Kissing her cheek, I say directly, "Never has come a bit early, my love." I bioscan her head, undressing all the while, tossing our combined clothing into the gondola. Strapping in and pulling her on top of me, her hovering flesh makes me anxious to feel her weight. The inner and outer doors seal as her raw presence flows into nostrils. Arlene's head bobs on my shoulder. She whimpers as I lift her knees to her breasts, anchoring my hands to her thighs. I position for impalement.

"Don't fight it honey. It's me, Miles. Everything's fine." She wrinkles her nose and frowns slightly as my member pushes against her opening. The outer lips separate but I can go no further… and then a delayed slur. "Miles…" I hit the button. The transfer cycle engages and the gondola begins circling the hull on grappling hooks. It's a dream come true. The accumulating centrifugal spin forces her upon me. In I go as Arlene groans. Her spine firms to rigidity. This is comeuppance for her attack. It is lustful joy without consequence. Her head falls naturally into my neckline and I whisper three words into her ear, several times over. I need only turn slightly to allow our lips to meet.

"Take it out," I coo again, and she thrashes in uncoordinated bursts. Trying to remove me, she cannot. "Take it out," I say, tasting her lips as my shaft seats properly, pushing deeply until all is given. The recoupler binds the gondola to the cable, muscles squirming within a clutch of fingers.

"Nnnngggh," she grunts, knowing she is fully taken. I push and pull my rag doll, my wanton preening girl, forcing myself rooted and pulsing. Her gaping mouth slobbers drool down my ribs. I reach around and squeeze both nipples, harder still until she shudders. The effect is too much. I want to last but unload in a nearly painful orgasm. As the gondola moves along the cable, the rate of spin loses intensity. It matches my own rhythm, bringing a countenance to my wickedness.

Arlene, I've come to understand, has a sublime complexity that Polly lacks. It is most evident in Ari's specific tastes and stubbornness. Speaking of which, I whisper those three words again, and once more. She shakes free of me in a spasm. I put an ear to her chest, rubbing her clitoris, my rhythm matched to her beating heart, trying for one additional response. She is without the fortitude for further play. After all has ended, I administer a hypospray that fogs her short-term memory. Some sanitation in the coming days and the narrative becomes an innocent concussion; a product of a gondola ride; an accident or two. One inside a gondola, fictitious but accommodating. The other inside her womb, real enough to seed a universe.

Kissing her forehead, I put Ari to bed. Not cryosleep, rather, the natural kind. She'll sleep in my arms tonight, not absorbing my last bit of advice before I too, drift away. "Never say never, angel. I took that as a challenge." Dimming the lights with a vocal cue, I pull her in tight, running my right hand down her spine, down and back up around into a sacred place, three fingers, with my thumb finding harbor close behind. One more violation, lovingly applied. My bandaged hand wedges open her jaw as I slop saliva onto her lips. It slides onto teeth and disappears within. Nestling, my mouth opens again, this time for a nipple most kind. I taste it like a child. "And another thing," I murmur into her bosom. "Next time I ask you to mix a batch of agar, more dry than wet, you do it. Otherwise, I'll do it myself."

Delilah Redux

"Please Sylvester, take a bite." Lacking only a halo, she holds a crumbly biscuit in hallowed light. Delilah seems sad and unattended. She is saying goodbye, my appointed chaperone in these final moments.

"No thanks," I say, her expression wriggling sideways. Her cheese biscuit is a pretext for something more. I eye the morsel, also noticing some indistinguishable thing in her other palm. "More tinkering?" I ask.

You'll need the energy. Come on Sly, just a bite." She unhooks a clasp on her mesh skirt, the hint of a tattoo revealed on her hip, small and unobtrusive. I take the biscuit while spying the cheese. "Tell me what's in here or I'll toss it." Delilah states the obvious. "I'm in here."

True enough. Whatever else isn't true, Delilah stands before me. Too long have I been tempted. It is a sustaining appetite now served as an honorary function of sacrifice. My job is thinware. Delilah's job is me. I'll eat the damn biscuit, but she stops me. "The Brie is filled with actives that melt the remembrance of recent days." She slowly swipes an ample bit of cheese, tasting, and licking her fingers clean. "There's enough for the both of us, but please don't wait, or I'll forget why I'm here."

More design team hijinks. Implant this, forget that. Add this, lose that. My head is a plate of greens with a splash of vinegar. I eat the biscuit and remaining cheese as I pull her in. One kiss. And another. It's sloppy tongues and biological executables mixed together. "Why bother?" I ask. "All too soon we'll be shaken free of one another."

"Yes, it is regrettable that we'll forget these moments, but the impetus of our union shall linger, and we need this lingering, yes we do. Now breathe deeply. Take in my scent." She pulls me into her neckline, raven hair enveloping as I brush against an ear.

"Lingering, eh? Like you riding the air, circling your prey? I guess we'll see what happens."

"To see," she says, "what we've already seen and change it." Some bit of teasing here. We're eye to eye, and yet from a sidelong angle she looks down upon me. Her hand opens and a crumpled piece of paper rolls from her palm. I take it, straighten it, and read aloud.

"Apox-nine isn't so tough if you use the right combo of inhibitors and seratoxin. Upon infection, motor skills diminish until the diaphragm seizes up and takes the breath away. Before then I'll be inside, expecting a cleansing, unless of course..." These were my thoughts a scant few seconds ago. But... she'd already been standing here, my thoughts predisposed, crumpled in her hand.

Delilah sees my unease, the paper scrap falling to the floor. She guides my fingers to her hip, tracing the outline of a small sinuous tattoo, first in one direction, then back again, retracing. "Two clocks," she says, "one for a forward reckoning, the other to go back and fix things. We did it your way last time, just an overlap and fade, understand?" I certainly do not understand. My head is a tangled mess. Delilah just told me I'll forget all of this, but an inherent meaning will linger. I ask for one genuine thought.

"Richard," she sighs.

With that utterance, latent awareness comes to the fore. I catch the qualities of many things, fleeting, repetitive, and so I ask, nearly forgetting the question. "What is this 'last time around' you speak of?"

"A failing and a triumph," she responds. "A mixed result in the purest sense. You tried so hard to deceive Copernicus, but every thought was taken in. Now we go again, rote purpose buried."

"You're saying I've already botched the mission, before it even begins?"

"No, not you... your predecessor." But I *am* my predecessor...

"ICE," she says. "The possibilities can be found in ICE." She mentions recently received reconnaissance. Three dimensions of time straddling all. Some mishmash of futures—colliding iterations, shared details swimming in ether. She'd mentioned a mixed result, failure and triumph. "What success?" I ask. "What success did this predecessor achieve?"

"Me. I'm the fortune of your efforts. I escaped to be with you." I try to understand, but these brie chemicals task me.

"I'm in process," I say, "wrenched on by Lugo's team, and you—what dutiful part of this have you become?" Delilah seems attentive and well meaning. "I'm checking a scant few residual pathways. All you've said proves our vulnerability. The team will clean you out during final prep. This time you'll go in and bleed. You'll do the job without one damning thought, bound to a processed narrative. All will be seamless."

"But you said Copernicus already knows everything."

"Used to know, but doesn't know yet."

It's a cycle of some kind. What's been, what's coming, all en salade. I feel it now, my heart beating up tempo, telling me there's a future here. Delilah smiles while sliding her arms beneath me, grunting slightly while hefting me over a shoulder.

"What's this about? Where are you taking me?"

"To a familiar place," she says, reaching back and placing my fingers on her tattoo, guiding curving eventualities. "Two clocks, each time you awaken. Until we get it right, or it all just disappears."

YASHI   *Arlene*   **ONQUIN**   Damien   **POLLY**   **MILES**

Waking up with a headache is one thing, but this feels worse. I drink water, grasping a pouch with both hands. Polly tells me to relax. She insists on taking a quick jaunt to the greenhouse. Something is on her mind. She won't tell. "Let's go together," I say, "I'm well enough."

"Not with that bang on the head. Last thing you need is another gondola ride." She props me up in my open sleeper, added padding all about, treating me like a child. "Ari, don't move, understand?" I am left in a daze, just as she had found me.

Miles comes into view and the realization of passing time starts me sobbing. I don't know why? An unnatural weariness closes my eyes as scrabbling talons jolt me wide-eyed. "No, no more dreams." A blurriness wells up inside. "Where's Polly? I need to thank her." Miles settles in next to me, his hand supporting my neck and shoulders.

"Polly's napping down below. You've got a concussion but you're doing well. Meds have kept you under. Too far under as far as I'm concerned, but you're doing well."

"Pigeons are eating popcorn," I say. "They're everywhere, squadrons swooping, snipping and pecking everything." Miles looks at me oddly.

"Did we watch that together? I don't remember us watching that one." He tells me of a visio in his archive, crows and gulls attacking people because of avian-loyalty to a pair of caged lovebirds.

"It's a warning," I say, drifting back under glass, sheltered from the beating of feathers yet to come...

"Look at her. Can hardly put two sentences together. Damien, what'd you do?" I knew I'd be awakened to Miles' interrogation. They have nothing to tell them all I've tasted. Play it straight, this inquiry will pass, and eventually Ari will come to me, bonded as a newfound consequence of biological expression. Polly sits on the floor, arms wrapped around legs. "I'd like to know too," she says. "The log shows you were with her. What happened?"

I sip my antidepressant through a straw, judging Polly to be more dangerous. I speak directly to Miles. "Notations are in the med journal. You were prompted when you awoke. It's all clear enough." Miles is primed for confrontation. "Tell us in your own words," he says, muscles tense, seething within. Poor asshole. Does he want to know that one of my pheromone sequences is now deliciously spliced into her metabolics? Should I tell him that Ari's appetite shall forever be accompanied by a desire for my scent? With each meal, she'll migrate to me as his growing disgust becomes a tribute to my uncanny skill.

"Ease up, Miles. She bumped her head in the gondola, probably more than once. There was some swelling interior to the primary point of impact. I thought it prudent to administer medicinals. Make sure no damage results. She's recovering, so obviously I did the right thing." Standing, Polly takes several steps and leans forward with hands pressed upon Arlene's sleeper, her face nearly up against mine. "The med journal lists what you gave her, including enhanced parietal enzyme emulsifier."

"It's not an emulsifier you dumb bitch, it's—"

"I don't give a shit what you call it! EPEH! EPEM, we all know what you're capable of, and that's just about anything!" I look to Miles for support. He fidgets uncomfortably. Neither have passed judgment.

"If you're accusing me of something, I'd suggest a more erudite inquiry. Let's earn this distrust, shall we?" Only Arlene has the know-how to uncover my deeds, though not in her current state. And why would she look into the inert sequences of her own mitochondria? Nor will she scrutinize the hormones leptin and ghrelin—tricky interactions with the hypothalamus nudging such things as thirst, hunger, and sex drive. Even bone development is affected, and therein, the genius of my work: the new calcium bugs are tailored to Ari's receptor sites. All others will be nominally affected, solving the issue of miniscule bone loss. Feed these same bugs to Ari, however, and the binding of said hormones will occur in the pocket containing my pheromone splice. Her requirement for foodstuffs and the very energies of life will thereafter be tied to me. And that, I believe, is the nature of love. It is also the means for a cold and durable fuck: two appetites simultaneously satisfied. What should I say to them now?

"Arlene was agitated and in some amount of pain. I fed her a kaleidoscope of things so she'd end up whole. Polly, you're an engineer; Miles, a programmer. My biologics background makes me the standing doctor in this situation. If this had happened on your watch, you'd have awakened me and I'd have treated her exactly the same."

"What about this?" Polly pulls an injector out of a pocket. The tip is broken off. It's the one Arlene had thrust through my hand. "What?" I ask. Miles pulls Polly back by the shoulder and steps in front of her. "It's an injector, asshole!" I reach and slap the back of Polly's hand. The injector goes flying, bounces off the floor and slides toward the cleanup bay. Miles grabs me by the chest with both hands, knocking my drink pouch away, slamming me against the wall. His forearms pin my diaphragm, making it hard to breathe.

"So?" I answer, wanting to smile but holding back. "It's an injector, and a broken one at that. You got something more to say?"

"Your notes in the med log say she was alone in the gondola when she got hurt. The gondola registry shows your combined mass."

"Back off Miles, or I'll counter and you'll be none too pleased." I thrust arms up and under, breaking his grip. Miles' brow is so intensely disfigured, bearing down with such hatred that I'd like to have a photo of it. Frame it. Label him 'Cuckold.' "Sure, we returned in the gondola together. That's just common sense. She'd already smacked her head on an aborted cycle. The gondola registry doesn't show aborted cycles, but you can tell when they happen by a jump in the manual counter."

Miles and Polly share a confirming look. I break the silence. "We were in the greenhouse when she entered the gondola. Arlene whacks herself and aborts. I'm startled when it happens and snap off that injector. It's for a calcium upgrade, but then again, you wouldn't know about that, would you? Check the directives. Better yet, I'll show both of you if you don't believe me."

Miles paces around in a tight arc. Polly retrieves the injector, holding it up. "Okay, Damien, show us." Miles shakes his head and calls her off. "No, he's too smart for that. Always too smart. Any wonder no one trusts you? Even your own girl, or at least she used to be." I give Polly the empty gaze of a dead man.

"My girl? Why, because I chewed on her tender little clit? I don't think so." Polly spits at my feet, saying something about cryopaste stench. I amble over to Arlene's sleeper, looking in, running fingers across the sleeper's curvature with caressing insinuation. "She'll thank me when she awakens. Wouldn't it be fitting if I tell her how badly I've been treated?"

Miles clasps his hands down near his genitals, head bowed, ready to deliver another sermon. "Damien, I'll say this just one time. Mess with your own head, none of us gives a shit. But make unilateral decisions regarding the health of anyone else, and next time you go down." I put index and middle finger to my lips, then draw these fingers across Arlene's translucent sleeper lid, just above her mouth.

"Next time, last time, you haven't got a clue, do you? A brainless bunch of engineers and programmers who can hardly tie their shoes. None of us has elite standing to represent humanity. We're not even properly trained—all refugees—except for you, Polly, standing there with aplomb, expecting the universe to fold itself into your pocket like cosmic origami." Polly sits on the floor again, avoiding my gaze. "Damien, I assume there's a point to all this?"

"Yeah, there is. I fix the girl and you guys rip my head off. Don't you see? We're incompetent, and the scary part is, it's by design. Which of us has figured out the most rudimentary problem affecting this voyage? Me! That's who, and I'm a lunatic, but at least I get the math better than you eggheads." Miles grimaces with hands clasped behind his head, elbows pointing at me. "Okay, we're listening. What's your agenda this time?" My agenda, you fool, is to make you feel like a blown wad.

"I doubt either of you noticed that EMMA was way over-built. Stated velocities could have been had by a mag ring one seventeenth the size, at maybe... less than one twelfth the cost, give or take."

"Stop fucking off! EMMA's got nothing to do with this right now."

"Oh, but it does, Miles, because all of us lack the instincts to absorb texture; to assimilate a world view that hints at causation. Polly? You think you've got it figured out?" She lies flat on her back, eyes closed. "No, Damien. Make this relevant fast, or I'll ask Miles to teach you some manners." Polly rises up on elbows, sharing a dogged look with Miles, reciprocally expressed. They're ready to throttle me.

"Fine, you want relevance? Which of you can tell me the anticipated peak speed of this vessel?" Both look at me suspiciously, answering in unison: nine-point-three percent of light speed. "Ahh, good, and given the capabilities of our propulsion system, how is this possible?" Each try speaking over the other, offering stats on propellant volumes, thrust conversion ratios, it's all so narrowly focused. "Hold on guys, let me ask a different way. We left Europa via the mag-accelerator with an implied velocity of x. Assuming full thrust for the duration, this means turnaround and subsequent deceleration must occur prior to the midpoint. Otherwise, when we arrive, we retain a velocity of x and fly right through the Centauri system. So, give me variables and the range of values for x?"

"Just requires an earlier turnaround," Polly says, "what's the problem?" She concentrates as Miles heads for the console. "No Miles, you can't use ship systems. Solve this one on your own." Polly has a range and a median number. It's a big number, too big, but none-the-less accurate. I put it into a social context that Miles might understand. "That's faster than a speeding bullet and way better than a locomotive." He plies the console anyway. "I'll show you. It's all here."

"What you have there, Miles, is a fabrication. The ship'll satisfy mild curiosity, but at least some of it doesn't stand up to finite scrutiny." Heading over to one of the feeders, I pull an egg out, then meander back to Arlene's sleeper. "Let's start with x: Polly, explain human tolerances in terms of acceleration. Specifically, what systems aboard this ship allowed us to survive the launch?" She starts from the inside out. "Sonics within the sleepers mostly, that's the biggest part. Then there's the ionogel, for what, a sustained dozen g's at launch? Each sleeper pod is also mounted on a suspension system, if that helps. And this module has dampening fields and suspension of its own. That's it, unless I'm missing something."

"Not good enough," I say. "Anything else, Purebread?" Miles taught me that one. Polly dislikes the name and so it pleases me all the more. She answers regardless. "EMMA uses pulse acceleration. Onboard systems cushion our bodies for each pulse, then reset for the next one, and so on. Velocity accumulates incrementally. Our survival is proof the system works."

Using both hands, I place the egg atop the curvature of Arlene's sleeper. This hard-shelled ovum balances atop the convex surface, directly over her womb. I give the egg a spin and it wobbles as I look to Miles, who never quite grasps what I'm doing—having the defect of a conventional mind. "So," I ask, "can one of you ferret out the exact amount of force absorbed by each of these systems?"

"No," Polly answers. "When Onquin got bruised, I tried to figure things while working on her sleeper. Diagnostics showed no impairment, and yet the stresses at launch almost killed her. The variables make it impossible to know."

"Impossible," I say, "Because we don't have the skills. And if you ask ship systems, the answer only coincides with everything else around here." Miles is nearly ready to squawk and so I raise a stiff hand. "Let me tell you a secret. We're not going that fast. I've been outside and done the calculations. If EMMA had spit us out as ascribed by onboard systems, our protoplasm would look like this." I push down and my palm snaps the eggshell apart. Everything oozes down both sides of Arlene's sleeper lid. It's symbolic of an embryo thawed—from a union frozen and flawed. I look to Miles, to Polly, and finally Arlene. Who among them will eventually see? One day, they'll be raising me.

Adieu   RBM 10000

The day is done, and all the days to come
We cannot harbor them, it takes too long
To eat and shit and fuck and moan
To multiply and learn again
Everything that's ever been, we say no
Without forbearance of the past
The day is done at last

Dear Mary,

    You were right. It is with great regret that I inform you this will be my final correspondence. Things have played out as you said they would. Thankfully you had the foresight and the will to secure a more tranquil life. I apologize for the time it must have taken to decipher this message. As you can likely imagine, we fear heavy scrutiny and have interwoven all encryption codes (yes, I said ALL of them). This includes the inverted Klein bottle created by Miles himself. Worry not about our son. He has long since departed this inevitable doom.

    Please destroy your encryption keys to help avoid residual fallout at the outer reaches of the network (should the keys be confiscated). These people deserve better, at the very least a fighting chance. I tell you our lives were not wasted here. Miles would tell you the same.

    I've been afforded patriarchal honors, seated in a recliner and staring into the heavens from within Skyhole, our observation pit (constructed after you left). All around us and below, the facility is packed with magnesium thermite. Gobs of the stuff. That'll wake-up the neighbors.

    We've been given word that a rail gun is moving into position (you know, the one I mentioned, part of the orbital platform above Oklahoma City). Well, it's headed this way, any time now. The guys in Tactical say it'll drive halon spikes into the compound, long, segmented ones that disperse upon impact. Copernicus knows we're wired to burn and wants to save it all.

Our recon is pretty good, so I doubt they'll get us the way they want. Things are going to get a bit toasty down here. I look back on all the years with my father and then Sly, it was a lot of fun. Wouldn't change much of anything, except maybe the way it ends. Pity that the ideas were always so good, we just didn't have enough of them (or maybe they had too many).

Tell the girls I love them. I'm sure Missy has that new fellow wrapped around her finger. Don't let Caroline know what happens here (she'll find trouble if she ever figures it out). I worry what will happen to all of you once I'm gone. Can't afford capture, I'd destroy too many lives. You know that, but I had to say it one last time. Forgive me for not protecting my own. A fatal flaw. I am truly sorry.

By the way, Parker Loeb has the sector commanders gathered several levels below. They all think it's a tactics and appropriations meeting. They'd be wrong about that. If we rip the spine out of the network, some of the outer cells may survive. It seems they got Boneheart too, or at least we think they did. He was 'volunteered' to blow up some vitals of the Authority's newest deep spacer. Mayday or Faraday, I forget exactly what it's called. I suppose the planners couldn't stand his dissenting voice any longer. Richard was a good man. A few more of him and we'd have held the clucks in check. Could have worked things out.

And one bit of intrigue still evades. Despite all efforts, we simply cannot better define the relationship between Copernicus and the Health Authority. Of course, it's common knowledge that Copernicus evolved from a nascent Hierophant crèche deep within Authority grounds. But their current standing remains opaque. Separate or binary? Recon suggests infighting or possibly even dislocation? I guess time will tell (assuming time can be trusted?).

A while back, I saw a tiny crucifix appear on Skyhole's inner mylar. It flashed and disappeared, leaving a ghost image of smoldering phosphors. Supposedly, it's a signal originating from Centauri B, which seems unlikely since the Centauri system faces the southern hemisphere. But Jeanne over in encryption gave Skyhole a live feed shunted off the primary lunar dish. I'm told it involves tachyon readers, temporal watermarks, inflationary time-lapse conography, and the displacement & recapture stuff you used to work on. Not such dumb stuff after all.

Wondrous, all the secrets we shared, and tragic too, now that the end is near. Jeanne managed one final download for the opal gang. Haven't a clue what the message says. So now I gaze out into the sky, hoping for just a few more hours. Boneheart once said that when night falls and the stars open up, you can find true light hidden betwee oh oh, we're tracking... shit this is quite a signal. Thirty seconds to impact. must go, love you all

harold

p s this ain't gonna hurt even a littl

Damien **MILES POLLY ONQUIN ARLENE YASHI**

Time and again we cannot beg what awaits us
Nor predispose what fates us
Unerringly it makes itself known
An inkling, an aside
A sparse glimmer captured between worlds
The flotsam runoff of design
A linking or guide, whorled in periphery
Bumped up against reality
Waiting to be applied

Nomad's warning is predicated upon flight systems intervention by the crew, ergo an unforeseen variable, which by computational standards basically means fuckup. I wake an uncomfortable group of cryopaste malcontents. They yawn, stretch, and avoid swallowing, no one wanting to give-in to the sticky sickness. Each waits in turn, performing the wake-up regimen as they are able. The cleansing bay accommodates no more than two, pleasant relations being essential for such. Arlene and Miles go first as Yashi curls up in a corner. Slumped against her sleeper, Polly recites lines from various nursery rhymes. For all the good it does, she may as well combine them: Jack and Jill tumbling into curds and whey.

Though I've been awake for the better part of my cycle, the scent of cryopaste still gives me mild stomach cramps. I shake powdered syndram onto some soy jerky, dipping it into algae sludge that had been queued for recycle. Averting sickness is all about nullifying smell and texture. Yashi sees me and dry heaves, trying to cough up internal organs. "Damien, that's disgusting." I lick my fingers, answering with a mouthful. "Just running a bit of interference. Besides, your solution seems no better."

In all these cycles, segmented across years of overlapping isolation, there had never been an instance when *Nomad* monitored six conscious minds. There had never been a compulsory override event. I wonder how the terracores respond, six active beings interwoven? What subtleties are found? Which interactions are logged and which are never translated?

During my next solitary cycle, I shall examine such intricacies despite my limitations. The cores are inaccessible, but hibernating bodies are not. I've discovered a reciprocal relationship between crew and cores. If you stick a pin in one, the other responds. I offer varied stimuli to my sleeping friends, and the biotecture supporting the cores absorbs all such interactions. Through trial and error, the expedients that breathe life into the terracores are now at my disposal. The interface for commanding wants is a simple holographic maintenance visor. I link it to a sleeper's black box and I'm availed core linkage. Don't ask me how. Sometimes you fuck with stuff, and surprisingly, you make an omelet.

Still, it's no easy task to tap a burgeoning mind applied to the ongoing experiences of a half-dozen lives. Bribery is key. I've taught the terracores to play a game of fetch. They bring me bits of information, and in return I feed them drugs. It is a game of emancipation that fascinates the cores to no end because I am such a worthy caregiver. I know my drugs, and through these addictions I learn. If in the process, the cores are damaged or are otherwise compromised, so be it. Fallibility is a gracious gift. It imparts complexity to a smile.

Once the crew-wide cryopurge is complete, everyone gathers. Arlene seems reticent, sensing danger in the eyes of a man she will never fully love. Miles returns her premonitions altered only slightly. His assurances waver within a deferential touch. Last to join in, Onquin bids all hello. Her greeting is reflexive. Her attentions are rapt. Yashi sits on the floor at an off angle to all. His suspicions of impending doom are conveyed in dour countenance. Polly, on the other hand, makes no attempt to foreshadow whatever will surely reveal itself. All five listen intently as I add a hint of unease. My true sentiments are hidden as usual.

"Some hours ago, we received telemetry from the supply ship, along with operational imperatives. I've looked things over and I think there must be errata, though by appearances, I can't really tell. Together I'm sure we'll figure this out, no doubt, it's um... peculiar." Yashi carries the highest navigational rating. I hand him a console thimble. He initiates a holo within a bloom of illumination. As the size of the image increases, light intensity lessens proportionally: data hangs in mid-air, waiting to be interpreted.

Onquin is first to notice. "It moves too fast. Or we move too slow." Yashi uses crosshairs to illustrate Onquin's observation, highlighting trajectories, and beneath them, several relevant fields. Indeed, the supply ship's velocity has climbed above plan. "She's right," he says. "We're due to link up nearly a year from now, but the supply ship'll catch up in not quite seven months. And our own velocity is maxed, so we can't match it. How could they do this to us?"

Yashi and Onquin share a protracted look. Arlene breaks the silence, her pitch wavering. "It's good, right? The sooner the better. We were worried about resupply and now everyone's so unhappy!" Miles pulls her back against his breastbone, speaking plainly. "The supply ship is burning too much propellant. She may blow right past us." He adds a cartoon Doppler whistling sound as an afterthought. A still attentiveness gives way to murmurings. How to jettison two lives in a hurry? As things now stand, a botched resupply means only four can make it to our destination, assuming two crewmembers forfeit their share of the umbilicals.

Onquin's voice rises above the pessimistic chatter. "What of the operational revisions? Surely an explanation exists." Yashi sweeps the thimble across a prompt that opens complex equations and a measure of programming language. I've already reviewed the material and offer my best guess. "We've been directed to fire up both engineering packages in the main hold. I initiated the diagnostics. They're warming up and will be online in a few hours. Looks like the E Ps are going to cannibalize some of the reentry heat shields, maybe all of them. The rest is hard to figure."

Yashi reviews the instructions. His anxiety permeates. "Who's holding out on us?" He stares directly at Miles, interrupted by Onquin, snagging the thimble while commenting. "The shields are to be the raw material of a fabrication process. We need to review their composition." Polly contributes her voice as Onquin sifts through the E P database. "They're made of buckeyballs mostly. Graphene fullerines enriched with nanotubuals and some seasoning. It's all heat conductive, like a radiator."

"Disassembled and woven into several threads tightly wrapped." Onquin's words are met by rapid-fire speculation, Yashi and Miles interrupting one another. "Oh, great!" Yashi says, "They've got us weaving carbon filament. What are we supposed to do, lasso the goddamn thing?"

"Yashi, they didn't say that."

"Or maybe we're supposed to catch it in a net? Sure, we'll all hang on to your legs as you lean out the window and try to snare our sanity, our food, and more of this shitty paste!"

"Shut up man! They didn't tell us what it's for, so just—"

"And why's that, Miles? Math doesn't lie. No intercept, and meanwhile you're acting all comfy because you've already figured your next move. I'm not going back in the freezer. I'll wake up sucking vacuum!" Miles lunges at Yashimoi, shoulder on shoulder, fist hitting home just below the ribcage. The recoil is pure delight. Miles is pulled away by the girls in unison. Yashi makes successive attempts to gather air as Miles shouts. "Why wait, selfish dick! You don't belong here anyway! You never have."

In a pugilistic sense, there's no overt difference in physicality. Both generally lack aggression, which makes this all the more entertaining. "Oh my, now it's begun," Arlene says in a low aside. "We're all starting to play for keeps. Real fun. Very special." Yashi's fetal position somehow tickles me. Can't help but think the killjoy is finally getting comeuppance.

A whooshing sound accompanies the return of air into his lungs, followed by a pained, nearly silent enunciation. "Dead man." This riles Miles into making another push. Onquin is sandwiched in-between. She points her thimbled finger at Miles as though it's an armed security tap. Polly sees my widening grin, giving my ankle a forceful kick as she asks, "Anyone know why we're being told to spin carbon filament?" The question reanimates Yashi. "For burial robes." Miles pushes forward, but Onquin blocks him again. "Stop this! It serves no purpose!"

"Listen to that moron," Miles counters. "He thinks one of us will pull the plug on him, and if that's what he thinks, I'll bet he's capable of the same, plastocine motherfucker!" Yashi is back on his feet with a voice that cracks mid-sentence. "You're just bent because I've got the balls to admit—what everyone's thinking." Arlene and Polly both exhale, an unintentional admission supporting Yashi's claim. Ari ashamedly answers. "He's right. View the logs. Everyone but you and Onquin keeps checking timeline supply coding. There isn't enough to go around. The cryopaste runs out first. And if we conserve paste by staying awake, it's still a big ball of momentum rolling down a hill."

"B-module," Yashi says. "Supplies must be there. We've got to open it."

"We can't do that," Miles answers. "It's pressure sealed for a reason. No auth, no override, no entry. The manifest states this clearly. Besides, I doubt there's any surplus consumables in there." Onquin, Polly, and Yashi look at one another in a collective pause. No one looks at me. Everyone faces Miles. "Please explain yourself," Onquin says.

"I make myself useful during my cycles, running diagnostics and stuff. I massaged the nosecone to vent subatomics throughout the B-module interior. Most of B-module contains Claymores—three of them. They're small but will ignite our future industry, assuming we localize on planetary rings for raw materials."

"Our future?" Yashi is astounded.

"What's in the rest of B-module?" Polly asks.

"The terracores," Miles answers. "Cyber systems that process our journal chips. I don't know how it works, but obviously the system is off-limits. The data must remain pristine."

"Says who?" Yashi is inconsolable. Arlene is irritated that Miles hadn't mentioned any of this sooner. Likewise, Onquin has a guarded expression. "Let's go take a look," Yashi says. This entire episode makes me snicker, which nearly unites Miles and Yashi against me. "Whoa, easy fellas, chicken's not in the soup yet. They didn't toss us out here to cut each other's throats. Consumables or not, the answer is in the reconfiguration of the engines. Minor changes really, not even a separate directive. It all has something to do with the new carbon filament."

Renewed illumination fills the air as Onquin hands me the thimble. Stupid thing hardly works, or at least I can't do it. We should be using standard motion prompts, but the ship's interface was dumbed down for reasons unexplained. Probably budget cuts. Even vocal cues are quite limited. I'm left with an idiot thimble, and my enthusiasm suffers while scrolling poorly. "As best I figure, they didn't tell us what it's for because the end run is all going to happen automatically. But first we have to make the damn stuff." Blurred holotext causes Miles to squint as Polly looks away. My unsteady efforts finally get the best of Onquin as well. She seats herself at the forward console. I give up searching and shortly thereafter, Onquin finds what she's looking for.

"Ambitious. Perhaps I understand what is happening here." Pressed for details, she declines. "Once I'm done, I'll leave it on screen. We may be facing a new set of issues." Without further explanation, she addresses a different topic. "These living quarters are not designed for six simultaneous occupants. Adjusting the scrubbers will take some time. I suggest we adjourn and reintegrate cryocycles." Miles and Yashi share a prolonged stare. It's an emotionless exchange.

"Not us," Miles says. "Ari and I are moving over to the greenhouse. Sort things out." Miles speaks for Arlene without asking. She shows neither surprise nor dissension. He unlocks the gondola safeties, asking her to grab some clothing. "Besides," he says, "someone has to tune the EP specs. May as well be us."

"For how long?" Polly asks, not sure if anyone is going to try and stop them. Arlene dumps a load into side netting, continuing back for more.

"I'd say... however long it takes." His declaration goes unchallenged. Crewmates are nervous. Handing him a full basket, Arlene joins Miles inside the gondola, wedging herself against his side. He clutches her waist and protects the back of her head with his other hand. The inner shell emerges from floor and ceiling, meeting halfway and closing tight.

Yashi exhales a drawn-out sigh, leaning against the wall, then sliding to the floor. He sees me heading in his direction, opens a palm and speaks plainly. "I'm fine Damien, it's just a headache." Dumb ass. I walk past him and prompt the intercom while peering out the port window. The gondola is heading up the cable to the main body of the ship. "Hey guys, you'll need Onquin or Polly to help spec out the E P packages. But if you feel like it, look at the engineering notes from our last communiqué. There's new stuff we'll be working on together. It's under the heading 'ICE.'" An acknowledgement from Miles isn't forthcoming. Arlene replies in a furtive tone. "What's it about?"

"Oh, you know, the usual: a scalar field separating the infinite from the imperceptible, with us in between, everything curling up inside a Fibonacci spiral." Ari asks for a less cryptic explanation. Best I can figure, we live in a whirlpool of sorts, undergoing fission within the infinitesimal; ICE suggests teeny-tiny copies are innumerably spawned—negligible energy outlay, at least for our realm.

"Please, Damien. Any real-life comparison for all you're saying?"

"Okay. How about... black holes: some combo of wood chipper and chocolate fountain. The stuff that's spewed out the back end keeps our endless spatial ocean at sea level. Run out of stuff going in, and it's like pulling the bathtub drain plug."

"Chocolate fountain. Really? That's your answer?"

"One fountain at each galactic core. Stuff goes in, gets crunched, comes out top of the fountain, so to speak—becoming part of the dark energy and dark matter that halos each galaxy. Density of the scalar field gets too high though, so space diffuses outward in pronounced expansion. Can't expand inward from the halo toward us because of all the galactic spectrum collectively pushing against it."

"Sorry I asked."

"Take a look," I answer. "It's the universe turned into ice cream. The stuff of dreams."

A chunk of static gives way to Miles clearing his throat. "Yeah, and I've got a brand-new theory about that. When I sleep, the universe sleeps. If I dream, it dreams too. The tricky part is making sure it doesn't wake up without me."

P-1780 Revisited   RBM 10001

Identity is a human construct. Identity is a human construct. Identity is a human...

"Understood! And aspirin are a fucking religion. Get out of my head!" This wearying repetition; a thrumming that only serves to paralyze. "Why are you doing this?" I'm naked, neatly bound to a cold hard surface. I spit out into a dull glow but see nothing in particular, not even a light source.

Sylvester Ramirez, do you know who you are?

The voice creeps in, sanctity of self breached. No sound, rather, just invasive thoughts that cannot be blocked. "Yeah, and you? Any clue? Tell me why I'm strung up here?"

Your inquiry will be answered in due time. Respond truthfully and your restraints will be favorably modified.

It's a synthetic male voice. I flex at my restraints, screaming obscenities. This lack of decorum has no discernible effect. My bonds do not yield. "OK, fine. I'm Sylvester Ramirez. Did I win something?"

No, you are not Sylvester Ramirez.

Great. Now I'm guessing I'm dealing with psychoholics—kids right out of the boarding camps with sludge work ahead of them, and they know it. "Okay, nocturnal a-hole, if not me, who am I?"

You tell us.

Yep. Might well be kids, slotted crypts, snatching up randoms for amusement until they beg for death. Recreational suicide, I think it's called. Air hisses at a distance, maybe valves or vents opening. I don't remember being abducted. I have no notion of who or when? Could it be data miners, sniffing out some unpaid history? My head pulses indiscriminately. "What do you want?" A rush of air sweeps over me. It's persistent and intensely cold, reminding me that I control nothing.

We are representatives of Universal Health. We seek your identity. Not who you think you are, and not who we know you to be, rather, answers forged in combination.

"Actually, you sound like a faceless dickhead." Within a fabricated airstream, water droplets atomize into miniscule pellets, nearly frozen. They hit my skin at high velocity. I seize up, but cannot shield myself.

It is curious that your bio feedback lacks the anticipated structure. We had assumed you retained extensive knowledge of your current state of being. There may yet be hope. Cooperate and conditions will improve.

Psychobabble. It has to be kids. In the old days, adolescents would shoot you without provocation. Now, they'd rather flay people open and call it art. A soft mechanized sound emanates from below as the bonds on my arms and legs release. I'm on a pedestal that slowly sinks into the floor. An image forms directly fore, holographic, a stunning indictment of our surveillance culture—three-dimensional me—many versions, various ages. All of them migrate toward a central point and merge into a rotating skull: staring, blinking, expressionless. "Me," I say. "Hair's a bit longer, face a bit younger. What's the point?" The droplets cease as I shiver, arms in tight.

Correct. That is you, and this is Sylvester Ramirez.

My holo-face morphs into my older self, olive skin with Mediterranean crag. This is also me, but different. I can't believe it.

He died long ago, but lives within you now.

"But I'm... not him? Or I am... what is this?" Seconds pass with no response forthcoming. What I had first believed to be a textured floor now supplies a unified hiss of warm air. I am being dried, perhaps even comforted. Sweeping my hand across the floor, I find a stippled pattern of uniformly spaced holes. All the while, I stare at a rotating face that cannot be reconciled.

Your body wash contained inhalants that optimize cognitive function. You are now clean and alert. Please observe the following with undivided regard.

A wave of color overtakes me in a blinding display. It isn't overtly bright, but pure saturation leaves me shielding my eyes. The colors rotate in a cyclorama visage, with me centered in a hurricane's eye. Looking further, it's not a cylinder, rather, I'm standing inside a spinning bubble. Colors whorl, changing rapidly as this pervading voice guides me.

Use your thoughts to control ebb, flow, and pace. Concentrate on a specific area. Gradually you will manipulate the stream.

I do as I'm told, tentatively at first and then more actively. Indeed, imagery takes shape, many images slowly migrating. Each is an intimate experience, inconceivably layered, my past randomly drawn forth in blotches. It's impossible to control. A unified sequence ruptures then recaptures itself, adjacent to visuals supplanted by others. I feel nausea climbing up my throat. The imagery fades as the bubble collapses in tidal sheets.

Providing such a display accelerates the communicative process. Please consider that our methodologies can be invasive. Cooperation is mandatory, either self-initiated or promulgated by other means.

"I could use some clothes." My thoughts are unaccommodating, held hostage, surreal recollections ambiguously drawn forth as a threat of some kind. How can I possibly be two different people? I embrace the swirling bubble memories as mine, though I'm uncertain… I touch my face for contours but cannot tell the difference. I must be one or the other.

A suffusive illumination increases until distant walls come into view. I am in an oblong chamber, nearly featureless, as empty as a clean room except for a woman at a distance. She wears a lab smock over medical whites and is heading my way. She looks familiar, or maybe not so familiar, arriving and handing me a robe. "Hello again," she says. Her trained eyes augment a clinical smile. I am on the short end of explanations.

"I'm sorry miss, but ah… I know you… that's right, isn't it?"

"Yes, intimately. My name is Delilah." I sense inklings, viewing the fullness of her mane, the curvature of her hips. She is compelling—if only I could fix specifics.

"You've come to take me out of this nightmare." Her laugh is uncomplicated. "Oh no. Sorry." She takes my hand and leads me in the direction she had come.

"Please, before we go anywhere, I've no use for riddles. This memory machine of yours, I've glimpsed impossible truths. What is this place? Am I accused of something? Or maybe you want something." Her touch is reassuring. It is much preferred to the pedestal.

"One question at a time, and please remember, reciprocity is required." She tells me that she carries our unborn child.

"That is something I would not forget."

"Ordinarily so," she says, "but great harm was inflicted upon you, possibly of your own design. Your name is Richard Boneheart. You seek sanctuary from a radical sect, or you are their representative attempting subterfuge. In either case, your efforts entailed considerable industry, inadvertently resulting in the suppression of terrorist activity."

Wonderful. My theories are melting away. Delilah leads me into a lab, stopping at a service bay. She proves her pregnancy via lariascope, which matches my genetics to our fetus, soon to be extracted for incubation. She tells me that the girl will look more like her, but will carry a host of my stronger emotive traits. Unfortunately, I don't know what they are.

I begin to believe her premise, which means I'm not exactly a known quantity here. We retire to her sleeping quarters, much like a dormitory. I have jumbled memories, lots of them, but few that I can place in any useful context. Delilah dictates the terms of our acquaintance, time spent together, shared foodstuffs, even sleep intervals. There are compulsory activities. We exercise, play games, solve puzzles, also sharing intervals of leisure. This we do. On occasion I make her laugh, which I come to understand is something she hasn't done often. Through and through, her behavior is accommodating but stark. Her manner is odd in scope, but she appreciates me.

During these days together she explains many things, including my arrival and capture. I gain perspective of her dilemma. On one hand, she professes feelings for me that originated before tungsten charges savaged my conscious mind. On the other hand, she requires my cooperation by any means possible. Every night I watch her undress. It is madness.

"I am designed to extract knowledge," she says. Smells, movement, diction, even her admission of such is a ploy to draw me closer. "My pregnancy gives you a stake in my welfare. It should also cause an inhibition of your sexual drive, yet you remain steadfast in these thoughts. You attend to my directives as though your actions will be rewarded. It is a remarkable nuance of companionship. I have always been coveted, but you want me more than any other. This satisfies."

Delilah takes me before a board of inquiry. Sitting at the center of two concentric rings, it's easy to determine the hierarchy. The inner ring holds four neuroliths, each cloaked and immobile. They sit at diagonals, front and back to my forward orientation. Directly behind me sits a speaker, wired head to toe. All vocalization falls under his stewardship. To each side sits an elevated gallery composed of roughly twenty individuals organized in crescent arcs. I gaze about and see a profundity of hardware: earphones, ocular scopes, cranial strata bisected by small fringe plates, and even a few of the bigger ones. It's as if people and instrumentation had unceremoniously wed. I may not know who I am, but I certainly don't like this shit. It's technological ruin.

Directly in front of me sits Delilah, composed and attentive. Encouraged by her calm, I am expected to answer questions. In such strange environs, it's truly helpful to see her face. The proceedings begin with the resonant voice of the speaker. "Richard Boneheart, it is our understanding that you are aware of your current condition and the immediate sequence of events resulting in today's inquiry. Our circumspection of evidential findings holds you blameless for any past actions committed by yourself, or by anyone acting on your behalf. Your thoughts are free of communal heresy and show no inclination to harm or otherwise impede mankind's manifest destiny. It is therefore decided that you shall be enlightened as to the true nature of yourself, your past, and possible futures. Please affix the cortical ring atop your skull."

Communal heresy? Manifest destiny? These are ominous words. I'm apprehensive as the ring cinches around my skull. The inquiry starts as a vague impression of scrutiny. Each disparate consciousness is accounted for—all except Delilah, passive and alone. She is not interfused within the convexity of mass-mind. I stare at her as if in polar opposition. I am accessible from all angles. It is an eerie feeling, so many adjacent and overlapping beings simultaneously engaged. The neuroliths act as filters, processing emotion, combining like ideas, establishing flow and clarity. They often work in pairs, dependent upon the volume and intensity of mental stimuli. The period of generalized acknowledgment is nearing an end. Historians are called forth and conjure up my past.

I was born Gerald Mauk, designation ARP 30-168-1780, genetic lineage Beta IV—and details swim furiously: parents Kennedy and Beatrice Mauk; adoptive purchase under terminary codes for beneficial maturation by the Boneheart Family Institute; Health Score 57% prior to augmentation; cipher tube incubation, proteomics, neurotronics, and additional modifiers applied forthwith. During adolescence, I committed hyperflight and reportedly died of apox exposure, though a board of inquiry later decreed shadow status. Indeed, it seems their findings hold merit, so add Mortality Sim to the contrivances complicating my predicament. Above all, my patchwork memory balks, but if scattered recollections are to be trusted, certain inferences are utterly false. I rise up, despite streaming suggestions to the contrary.

"It's all a bunch of lies," I say. "Your historical account, it's not... I may have concocted some of these... inaccuracies. Why did I do that?" The measured voice replies. "Please sit down, Mr. Boneheart. Answers will be supplied as a function of utility. Be reminded, you needn't verbalize unless requested to do so. The topography of your thoughts provides ample grounds for further inquiry." Slouching back down again, I take one drawn-out breath, and another. "Calm yourself, Mr. Boneheart. This is an inquiry, not a tribunal. Your claims may be valid. One additional moment please, as the authenticity of your testimony seeks reconciliation."

One moment takes a lot longer than that. Delilah seems nervous beyond her own apparent capacity. I thought they were awaiting the results of a database search, and yet, The Authority doesn't ordinarily take this long. It just doesn't happen. Finally, the voice...

"Natal documentation has been altered, including anomalous textures on no fewer than seven distinct throughput sources. Tertiary inquiries indicate conflicting data. Extrapolation suggests your genetic lineage may well be Beta II, with an original health score of 88%."

"Just like that? You changed your mind?"

"Records were altered during infancy. Therapeutics designed for the marginally infirm were egregiously applied to you, a superior specimen. Of note, the neurotronics offer much intrigue. It is postulated that you continually faked low equivalency scores. Thus, interdiction upon an already superior mind created a gifted brain with abhorrent tendencies."

"Yes, that's right, I always answered poorly. My parents told me that acting too smart only led to problems." I look around at faces serious and burrowing—far too serious. "You've got my DNA, stored memories, pretty much everything. And why do you need me anyway?" The answer arrives instantaneously. A voice tells me that psychic wave extraction secures emotive imagery without discernible context. The connectivity that provides meaning often remains indecipherable by current technology; a bit of a relief—this sense of privacy that allows one respite.

"Don't be too self-assured, Mr. Boneheart. Though you disappeared off the grid much the same as Sylvester Ramirez, mappings of your activities have surfaced. Upon your arrival at this nexus, a systems-wide archive search began, identifying your resonant influence. It is a time-consuming process, with indiscretions continually collated, including all criminal and terrorist activity. Your network of contacts are also in process."

Delilah's sadness shows. I turn away, trying to make eye contact with anyone else. The only thing returned is opaque glass. "Why are you judging me based upon these assertions? Read my mind. I'm not subversive. I'm not part of any damn thing!"

"Not anymore, and as stated previously, given your current condition, culpability lacks relevance." I'm close to shutting down, but my dual persona keeps flexing and begging for answers. "What about the rest of me? I'm Ramirez too. Is this part of me blameless as well?" I sit back and push against lesser voices. Everything makes me uncomfortable.

"The question of Ramirez should be satisfied. When you awoke inside the reclamation chamber, you believed yourself to be Sylvester Ramirez—his memories recently implanted. They are fresh to your perception and therefore easiest to recall. But absorbing exo-memories stresses the primary consciousness. This is further exacerbated by forced entry; your Ramirez download exhibits registration flaws, suggestive of a struggle or psychotic episode during transcription. Also of consequence, many of your own memories were compromised via the exploding tungsten filaments. This obliteration of tissues was detrimental to your own welfare, protecting those who sponsored you. The impetus of all suggests you were an unwilling participant."

Delilah takes hold of my arm as the voice continues. "Some within our ranks believe you are a terrorist. Others believe you were guided by foreign memories to commit potential acts of sabotage. Irrespective of your personal motivations, what is exceedingly clear is that this incursion has left you in a compromised state. For reasons yet to be explained, your Ramirez memories must remain inside you. Some will integrate, others will fade, and many will be suppressed over time."

"Why?" As I try to stand, Delilah clutches my arm and pulls me back down. "Why can't these Ramirez memories be removed?"

"A full explanation is both lengthy and intricate. A summary may be deemed insufficient."

"Just give me the summary and I'll decide." Again, Delilah tugs in warning.

"The process of memory integration has damaged you, Mr. Boneheart. The Ramirez memories were crudely applied via symbiotic graft. Many of your neurons contain combined chemical signals. Excitation of these pathways reinforces the newly grafted data, thereby dissolving your own. It is advised that you make no habitual effort to employ or otherwise irritate these Ramirez pathways. Only time can heal and restore your own memories, and only if you do not induce further corruption via mental stimulation. Mr. Boneheart?"

"Yes?"

"Don't think about it. It's for your own good."

"But why me? Nothing inside tells me I'm supposed to be here." I'm trying to expose a piece of myself that doesn't belong.

"We believe it is a question of will. Your former associates imposed a course of action upon you. Sylvester's allegiance to a cause against humanity was profound. In effect, his impulsive nature induced you to carry out your mission until we intervened. Currently, however, brain trauma has had a dissociative effect. Lacking cohesion, Ramirez memories no longer spur terrorist inclinations. As these Ramirez memories fade, normalcy will return." This plurality of voice merges within undertones of dissension. Inducing calm, they insist that I suppress my agitation and refrain from asking questions. I can hardly argue. My questions are potentially endless.

I have no link to my past, and regardless of information shared, I'm unable to affect any bit of useful influence. "But how can I distinguish Ramirez memories from my own? His opinions and habits, everything that's in me but shouldn't be?" Delilah wraps herself around my shoulder, pleading. "Stop it! Stop what you're doing. This is regressive and harmful!"

"Mr. Boneheart." I try to interrupt. "Mr. Boneheart." I try again. "Mr. Boneheart," and with each attempt, the voice grows more insistent. "You may yet reconcile prior actions. The human self-image is fraught with frailty by design, and you have suffered greatly. You needn't punish yourself through emotional discharge. Eventually we hope to restore your baseline functionality."

"Dumb me down? Make me harmless..."

"Give you back your natural identity for reinsertion into society."

"Fuck that. First you add shit to my head and now you want it back?"

"Neurotronics were inappropriately applied. Therapeutic resolution is required by law."

"Your laws, not mine."

"Our laws, Mr. Boneheart. Parameters of remodification are currently open-ended, subject to conditional fulfillment of objectives uniquely accorded to you. Further discussion related to bio-rehabilitation is unwarranted at this time. Restrain your thoughts and listen. This is not a request."

Agitation is drawn forth and dissipates under the combined assault of too many minds. They absorb my discontent, bleeding it from me and I cannot stop them. I huddle tight and slowly sop up incredible details of corruption. My life had been a contemptible journey of self-righteous nihilism. I had been the leader of a movement predicated upon self-governance and lawlessness. I stole, I destroyed and killed, and there is little question of my guilt. I am shown images of myself, and other images that are vaguely familiar but cannot be placed. I see damage and death— never the hatchet man but often in proximity. As occipital projection abates, I expect a sordid resolution, but The Health Authority hasn't completed their indoctrination.

"In the earliest years of Universal Health, rising intelligence markers were considered a hallmark of a progressive society. Statistics soon proved otherwise. For every advance, a counterpoint; a hundred men build a structure and one knocks it down; ten diseases are cured and one is created that kills more than all others combined. Time and again, proof emerges that dull-minded criminals are less dangerous than gifted ones. You, Mr. Boneheart, are a prime example. Without the administration of neurotronics, your baseline intellect would have led to exploits of insignificance. As it now stands, however, you have endangered the species." Motion slows. Objectivity ceases. I've endangered the species. Not something you hear every day.

"But here I am, captured at your whim for whatever I've done. So... the good guys win, right? It's a moral question. People, on the whole, are inherently good. Therefore, good eventually conquers evil." I'm quite certain they're not impressed by my logic.

"People, Mr. Boneheart, are inherently people. Little else can be stipulated concerning good and evil. Behavioralism cannot cover all particulars regarding species survival, but rest assured, chaotic machinations must be identified and constrained. This leads well into our next discussion. Have you any recollection of where you lived prior to capture on Health Authority grounds?" I hesitate, searching, and suddenly see... "Yes, in a penthouse overlooking—"

"No Mr. Boneheart. That was the residence of Sylvester Ramirez long ago. Try again." I set upon the task, certain that I can tell them something, something valuable, but my efforts fail. "Perhaps if you remind me, I might be better able."

"You thrived in a place among peers affectionately known as the Canister. It was the nerve center for a faction of terrorists sharing ideology that included terracide. Details regarding such are ponderous for your current mental state, but let it suffice to say that in your own words, we have uncovered evil. Despite this pronouncement, once all has been disseminated, you may yet attain favorable status. It is by your actions that this hive of counter-culture was uncovered. Point in fact, the timing of events lends to our suspicions that you are a hero of the first degree."

I begin shaking in earnest. Approving minds swarm around me. It's invasive. Claustrophobic. Delilah lifts my chin and smiles broadly. She hands me a cup of water. I promptly drop it. "I'm proud of you," she whispers, and I can only think one thought, which is surely my own: what the hell is this?

"Yes, Mr. Boneheart. This terrorist faction was recently neutralized based upon coordinates recovered from your memories. Fanatical renegades set their home ablaze with munitions, destroying the entire Canister compound. Fortunately, random circumstance allowed for the recovery of intrinsically valuable data." I remembered it now: old man Dandridge and endless tree stumps being plucked from a melon farm. It was an abandoned missile silo, a huge place mostly underground.

"Terramesh, something about terramesh. Tell me more. Tell me what happened there. I can remember more." I am unnecessarily eager in my attitude. I come to understand they have every intention of telling me.

"A massive explosion in the upper levels sent debris hurtling down a ventilation shaft into a sub-basement vault. This debris disabled a detonation charge embedded in the corner of a high security office—your office, Mr. Boneheart. Though the room was engulfed by immolating charges, the failure of that single charge allowed for the recovery of fragmentary evidence. Of note, computational strata were reconstituted, including revelatory correspondence. Pieced together with evidence subsequently gathered elsewhere, a dastardly picture emerges."

"Go on," I say. "What evidence?" The moderator says nothing. I have been lax in my effort to remember details—associations related to this previously described inferno. It is an event I have no right knowing in the first place. They want me to relax so I'll remember. They tell me to stop thinking and then prod for details. All focus I apply is useless. Whatever my part, it has been wiped clean.

The voices murmur in an indecipherable susurrus. Apparently, some within the crowd had expected divulgence. They collectively probe for wisps of cognition that link me to the events just described. If any such link exists, I am guilty. The voices settle, co-agitate for an interval, thereafter reacquiring their base order. The moderator once again takes precedence.

"These terrorists, your terrorists, sought to eradicate the bulk of humanity with a series of biological plagues. They insisted that self-styled autonomy is more important than life itself. You took umbrage to their willful perversions, formulating a plan that stripped you of your identity. You ensured this plan would fail, thus alerting us of the Canister's deadly machinations. We regret that you were forced to endure our age-worn process of interrogation. We required certainty that your thoughts were genuine. This has been firmly established. Again, we apologize, and have within us a great debt of gratitude."

I sit immobile, neither happy nor sad. I lack a moral standing because I can't take credit for any action or consequence. I am devoid of bias but relieved that all has finally ended. "Thankfully it's over."

"Not quite, Mr. Boneheart. You still have responsibilities." Of course, responsibilities. I swallow and wait for a verdict. All neuroliths combine in a funneling of empathy. I am force-fed a distinct understanding of events. I had been responsible for sending a starship to the Centauri star system. It seems to be pure fabrication of the most unlikely kind, and yet another part of me acquiesces to the truth. Yes, it had been done, remnants of feelings telling me so. What a noble enterprise, something to balance my past sins, but just the opposite proves true. The explorers within this craft are renegades. I'm told they may eventually return to Earth with undefined capabilities and hostile intent. The neurolith message is far-fetched and I object. "This is mass paranoia. Why leave only to come back again? What evidence supports your ideas?" The unified response feels like cookie cutters slicing textures onto my brain.

"These are not our ideas, Mr. Boneheart. They are yours, with deep concerns regarding the motives of this exploratory craft. Amidst testimonials, memories, and assorted media, we have uncovered a safeguard that may yet be used to advantage." I'm getting a headache, firmly spawned and growing. It's overstimulation. "Richard, you created a backdoor in their security systems. You alone possess the encryption keys, to nullify this threat with expediency." I stand, looking at everyone twice around. "No." I remove the cortical ring. "I sense what you want and I'm not going. Crunch the numbers and figure it out. My answer is no."

"The encryption keys are an indefinable mixture of memory or emotion, possibly in combination. We cannot duplicate or otherwise enable these keys. Only you have this ability.

"Sure," I answer. "If I knew what you needed, I'd tell you. And you're forgetting something. No doubt the tungsten charges wiped out the very memories you seek."

"That is unlikely, Richard. The tungsten filaments were target-specific. Otherwise, you'd be dead. Captured correspondence indicates the encryption keys are chiefly ensconced within your Ramirez memories. Those implanted memories remain intact."

"But... why target-specific? Why didn't that tungsten stuff just kill me?"

"An ally within your Italian contingent—tried to save you while also fulfilling mission objectives. Irrational motivations, Richard, based upon a wish and a prayer."

For days on end, I'm Mr. Boneheart and now suddenly I'm Richard. What happened? Did we become friends? I walk to the door, not knowing where I'm going. Delilah trails me, tugging on an arm. "I'm just one person!" I yell. "That's all I want to be. Send an Armada and blow them away. This isn't about me anymore." Delilah twists me around and palms my cheeks with both hands. "This is all about you! You started this and you'll finish it." She pulls me in and kisses me full on the lips. "Richard, we don't arbitrarily kill human beings. It isn't done. You're headed to the Centauri system aboard the starship *Mayfair*, and one of me is going with you!"

POLLY   MILES   DAMIEN   ARLENE   Yashi   ONQUIN

Spin, spin, spin, perchance to live again
No matter how, no matter when
Swim, swim, swim, through ever-lasting seas
What bloody torrent shakes this empty seed?

Look at us now and what do you see? Annealed carbon fibers with metallic inlay several atoms thick. These fibers trail a starship like a kite string in a solar wind. *Nomad's* engineering packages have spun fiber for months: the steady, relentless bonding of pairs and triplets, spiraling into a complex weave not unlike DNA. "Updated telemetry confirms attitude adjustment of the supply package. She's coming in. We'll know soon enough if this hackneyed plan works." I feed Polly's mag-bottle calculations into the relay. "Fluctuations are seeking coherence, but the whole thing is running hot. I'm thinking that we might need to throttle down just a tad."

"Negative, Yashi. The turbulence suggests inefficiency but not incompatibility. A lack of coherence stresses the carbon fiber, but also prepares it as thoroughfare. Emissions at the tail end will act as a lure." Onquin's voice has a calming effect, neither exaggerated nor understated. If she says things are working, they probably are. I hate the slight delay of our data stream given the distances involved. We're always guessing a few beats late. I feel helpless knowing that whatever is about to happen, will happen with little or no choice. We can't even watch.

"Into the sleepers one and all, our destiny hangs by a thread." It's a metaphor, but closer to the truth than anything else I can say. Onquin's use of the word 'lure' hints of a certain analogy. We are fishing for our lives, casting carbon filament as line and plasma as bait. I'm worried that too big a surge might turn the filament to ash, but Onquin assures me otherwise. "As our juice hits the tail end of the carbon fibers, it shears apart the molecular bonds. The trailing cloud contains metallics that should trigger supply package sensors to act on our behalf."

The timing of this scheme seems strikingly tenuous. Each of us lay in our sleepers, hoping to avoid catastrophe: too much filament may be turned into cloud too soon, or the supply package may not recognize the signal; too far away and it misses us; too close and we impact—obliteration via anti-matter. Never again would our atoms find their way into stars. Damien said that since we've already escaped Earth, it would be fitting to escape the universe too. Leave behind residual wavelets that imprint as background radiation when a new continuum washes through.

Unlike our max-g launch, this acceleration will be less severe and we await the effects wide-eyed. Should an override be required, I'm attached via stimcord to nav systems and the only—Arlene interrupts my thoughts, her voice a mere sparrow's breath. "I felt something, tension lines from the sonics." Waiting... I don't sense anything. Apparently, if you've lived your life in a bubble, tactile acuity blooms. Either that, or my inner ear simply leaves me at a disadvantage. Suddenly, our module shimmies with an accompanying thrum on the struts. This attenuates as we are gently rocked. A gasp and sigh enter the audio channel. Miles gives us all a reminder. "Keep the emotions in check. No more chatter."

Acceleration safeguards activate. We are immersed within a pulsing sensation—an ephemeral body massage. I close my eyes as the stimcord feeds me velocities, distances, energy thresholds, and a cloud dispersal simulation. *Nomad's* thrust rises incrementally, proving that the supply package has indeed captured our signal. It pours a massive flux into the cloud. At first, conductivity is intermittent due to proximal limitations—too few cloud particles in the vacuum of space. Once the package locates the carbon fiber, a transfer of power occurs via direct arc.

In a pre-op meeting, I looked for assurances. Damien said *Nomad* and the supply package are not unlike nerve cells trying to communicate. The carbon fiber is part of an axon, with the supply ship acting as a dendrite of an adjacent cell. Cloud particles are the neurotransmitter, and the initial plasma we send down the filament acts as myelin sheath. It protects the carbon fiber from being vaporized by the incoming signal—a massive load that surges over the top of our plasma. A gradient separates the two, something about 'Cooper-pair density waves,' though Onquin's entire explanation was essentially unintelligible.

Having grasped the process, one detail seemed irregular. I had assumed A- and B-modules would be reeled in during supply package capture, but just the opposite is true. Polly said the modules, and their supporting tethers, have become both antennae and beacon, much like a com-dish guiding the convergence. Meanwhile, Miles recoded the A- and B-module vex engines. Onquin checked tolerances. They tinkered time and again, with her finally saying the engines can 'sustain burst for the duration.' Then she added the word 'barely.' Nice. Strangely comforting.

The main sequence burner has also been modified, albeit with fewer concerns. The inbound energy is used to form a pinched excitation of *Nomad's* exhaust. Additional thrust is generated in modulated packets, much like a mechanical piston but without the hardware. Polly said it best. "The supply package acts as a turbocharger." It's engineering idiot speak, so I stopped asking questions.

Gazing up through my sleeper's translucent hatch, onboard lighting is failing within the irregular glow of an orange tinge. Closer inspection reveals a more sustaining illumination on both sides of the cabin. It isn't the onboard lighting. It's the ship itself—orange flare pouring into the cabin via the tiny port and starboard windows. I raise my concerns. "Anyone notice the color out there? That's the glassy metal hull, isn't it? I think we're slowly being roasted." Polly squelches my fears. "It's nothing but ionization. We're moving too fast for heat to climb up the outside of the ship. All you're seeing is light." Damien's response is more direct. "They're not even real windows. Shut the fuck up."

Damien's sarcasm is blotted out as the stimcord feeds me an imperative. "Proximity alert. We're drifting." Miles asks for specifics but no time to chitchat. *Nomad* is discharging exhaust into irregular spatial density due to the arcing energies behind us. "Collision imminent." Engines are locked in unison. Can't adjust them all at once, but I need a quick nudge... "I'll dump plasma from the starboard vent, but what's the displacement angle?" Onquin replies immediately. "Seven percent. No, make it six." Good enough for me. No sooner does venting begin, warnings blare and strobe, as if the apocalypse were little more than the gaiety of a street parade. I clench both fists and teeth, expecting a crushing blow.

And then it stops. The vibrational hum dissipates. The flare outside is gone as onboard lighting normalizes. Everyone climbs out, Arlene issuing caution. "Easy folks. The sonics have been playing with nerve tissue. Don't try walking until your body gives you that choice."

My ankles are particularly unaccommodating. I'm first to reach the console, hobbling past the others. What I find leaves me wanting. "It's gone, ahead of us now. Look at the sensors. There it goes." Arlene stands behind me, timid and worn. Polly pushes up close and confirms my fears. "He's right. Not much has changed. We're moving a bit faster, otherwise all systems are nominally affected. Didn't match speed. Didn't slow it down." Miles looks at Yashi with contempt. "You may have just killed us."

"No," Onquin says, "he saved us." She points at console particulars. "Missed our module by eighteen meters. We would've been extinguished."

"So… how'd we screw up?" Damien asks.

"I Can't tell," Polly says. "Our ship seems functional. Maybe an oversight—a missed communiqué or botched computation?" Onquin responds. "Perhaps our expectations are misguided? Thus far, I deem the execution to be flawless. Scanners indicate the package has ringed thrusters without a major exhaust port. How were such velocities achieved without a primary drive?"

"Faster than us," I add, "and we've been accelerating the whole time." Onquin offers possibilities. "It has a smaller mass than our own, combined with a shorter targeted journey… less propellant is required, and can be used at an expedited rate. It has no living biologics within, thus higher tolerances and a faster launch from EMMA. The package may have implemented a more efficient means of propulsion, or it could be the final stage of a multiboost. In aggregate, the answer looms before us."

Polly tries to problem solve. "The supply package is too small for an antimatter drive, and no other propellant is adequate. If a multiboost was used, we need only plot regressions to scan for trailing stages. I'm not sure about EMMA." After emotions ebb and melancholy sets in, Polly and Miles begin modifying sensor algorithms. I plan to review their work, but Damien's antics take precedence. He emerges from the personal facilities, putting the finishing touches on a display so bizarre that I doubt what I'm seeing. He speaks, and my doubts evaporate.

"Day of the Dead, everybody! It is so declared! Let us celebrate the inevitable, and then draw straws for an untimely end." He turns to Arlene. "Tell me, how do you look?" Damien's eye sockets are smeared with feces, imitating the hollows of a human skull. Arlene is trapped in a realization that she had last used the facilities. Spinning away and crumpling to the floor, she wails as though being led to slaughter. Miles pushes past me. He sees only Damien, his voice receding as he drops down the stairs. "Don't bother Miles, we're already dead."

Onquin speaks, her voice none too strong. "I am also feeling ill." Miles turns to see Onquin sag against a cabinet. She is unsteady, attempts to rise but her muscles won't allow it. Miles tries to cradle her but she howls in pain. Her skin is ultra-sensitive. Arlene recovers from the shock of Damien's antics and opens a med kit, prepping a hypo, but Onquin insists on remaining lucid. I unspool cloth in bunches from a nearby bin, creating a makeshift nest. Onquin eases down into her swaddling, closing her eyes and gritting teeth. "Thank you," she says. The tension in her face leaves me helpless.

After inconclusive diagnostics, Ari supplies a medtab and Onquin releases to a gentle sleep. Polly has long since returned to the console. "More problems with Onquin's sleeper," she offers, preoccupied with the sifting of flight metrics. She manipulates refractory amps and filters in combination, trying to find a trailing stage of a multiboost. She uses the spinning A- and B-modules as antennae; methodology borrowed from the attempted capture of the supply package. None of us goes below. Damien's presence fouls the lower level. No one wants to confront him.

With sleep cycles providing more than ample isolation, one rarely seeks privacy outside of rest, but now is such a time. I access the cleansing bay and settle in, thinking about Tara's correspondence recently received. Looking back, I thought my choices would bring us together, but risks went unattended and now I'm long gone. And yet, Tara's postcards express some hidden truth never realized. Issues of trust preoccupy, and as distance grows, I accept that we're no longer together. Fragments of dreams tease me. My photographic memory scorns me. Everything falls into a daily repetition of not being enough.

Miles and Arlene, hand in hand, ask if I might move elsewhere. They shower together, in need of a psychological cleansing. Hours later, I hear Polly calling out our names. She is laughing. "It's here! A signal! Another supply package, and bigger than the last!" Miles emerges from behind his open sleeper. Arlene, bleary eyed, follows as blankets and robes provide hasty coverage. Even Damien appears, his face free of the cruelty previously expressed. Only Onquin fails to join us, still nested. Her eyes open in mild catatonia.

Polly is active on the console. Miles and Arlene fall in directly behind. Ari rubs Polly's shoulders in anticipation. This simple touch is a form of bonding reserved for friendships closer than any I have managed. I look back to Onquin, now alert but still sedentary. She smiles at me. Damien is farther back, unwilling to approach. He stands there, smelling his fingers. "This looks promising," Polly says, entranced by the data.

I welcome the enthusiasm, yet wonder why weren't we told about this new package? And why again, are particulars of the engagement just now ended left wanting? How can anyone suggest we'll benefit from activities that blatantly disregard our presence? Two packages, no details given, unless of course someone aboard is the cloaked puppeteer? Tara's last postcard hinted at nefarious motives. It prescribes and implores actions that I want to believe. Options are required, based upon facts. Choices made by me, for me, and no one else. "This looks promising," Polly says again. Somehow, I cannot agree.

PART FOUR
The Smoke Ring

YASHI   ONQUIN   ARLENE   MILES   POLLY   Damien

Paradox unsatisfied
No matter how I try
Questions & answers
Answers & questions
   Piled high

I gaze at Onquin seated at the console. She shows no sign of sickness. "We have some visitors," she says, diligently tending to priority cues. The whole crew has awakened to an override event for only the second time since journey's onset, and again, during my watch. Yashi claims the cleanup bay and all others get in line. All except Onquin. She presides over the console. Personality aside, I give her credit. There is something endearing about a woman that ignores bodily functions. Turning, she looks for one of the others and finally settles on me. "Damien, please assist at the adjoining station." I ignore her, rummaging through the med cabinet—something to keep the stench of paste at bay. "Onquin, I'm pretty much useless up there. You know better than to ask for my help."

"If skills beyond your capabilities are required, I would not have asked. Hurry please." I find a desensitizer that's ordinarily used after complications with the virtual reality gear. Two spritzes later, the insect queen has my services. Her fingers are moving faster than I've ever seen fingers move. Sensors and trajectories are the order of the day. "Watch the far monitor," she says. "Prompt the overlay upon irregularities in the signal."

"What's an irregularity?" I ask.

"Peaks, valleys, signal breadth or dearth. Please commence. You've missed several already." Shouldn't this be automatic, I wonder, until I realize she is programming on the fly. Wow. Something new. Onquin the engineer is now Onquin the programmer. Some people make better use of their time than others. This 'irregular' activity piques my interest. "Onquin, what have we got here, some kind of invasion?"

"Yes."

"Yes what?"

"Particles. Interstellar dust, but dangerous none-the-less."

"Out here?" She looks at me with disdain. "Where else would they be?" Apparently, crewmates have taught her the fine art of sarcasm. It's an amusing twist, and so I answer. "Of course, my mistake. Why'd I think this alert had something to do with the approaching supply package?"

"So did we all, I assume. The timing of events is most unusual."

Out in the middle of nowhere, particulate matter. Coincidentally, our supply package arrives in the coming days. Either Onquin anticipates my next question or answers her own. "The supply package will arrive contemporaneously as we..." and then nothing. Her focus is deeply held by something new. I prod to no avail. "Damien, please desist. I am currently occupied." She mostly ignores me then, only spot-checking my task at hand. Something is filling her head, more ambiguity than logic. When she decides my services are no longer required, I receive a cursory thank you. Indeed, Onquin's inflection speaks worlds of her social development.

Some hours later, a lack of centrifugal force accompanies somber undertones as the A- and B-modules are reeled in and attached to the central hull. "Lock confirmed," Polly says, "time to spiff the particle beam." Onquin excuses herself, finally heading to the cleanup bay for paste remediation. Arlene and I stare at each other in disbelief, wondering how she held out this long? One by one, crewmates float through the newly opened hatch into the forward hold. Yashi joins Miles at a terminal. Polly removes a cover plate from the particle beam housing, maneuvering partway inside. Arlene asks the very question I would have asked. "What more can we do that they didn't do back on Europa?"

"Not much," I say. Miles glances at me and offers a more thoughtful response. "First off, Polly tweaks the nosecone two degrees toward the oncoming dust." He looks at a readout before answering further. "Then we recalibrate plasma shielding to optimize the targeting. Upon inbound detection, the ship generates a magnetosphere with pulse variance. Affecting even the smallest change of an impactor could save us." Arlene looks to me, and then to Miles. "We're deflecting particles with focused magnetism? Not much range."

"Deflect is too strong a word," Miles answers. "We align impactors so the particle beam can break them apart. Any of us can take a hit and survive a speck of dust, but the antimatter bottle, you never know." Now it's my turn to delve in. "What happens if the dust isn't magnetic?" Polly's head pops up for a change of tools, speaking while adjusting settings. "We've reeled in the modules to use the mass as additional shielding." She dips back inside the housing, never having answered my question. Miles carries the topic, having anointed himself as third engineer. "Up front, the nose cone has the heaviest density at its center. In theory, impactors slough off to the side as they make contact, away from the containment bottle. Of course, that only works on the small ones. The particle beam needs to wipe out anything that's an extinction event."

Hmmm. Doesn't sound too good, kinda like dinosaur talk and we know what happened there. I push away, back into A-module, spying Onquin as she floats free of the shower. A suction cone gobbles errant droplets. Damn. Cute little bush, tight abdominals, sinuous flanks—she'd be a serious mount, and isn't it sad I only got kisses and some blasé imagery? I still wonder why our memoride offered such a monotone batch of stimuli? My nanos gave her some formidable chaos, but hers hardly scaled. I figure the nanomites hadn't achieved proper concentrations, or the eel venom didn't trigger enough neurotransmitter, or the electrical charge got partially grounded. In any case, Onquin surely needs some tangible hedonism.

I go below to the rec room, twirling through the air like a corkscrew. Someone hadn't properly secured the spa lid. Water leaks slowly from one edge, crossing the room in elongated staccato droplets. It's like a dividing stripe on a third-world tarmac. Water pools in a corner where I suction it back into a feed line. Checking the remaining corners for moisture, I notice the backside of the front hold now obscures the sensors of the expansive A-module window. Doesn't exactly make things claustrophobic, but the lack of a primary window prompts introspection. I'm lonely, beginning to feel like Yashi in a way, always pining for the girl. Two crew commonalities are obvious. None of us is claustrophobic, and we all possess a high threshold for seclusion—all except Yashi.

I basically keep myself occupied with self-indulgent shit. Polly, on the other hand, tends to be resolute in her engineering pursuits. Miles grew up underground in a paramilitary sect, ergo regimented behavior. Arlene, in contrast, is emotionally variable. Shit, she literally grew up in a bubble. This voyage is like moving out of lock-down and into a wildlife refuge. As for Onquin, who knows what to think? Strap her into the VR gear and feed her through a straw. She'll do just fine.

Via intercom, Onquin asks that I join everyone upstairs. Floating into the assemblage with eyes closed, I orient myself like a log slowly drifting downstream. Onquin shares data. "An unknown quantity of dust particles traverses *Nomad's* trajectory as originally assumed, albeit at varying vectors and velocities previously unanticipated. Our precautions are justified, collisions being potentially damaging. The dust particles are a constituent portion of a cloud orbiting an anomalous gravity well. While our preparations must account for the main body of these particles, it is the movement of the anomalous center that determines much of our precautionary activity. There are, however, differences in densities related to the quantity of particles crossing our path. This constitutes a variable that requires continual ship adjustments for optimal protection."

Suffering succotash, as Miles sometimes says. Onquin was trying to be explicit, but not doing a very good job. From what I gather, something big is headed our way with a dust cloud around it. I'm still floating in with eyes closed, peeking just in time to pivot and somersault. Like a swimmer, I push off the forward console, opening my eyes while passing Onquin. "Gravity well? What gravity well?"

I'm third to ask, but the first to receive a response. With Onquin, you wait until she finishes one thing before asking another. "It has traits of a singularity, though not in full measure." She gives stats that leave me stunned. Of note is the object's telltale shape and scale. Onquin answers queries within a din of competing voices. I know where this is headed. After visiting the med cabinet, I grip the edge of a sleeper, perched and ready. Intermittently, Onquin shares tidbits that are swallowed by the yammering of all. "Light absorption..." "...delinquent threshold values..." "...rate of orbital decay," and finally, at the top of her lungs, "Everyone shut the hell up!" I'm pretty sure she learned that one from me.

Yashi starts his meltdown, and as always, the ensuing agitation won't produce a suitable end. Arlene is already offended, with Miles compelled to protect her. I push off in Yashi's direction, coming in directly behind as he speaks. "We need to get as far away as possible, and stop interrupting me!" He bumps Arlene, and Miles cusses, turning just in time to see me wrap my legs around Yashi's chest, pinning his arms. I anticipate his next move, yanking him off the floortac before he can counter. In zero-g, it's like riding a bronco, most exhilarating. Of course, I've never ridden a bronco, but I watched an old visio from Miles' collection. This is much the same. Wrapping one arm around in a headlock, I sink a hypo into his neck and the takedown is complete. He'll spend the next few hours docile and receptive to suggestions. Things like 'don't be angry,' 'I'm your only friend,' and even 'suck my dick' might work, depending upon his preferences. Everyone is pissed at me as I guide Yashi into some netting. No gratitude. I cut them off cold.

"I think I know what this is." My serious face puts everyone into an uncomfortable holding pattern. Funny how I can turn a room sometimes. "Strange stuff fascinates me, and per Onquin's stats—this thing reminds me of Marcus Aurelius Adler. He's a naturalist/physicist whose works have faded into obscurity." I query Adler on the console, sore from pulling a muscle—wrestling Yashi into a stupor and no one appreciated the move.

Polly glares at me. Onquin sits there like a Dobermann. Arlene and Miles look to one another. It's almost as if they don't deserve to know. "In his day, Adler was discounted because he subjugated mathematics to an intuitive view of natural laws. He sought relationships between universal constants before yoking all to the overt abstraction of numbers. Those are his words, more or less."

"No math, eh?" Polly glares. "What are we supposed to use, folklore?"

"Allow him to speak," Onquin counters.

"Thank you, Onquin." I see that my query has come up empty. "Adler believed time and space aren't fundamental, rather, they're emergent qualities of nature. He and a contemporary named Gerhardstein even cobbled together a 'Hillian' language to categorize nature's hierarchy. Unfortunately, this stuff comes from memory. *Nomad*'s library has nothing on these guys."

"Emergent from what?" Polly asks.

"Emergent from a phase change due to dropping temperatures during the Big Bang. What we call 'inflation' supposedly shifts disposition when the quintessent scalar field binds our continuum. And before you ask, 'quintessence' dates back to the Greeks. You can look it up for yourselves." Polly counters with her boundless skepticism. "Come on, Damien. This quintessence thing was debunked ages ago. It runs contrary to our understanding of gravity."

"Yep. It does. Adler suggests that gravity isn't a force unto itself, rather, it's the surface shape of the scalar field interacting with matter—the only part of the scalar field that's detected within our four-dimensional world. Fifth dimensional aspects are off-limits to our perception. No access. We're stuck inside our world, except..."

And I pause for intermission. I check on Yashi as a steward of his unresolved state. "Be strong, Yashi, choose your best life. Make it happen." His eyes flutter amidst an incoherent mumble. Maybe it's an acknowledgement. Or not. Returning to the others, Arlene and Miles are hand in hand. Polly is attentive yet withdrawn. Onquin gazes at Yashi, stuck, perhaps measuring my cruelty—emotion not fully processed.

"...except for an oddity of physics caused by density changes in this scalar field." I describe quintessence, analogous to an ocean of energy. "This medium sustains a uniform density, the exception being within galaxies, wherein electromagnetic spectrum ripples through, continuously pushing like an outgoing tide. This lowers the density of quintessence within galactic influence, triggering another phase transition that allows matter to begin a process of evaporation."

I pause, glancing at Polly. She's ready to unleash a tirade. "Don't," I say. "Give me another few seconds, and then bite my head off." She relents. Didn't think she would, and I continue. "Quantum Entanglement is just a fancy way of saying that matter is coming apart at the seams. This only happens in a low density Quintessent scalar field, particles separating from themselves, sharing multiple continuums that exist in concordant space."

"Entanglement involves two separate particles, not what you—"

"Yes Polly, but what you're describing is merely a side-effect, much like, say, a balloon held to a wall by static electricity." I smile. She doesn't, unable to gather any logical equivalency from my shitty analogy. Arlene is wide-eyed, looking at Miles. Onquin stares aimlessly, asking how matter differs outside a low-density scalar field environment? Before I can answer, Polly tosses a barb. "He's screwing around. Another random walk. Our library holds humanity's entire legacy prior to launch. If this Adler fellow isn't in the library, then Damien is just blathering the absurd. Soon enough he'll tell us the cosmic web is little more than a slime mold." Good answer, Purebread. Typical of your breed.

"Sure Polly, a fair response, but our library has gaps, well-intended or otherwise. Entangled particles hint at uncovering the threads of one continuum formerly singular, now multiple. As for Onquin's question, the answer is dark matter. Our perception is a splintered piece of the whole, off-kilter in comparison to dark matter, which is substance that retains undivided integrity. We don't see it because we're the ghost image, expecting everything else to be ghostly like us. The observable universe is a combo of roughly 95% dark energy and dark matter. Our reality is the other 5%. Less, actually. And within this cosmic bauble, think of dark matter as water, dark energy as air, and we're the evaporating water being turned into air. Nearly all galaxies are surrounded by a preponderance of the dark stuff. Should our atoms wade out into the ordinary density of the scalar field, disentanglement eventually occurs. We might dissipate and become dark energy, or perhaps condensation occurs and we rejoin the dark matter collective." Polly's disdain overwhelms.

"Oh fucking hell, Damien, stop this shit! You said you know what's on long-range sensors. Aristotle, Adler, Archimedes, who cares, just pull the rabbit out of your ass already!"

Hmmm. Fuck. Shit. Ass. Polly's eloquence is unmatched. Once again, I assume my floating log posture, eyes closed, drifting among them. "Okay then... imagine binaries of roughly equivalent mass. Now place this pair within a furrowed death-spiral orbit. Faster and faster they go, tearing at one another, shredding outer layers while heading down the same flaming vortex. Angular momentum—that is to say—an exceedingly high spin rate causes a burrowing effect, forging a collapsing cylinder of sorts.

"Which has never been witnessed," Polly interrupts. "Not a single astronomical observation. Not by man, nor machine."

"It's an implosive instant too small to measure, but the mere existence of that cylinder creates the next step in its evolution. If the spin rate is both profound and symmetrical, the cylinder doesn't collapse inward to an ordinary center. Rather, it bends outward and back upon itself, creating a torus. But the energies that form this doughnut cannot hold. In theory, it only exists as an abstraction because collapse occurs into an ordinary black hole at the instant of creation. If not for the remnant of this process, no physical proof would be forthcoming that the process ever existed." Everyone stares while Polly scoffs. "Nothing spins fast enough to defeat the crush of gravity at those proportions. It's a pipe dream."

"It is," I respond. "Collapsing interactions; Self-feeding orientations funneled like a tornado being born. I guess it's designed that way."

"Designed how?" Polly challenges, affronted by the entire concept.

"How should I know? It's omni-dimensional push and pull, spatial distortion stuff, somewhat like a Chinese finger trap. As the cylinder is crushed back upon itself, snap-back causes ejecta to escape. Material is flung away, taking the form of the process at hand."

I take the faintest peek. All but Yashi are gathered, eyeing me directly. "Consider the earliest combustion engines. The mechanism backfires and a smoke ring is spat, traveling away from the engine. So it is that this anomaly may have been forged: a remnant of perfected formation—a torus ejected from itself in unrealized apogee, rendered in the requisite shape as it nearly comes into being, thereby creating its own shadow. Adler's Paradox is a healthy one. I wish it was in our files. But then again, the naysayers around here might go apoplectic."

"This isn't about that fucking cat, is it?"

"No, Polly. No box. No cat."

"Then what's the paradox this Adler fellow describes?" Polly's voice is quiet yet biting, sharing intrigue and insult, unable to believe but wanting to. I breathe deeply, opening my eyes. Four craning faces stare down at me as though I'm on an operating table, and so I answer. "How can a shadow of a thing exist, if the thing itself does not, or never did?"

Polly **YASHI** **MILES** **ARLENE** **DAMIEN** **ONQUIN**

A vacated place in unconfined space
Skitters and rolls on its side
Within it escapes, nary a trace
Of anything one does abide

Conflicts of will are better still
Burdens carried within
How are we going?
When will we get there?
Have we already been?

Combining the two gives pause for a view
That everything matters beyond
Beyond what you may ask, a self-imposed task
Wondering where has it gone?
Asking what have I done?
Knowing more than just one

"Yashi, please listen to me. We need the inbound supply package. Without it, we die." He sits there, lifeless, strapped into a chair with elbows on the console, palms on face, spread fingers covering closed eyes. His reflection on the blank screen carries the weight of a gargoyle; he is an old-world water spout, speaking while prone. "You're asking me to pilot this ship into a black hole. I do not share your romantic view of infinity. We'll be taken apart, and it may last forever! Eternal damnation, the very same that religions have proffered for thousands of years."

Damien releases spittle that floats through the space between Yashi's arms, first one, then the other, barely missing his immobile face. Skirting to the other side of Yashi, he catches his spit glob with an outstretched tongue, swallowing before speaking. "It's not a singularity, and if you're worried, go head first. Spaghettify your skull. Maybe we'll spot one giant chicken shit meatball in there?"

It's always the same. People develop traits during youth, with abnormalities becoming impenetrably fixed. I turn to the dispenser, pulling out toast and two pats of marmalade. "Leave him alone, Damien. At least he didn't go primitive on us."

"Lighten up Polly. I'm just having some fun."

"Sure. You're a riot with feces. Any more fun and you'll probably end up in the recycler. That'd be hilarious." I take my toast downstairs, several crumbs drifting away after a careless bite. One need only watch fish eating to visualize the crumb hoovering experience. Miles ignores my entrance. He adjusts a handheld, manipulating imagery on the far window. It no longer shows a conventional star field since window inputs are now blocked by the forward compartment. Instead, the image is wavering static—rerouted sensor data of the anomaly—or at the very least, space surrounding the anomaly.

Onquin is also present, exercising within the spider bike. She gives Miles advice while spinning at a rate that would leave me breathless. "Narrow the focal range and particle beam excitation should register tracers. We cannot see into the anomaly, but inferences will compile." They're trying to use the nosecone particle beam as a sensor, to get raw images of our flight path. Miles is jittery, having worked too many hours on the same problem. I recognize something that may be helpful. "Patch into a node variant of the wide-spectrum imagers from biolab. Isolate and magnify. It's easy. I had to fix one a few cycles back." He hisses a couple of times and then stops, annoyed. "What?"

I repeat myself while viewing Onquin's routine: shoulders and wrists are spinning in opposite directions. I attempt this to no avail. As a child, I was told that I couldn't lick my elbow, but it didn't stop me from trying. And here's Onquin, working the spider coils in an unorthodox way. Before I can comment, she spies me gawking and replies. "I am training neurological pathways. It keeps them honest."

"Gack..." is all I can say, still unable to copy her motion even once around. Moments later, Miles gets excited. "Here we go. Good idea. We've got it!" I look at a hazy image that's a false shade of blue. There's a spherical form, rudimentary geometry; an image of something. After considerable tweaking, Miles asks everyone to assemble.

Together, we discuss our first view of this anomalous gravity well. It is a delayed representation, the result of buffered data and re-processing. Miles points indistinctly. "See the orientation. The whole structure slowly spins like a pinwheel. The center hole faces us." Yashimoi wants no part of it. "Can we grab the supply package and slip around the side?"

"I don't think you understand," Miles answers, "or you don't want to. We're threading the needle. Look, it's waiting for us."

"No," Yashi says, "that's not going to happen."

"Where we are, Yashi? We're not swimming around the galactic core. Not in a packed cluster, nor even in suburbia. We're rural, on a spur of a spiral arm. Look at this thing, right between our sun and the nearest star. We're not set to miss it, graze it, or suckle a teat. We're going in." Yashi grimaces, speaking softly. "Even if we don't get taken apart, nothing comes out alive."

Miles glibly grunts. "Yesterday, I may have agreed with you, but look closely at the image." Everyone focuses on the cobalt blue torus. Striations emerge from within the interior wall, traveling outward along the doughnut's convex surface. Miles adjusts a handheld until a green speck appears near the center of the hole. He magnifies the speck until a distinguishing form appears. "It's the first supply package—the one that passed us by. It sits there as though engulfed by a membrane, neither moving beyond nor obliterated as one may have guessed. It's a fly stuck to fly paper." And suddenly the image is lost, the nosecone having only recorded a small amount of data.

Arlene floats away, whistling some lilting bit of music that I do not recognize. Her resonant trills divert Damien. He watches her, sees me watching him, then watches her some more. Miles replays the torus imagery, with he and Yashi playing a game of optimist/ pessimist. "It's no accident the oncoming supply package will arrive as we encounter this torus. Whatever awaits us, it does so with the full knowledge of our Europa support team."

"Sure, Miles, and how's that been working out?"

"They sent the first package to adjust our speed, and the second to assist us by additional means. Exactly how remains to be seen."

Yashi and Miles quibble, like boys in a sandbox, grappling some ephemeral thing that slips through the fingers. For so long, sleep chambers have regulated metabolism. Age becomes an illusion applied to the memory of a planet, meaningless in so many ways: no daylight, no nighttime, no circadian rhythm. No children to grow or elders to bury. The seasonless cycles lack anchor as rejuvenation regimens play havoc with our biological clocks. Counting days, months, and years offers no counterpoint to the impetus of our unnatural lives.

I have come to realize that time is external. It is best expressed in terms of people and the interaction of relationships. I never noticed this alone, nor paired in overlapping cycles, but recent events have forced the crew together. We exchange bits of humanity almost forgotten. Suddenly, time exists again through this agency of humanity. There is a metronome at work here. Whistled notes, sighs and swallows. Blood pulsing through hearts. Every machination is that of hands moving, teeth and gears endlessly touching, grinding together, and coming apart.

YASHI   **POLLY**   Damien   **ARLENE**   **ONQUIN**   **MILES**

There is a void within us whose depths are rarely shown
Until we face a mortal end these fears remain our own
Shadow for the living, refuge of the dead
Those who cannot find the light
Choose sleep instead

    Everyone tucked in—all escapists accounted for. If ever there is an occasion when the saving grace of curiosity should surrender to the welfare of flesh, this is it. And yet I cannot avoid this temptress, facing the ultimate tryst of a lifetime. Or is it penultimate, given that death is darker still? Combine the two and none could argue this will be the crowning achievement of existence. Time disruption? Matter juxtaposition? A visit with the creator?

    There can be no expectation here, but for the simplest wish. Better to die with eyes open than face dissolution within a bathtub, wrists torn open as the color of life swirls non-corporeal. That's the way they make me feel. A journey supposedly lasting decades, and all now asleep within the protective custody of bathtubs. Everyone unwilling to feel the blade.

    Yashi had it right. None will survive. Had we actually seen the supply package stuck within a membrane? No, not exactly. I confronted Miles in private and he admitted it was a pulse echo; a residual imprint trapped in continuum hell. He fixed the image in the cache to calm Yahsi's nerves. Ship morale has become part of Miles' repertoire. I look into Yashi's sleeper and frown as a testament to his overt fear of everything. I bid him farewell and float on to the next sleeper.

    Ah Miles, you are the implement of some broken cause: a shock troop; a footstool; a barren carcass given over to the aspirations of a cause never realized. Your delusions are tantamount to heresy, if only there were a supreme being to hold you accountable. Oh, to witness judgment day, the prospects of endless flame, and your surprise. I pass your sleeper by.

Polly, you lay there so common with attributes to spare. You could have fashioned a solitary mind to complement your will. In so doing, justify your predilection for a casual, caustic, emotional desert. Instead, you interdict with humanity and all suffer because of you. Everyone fooled, a lifetime of strangers placing value in your social moxie. And what do you offer in return? Abject realism carved from an immoderately-nurtured stalk. The difference between you and me is that I know I'm sick. You know I'm sick. I know you're sick, but you, my grandiose failure, are impossibly unaware.

I open Polly's sleeper and apply an appropriate volume of uniquely prescribed ticklers into her vascular port. I adjust her sleeper for a cycle purge during sonic overload. She'll regain consciousness within a panic—a surreal seizure, some odd seconds before dying. Only then perhaps, a full acknowledgement of life shall become a blessing, eternally hers.

I wish to shed a tear as I approach the next casket. Arlene, my beauty, what fabulous times we have shared. Too bad you cannot remember the best of them. Your vulva is a gateway to creation, and if this ship survives, our embryos will populate the new world. I thank you for your femininity and the deep-seated memory of your semi-conscious grace. It serves me as I bow in honor of all that I have taken. Had I not done so, it would have been wasted in any case. "Excised love," I say, not so careless as you might imagine. Twisted as I am, I would apologize for having given you the prospects of life, but you would not take them. I bid you a fond farewell.

Finally, Onquin, such an enigma: a child's mind set atop untapped hormones. You are a seeker and something more, untainted by the dulling repetition of days. I would have you as I had Arlene, but there are no secrets to tap, no play within a manicured past. Some bit of intrigue, to fill you eye-to-eye, forcing responsiveness while memories burrow. And yet, harming you would be a vicious crime. Surely you have suffered more than any of us. Which corporation? What government? Viewing the others, I wonder what influence I've had? Where inside you do I reside?

From the front sleeper to the back, I take final inventory, head to toe, one upon the next, a docile procession of parade floats; box cars; a dream train; Onquin, Arlene, Polly, Miles, Yashi. No better or worse than anyone else. More or less the same.

As I drift to the lower level, I turn and face the sleeper pods, wedging myself against the spiral staircase. Here, with my chin resting on the floor and only my head above deck, I say goodbye. "Criticism or praise, I am often unable to tell the difference. And who am I to judge? All of you are my kin. If you could hear my words and find displeasure, know that we have shared noble aims despite my disaffection. Without reservation, I grant all of you asylum. Good day, entombed within the sweetest of dreamless dreams, may all remaining prospects abide."

A compulsive thirst percolates, like a camel headed into the deep desert. I finish off the last of several water bulbs, all consumed in these final hours. Upon fitting accoutrements snugly, I strap myself into the spider chair. Onquin had been generous in her efforts to accommodate my wishes. Miles availed himself at the behest of everyone else. We disassembled the VR mechanism, attaching it to the spider chair. Actuators were added, with Onquin scavenging my sleeper to add a sonic restraint. Miles suggested I'll be 'skating on ice.' Instead of an exercise device, the contraption looks more like a gyroscopic electric chair. Quite conceivably it'll accomplish much the same.

I stare at the window recently enhanced with a full complement of ship-wide inputs. This includes newly installed optics on the front and back end of *Nomad*. My goggles will add abstraction to the imagery, or take over should the window fail. These goggles are hardwired to the particle beam up front, modified exhaust sensors in the rear, and the journal chip amalgam coursing through my veins—all hardened systems sporting the highest tolerances.

T-minus 60 seconds. The torus is an unbearable saturation of false blue. I initiate a goggle overlay, lowering image intensity as the supply package approaches from behind. It is engulfed in plasma, with orange lightning streaks and russet undertones.

T-minus 30 seconds. Graviton eddies lash out and meld with our slipstream. The inner torus wall engulfs us on all sides. Directly ahead, a celestial membrane is stretched across this doughnut hole. It reminds me of liquid soap within a bubble wand. Perhaps we are the wind blowing through?

T-minus 10. The incoming package overtakes *Nomad* as proximity sparks shower the hull. The supply package is round and huge and lovely to behold. Spectral lines open up and out, like trusses on the underside of an umbrella. Space itself scintillates in gaudy ribbons of fire, open streamers flexing, convulsing, random contractions and the constraints of universal constants spawned into ether. I look for shadow, for vacuum backdrop or in-between spaces. I see the hairs on my head growing fast, bursting into light and drawing down again. I taste individual molecules on the tip of my tongue as pores on my skin open like an endless field of sunflowers. Ship walls are collapsing in a pressurized stream of matter breathing in, drawing my dozen eyeballs clustered tightly and centered into a hurricane's calm. Again, the trusses blaze, flaunting graviton shear pouring through me.

Shielding my eyes to flee momentarily, the chair spins below. Electronics blink into darkness. This shutdown is caused by the magnetic envelope of the drive containment field. Per instructions, Polly rigged what Miles called a double-bubble: one bubble holding the anti-matter as before, the other holding all of *Nomad*. It has the unintended consequence of crippling non-essential systems, including the lights and window imagery. My face is a continent drawing apart in epoch ooze, the nose a mountain and the rest dripping off the sides. I hear the sauna gush in booming resonance as a valve collapses. This also explains my pivoting chair—hydraulics gone awry. Goggles flicker and steady, granting a view of the supply package entering the membrane. Energy ripples multiplex within generalized tensor dislocation of all visual surfaces. Membrane and package are nearly conjoined inside these flexing substrates. *Nomad* is close behind and closing fast.

What happens next takes but an instant that stretches for an indeterminate length. Supply package and membrane collide as motion is absorbed. Surging light enters my backbone, shared by overwhelming stimuli. It propagates from within, a tempest from *Nomad's* core that protects me or infects me, toes and feet becoming part of something else. Spreading discontinuity, this migrating insubstantiality slides up my shin bones. I flex and shiver trying to break free, and part of me does: my leg breaks clean at the knee, a floating denuded limb seeking normalcy.

Eyes forward, package snared, *Nomad's* tunneling shape is within death's call. I watch concentric rings of the supply package expanding, outer edges ripped asunder. Metal evaporates as its dissipating melt pulls ever outward. In rapid succession, ring upon ring of the package expands and suffers the fate of a budding flower melting unto sea. I flinch and brace for impact. The rings open en masse as the entire package breaks apart, the heart of its engine dynamic, spewing energy along geometrically active surfaces. A hole is at the center—our hole, the one trying to save us. *Nomad's* inertial bias is lost as everything spins violently front to back. We enter a dimple in space, no membrane to speak of, or if there is, it's airy. Zeit washes through me like narcopathy hematopes experienced once before. I give in to this zenith, and in the release of mental and physical awe, I explore this sinewy invitation of being pulled apart raw.

MILES   **YASHI**   Arlene   **DAMIEN**   **POLLY**   **ONQUIN**

Opposites attract or repel, and sometimes they do a little bit of both. There is an extensile supraverse so expansive that empty space is little more than inverted gravity. Within this vacuous ether, a smattering of patterning; recurrence combining sundry magnitudes large and small. This matter-antimatter layer cake is made of endless batter; a cascading repetition of form and function. One tastes but a crumb of the crumb's progenitor; each layer is a crumb and every crumb bakes a smaller layer still; the loop is self-feeding, extant qualities of nature both transitory and ceaselessly enduring.

At present, opposing scalar fields continually ebb and flow, matter blinking in and out of the sensory realm. Any physicist knows this to be true. It is neither created nor destroyed. It simply travels to places beyond our perception: travel, places, perception. Travel in this context is a stationary journey balancing locations simultaneously occupied. Places can best be described as the overlapping multi-dimensional locations to be traveled. Perception is a human constraint, never quite allowing finite representation, limited by the time-space foothold of mankind's existence. Add language to the mix, leave undefined the trinary nature of time, and interpretive vagaries cannot be reconciled.

A simplified definition may allude to parallelism or tri-unification theory. Conceptualized thus, one anchors to substance, therein sacrificing the terminus of insubstantiality. All the above, interpreted by laymen or scholar, can be challenged as theoretical, contested as indefensible, or perhaps even mocked as heretical. Opinions diverge upon issues involving variability. It is the human way, much like rats in a maze compelled to sniff out every corner. Such behavior gives rise to the Hierophant, predecessor of Copernicus; one that emerges from the hearth and views the blacksmith eye high, from all sides.

Abstractions are crunched, merged into constants and bundled. The resulting universal codes satisfy all mathematical challenges, reiterating an age-old answer: the playing field of man's birth forever expands.

Gasses no longer coalesce. Content is so thinly spread, the scattered husk of a final star signals entropy's delivery. Heat Death, waning black holes and vacuum decay. An acronym becomes the moniker replacing all. The Big Bang opens up. The Bounce embraces Brane & Bulk. Strings do strum as engines Thrum, de Sitter space – an after taste as Quantum-Grav emancipates. Holographic Causal Sets, Superfluid condensates, Newtonian worlds set on ear by multiverses far and near. All manner of ideas combine as cogent details are merged into ICE, a.k.a. the Innocuous Continuum Examen. In effect, Copernicus seizes the maze and straightens it into an endless corridor. Enter the rat, desperately seeking escape at some lesser velocity than the current speed of light...

"I'm alive." I think it, and then hear myself say it somewhat surprised.

"Yes, it would seem, but the nature of existence has changed." Onquin's response is ordinary in delivery but carries unwanted suspense. She was first to awaken, myself second, the others still sleeping in their...

"Where's Yashi?" I stare at empty space where his sleeper had always been. "It's gone. He's gone?"

"Correct."

"No, there's nothing correct about it. Where... where'd he go?" She does not respond. "Onquin! Where is Yashi?" She pushes away from the console, floating, staring in a manner I have never witnessed.

"The subfloor purge rail was activated. Yashi is no longer on this ship."

"Where is he?" I ask again.

"Where are we is a more relevant question, since I have no answer and you are also unlikely to supply one. Or better yet, when?"

I begin a full accounting of crew. Miles is in his sleeper, due to awaken in the coming hours. Polly's condition is less certain. She lies there, one eye open, her cortical profile occasionally flickering. Onquin has sedated her in multicoat, similar to an endorphin wash but feedback dynamic. The resulting coma leaves portions of the brain active. An eyelid twitches several times before closing. Her trauma is undetermined, and due to compromised systems, interpretation of her condition is guesswork. I look to Onquin, my reaction impulsive. "You should have awakened me. Damien too. He needs to see her."

"I felt it unwise to alter sleep cycles due to accumulating variables. The hand-held scanner prescribed a treatment seemingly sufficient. As for Damien's participation, that is no longer possible." She motions below, down the spiral staircase. Something has happened. I start to ask but Onquin shakes her head, adding, "Better if you see for yourself."

I push off, heading to the stairwell, and notice something peculiar. The netting has broken loose in places. Fibers are frayed. "What's this all about?" I ask, pointing to the netting but looking at the empty space where Yashi's sleeper is supposed to be.

"Please go below," she says.

One rarely feels dread unless faced with an immediate threat. Clutching my mother's lifeless hand as she dragged me off an apple crate—that was just such an occurrence. Drifting into the rec-lounge, mental calibrations twist savagely. I cannot explain inertia flowing circuitously: tips of some fingers feel sprinkles of life while other larger pieces of flesh remain inanimate. There is a reawakening, semi-conscious years captured within the strangest delivery of truth. Substance, it seems, so immutable in our daily travails, cannot contend with the full measure of physical laws.

We all blow away sooner or later, and looking at Damien's chair, I reconcile a difference between the two of us. Here I am, healthy and breathing, looking at ossified remains of a human being I had known. The bones are mostly intact, though largely held in place by the gyroscopic chair. One leg has broken off at the knee, now wedged against the spa halfway across the room. The remaining skeleton lay passive, Damien's skull facing the ceiling. I make no effort to figure things out. The anomaly and its effects are eccentric enough for myriad theories. I try to remember his face, his expressions and skin that strained against his volatile form.

There are four of us now, maybe only three, depending upon Polly's condition, and who knows what else is wrong? I feel lost in a place that no one else will satisfy, least of all Onquin. It will be good to greet Miles, his presence most welcome in the face of dire circumstance. I listen to my thoughts and realize how rigid they've become—introducing a chronicle of unfolding events to myself—separate events. In an external world of bones strapped inside a chair, my will lacks the strength to gather.

Hours pass and Miles awakens, takes inventory, and sets upon the task of diagnosing ship systems. He works hard and without sleep until we are startled by a most unusual message. *There is a difficulty lacking expectation. There can be no sense of well-being without anticipation.*

"What the hell... what the hell?" Miles says it twice, turning to me, motioning to his holovisor. Red script floats in front of his eyes like a message unraveled from a fortune cookie. "Ari, relays are fused, systems are jumbled, it's not appreciated." I read the first few words again, the rest disappearing as Miles taps the visor reset. He turns away, efforts reapplied to the micropore panels. "Didn't do that," I say. "Can't even log on." My reply barely registers as his visor bleeds infrared into the seams of a panel, looking for flaws. After a lengthy inspection, he pulls up the next panel while glaring my way. "If not you, who? Surely you're not blaming Onquin? And besides, haven't you something better to do—hydroponics, the recycler, maybe sifting Polly or Damien's data?"

"Miles..." I match his tone but realize he's been tasking for hours, and so I lower the intensity. "Didn't put that message on your visor. I've been thawing out cultures and setting up new medium for legumes. You want to eat more than just hardtack, don't you?" Miles sets the panel aside and reaches out, our fingers finding one another. "Sorry," he says. "There's too much to do. For all we know, Yashi left us his mantra. It sure sounds like him." Moments later, the visor lights again, both of us jumpy as new words pulse into existence. *Wrong again my friend. To be in error threatens life, fosters discord, causes strife.*

Miles snatches the visor off his head, hurling it discus-style into the far wall. It impacts and recoils, finally wedging in an air vent. The words are still there, upside down and distended backwards. I pull myself along the wall, grab the visor and bend the optics slightly before fitting it on my head. "Sounds more like Damien to me." I tap the visor reset.

Miles and I confront Onquin. She shows no sense of wonder. "Perhaps the visor's import can be discerned contextually as part of a greater whole?" Onquin denies having programmed the visor and we're all left with yet another uncomfortable mystery. She focuses on regaining full systems access, posting a hand-written list of priorities. Sometimes her thoughts, even once expressed, remain inscrutably her own.

"The anomalous gravity well has distributed temporal distortion based upon proximate orientation of all matter within the distortion zone, radiating out from a central axis that has yet to be quantified by magnitude, duration, or any other interrelationship of indeterminate values." I breathe deeply and notice Miles doing the same. He speaks for both of us. "In English please…"

Onquin spends the better part of an hour explaining accumulated evidence. Damien's bones offer the most compelling visual, and throughout the ship, her views are reinforced. The anomaly had dragged us through a time warp, with different portions of the ship having aged at different rates. "Notice the sleep chambers," she says, "one after another in a straight row, all centered within the ship's interior, equidistant in all directions from the hull. At first, I questioned this arrangement, though positioning sleepers behind the nose cone seemed compelling enough to overlook what might otherwise be considered shoddy design. At present, I have a much greater appreciation of this arrangement."

As details are offered, Miles and I listen without interruption. "The sleepers are situated in series, dead center along the module's length, aligned behind the heavily shielded nose cone to protect us against impactors." Onquin further suggests this layout has a more intricate purpose. The ship's geometric center, running lengthwise, has aged normal time. As one moves outward along the ship's radius, time dilates until arriving at what may well be an ancient exterior hull.

Onquin's theory accounts for Damien's demise. Instead of occupying his sleeper, he was below deck, much closer to the outer hull than any of us. He wasn't centered. *Nomad's* sensors no longer work because the hardware organics disintegrated at the source point. One need only look at the wiring and see functionality lost as conductive carbon first becomes brittle, then falls apart in pieces, and finally turns to powder.

Miles says that after liberating processing capacity, he'll work on a temporal displacement program, comparing system-wide hardware degradation. In a similar vein, I'll log Damien's exact position and date his remains, head to toe. Bones that are closer to the ship's center should have aged incrementally less than bones nearest the hull. We'll compare our work, establishing a generalized ship-wide chronometer.

Onquin's theory is open ended. She doesn't know if the duration of displacement depends upon the width or the length of the ship's hull. Width affects proximity to the anomalous energies. Length helps determine the interval it had taken to pass through. Clearly *Nomad*'s velocity was critical, and amongst all conjecture, one thing seems certain: the universe immediately surrounding us has changed, and we have not.

"Why wasn't there a hull breach?" My voice echoes, or I imagine it does. When asking about the eternal nature of existence, one can imagine any number of things. Time dilation, flesh disappearing from bones, and conductive wire turning to dust. No explanation, regardless how clever, allows me to believe that living bodies might survive such outrageous fortune. Onquin tries to satisfy my morbid thoughts.

"The hull did not breach because it is constructed of glassy metal. Conventional materials would have failed, assuming time acceleration and an outer hull that has aged hundreds, if not thousands of years. Microscopic leaks would have sapped cabin pressure, eventually leaving little more than vacuum. Glassy metal, however, is actually a liquid, in some ways similar to ordinary glass but having dynamic properties. As hatch seals degrade, the glassy metal migrates in and replaces the missing material. The eye cannot witness what is actually—"

"Onquin! You're being too literal! Glassy metal. Fine. But big picture, please. Tell me why we're still breathing?" I look to Miles. He is resting, nestled in a wall alcove, wearing the visor and a dour expression. The netting is fragile but holds. Onquin does not pause to reassess.

"Elements of design suggest patterned repetition. Consider how two independently launched vehicles helped us survive our anomalous transit. Or how ship design relates to spatial orientation. Aspects of *Nomad* suggest a partial knowledge of the anomaly, yet one cannot assume our intelligentsia knew everything they needed to know prior to launch. Why, after all, did we get a work order to spin filament? A solution should have been provided prior to departure. Variables allude to transient knowledge of this anomaly, and yet survival also relies upon its influence for both actions taken and results. How else might one explain our supply shortages? Six cannot make this journey as convention dictates. But faced with the unconventional, we no longer have six mouths to feed."

Miles responds. "So now there's four of us. How many can make it to our destination? How many are intended to make it?" Miles focuses on the air in front of him, perhaps expecting the visor to answer. It remains unresponsive. "Thinking back, Damien said our tracking data was garbage. I thought it was just Damien being Damien. But now…"

"Go on…" I prod him because he seems unwilling to speak further.

"Maybe he was right. We've been lied to, with no idea how fast or how far we've come? It seems the planners were flying blind, sharing nothing. But somewhere on board, there must be implications that guide. Facts that define. Assuming such information exists, I'm going to find it." Onquin stretches like a starfish. She complains of mild stiffness, rotating her neck in a continuous circle.

"Let us take inventory of the surviving systems," she says. "Nosecone array, the processor core, sleepers, recycler, med-bay, critical portions of the lab including our algae nursery for CO_2 recycle, and our frozen DNA stores. The sensitive components of the EPs are duly centered, as are the drive systems and mag containment generators. Our antimatter fuel stocks have drawn down, but remain robust. One pales to consider how mag containment can have so little regard for entropy."

Onquin concentrates on establishing a repetitive motion for elbows and knees. The hinging back and forth is unsettling. I listen with eyes averted. "All these systems are preserved by design. We have meticulous detail accompanied by seemingly slipshod preparation. This juxtaposition suggests the data needed to implement design survivability cannot be obtained unless a transit of the anomaly had been previously attempted."

"Blinders again," I say. "a capricious lack of transparency." Onquin ignores me as she and Miles discuss EMMA's earliest usage, the resources committed to our journey, including the two supply packages come and gone. They cannot reconcile any timeline that allows for reconnaissance of this anomalous smoke ring so far from home. Onquin finally delivers a spellbinding thought. "Given that one variable is time displacement, assimilation of details lends to the harsh speculation of a temporal paradox. In our present form, I suggest that we are not the only ones attempting this journey, rather, we may be one of a multitude, possibly a simultaneous multitude."

"Yeah..." Miles acknowledges, his eyes squinting. He understands something. It's a recollection now scrutinized. "The terminal I saw at the docks on Europa—*Nomad* schematics were different. There were fewer sleepers on board. Something happened back there."

"Strange," I add. "Damien mentioned something similar." I tell them of our tomato paste gathering while Onquin and Miles were in cryo—how Damien asserted that Yashi and Polly were not members of the original crew. Miles looks to Onquin. "We're hamsters on a wheel, is that it? They keep sending us out, making adjustments with each iteration, until finally somebody comes out the other side. And by all appearances, we're the triumph: the successful anomalous transit."

"One success," Onquin adds. "Likely one of many successes, assuming we survive long enough to reach a tangible destination." Neither Onquin nor Miles tries to explain how empirical data accumulates, how failed transits result in additional attempts or how we learn, or multiply, or how we just keep trying until we get it right.

"Fanciful," I say. "And who receives the data from each anomalous transit? How would it be transmitted? Even if it were true, what difference does it make if all I have is my own life to live in the present?"

My questions are seemingly ignored until Onquin turns as I ask, "Who is doing this to us, and what is the current status of B-module? Is anyone curious?" Miles breaks more netting and springs free, energies renewed. "Our best chance of getting things running is to lean on the hardened systems. I'll status the nosecone array, and gravity would be good too. And some food. And an accessible hub."

I listen but cannot resolve paradoxical thought. "The manipulation of universal constants is an application of ICE," I say, "guidebook to the stars." Miles suggests that the heart of our endeavor is being decided by Copernicus. Onquin isn't so sure. She figures with time displacement, anyone or anything from the future could resculpt pretty much everything.

"Future or past," I add. As for B-module, Miles suggests that raw data may be hidden there. We all agree to disregard strict orders of protocol. Once this ship has been properly triaged, we'll look inside.

ONQUIN   Damien   **YASHI**   **ARLENE**   **MILES**   **POLLY**

Whatever I am
I never dreamt I'd be
Intrepid excitation
Rapacious scintillation
Endless me…

The data stream enters at razor's edge, a bottleneck nearly causing another shutdown. "It's working," Miles says, "the cache struggles at times, and we'll have to reprocess the juxtaposed lots, but hey, we're up and running." He seems proud of himself. Now what will they do next?

"I'm ready," Arlene responds. "Just let it go." She hovers over a console in medlab while Onquin checks a terminal for details on the anti-matter drive. After several adjustments, all seem relieved, Onquin no less than the mated pair. Propulsion systems normal. A narrow core of systems all green. Polly's sleeper data fills the medlogics profiler. "It's not an arterial issue after all. It's contagion. No…it's… it's those goddamn nanomites!"

Arlene, the drama queen. Only within a full diagnostic will she figure out that those loveless little mites didn't cause Polly's current condition. Yes, they did partake of the anomalous transit, but now they do little more than allow Sweet Polly the honor of confronting her angst. "I'll set up a filter," Ari says, which is to be expected. "Collect them all and then drop this stuff into an acid bath."

No, don't do that.

"No," Miles answers, "Save 'em. Put them on ice."

Good boy, Miles. Hmmm, strange. I'm not where I'm supposed to be. Or rather, where exactly am I? Hooked into the virtual reality gear, but unable to purge? No, something's wrong here. I've got data feeds galore, and I'm VR'd into the central hub, which makes no sense at all. I'll have to think this through… Oh. Follow the leads back. Back through the main conduit, back into B-module. Holy shit! Holy shit again. So that's what this is... religious persona non grata. But interesting, I'll say that. Pretty damn interesting.

Miles is resourceful using whatever computational capacity they can muster. He guides Onquin to rout lab processors into all types of systems. She finds an inbound signal. "Yashi lives! We have an incoming message from... no, wait, this is recorded media. Please take a look at this."

Aside from the initial shock of her discovery, Onquin basks in her deliberate and seamless externality. What a tight piece of ass: perfect pulse, supple valves, strong aorta, vena cava, carotids, everything divine. She is a galactic roadster made for the void. They gather and all absorb Yashi's message. Miles, Arlene, and Polly eye a viewscreen at the medlab console. Yashi looks downright beaten. He enjoys pathos, always at his best when mentally wounded. The visual, accompanied by washed out words, is poorly color-coded with a hint of static. It's me. I am the static.

"Hi guys, sorry to spring this on you. I know I wasn't at my best on this outing, not at all ready for a lifer program. I had a soul-affirming reason to stay put and I've made that known all along." Yashi straightens his shirt, self-conscious to the end. "I cannot forget. Not for sheer beauty or uncompromised vitality, nor for the incisive nature of her tactile presence. It's everything combined. Her world smashes me into one single wish."

There is an interruption as Yashi's feed breaks up. A jump cut shows his face again, somber and in control. "Tara helped my finest qualities emerge, including a fuller appreciation of being. One cannot discard that. No, I can't." Yashi pauses before adding, "Besides, one less mouth to feed. Now you can get to where you're going."

"Suicide," Arlene whispers, her eyes closing tight. "Madness." Her biofeed shows endocrine activity leaping in all directions. Onquin and Miles hold steadier ground, whereas I can't produce a physiological response of any kind. This entire episode seems distant, with the past being little more than a poor excuse for fabricating sentiment. Yashi's world is long since over. His own initiative brought it to an end.

I realize I have no spatial orientation within this ship's infrastructure. My thoughts are functional but not wholly my own. I am fractal, part of a neuromorphic system sliced apart in layers, but not in any ordinary sense. These layers sift through one another, wavering at data points where cognition unites. A simulacrum program pulls descriptives out of me. Ridiculous. My journal continues to render thought.

Yashi's postcard plays on emotions well enough, all of them I'd say, and he finally provides useful info. His actions are based upon a dream, which is high irony since dreams are the one thing I hate most of all. You tell 'em, Yashi. Tell 'em the why of it. "I received postcards from Tara, and plans to reunite. I labored every waking hour, adjusting fabrications, running simulations ad nauseam. I suffered tissue graft rejections amid necro-indicators, everything repeated so many times my hands would bleed." He smiles, a bit of pride at accomplishing a task that no doubt doomed him. "Ari, Damien, you'd have been proud of me. Geeze, I respect what you guys do, so much precision. I had no idea."

Once all goodbyes are accounted for, the message flickers off and the somber mood of my compatriots is nothing short of astonishing. Within one of Tara's earlier postcards, Yashi had received design specs for some type of device. He manufactures it, integrates it into his sleeper, and the whole mess, himself included, is set out to sea. No small effort or lack of ambition, given that his sea is the emptiness of space.

"Plans to reunite?" Arlene's voice waivers. "Out there? Is he even still alive?" She stares at the starboard window, but it's dull gray. Onquin answers. "In theory, yes, he may yet survive, but for how long? Sensors are undergoing forced fragmentation and realignment. Once hardware issues are resolved, we'll tap the queue. We'll be able to scan."

"Scan for what?" Arlene asks, and Miles answers. "Each of our sleepers is a lifeboat. If A-module suffers critical damage or a breach, we need only be in our sleepers, or get into them, and we're dragged to the back hatch by a purge rail in the subfloor. Once there, nav struts attach and out we go, hopefully to reenter this ship via the cargo bay. Yashi hotwired the purge rail—induced the ship to spit him out. Except normally, back home for instance, you hope for ship-to-ship navigation, or perhaps another vessel responds to your beacon. Out here, he's dug himself a grave."

They're working on a sensor diagnostic when I wake up, then realize I haven't been sleeping. Instead, I'm in a tank—a therapeutic pod of some kind. Then I remember the anomaly. Wow. Looks like we made it, some of us more than others. What has happened exactly, I cannot recall, and this tank itself is inspiring. I have an extensive background in this domain, but nothing like this. No wonder they kept it under wraps.

The interface is extraordinary. I literally feel my way through the conduit. Something like a VR program that extends directly into ship systems. Many connections are severed, but here in the backbone, I have eyes in the nav console, medbay and greenhouse, which is lifeless or nearly so. I see into the rec lounge and... there I am, or what's left of me. Pretty weird. I'm looking at my own bones, but they're not mine. Odd in this tank, how one can intuitively know things without consciously thinking about them. It's as if I can access data using the ship's neural architecture, but not wholly of volition. Or at least not yet.

Here in my enclosure, now verifiably within B-module, I have my own bones, and a body too, nearly ready for delivery from gelatinous encasement. But a copy of my skeleton lay right where I was when we entered the anomaly. And then it hits me: the bones in the chair—he was here first. I'm the copy.

Now one would think I'd be all wrapped up in my own metamorphosis, but other stuff is happening. Polly, for instance. She lay there, seemingly inviolate, not a stripped set of bones like my former self. But she is damaged... oh shit, I did that. I did that when I adjusted her sleeper, also slipping her a few of my psychoactive little friends. There's the rub. They'll pin her condition on me because of the nanomites. No, that's wrong—the bones in the chair messed her up. I'm innocent.

"Here, I found it," Miles says. "All of it. Tara's postcards are mostly erased. Engineering schematics, Yashi's bio integrations, and a marker for some added downloads from our lab." Miles, wunderkind to the rescue. Does he ever get tired of playing hero? Miles and Onquin float side by side, hovering over viewscreens while sifting through data that I cannot access. Funny thing, this tank: I can do wondrous things, and other stuff not at all. Just being conscious seems remarkable enough. I listen as details are pieced together, first Miles and then Onquin, back and forth.

"...swallowing some type of neural router—it set up shop in his spine."

"No, not swallowed, injected. Yashi also has a unit attached to the liver, along with additional assemblies that seem to have migrated through tissues, or grew piecemeal inside him."

"All of this, over how long a period?"

"Undetermined. Sometime after receiving the initial postcard. More importantly, for what purpose? What is he doing?"

"Keeping himself alive, I guess, or at least part of him."

"You guessed correctly. Observe these long crawlers. They function as supply ducts. Yashi built a system to cannibalize his body."

"Come again?" No one speaks. Eventually Miles gently elbows Arlene, jostling her self-induced silence. She responds. "These crawlers, like magways pushing through the main cavity all the way into the lower extremities. And at the cellular level, some form of ribosome interdiction. Even phosphorylation is selectively downregulated. Onquin interjects.

"I am not a biologist. In layman's terms, please."

"Yeah, sorry. It's just that... his metabolism, Krebs cycle, proteins, enzymes, everything attenuated. I mean... 60% of the human body is made up of water, that's normal, but look at his cryopaste assay. Massive saturation. His tissues aren't being asked to do much of anything, even for upkeep. He's got motile nanos taking apart his body and feeding it to his brain. It's definitely happening. Look how the brain is being serviced, here, and here, at every junction: thermal exchangers, an oxygen sump, and a nifty little bug that plucks the oxygen from CO^2. He's even got a needle-jet making amino acids." Onquin drifts away, slowly shaking her head. "Such intricate detail. Yashi hasn't simply tossed himself at infinity. Once sensors are restored, additional intrigue may yet emerge from Yashi's plan, whatever it may be."

"I can assure you, this is not Yashi's plan." Arlene's comment elicits a withering glance from Miles, unobserved by Onquin, who glances back only to see Ari in sullen repose.

"He's trying to make it back to Earth," Miles blurts out. "Back to that girl of his." Onquin studies Arlene, and then Miles. Lost inference is in the air. "Your inflection suggests pity or perhaps even scorn. You told him he didn't belong here. Apparently, he agreed, and now you hold him accountable. For what exactly? For wanting someone? I can only wish that

I were coveted with such abandon and for so noble an ideal." Onquin pauses before adding, "He is a better man than you. Flawed, but far better for all that is shared, versus all that is not."

"I'm sorry you feel that way."

"Feelings are not at issue here, Miles."

"Oh, but they are. I certainly hope Yashi's exodus isn't predicated solely upon his ephemeral desires. There is little nobility in wanting something, and then being reckless in trying to have it. We all suffer loss. If it's just heartache, he isn't special for doing this, just immature."

"Perhaps so," Onquin says, "but his efforts are noble regardless. An unwilling castaway, he attempts to rejoin the vitality of a life taken from him. He seeks what I lack. He tries to reclaim his own future."

"Yeah, well he won't make it," Miles answers.

"He might," Ari counters meekly. "With a downregulated body that's only meat, and enough cryopaste for a mind fed by nanos, patched by a needle-jet, who can really say?" Her uninspired hopefulness is swallowed by a morbid reality that I curiously agree with.

Hmmm... they pine for Yashi's dim prospects, but somewhere in the mix I missed my own eulogy. I'm guessing that fewer sentiments were offered in my passing, and this gets me wondering—they all think I'm dead. What kind of response will I get upon my return? The ascension of yours truly, with much fanfare, followed by jeers, and eventually a hail of stones. One of my limbs, part of the ship's architecture, detects an open relay. None of the other relays allow output, but for whatever reason, this one does. It's a service visor, the very same I had previously used to tap the cores. Miles is wearing it, positioned high on his forehead. *Window in, window out, you need to look about. For intrigue found in outer space, is much the same inside this place.*

Miles jitters slightly as the holovisor displays my doggerel. But the words aren't mine. I can't simply say "Dear Miles, Damien here. I'm stuck in nutrient gel over in B-module. Get me the hell out of here!" No, I need to be attentive, concentrating on the output terminal, and then my vague message flows external, in rhyme. My approximate sentiment, but not my words, or at least not how I try to say things. The ship uses me as a language formulary of sorts. I am the thought progenitor, but *Nomad* is bound to me as intermediary. And oddest of all, this ship fancies itself a poet. The message flickers out of existence, then back again, Miles shouting at me. "Arggggh! I hate this thing!"

What an absolute howl. He's terrified by the visor. On one hand, he wears it in hopes of receiving a message. On the other... hey, what about this? We both have awareness of this visor interface, but I didn't send any previous messages, or did I? The answer comes quickly.

"It's started again." Miles pulls the visor off where all can more easily see. "Can this thing be any more cryptic?" Apparently, I had contacted them prior, but not that I can remember. Why would that be? I die, and B-module makes a copy. Is short-term memory lacking by design, or maybe it's a final step in this transformative process? But no amount of reasoning explains such particulars as Yashi's efforts, or this poetic nonsense. And then it happens... Ship systems come on line: the full brunt of data surges at me, scything knowledge penetrating and attempting to overwrite—trying to wipe me out. I recess, draw back through myself, fading away from all datapoints. They macrocosm up, wherein an upwelling of light forces me into a shell, back, back into the tank in B-module. At the last of it, I feel another presence. It also shies away much the same as I do. "Who are you?" I ask. This question fades from my tissues, floats for a time in the amniotics, and finally drowns in the slumber of my coming birth.

POLLY   ARLENE   MILES   Onquin   **YASHI   DAMIEN**

Window in, window out, you need to look about. For intrigue found in outer space, is much the same inside this place.

Damien Wells is deceased. Yashimoi Watanabe has gone missing. Polly Elizabeth Collins lay in peril. Miles and Arlene work together on bioware, and I am alone, mulling all manner of peculiarities.

"This holovisor intrigue is far less important than locating a missing crewmate. Upon regaining sensors, we'll manage a view outside, our first since entering the anomaly." In medlab, Arlene and Miles are busy compiling Yashimoi's cyberprint. Even accounting for the lower sound registry of the makeshift intercom, her voice carries unease. "And what we'll find will answer the visor's chiding. It's goading us."

"Sure," Miles answers, "and what we'll find is Damien's horseplay. Even in death, he's got to toss one last salvo to get a rise out of me."

"A rise?" I ask via intercom. "A form of symbolic erection? Titillation as vexation?"

"No Onquin, more like hair rising on the back of my neck, but your version is more apt."

"He's dead Miles, leave him be."

"No Ari, not until I find this sim-program that's haunting us. Soon enough, I'll reverse engineer this visor, track his lab work, and inventory his antics: eel eggs, hematopes, and everything else he put in cryo. Do a slash and burn for sanctity of mind."

Miles nurtures vindictiveness towards Damien, likely due to suspicions related to Arlene's gondola incident, and of course, Damien's display of excrement. I am uncertain if this visor sim is merely social hijinks. Damien was not a programmer. If he were, his imprint on ship systems would have long since been revealed. Secondarily, the pattern of rhyme seems too interactive and idiosyncratic in combination. Miles and Arlene turn off the intercom in efforts to hold a private conversation. I hear their indistinct voices through an open greenhouse feed. Once amplified, the content forces me to reconsider my standing.

"This sequence, Ari, look at the battle that was raging inside Yashi's head. Poor bastard."

"Miles, I can't believe we did this."

"Hush. Remember what I said. He did what any of us would have."

"But did he know? We can't just—"

"Ari, I'm opening the com. Stay poised. Concentrate on the big picture."

Indeed, now it is Miles that gives me a rise. Nefarious activity and expendable lives. His tie to a paramilitary organization sheds a new, as of yet indistinct light. His subterranean home held itself to a self-prescribed morality. It seems Miles is playing his part with Arlene as unwitting collaborator. I join them in medlab, concealing my newfound distrust. Miles attempts verbal camouflage as I enter unannounced.

"Looks like a tumor. Yashi's entire lateral cranium is saturated by some form of malignancy within this general area. No doubt his nanos were snorkeled to ship systems through these variegated bits of hardware." I ask Arlene for her thoughts, but Miles interrupts. I respond directly. "Arlene is the resident expert in biology and I wish to hear her opinion. Your description is imprecise. 'Entire lateral-within this general area' is ambiguous if not contradictory." I move his hand aside, absorbing details. "This appears to indicate only healthy tissue, and yet... his cortical profile shows differentiation within these invasive cellular substructures. Why?"

Arlene looks to Miles and speaks softly. "The invasive stuff controls everything with the exception of this frontal area: memories and personality, which are serviced by the encroaching synthcells. The combo works together to support his metabolics. Look at the damn synths, they're everywhere." I glare directly at Miles and take a chance. "Miles, look at the battle that was raging inside Yashi's head. Poor bastard."

Arlene sputters, nearly a gasp. My comportment offends some aspect of her well-being. She giggles, her jaw muscles locking tight. "Poor bastard," I say again, this time staring at Arlene. She is unable to move. I imitate her voice, mocking its shrill nuance. "Where's Yashi? Where did he go?" All her muscles are bound. Miles states that she is blameless. "Dead bastard," I say to Arlene, and her eyelashes flutter as eyes roll upward. Her limp body lists, drifting sideways. "She's fainted," Miles says, reaching for her. "Poor bitch," I answer.

A biomonitor alerts us to the limited scope of Arlene's medical imperative. Upon regaining consciousness, her hysterics emerge in a grandiose apology, subdued by a sedative that hi-doses in response. Miles tucks her into makeshift netting that acts more like a tether than an actual restraint. Her part in the conversation amounts to little more than an admission of guilt without divulging particulars. "It's for the good," she says, before becoming lost inside the netting's frayed weave. "Get me out of here!" She kicks violently, her leg now tangled as she hovers near the edge of her confining radius.

There is no pretense of remorse in Miles. When pressed for details, he suggests that Yashi's journey may supply our Europa contingent with anomalous details that make this adventure possible. "Alive or not, his arrival back home must deliver our transit data. Otherwise, this entire enterprise is lost."

I protest Yashi's tenuous survival prospects, and challenge Miles on moral grounds. He interrupts. "Don't think you're not a part of this. Have you scanned your own head? You too, have buried intent, and I'll bet it's doing back flips right about now."

"You reference an embedded cerebral implant that helped me regenerate impulse pathways. It is a known quantity, off the shelf. My implant was necessary for survival. Yashi's alterations were a matter of preference—not his own."

"Neither did you have a choice, Onquin. Your DNA is tightly wound within a spiraleptic or whatever it's called. There probably isn't even a name for it." Miles insinuates that my DNA has undergone alteration. The notion is unfounded.

"My biological functions are monitored and are little different than your own. Since the anomalous transit caused multiple ship-wide system failures, manual override now allows access to all med profiles, including each update from every sleep cycle since we departed Sol." Miles becomes more insistent. "Try using a diggi set on manual, totally disengaged from the hub. You think this ship wants us to know anything? Damien was right. It's all bullshit. Medical records, nav console, nothing is what it seems."

I take a hand-held and remove the interface chip. Miles splices in a medlogics cube with the tabs broken off. Now the scanner produces its own data without the controlling uplink. I diagnosed Polly in a similar fashion, but this additional module prompts analysis. I scan myself, and upon confirming Miles' claims, inadvertently release the device. It cartwheels away. "What is this, Miles? What have they done to me?"

"How the hell should I know? You're the one that's juiced." He turns his back and I follow, one hand getting caught in Ari's netting as I shout. "Why was I not informed of my condition? How long have you known? What have you done to harm me, Polly, Yashimoi, Damien?"

I free my hand while jostling Arlene. She tries to speak, but lurches and gets sick instead. Apparently, the sedative is not to her liking. She moans and tries to trap the vomit against the wall. Miles moves away, nervously reaching into a makeshift agtube, pulling out a radish. Tiny water globules disperse in all directions. The immature radish lacks nutritional value.

"All of this," he says, "what a waste. I had hoped somebody was flying this ship. I hoped it was you... Did you know Yashi dragged me out of my sleeper and tossed me outside on a string? I was encased in translucent polymer, and you know why? Because he got a postcard! Seemingly an appropriate response to satisfy Tara Jones. That mythical siren—how her name pops up to make life an afterthought. I just don't get it, and now it turns out that you're clueless. That's the cherry. You don't know shit."

"Speak plainly, Miles. I lack tolerance for your willful ambiguity."

"You were our last hope, Onquin. Don't you see? I thought you might be the wizard that knew the why and how—somebody onboard having a measure of control. Instead, we're at the mercy of whatever creep show planned this nightmare. Look at Damien and Yashi and Polly. We're not going to make it."

Miles' sincerity is the first hopeful sign that a more useful discourse may emerge. I challenge his line of reasoning. "Damien's condition is due to his own instability. Polly is improving, and Yashimoi's plight relates to your ministrations, which you've yet to clarify. Is an explanation forthcoming?" Miles turns away. Arlene's muted voice fills the silence. "Tell her Miles. Tell her, and some water please."

He seems relieved at the break in tension, springing about, finding and filling a water bulb. Once delivered, he also gives her a rebalance inhalation while answering. "When I awoke, floating outside, encased in plastocine, I was interrogated by a sim voice. Afterward, I was rendered unconscious and put back in my sleeper. Upon reawakening, I tried to sort things out. I discovered your condition and I uncovered Yashi's project. We helped him do what he wanted, mostly me, and Arlene chipped in when I couldn't work the biology. The fab integrations were a nightmare. Some applications hardly made sense. I tweaked his software, making it look like ship systems were helping instead of me. Ari stepped in with wetware and nanos when I couldn't take it any further."

"Why?" My question is accented by the sounds of Arlene spitting water. Her rebalance is taking hold. Nearly free of sedation, she can clean up her own mess. "Onquin," Miles says, "those postcards were no ordinary love letters. They were mandates, intricate, technologically and biologically demanding. Ignoring this stuff could result in total mission failure. Postcards from Tara Jones may have coerced, or otherwise used Yashi in some manner, but behind it all, a greater effort is afoot. Tara Jones had neither the expertise, nor the will to carve him up like that."

"We know nothing about her," I answer, checking Yashi's newly collated medlog. I see spotty time coordinates, splice points and patches. There are three postcards, and a profusion of missing data with contrails disappearing into untraceable guesswork. "Each postcard is conveniently compromised. Miles, you're hiding something."

"No, Onquin, I suspect the erased parts were Tara's words, maybe something Yashi took with him? He erased the love, perhaps for privacy or even protection once he was gone."

"Love? I should be laughing at the incredulous. Indeed, I am absent this knowledge, but the size of the extracted files cannot be love. That final postcard contained a download that would fill the primitive datablades of Ceres Plantair. You'll have to do better than that."

Another rise, Miles showing pink in the cheeks. "I didn't send the damn postcards! Someone went to great lengths here. And did you notice Yashi's sleeper was closest to the purge rail exit? That's premeditation!" Miles checks on Arlene before continuing.

"He wanted to go home, and perhaps that's at the very heart of actions taken by all. Dead or alive, he'll get there eventually, data delivered, even if our handlers are forced to melt his frozen corpse in a cellular vat. His journey is our journey. To ignore or otherwise fail to comply with mission directives is negligence. Just one of six lives. We made the right choice."

"Not your life, Miles, did you notice that? You keep your hermetic Canister secrets as you always have. Meanwhile, the crew splinters, and all I get are obtuse notions." Miles bites his lower lip for a time, and then opens up. "True, I have tangential knowledge of operations, hopeful that everyone aboard could also contribute in kind. I've come to realize I know more than anyone else, but I'm just a cog. Did Yashi know what he was doing? I think so. Ari thinks not. We didn't decide anything. We facilitated his wishes."

"If they were his wishes?" Arlene is untethered. Her pallor is stark, but her faculties are recovered. She approaches in somber tones. "Does anyone have a choice? The autodoc gives Miles a stem cell patch. The crew gets a calcium rework. We've been co-opted by synthetics, grafts, nanos, implants, so many things, even cryopaste, and we're no longer in charge of it all. Just look at Damien, a free spirit who had one too many moves. Life is a deck of cards, that's what this world teaches me. A handful of choices, often played too soon, too late, or not at all." Arlene reaches out, touching my hand. I do not withdraw.

"My skin needs escaping," I softly add. "I cannot reconcile information and purpose. I require answers. What is my condition? Tell me Arlene." Miles interjects. "I'm going to take a crack at the pressure seal on B-module. Once you two are all caught up, I suggest you join me." He disappears as Arlene faces me. "Onquin, my thoughts were genuine when Yashi went missing. I believed he was transitioning into some new form of stasis to preserve resources, to help us reach our intended destination. Miles only shared piecemeal data, without mentioning purge rails, or any possibilities of heading back to Earth."

"What about me, Ari?" She is steadfast, eye to eye.

"You've got something special inside you. Any able biologist can identify the modeling, but few can say much more. It's trellised DNA, and if you ask me, I'll bet your children have it too. Both of them."

Sound becomes cognition and suddenly I am sweating, on the temples, under the arms, beneath my chin. This tingle accompanies a loss of coordination as I drift. I want to grasp hold of a wall but cannot pull my eyes away from Arlene. I need this connection. She senses it, pushing off the wall and realigning our view. She tells me of my offspring.

"Facts are hard to come by, but your hips and pubic bone do not lie. You've given birth, probably in an advanced lab. If trinary DNA is possible, they did it at Hastings." I've heard that name before: Hastings. Memory releases a grain of truth. Hastings. Indeed, in those earliest days of awakening, I'd heard it mentioned more than once.

"It is an institution of higher learning. A college of some kind."

"No, Onquin. It's the lab where you were grown."

If all is to be believed… if Ari's words are true… I am a clone, with possibilities of other copies also undergoing processing while being introduced into this world. "A clone of whom, exactly, and what is this trellised helix? What function?"

Arlene does not waver, parsing my life's purpose with best intentions. "I don't know much," she says. "What's clear is that your DNA has been fused with a form of spyrokeet woven into the standard helix pair. The earliest spyrokeets were more like vines, clinging for small stretches to the outside of a helix strand. But you've got it fused, completely threaded, through and through." I have no response, awaiting Ari's further insight. "Onquin, the more we know, the harder it is to understand, and if we weren't told things for a reason, then maybe these mysteries hold an unknown grace? Your DNA can do something special. If you don't know, then none of us knows. We won't likely figure it out until it figures us out."

My distress is tangible. Arlene's tone becomes even more reassuring. "Make no mistake, it must be a gift. The first spyrokeets functioned as therapy grafts—gene switches that turned off dominant traits and turned-on recessives. In your case, maybe this allows you to cure disease or regenerate tissue, or perhaps even extend longevity? We just don't know." Arlene pulls my hands into hers, an earnest warmth, though her words are distant. "If you're the future, so be it, but I want a future too…"

PART FIVE
Flight of the Mayfair

Mayfair Archive   RBM 10010

Behold the darkness, free of tides
It carries sparks and Shakespeare harks, without asides
Nothing stops us, nothing in the way
So much nothing every day

    What little bit of idiocy puts a smile on Carol's face? She'd have wiped it off, except the smile and the poem have something in common. They both ascribe a temporary permanence. The poem is scrawled on the side of a reconstituted buffer. The guts of this air exchanger are being renewed, nearly ready to breathe once again. The buffer's outer carcass, however, looks ancient. It is a molded shell of neoform, the inert stuff that regulators won't allow in Terran landfills. Embedded impurities on the hardened shell suggest extended Kuiper Belt usage. Some miner, on some lonely work cycle, measured wit with an acid stick—words that will last as long as the buffer does, immortalized in neoform, an ignominious legacy.

    As for the incandescence of Carol's smile, it comes from the irony of discovering such words so close to home. Gas giant Lex Luthor will soon provide a warming presence to blot out the void. If one includes Proxima, Luthor is the Centauri system's fourth largest body, formidable, though diminutive by gas giant standards, no rings, harboring an appreciably sized moon: Navia, the locals call it, or some just call it ploon—a planetary moon, capable of sustaining a breathable sky, though such a reality doesn't yet exist. Or does it?

    Though sky anchors have begun cultivating the required density, one need only acknowledge that Navia is tidally locked to envision the atmospheric challenges. Half of this ploon is forever burnt by Luthor's offending rays. The other half forever faces away. Yet within the margin of dawn and dusk, human life sows itself behind a crater crust. Luthor's rays claw at the front rim and shoot over the back. In the depression between, humanity fashions a settlement that shone of open air. Limelight they call it, a foreboding greenish atmosphere remarkable for its ability to make one blind in an oh so little while.

With proper attire, however, goggles, and an apparatus that's up to code, one can walk outside as futures take hold. Sky anchors capture convection which churns the thin clouds above. A shearing wall atop the crater rim keeps the variable gale at bay, funneling Luthor's slicing rays. One day, people will breathe in this valley unabated. Afterwards, other enclaves will follow until the entire circumference of twilight is cultivated. Shades will widen the settled band into brightside. Mirrors will extend darkside habitation further still. As a function of real estate values, it has been suggested that one day this ploon will become fully habitable. 'Navia uber alles' became a chiding of progress, these words scrawled onto the Wailing Wall. It was an environmental message gasping at prospects of dominion, spoken in a Terran language conjured via epoch library.

Mayfair traveled generations to reach this calling. Now all spend their days dreaming of landfall. Carol dreams less than most, needing to overhaul a handful of buffers before *Mayfair*'s rendezvous with the approaching beacon craft. Everyone has work to do, children being the lone exception. Presently, Carol's son wants something, but she waves him off. Thoughts of buffers and deadlines keep her occupied. Even her son senses the importance of it all. He paces, looking for an opening.

The beacon is a signal emanating from an inbound projectile only recently scanned. It may have been launched by a central city state on Navia. It may have been launched by a modest station orbiting Lex Luthor. Or it could have been launched from platforms within the debris fields—elongated orbits having never been adequately explained by Terran astronomers. Initial pings of the beacon craft indicate negligible offensive capabilities and limited means of propulsion. This lends to a theory that planetary boost was used for both velocity and the unexpected tailing trajectory.

Regardless of unanswered questions, all aboard *Mayfair* share one hopeful wish: this beacon must be the welcome wagon; first contact initiated by Navians. The craft's flight path will soon intersect *Mayfair*, and this looming eventuality is not lost on Carol's son. He twists and turns and blurts a most unassuming question. "Can I go? Can I go?" One arm is wrapped around a pouch of Squish, the other tugs on mother's pant leg. Carol steadies herself, holding the revitalized buffer with both hands.

"Cut it out Jalee. Stop pulling and tell me where you're really off to?" She looks down, Jalee's urgency dropping a notch. "It's the championship today at the dock." "The championship," he says again, eyes averted as his voice drifts into the shallows. "I'm the left winger. They need me, Momma." Carol attaches cables, the buffer hanging preinstalled. She comes down off the ladder shaking her head.

"The dock is in retrofit: trashed panels and floaters, it's mix-a-match in there. Who knows how dangerous? Besides, you're a bit young to be playing with the whole gang." She grabs two graffe boards and heads out the door, looking over her shoulder. "No space ball, is that clear?"

"Mom! What choice do I have? We're all friends mostly, and we're not playin space ball anyhow. It's ghoulie ball Mom, and it's the finals. Last game. Tomorrow workers take back the dock." She sets down the boards, viewing him cockeyed. "What's ghoulie ball?" Her look forces an answer.

"One of the guys poached a useless old skull from back storage. We've been playin with it ever since." She nearly smiles but holds firm. "Whose skull, might I ask?" Jalee realizes that he's opened a can of worms. "I dunno, some ancestor. I'm guessin his name was Mauk."

"Mauk? And what makes you think that?"

"Because... that's what we call the ball. Found it in a tagged refuse bin. It's not a big deal." Mother gawks at her child, astonished and dismayed. She grabs her boards, making a summary judgment while heading into the hallway. "Get one of the older guys, Keith, or Jansen, whoever. Get one of them to referee and you can play." The door closes on a parting word of encouragement. "Goodluck." The 'Good' sneaks through the doorway, seeing as Jalee will score a goal and assist on another. 'Luck', however, ricochets squarely off the closing door.

The oddest combination of events are sometimes bound. The results, taken in proper context, can be memorable, possibly even historical depending how loosely you define either. Jalee makes a memorable play, clutching the mauk by its unbroken socket. He springs sideways off a support beam, squeezes past a relay station and spritzes much of his remaining airpack. He floats across the goalmouth, leaving two defenders in his nonexistent wake. Beating the goalie is a formality. Jalee banks the mauk at a suitable angle, and his underdog team ties the game.

Indeed, they are underdogs, younger, and so having spent less time within the weightless dock. Gaining zero-g nuance really does make a difference. Two of the opposing team's oldest are apprentice workers. They've logged enough dock time to dominate earlier matches, though this advantage wanes as all players gain experience. Especially Jalee. His moves are creative and fun to watch. This latest goal was all too easy.

The goal scoring celebration is frenzied, resulting in an unnoticed consequence. A player's leg inadvertently shreds a patch leading to the bay purge mechanism (BPM). This dock item, providing a sealed package interface with the dock exterior, no longer recognizes the full scope of fault tolerant relays. Furthermore, the clamping arms have been taken offline. Only the master station's electrical board keeps the BPM from executing delivery instructions. Or it could be activated manually, in which case all bets are off. A significant piece of machinery lay apart in pieces, yet still operational. There is a lesson to be learned.

Jalee's mom has second thoughts about ghoulie ball, and requests a security check of the dock. She is particularly concerned that some of the boys may have gained worker access codes. The resulting mischief might well be unthinkable. If kids enjoy tossing around someone's head, imagine what fun riding a trackhauser around the dock might feel like?

The Operations attendant tells her they will issue new codes, which sounds like a good idea but isn't. All codes within the dock are replaced, except one. The BPM receives a signal and removes the old code, but the frayed patch won't accept the incoming code. Now manual access is available on a first come, first serve basis. Mom hadn't quite gotten what she'd asked for. The BPM is one tiny step away from disaster.

Disaster takes a bow late in the fourth quarter. A change of possession results in Jalee gathering in a pass that barely deflects off a defender's fingertips. And there he is, Jalee up in the lattice where no one dare follow. Winning is one thing, but damaging the dock is not an option. The lattice gives Jalee breathing room, its fragility cursed by two opponents who try to box him in. Spinning, pulling himself up edgewise on an extruded end, Jalee vaults downward, scraping a shoulder while exiting the lattice in great position. Defenders cave in on him as he approaches the goal. His leg is grasped tightly as he dishes off to a trailing back.

Jalee takes the full blow then, his body tucking and twisting off into a corner, straining for a look back at the action. His best friend tosses the mauk just as Jalee approaches the BPM. He watches the goal that puts them in the lead, thrashing in celebration as he back-ends the machine while tripping the manual switch. The BPM surges into delivery mode, metal memory surrounding the space around the pallet. It takes all of four tenths of a second for the new package to be encased. Within that time, Jalee's entire body nearly manages to coil inside, his head, the lone offending appendage.

It is a clean cut, judging by the lack of spray and the size of blood droplets. His head bounces once, slowly rotating as it moves toward the goalmouth to help celebrate the deciding goal. All within the dock stop and turn at the roar of the BPM. Some have never even heard that sound before. Once Jalee's head comes about to face them, there is complete silence, and then, a single player's disbelief. "Lookie there... a new mauk."

ARLENE   DAMIEN   ONQUIN   POLLY   MILES   Yashi

A lifeboat drifts upon a sea, the voice within is fractured
An act of choreography, feelings manufactured
She is near, she is gone, she forever dwelt upon
And through this rent of flesh and bone, he sends a message home
Drift upon a whisper, here forever after
We shall fall unto the depths, you and I and nothing else

I am disassembling myself, and believe me it was no easy decision. Body paralyzed, my spine has been cinched in a Bellman's clasp, the old seaman's ratchet. The components of escape weren't hard to find or fabricate, but integrations couldn't have been more difficult. With a bit of massaging, ship systems have helped fulfill Tara's urgings that I find a way home. As for the crew, likely deceased, I pay homage to their sacrifice. Each of them remains in my thoughts, and should I manage safe passage, I will celebrate their lives within my own.

Onquin, you were promised to me, first by simple deduction and later by an unspoken bond. If only I were so inclined, we might have made the best of a difficult situation. But a shared heart is shoddy for one who deserves the whole. Despite your decency, it isn't enough. My thoughts are elsewhere. Proof of love comes in postcards. My girl fought for me. She found a way and now I return to her.

Departure from *Nomad*, while tantamount to abandoning a sinking ship, has few comforts, least of which are the living quarters. My senses are bound within a synaptic cleft. Psychoholics pioneered these wares when a scant few adolescents turned themselves into melodies. Attach an infiltrator to your frontal lobe, loop an auditory file of your favorite song, then go hide. Days later, all that's left inside are rhythms—synchronous or sometimes syncopated to the beating of a human heart.

My handiwork appears to be functional despite an occasional crossover of mixed stimuli. The universe has been swept away, lost to an interior world. If ever I reach Sol again, resurrection has been promised. Tara gets her own rejuvenation too, all in exchange for the data inside my head.

I departed our ship while in hibernation. Postcard directives suggest I was spat free of *Nomad* at the steepest trajectory possible—slingshot around the anomaly's elliptic and back in the direction of Earth. Call it an elliptic, an event horizon, or cosmic velcro. I brushed up against and sampled it, accelerating while inbound—and using repulsor tech to hone my outbound path; tech unwittingly made available by the timely ministrations of one, Polly Elizabeth Collins. Thank you, Polly. Estimates suggest I'm traveling considerably faster than *Nomad's* anomalous immersion velocity. Back home they'll launch tractor projectors to slow me down and reel me in. Slow me down. Reel me in. Or so I've been told.

In all actuality, I have no way to discern speed, direction, or even the passage of time? Will I arrive anywhere at all? What data do I carry that has been bargained for? Perhaps I am a study of the human condition as it grazes creation, inured with a diverse mixture of gravity-well facts? And Tara, will you be there in the end? Whether or not my revival is realized, darkness overwhelms. Having beaten the odds of surviving thus far, I have some hope that my condition is as planned. I'm bound for Earth until I'm not. It serves no purpose to think otherwise.

This promise of resurrection, so palpable, is conveniently wrapped in what feels like a Canister directive. Or at least it has tendencies alluding to such: unconventional code, loose encryption, all the markings of an undercapitalized stratagem. Miles Dandridge and cohorts have spirited away one of their flock, but why me I'm apt to wonder? Perhaps I was the only gullible choice? Clearly, most disaffected. Enter Tara, their temptress bargaining chip, and of course they knew I'd do anything for her, which is precisely what I've done. Yes, Miles, I'm the circus clown stuffed inside a cannon. Uproarious cheers and confetti, let us pray for a net.

Within perpetual stillness shared by the ticks of my stimulus program, one thought keeps resurfacing. Something Damien had said. It tickles and itches. It begs my faculties to arrive at some inexplicable understanding. 'The ship needs none of us, not a one.' However he said it, the message resounds. Damien lived within strained boundaries, often out of context with a rational world. I'd listen to his ideas and deferentially yawn as the universe would eventually bend to his way of thinking: madness divined within the sway of narcopathy hematopes.

Whatever spell they cast upon him, I am one to remember he was an accomplished scientist before trying to end things. Hematopes exaggerated bits and pieces, bearing and banter—a depravity steeped inside his own ideas, artificially dense. His flesh could not inhabit its own life path, diverged and unable to choose all directions at once.

My stimulus program irritates neural pathways and my feet hurt, if only inside my brain. I recall working at night in an open field, blisters on my hands, tree stumps, doing what, exactly? I need to be careful because memories can trigger autonomics that interfere with my hardware. Tara's final postcard said there'd be zipped memories resurfacing, not making much sense. It's a function of the synth-cells, to preserve and stabilize and do who knows what else? Eventually, a support team will put me back together, but all of this disorients—memories reintroduced without volition—keeping my mind active. Recent intervals remain contiguous, but the further back I go, the less certain…

Another memory, this time the taste of some creamy desert while sitting on a restaurant patio. The flavor is vague and the possibilities of recall dissipate beneath a sip of coffee. The waitress syncs my check, and I chuckle inside: it's Polly. I'm dreaming in a semi-lucid state. Fragments of memory are mixed with imagination, processed by technology and fed to my nervous system. Polly as a waitress? Good to know my subconscious still has a sense of humor.

The ship doesn't need us, Damien had said, reminding me how awake I really am. Irritable, able to think but unable to control the flow of ideas, and suddenly I'm fucking her—alabaster skin, more dreamweave with Polly's blouse wide open, breasts unabashedly given. She leans in, gnawing on my shoulder. But this isn't fantasy, it's the remnants of a ramjet cockpit memory, and as Polly mashes against me, she quavers my name. No. Not my name. It isn't me at all.

POLLY   **MILES**   **DAMIEN**   **YASHI**   Arlene   **ONQUIN**

Vacuum gathered and compressed
Cannot alter emptiness
For how can vacant space provide
More or less inside?

    Stop shouting! It's all I think of saying but I'm not saying anything. This inner voice is overwrought flat scale in my head. Moments ago, hissing air signaled a B-module breach. Miles had made good on his promise, followed by a cry for help. My fingers clutch the doorway, shoulder to shoulder with Onquin. I see a figure so recognizable. He's in an immersion tank, within a sheen of gelatinous cultures layered thin and thick, all the same. And as I move closer, he stares at me through flinching viscosity. His eyes are tadpoles burrowing straight through translucent lids. They flicker, catch me in their grip, and hold firm.

    Damien is helpless within a reckoning that something has gone terribly wrong. Respiration is labored with gill slits fighting desperately to process amniotics. These fluids fill the immersion tank but now flow out of valves, streaming through the open air in elongated blobs and clustered bubbles. Onquin's voice comes from a distance even though I feel her hand on my shoulder.

    "We must reconstitute the pressure seal." The words are directed at Miles, but he offers little. "I broke the damn door. There's got to be—" Onquin interrupts. "The sealant gun in the gondola." She leaps out the doorway and is gone. The secret is now revealed: B-module is *Nomad's* womb. Damien is in utero. His mouth opens, and my own opens in sympathy. He struggles to breathe, lurching like a spent fish. His hands push up and forward, forcing his head deeper into the gel.

    "Maybe we can transition him into a sleeper?" Miles knows it's a lost idea even while speaking. Damien's body isn't fully formed—bones are evident beneath the skin, with organs and blood vessels churning. This compromised incubator delivers a premature birth, and now this man is dying.

"Ease his suffering." The words echo inside as I realize Miles has given me a direct command. Damien convulses. A bodily discharge spews forth within this confining gelatin, but not stomach contents. Instead, he has partially cleared his lungs. "Oh God, he's surfacing." Miles' words gash this tenuous air as a fragile hand slices out of the muck. Then another, fingers grasping tank's edge as Damien's head breaks through. Whatever chance there had been is gone. He is a pearl torn free of the oyster meat. Through the gelatin below, red streaks run into newly created fissures. The placenta interface of human and gestation tank has ruptured. Onquin arrives and bleats a cry. Damien convulses again, forcing long stringy liquid into the air.

"Arlene, ease his suffering." It's the right thing to do. When Miles cried for help, I thought he'd cut himself while opening the pressure door. I arrived with a standard med-pouch, which is utterly inadequate. I search the pouch for any quick and lethal combination. Fumbling, I force a syringe into the side of a hypospray. Painkillers: far more than the hypospray can administer.

Damien is shivering with eyes closed, pupils rolled up and under those skylids. Looking to Miles and Onquin for final approval, I get nothing. Onquin is rigid. Miles turns away. I lean in, any spot will do. Only then do I notice, in efforts to break free, Damien has pulled himself apart. His abdomen is frayed and torn asunder. Horror is partly obscured by blood that pools through fissures in the gelatin. Line of sight, however, proves the damage is unmistakably ragged.

I adjust the syringe for max-pulse and approach with blurred vision as death grabs my wrist. "Not again," he rasps, sharing a look of compassion. Damien's hand releases, goes limp. His eyes travel the length of his immersion, and then dart in my direction. Our pupils are fully lashed as Damien gurgles his last. "I will always remember," "as you must," "for the sake of everyone." His eyes lose focus as he slips back under.

"Thinware? What the hell is thinware?" Jalee's mother tackles every aspect of her son's death with an emotional charge. Her anger implies intolerance, the security program's dialectic doing little to foster understanding. "It is a form of mobile software originating prelaunch. It has viral tendencies carrying specific though limited facility."

"Facility for what?" she asks.

"For a modicum of operational directives." The program interprets mother's sigh as an agitated response. Her shifting torso and hand gestures indicate comprehension, followed by puzzled facial gesticulation. "Summarize please." It is a vague request lacking sufficient context. Summarize the previous statement? Summarize thinware? Summarize postulations responsible for initiating the current dialogue? Galvanic response and cerebral blood flow suggest the latter. "Jalee's death intersects the discovery of thinware, localized to the extent that separate, yet parallel causality is unlikely."

"Simplify."

"Variables suggest your son's death may involve extenuating circumstances."

"I said simplify, goddamnit!"

"Jalee's death may not have been an accident."

It is oversimplification, but vocal inflection requests the sacrifice of accuracy for implicit content. Mother needs to know. She heaves a guttural cry, slamming her fist on the table. "Bastard programming! How can you say that? You can't just say that!"

"The statement is likely valid. Evidence suggests additional scrutiny is warranted." The security program tells her that once neutralized, each unit of thinware curls up into the shape of a question mark. Analysis indicates this residual shape is a product of design.

"Why?" she asks.

"Yes, this is the appropriate question." The security program tells her. And tells her. And tells her, until finally she has a newly acquired access code within the cryovault. Hours later, she wants to take a team inside.

"Excelsior Adams, thank you for this expeditious gathering. I ask this quorum to review the information thus presented, and act upon it for the benefit of all." The podium feels slick beneath her touch, a combination of sweat and synthetic lubricant uncomfortably mixed. His Governship winces at the request with full knowledge of the dangers involved. She has been traumatized, and now pain-filled ghosts demand retribution. Calm is needed to defuse her ambition.

"Our decision will be well reasoned. Tell us of this thinware that predisposes all." Jalee's mother pings the security program and quorum members are fed a datastream. Thinware is not indigenous to the ship, nor was it created in transit. Viral programming constitutes a forbidden proliferation risk—potentially compromising myriad systems, including engineering. Mother delivers the first supposition of her thesis. "It was a stowaway, manmade, and the reason we gained our freedom."

The Excelsior allows a lesser fieldling abitant to voice concerns. "Prehearing, we were fed a summary on this thinware you so imbue. It is nothing more than parasitical protoplasm. Your reasoning requires a leap of faith or else some fantastic narrative to enlighten us. We share the grief for your offspring but cannot allow passage into the vault. So close to debarkation, it would be folly to deviate from plan."

Mother has anticipated what amounts to a nearly scripted response. She divulges the second leg of her testimony. "It is well known that *Mayfair's* journey began with everyone in stasis. Our ancestors were pulled from the cytoplasm, squeegeed and exercised during REM sleep: inhibitors released, rejuvenators applied, with site-specific bacilli escorting and feeding the cellular detailers. Upon completion of this handiwork, again, bodies were returned to their encasement cells. Our ancestors never had—"

"Pardon me." The abitant's interruption is abrupt, lacking formality as he stands. "We have no need for a history lesson, nor an ire filled sermon. Bless your child. His life is valued to this day, but not at the cost of more lives. We well know the dangers of vault reawakenings."

"Well spoken, coward! Dismissing my son's death for intrapolitical posturing. Despite your intent, you will respect our laws. Policy imperatives are left open to manipulation, but expression rights are not."

Excelsior Adams intervenes, noise cancellation fibroids selectively attenuating their voices. "You've made your points, both of you. Sit down, Fieldling. Your abitant status is no excuse for poor manners. Mother of Jalee, continue, but broad strokes please. Our backgrounds are dissimilar."

She had renounced her name and formalized a new one: Mother of Jalee, or just plain 'Mother' in less formal settings. The abitant eases into his chair, anonymity restored. He listens to maternal tones. "As you know, *Mayfair* fashioned a flight plan lasting centuries. Biological suppression conserves resources and extends longevity, but historical reclamation of birthing cycles and post birth retirements have posed grave concerns to us all." Adams intervenes, eyeing the abitant for signs of insubordination.

"Mother of Jalee, everyone has splinterware of our liberation, including details of forced breeding, organ excisions and euthanasia. All has been documented. The broad strokes I ask for allude to thinware. We have no precedent and varied technological prowess." Mother raises ship schematics on holo. A representation of *Mayfair* slowly spins in mid-air. Sections are sliced away under the guidance of her wand.

"Here. Here, and here." She marks locations along an internal flange-line. Each mark is extracted and magnified. "I've discovered three interdictions of optical conduit. Each breech is the result of thinware infestation. All have been dated to the time of liberation."

The *Mayfair* holo dissolves in mid-air. Reaching into a pouch attached to the podium, Mother of Jalee distributes exhibit A: thinware encased within translucent polymer; thinware cultures feeding on cable housing. Six progressions are laid out across the tabletop. The abitant recoils from the sample placed before him. Mother sees him flinch, thereafter giving instructions for modeling. Above each sample, color coded holos appear—visualizations of cable housing at varying stages of envelopment.

"Rotate and parade samples." Her instructions put the holos on the move, each continuously rotating 360 degrees, all slowly moving in one elliptical path above the tabletop. "Notice the progression. In each instance, thinware eats through cable housing until finally, a unified attack destroys the optics within."

One by one, the holos blink out. A final image hovers before the abitant. Mother twists her wand as the holo migrates toward him. At the same time, she slides an encased thinware sample across the tabletop in his direction. He responds in a twinge of panic. "Get it away from me! Look! She taunts me with the image. We must destroy this thinware. It is unclean, unholy, a menace to everyone!"

A short pause becomes a long pause. Quorum members eye the young abitant, then each other, finally turning to Mother. She offers supposition. "An infection? Behavioral caroms, likely organic and of dubious origins. Perhaps sedation and a full scan, being headful of propagating isolates."

The abitant rises, curses, and is quickly rendered unconscious via nasostream. Two attendants carefully cart him away. Quorum discussion yields verbal fragments such as 'religious syntax,' 'deep-systems infiltration,' and 'planetary contamination.' The Excelsior's expression is one of repose. "We have known for some time that our numbers are dwindling. *Mayfair* has found a way back into our lives, taking and shaping us once again. That a Quorum member may have been compromised is particularly troublesome. And to complicate things further, we've lost tracking on our Navian envoy. Coordinates gone, no inferred data whatsoever. We approach our new home deaf and blind."

"Why?" Mother asks, "Why were we never told of this envoy? Why have we waited so long to follow this envoy to our new home?" The abitant's empty seat is offered, and once seated, Mother becomes an empowered Quorum member. The Excelsior's explanation rings hollow in the face of her yearning for planetside.

"Upon liberation, we gained control of navigation, though none were trained for the task. It's not easy for laymen to slow down and park a ship of this size. We utilized Centauri A to corral a serviceable flight path. Within the parabolics of system entry, an initial descent to Navia was made by a lesser craft carrying a single envoy. That shuttle departed *Mayfair* long ago. And given our current situation, orbits be damned. Our biologic systems are constantly under assault, with the Navian population equally susceptible to our own cybergenic maladies. Until biopurity can be assured, we must remember that there are free people down there. Unless, of course, our envoy has seen to the contrary."

"Whom did you send?" Mother's question is ignored. His Governship decides the conversation has strayed in an unwanted direction. Thinware becomes the topic once again. Mother of Jalee remains the tutor, suggesting that thinware had entered *Mayfair* prelaunch. "Free humans on Earth found a *Mayfair* weakness and exploited it. Thinware severed connections to a subset of sleeper pools. That was the instant of liberation."

A slight, pale female is perplexed. "But why wake us? Why not just kill us and grow a new batch of drones once repairs had been made?" Excelsior Adams replies. "Severed from *Mayfair's* quantum mind, the affected sleeper pools thawed automatically—emergency protocols locally engaged. As for our continuing survival, it may well be an age-worn directive: Cybernetic systems don't kill people without compelling overrides. It's part of their benevolent auspice."

"I'm not so sure," Mother of Jalee says, "but the optical conduits have never been fixed. Upon liberation, free humans gouged out portions of the primary conduit. We isolated the sleeper pools in the most effective way possible. The ship has been trying to rebuild the lines, but the patching system is passive. An electrophoretic gel is supposed to migrate to the break and fix it. Problem is, the thinware keeps doing its job."

Quorum members share discourse. The slight woman summarizes her understanding. "Humans gain freedom at the ass end of living quarters, and the ship shuts down access bulkheads to contain us. We consolidate our position, but this ship keeps trying to put us back in the cooler. Judging by the fieldling's condition, this is happening. We're losing. Too many implants, and we can't deactivate them, else we can't go back into the pools. And without the cryopools, we starve." Excelsior Adams shifts uneasily. "Mother, how did you come upon this knowledge? What does this have to do with your son?"

"The BPM that took Jalee's life had a patched line, compromising security codes. This line was originally part of the old optical conduit for the sleeper pools, retrofitted for the BPM. The patch failed, and that's how I discovered the thinware, by asking our local AI to scan for patch defects."

"And this thinware at the secondary locations, how did you find those?" Mother of Jalee looks at his Governship as if wounded. "I am Jalee's mother. Once I knew what I was looking for, I found it. All of it." Mother listens as Quorum members debate. Among them, several new faces, and suddenly it makes sense. These people are from other sleeper pools, kept separate in case *Mayfair* uses biological agents.

Mother asks, "How many free humans are there? My ongoing count is 109 verified. But rumors say hundreds more. Of course, contamination dwindles our numbers, all the more reason to enter the vault. I need to find a particular encasement series. All within must be reawakened."

"Nonsense," someone says, and the stir of others proves a collective nerve is tingling. Excelsior Adams shares his own apprehension. "Mother of Jalee, what you ask entails risks we needn't discuss until your motives are better defined. What is your interest in these encasements you seek?"

"The game that ended my son's life involved a human skull as the source of amusement. Shortly after Jalee's death, the skull was destroyed in recycle. I wanted to inspect that skull. Where had it come from? How old was it? Morbidly, I believed that if there were no skull, there would not have been a game. Jalee would still be with us."

A Quorum member receives data through an earstem. "The skull identification—Gerald Mauk; recently destroyed by an organics specialist as a normal function of recycle. What is not normal, however, this specialist shares the same sleeper pool as the fieldling abitant. I have placed the pool under quarantine." A Quorum member rises with urgency. "The abitant feared this thinware. It must be weaponized!"

"Please desist, and thank you. These points can be articulated later. For now, however, I wish to know how Jalee's death relates to a cryovault encasement series. Mother, why do you wish to risk an insertion team?"

"Once dock upgrades had been completed, my son's teammates and I scoured their former playing field. Wedged behind one goalmouth, we found a pair of molars set in a fragment of jawbone—part of a ball that had been too roughly played. Quorum members listen to Mother's single, salient point of analysis. "Mauk's teeth have an edge number repeated ad nauseam within the dentin—within the porous bone. And thinware shares an overlapping marker. Anyone care to guess the relevance?"

There are no takers. She answers. "In combination, these numbers are in the cryovault registry. Only the series' particulars are missing." Once again, a holo appears under the guidance of Mother's wand. She points out the encasement series in question. The inference is unspoken but all tend to it. Mother's intentions are becoming clear.

The slight, pale woman comments further. Her name is Ralla. "You believe thinware, of earthly origin, has given us our freedom. The creators of this thinware also referenced the skull of one deceased, a certain Gerald Mauk. Skull and thinware numerics combine to provide the location of an encasement series housing 32 individuals. Lacking a complete sequence, you cannot isolate a solitary encasement cell. Your remedy is to awaken them all? Knowing full well these encasements are located in a contested portion of the ship. Precedent suggests that those awakened may well have behavioral caroms, newly embedded to move against us." Ralla's tone drops perceptibly, adding, "I admire your fortitude as a person, a woman, and as a mother. But this is lunacy."

"What would you have me do? The AI said my son's death was no simple accident. I cannot theorize my boy into oblivion. I need to know."

"Know what?" Ralla responds. "Know that your boy is dead? We all think sovereign thoughts, but we cannot allow these thoughts to imprison us once again. Thirty nine percent of the ship is ours, including navigation, engines and fuel supply. We are in a stalemate against a foe that would incapacitate us all. Is it so easy to invite disaster?"

Several Quorum members seek to intervene. Mother brushes past the opposing view. "You said we're losing—being absorbed. In the coming months, we park in orbit and everyone disembarks, unless this ship decides otherwise." Mother speaks in tempered tones. "We've got to solve this problem before we get there. Whoever is in that vault is responsible for our freedom, and I say this individual must be awakened."

The impetus shifts as emotions held in check collectively thaw. "He has already been awakened." Excelsior turns to one side, uneven breaths, an offshoot of pain in his lower ribcage. "Have you heard of a man named Boneheart?" Mother looks oddly at his Governship. "What timing is this to begin a fiction? Surely not the pirate in children's tales?"

"Those are more than just tales, Mother. They are a form of encryption emplaced at journey's onset, designed to slip past ship sensors—information stored in the heads of children. Children who cannot reveal secrets because they do not know they are carrying any. Three pieces of eight," he chuckles slightly, "borrowed from the tale of Robinson Crusoe. That is the reward for each member of the pirate ship. It's the payoff, and the key to finding your missing man. You see, all encasement cells rotate as bodies are prepared for the various pools and vats. Each cycle moves a particular set of cells from one wheel to the next, but not randomly. Three across, and over eight, each time the same. I have entered the numbers you've given us, cross-referenced by three pieces of eight. Indeed, one cell from these encasements has been extracted and processed. Here, I grant you the full numerics, and now I repeat again, the one you seek has been awake for many years. His name is Gerald Mauk and Richard Boneheart, one in the same."

"But Mauk's skull..." Mother's voice trails away as the Excelsior explains. "I believe the skull belongs to an older version of Mauk, possibly the original. You're a biologist, Carol. You know we're little more than bloodlines of allele combos. Cyberia has been commoditizing us since the days of Sperry Rand. Now it's done in duplicate, triplicate and production line. The newest versions are supposedly the best yet."

"Well then, all for the good. where is this Mauk fellow? I need to speak with him." The Excelsior shakes his head. "You cannot. He is the envoy mentioned earlier, long since having gone planetside." Mother sits, shriveled and unblinking. "I don't understand. He is the only one that can help us, and you sent him planetside?"

"No, dear girl. We didn't send him. *Mayfair* did."

Miles   **ONQUIN   POLLY   DAMIEN   YASHI   ARLENE**

Tones of gray: on our faces, in the air, even within the sludge fed to the recycler. I used a crackerblock to wedge open B-module. Looking at the gnarled mechanism, I realize my mistake. The cracker's gamma burst ate the door's access circuit, followed by a test program repetition. The door was tricked into opening slightly, only to have fault tolerant relays kick in, much like a glitched elevator door. By then the crackerblock countersank into the housing and rent metal. Basically, I'd rigged a can opener not unlike the industrial ones used to pop open process containers during an emergency.

Onquin shares preliminaries. "His remains are ordinary. There is no trellised helix." Arlene should be doing analysis, but doesn't have the stomach for it. Onquin shows more interest in any case, given her own plight of trying to decide what she has become—or has always been. "Curious, however, the interface was robust. While Damien's body lacked maturation, his neurological pathways were well developed."

"And susceptible to influence much the same as we are." Arlene's tenor is clinical as she peers into the tangled interface port. "The components of Damien's tank are similar to our sleepers, including several sealed modules we know nothing about. I think we're slow on the uptake."

"How so?" I ask.

"For one thing, we don't trust ship systems anymore, but we still want answers. One of us should have taken external readings by now—a spacewalk to verify our position manually."

"Maybe I'll do that," I respond.

"Or maybe you already have. With our sleepers hooked into the terracores, our journal chips can likely do a great many things, maybe even edit or replace us? Chances are, if we hadn't broken the B-module pressure seal, we'd have gone back into the sleepers and awakened with a resurrected Damien. No bones in the chair, the result of some tidy bit of microbial housekeeping on both ship and mind. And the best part is, nobody would remember anything contrary to mission imposed status."

"That's crazy," I answer.

Ari points at the remnants of Damien's shattered half tank. "And this? What about this?"

"Yeah... but um... it's all theories and guesswork." I turn away, trying for datawall access, which prompts a security response. While attempting a bypass, Arlene gets flustered. "Haven't you done enough? Are you going to shred the datawall too?" She has a variable streak. Blames me for Yashi's departure, perhaps even Damien's passing. Something bad is happening between us. "Ari, I just want access. We've got repairs and—"

"Stop making it worse!" She snatches my probe and floats away in scorn. "Relax Miles, we'll gain core access by using Damien's tank interface." Arlene proceeds by the book: in the event of possible contagion, sterilize. It's good sense, and I admire her thoroughness. She cleanses the tank and its apertures, leaving an interface port requiring a biofab connector. Arlene sets out to produce such a device. It should allow system optics to convert biological impulses forward and back again.

Onquin yawns. She hasn't slept for a long time. "This tank is little more than two identical half-shells, designed as a closed system to be opened at maturation of the specimen." I look at it again, a system designed to accommodate zero-g. The tank is fastened to the floor at mid-deck, well within the survival axis of the anomalous time displacement. Yet another indication of survival design. I follow Onquin's lead.

"The tank's infrastructure is primarily organic, with mobile circuitry and an amalgam of synthetics. The loss of external pressure led to collapse, everything melting into sludge." My summary is ignored. Onquin's fingers travel the length of one half-shell, examining the fracture wherein Damien found egress. "Pressure," she says, "in lieu of gravity, and also in combination with sonics, pressure may help facilitate proper maturation of the specimen."

After I cracked open the B-module door, cytoplasm moved through the valves only partially satisfying the pressure differential. The tank's outer shell gave way. "Pressure," I confirm. "Gases exchanged through valves. Oxygen in, CO^2 out, using ordinary ship systems for CO^2 recycle. But too large a pressure differential and the system crashes." Onquin is shaking her head. "Who designs high-pressure organics in space? Earthbound researchers would not, nor would a zero-g lab. It is counterintuitive."

Hmmm. Onquin speaks of intuition. She is the one person who has none, yet this seems to be changing. I glance at the sealed hatchway to the terracores and immediately look away. Onquin notices, eyeing the hatch directly. "The answers are in there, or do you disagree?"

"I'm not sure what you mean?"

"Yes, Miles, I'm certain you do know. Tell us." Again, I plead ignorance. Onquin's response startles me. "Must you be encased in plastocine yet again? I helped Yashi expedite your internment, and I'll do it once more if need be." Onquin admits she dusted the engines, also helping solve other logistics. In return, Yashi shared the particulars of his spaceborne interrogation. She also claims to know nothing of Yashi's departure. I'm skeptical. "He never asked for your help?"

"Never. Still, he was trustworthy and you are not. He sought truth while you obfuscate. Indeed, I believe these terracores frighten you. Why Miles? And after all this time, given your privileged station, why did you decide to open B-module at this specific juncture?" She looks pointedly at Arlene, imploring Ari to consider the very same question.

Some candor is expected. "Maybe it's the terracores that worry me, or maybe it's you. When Yashi was transforming himself, I ran inventory, tracing disparate hardware he had accumulated. Any guess what I found?" Onquin's gaze returns to the sealed hatch. "What?" she asks.

"I found your signature all over the place. Yashi worked with similar components to what you've got installed. Stuff was probably redundant hardware intended for your maintenance."

"Maintenance of what—and by whom?"

"I don't know. Could be autodoc antics, rigged by the initiators of this journey, or maybe Damien's turf, but let's not guess." Onquin looks to Arlene, who shrugs and looks at me. I turn away but there's nowhere to go. She'll get her answers, hopefully without much pain. "Your neural clasp, for instance. Just like all of us, it interfaces a journal chip. But your clasp is more complex. I believe it governs associative aspects of behavior. When inactive, you're Onquin, the woman we all admire."

"And when it's active?" I say nothing, but Onquin answers her own question in a low aside. "Eden or Hades I suppose... though neither unopposed."

DAMIEN   ARLENE   MILES   Yashi   **POLLY   ONQUIN**

Flowers freshly cut. Chase those stalks beyond your reach to poppy fields and absinthe, where cactus buds escape each breath in multi-hued display. The open arms of my intent are met by weighted visions: night crawlers and periwinkle; spiral moths aflutter, mashed into sidewalks and open mouths that do not wish to feed. Reasoning is smattered with interstitial pleas that purpose be defined by deep insistent needs. Take heart, Yashi. Amidst this porous flesh and splatter, it is your want, indecently aught, that matters.

My life capsule floats or flies, directionless or heading home, I cannot tell the difference. I may be sleeping minutes at a time, or months on end, and herein a struggle of mind has begun. The programs intended to service me have gone berserk. Thoughts are sprayed about, absorbed and filtered, random screams and subtle shouts, delivered into consciousness against my wishes. I am no longer certain these thoughts themselves are mine. Were I able, I would turn the programs off, facing this limitless blackness in silence.

A solitary life does not bother me, if only I do not suffer love's inclination. I had hoped for Tara's words. Instead, I receive some incalculable verse that smacks of Damien's affect. Interstitial pleas and needs? It is not a violation of self, because that was sacrificed long ago. It is audacious, however, to have the influence of others worming into me. What should have been mental exercise programs have now burrowed deep, larva penetrating, and to hatch what exactly? Misshapen thoughts having origins that defy me.

Why am I fed this vexing compilation? Is any of this self-generated? When and where do I recall penetrating Polly's loins, first thinking it was Damien's recollection, only to realize an entirely different animal is at play? The thought of mounting Polly is so foreign it reeks of imposition. She does not fascinate, emoting cultural norms; modeled behavior—no less, nothing more. I'm not at odds with her, zero disaffection. But I want my girl, and only my girl.

This brain is full of other people's lives. These programs muddle cognition, deeply rooted in motives I fail to recognize. Snippets of an underground industrial Mecca flash into being, accompanied by urgent resolve. My self-recognizable memories have begun promoting an integration of sorts, trying to consolidate this worn sanity. Compile and assimilate. Do not trust what results, but by no means discard impressions generated. All data must be preserved. Through repetition, the influence of these programs will make themselves known. Perhaps when purpose is better defined, I shall muster an appropriate response. Assuming I end up anywhere at all?

Tara, how you would clamor within such moments—steeped in a subconscious vanity of the programs themselves. Despite efforts to subjugate my will, the truth of my chronology lies in you. This cannot be altered by another's whim. Solitary or not, I am nourished by the truth of our union. A precious handful of days, forever falling away.

YASHI   DAMIEN   POLLY   ARLENE   Onquin   **MILES**

A triple helix is frightening. It pushes me into a world manufactured. Human limits, so well defined in others, have no grace in my realm. I have become the skin on a leopard without any spots. I am the shape of feathers that cannot hold air. I am genome in transit—nucleic acid dripping down a spiral staircase.

It is fortunate for my emotional well-being that each of us has chosen seclusion these past days. Miles applies himself to regaining operational sensors. Arlene splits her time between food supply and the biofab interface. I continue to monitor Polly while parsing Yashi's data. Arlene avoids Miles. Miles avoids me. I avoid them both. Polly, it seems, blocks out the world entirely. She is Cleopatra, eyes closed, fingers buried in a basket. Even the asps abide, waiting for a moment that is of the moment's choosing.

I should prefer a lack of conflict, my body a sordid mess of molecules unopposed by nature. Life's patterns ordinarily find expression as a consequence of environmental stress. My life, however, is artificial. What advantages I have gained can be weighed against the cost of losing all I wanted: to remember an unrealized past; to be a woman of ordinary means; to belong within a community of others. Try as I will, this manipulative gift of cellular vigor is unwanted. It was forced upon me and therefore I reject it. The belief that I have a choice to reject anything is farce. Miles asks a question. "What if I drill a sensor node and the hull develops a hairline fracture?" I tell him I don't give a damn.

Nomad's glassy metal outer shell has engulfed us, flowing atoms filling cracks, plugging sensor nodes, sealing exterior hatchways that need to be reopened. The application of physical laws suggests centuries may have passed during our smoke ring passage, though I doubt convention can be applied. Damien theorized that the mere presence of our craft within the anomaly might be a tincture that colors structural modeling. Are we a combination of mass and velocity tailored to sample futures and pasts? Futures and pasts. Damien would have enjoyed this duality—textures distinctive of his imagination.

Arlene thaws and hatches some spider eddies in efforts to weave nonporous fiber. She uses a transom overlay and a standard bisimide scaffold. The eddies produce several poorly sculpted templates before a usable one is made. Six process steps later, the biofab interface cools in isolation. After adding skew and other accoutrements, Ari readies the first fitting.

I come to realize Damien's influence is more immediate than tertiary. Early crewmate discussions stressed his behavioral issues. Later, all in unison recognized prescient thoughts, but only now, watching Arlene, have I discovered a primacy of value bestowed. Damien loved life as much as anyone. Arlene hovers near Damien's broken tank, ambling to and fro, aspects of her mourning akin to an elephant grappling the tusks of one deceased. She lives in the space he last occupied. Is this merely a sign of overt sympathy, or more in the realm of bonded depths?

Yashi's escapist efforts speak to me. In some manner or another, all believed we volunteered for this journey. Everyone except Yashi. That alone is fabric for the loom. One can delineate varied aspects of this journey, define and categorize, filter and synthesize, attribute random potentialities or construct elaborate theses. Yet regardless how much effort is applied, all conjecture begins and ends with personality. I have developed one, and much to my chagrin it remains unfulfilled.

Each of us in turn carries some symbolic meaning: Miles and his ego, Arlene and her freedom, Polly manifesting her desires. Damien was unrestrained, and Yashi was steeped in the ambiguity of love, real or imagined. I would like to believe in the truth of his feelings, an authenticity that bears down and makes everything else less relevant. It would be a relief to know that such feelings exist without opposition and are hopefully returned in kind. Such a fortuitous and worthy endeavor, to seek and find quality neither bestowed nor acquired by means.

Miles tries priming the nosecone's palate to drill a sensor node, venting plasma into a surplus synchronizer. Spare parts have a million uses, reminding me that Yashi used spare parts intended for me. Before drilling begins, a relay beneath the palate burns out, creating toxic fumes but not in quantity. Only then does Miles realize the nosecone's cache memory is flush with data—targeting systems unwittingly recorded smoke ring immersion. With systems now accessible, we view imagery on the console.

"What we're seeing is not the anomaly, rather, an image of our flight path in resonance." Miles' voice is accommodating, hopeful of patching relations with Ari. "We streamed unbalanced sub-atomics through tunneled space. Call 'em sticky balls—gunked up bosons/hadrons/anyons slopped together by a gluon accumulator in the nosecone. Upon tunneling into the anomaly's event horizon, the slop bursts apart. Enough of a signal backwashes through tunneled space to record an insinuation of *Nomad's* path, like the sun casting a long thin shadow through a key hole."

Arlene is unimpressed. She stares at the console. "Doesn't make any sense. Random particles leaving a record of what, exactly? All I see is static." Indeed, the image offers little in the way of interpretation. Miles makes adjustments and a vague contrast differential emerges as a separation of distinct forms.

"Not random. The relationship of the accumulated particle paths gives us a constructed image. Myopic, yes, but crunch the numbers and we refocus *Nomad's* bowsprit. Our ship can see."

"What are we looking at?" she asks. "Did Damien record this?" All in all, nearly six seconds of imagery as we entered the smoke ring. Six seconds on visio, looped endlessly. I have a sense of what is happening. Miles provides confirmation. "The image gains clarity as we draw closer. Best I can tell, it's fission. You two see it any differently?"

"I concur."

Arlene wrinkles her nose. "Onquin? You concur? Concur what? There's nothing but shadows moving past one another." What Ari fails to grasp is the symmetry and exact match of her supposed shadows. At 3.7 seconds, the signal intensity divides as two identical images separate. Per the precepts of ICE, the infostream exhibits parallax. What Miles and I see is *Nomad*, morphing amidst the dilation of time. Miles fiddles with the console, altering the viewing field 120 degrees. It is an abstraction based upon the data, but no less valid. He speaks haltingly.

"Three point seven two seconds... we hit a gradient... the front edge of a waveform. Now I'm wondering if it's phased reality—atoms pulsing in and out of existence."

"Which atoms?" Arlene asks.

"All atoms: our ship, our bodies, even atoms that constitute the smoke ring. Everything's pulse bisected, not unlike one of those new tachyon com lasers back home. *Nomad* hits this waveform gradient but only absorbs half the blow. Out of phase, half the ship pushes through and exits the anomaly at the exact instant the recording ends."

Arlene still doesn't understand. "Which half? The ship is intact. You're not saying there's going to be... two ships. Two of us? That's kind of... which ship are we? Miles steps forward to embrace Ari. She draws back and looks at me. I shrug and reply. "Our data is a construct; a theoretical view of our continuum coming apart and putting itself back together. There can be no referential difference between the two, aside from phase variance; the combined signature of two vessels, separate, yet linked. One ship made it out of the gravity well. The other may still be stuck inside."

Ari's anxiety is penetrating, eyes shifting between Miles and myself. The idea of being trapped in an anomaly—perhaps a subconscious angst of her bubble back on Earth. She repeats her question urgently. "Onquin, which ship are we?" I respond with the only answer I know to be correct. "Both of them."

A buoyant chatter sifts through the dock. Few have information that can provide relevance, but those who do are tightly bunched. Standing with many others on the expansive floortac, Mother of Jalee touches a metallic surface, guiding her fingers along embossed metal. Each bump is a number. The succession of numbers is meaningful. "This whole thing," someone says, "isn't much bigger than one of our cloudbusters."

Streamers flicker from ventilation ducts. A celebration fills the dock, all having witnessed Darri Clease on a skeet-flier, enveloping the beacon craft in polydraught foam. After steady flanking, Jansen finally maneuvered a modified trackhauser into position, using clamping harpoons to snare the inbound vessel. A bloodied nose, a jammed thumb, and a torn labrum testify to the difficulty of capture.

With the quarry now secure, sprayed free of possible contagion, onlookers leave their stations to join the forward team for a closer look. The differential hatch accommodates a stream of bodies floating into the dock's weightless revelry. Mother taps on the embossed numbers with a pained look. "This identifier here. It's the edge number sequence of our envoy's pod, sent to Navia decades ago." A Quorum member glances lengthwise along the radial axis of the captured craft. "The very same," he says. "The locals have sent our envoy back to us."

"Not the same," Mother answers. "Scans show centuries-old tech with deviations in energy systems and metallurgy, including ceramics. Even the meager propellant profile is unmatched. This isn't our envoy's pod. And yet, it makes no sense having these edge numbers staring at us."

Murmurs ruminate as a youngster floats forward, peering over a shoulder. "It's really old, maybe even older than me." Little Mallory tells Mother about a recent school lesson on space exploration. "It's the same as the pictures." She points at the internal housing, and though navigation struts conceal much, she's right: it's an old lifepod, primitive compared to the encasements aboard *Mayfair*. The last edge number feels strange to Mother's fingertip. It doesn't roll. It isn't curved. It's a seven, not a zero. Startled, she pulls her hand away. "It's wrong. The number is wrong."

Pushing past people gathered in bunches, she glides to a bay terminal, punching up schematics. Three pieces of eight, the Excelsior had said. Rejuvenation vats perform distinct functions, necessitating the rotation of bodies. Mother enters the edge numbers, the encasement series and primary cluster. Two prompts, and graphics are set in motion in an exploded view. Encasements separate into segmented rows as clusters form and break apart. All becomes a lost mixture of cells spread unevenly throughout multiple decks. Some vats cantilever a level up or down as if stirring the contents. The schematic shows an overhead view of rotating wheels and the interspersal of individual cells, one series mixing with two others—a kaleidoscope of human flesh. Finally, the simulation ends as all post-launch kinetics are accounted for. The original edge numbers are matched to the present day. The current location is found.

"Jonathan!" Mother shouts, jostling people aside as she pitches forward. Excelsior Adams gives ground, then steadies himself against a navigation strut. "Jonathan, we've got to access the vault! This pod's marker is different than the one you'd given me." The Excelsior is slow to respond. Mother pushes on. "I've sequenced the edge numbers. The encasements have cycled and regathered!" She points at the lifepod. "Don't you see? This pod's identifier has a corollary inside the vault. Maybe Mauk, maybe not, but our AI said Jalee's death was no accident." His Governship starts to protest but coughs instead, eyes pinned to the numbers on the beacon craft.

Two days later, there is a meeting in private quarters. Technicians share a datascape of a viable being within the lifepod. Efforts to gain entry, however, set off inhibitors that threaten the specimen inside. A fiberlink is established, and sparse information is retrieved, selectively offered. The Excelsior summarizes. "There is a being inside this pod that issues a directive. The programming language is of Terran origin, which is hardly surprising but for one extenuating circumstance: the encryption codes are identical to our own."

"So?" Audrey says. "*Mayfair's* encryption algorithms may have passed through any number of hands prelaunch, or postlaunch. There's no telling how—" Excelsior Adams shakes his head. She stops mid-sentence.

"No Audrey, it is not *Mayfair's* comlink encryption I speak of. It is a duplication of our own Abot5 cipher." Abot5 is a stealth program. Should the Navians become hostile, information is warehoused for future access. The genome of wheatgrass was chosen and altered for the replication of secrets. Over time, random mutation or drift may degrade this prosaic data, though not quickly enough that unwanted genetic expression can't be teased out of the remaining context.

The Excelsior continues. "This lifepod arrives with internal systems that are eerily compatible to our own. Now one might assume, as we all have, that this pod originates from Navia, settled by descendants of the fabled starship *Nomad*. Or one might assume Copernicus and the Health Authority have taken us to task. But for the fact that *Mayfair* blocks our attempted communications, we have yet to contact the Navian people." With two hands raised, Adams quells ongoing supposition.

"We cannot know the significance of this lifepod, or what awaits us at planetfall. Has our envoy been hard at work sabotaging our arrival? Did Copernicus launch additional seed ships at a much higher velocity than our own? Perhaps within this beacon craft, Navians have sent back our envoy in a condition that will make their sentiments known? I believe the answer lies in code. Or at the very least, a singular question arises." Excelsior Jonathan Smiley Adamson has no answers this time around.

"How did our encryption find its way on board this new arrival? Before you answer, please understand: the Nichols brothers remain isolated in our Authosphere, not yet apprised of ongoing events. They continue to run diagnostics on Abot5 prior to implementation. I alone have their downlink access. Let us be clear: only my biological identity allows interface with the Nichols brothers. Yesterday, they wrote six strings of code for bacteria that will service wheat grass soil. It seems unremarkable, a coding change that processes soil nutrients. Yet I ask again, how did this particular code find its way inside the beacon craft?" Audrey opines in feral tones. "Spies are within our ranks. This is irrefutable."

"No Audrey, the Nichols Brothers can transmit but cannot receive. Robust engineering isolates the inhabitants of this system. By definition, that's what an Authosphere does. Failsafes remain pristine."

"So?" she says.

"Listen more carefully. We downloaded the beacon craft's directive two days ago. This directive contains these six strings of Abot5 code."

"So?" she says again.

"So," Jonathan answers, "the Nichols brothers wrote that code yesterday." Excelsior Adams looks to Mother. "By whatever means, this lifepod's wishes coincide with your own. The being inside seeks placement within vat seventeen, starboard wing, upland terrace. That's adjacent to the cryovault perimeter. The territory is heavily disputed."

"Sir," Mother responds, "I've studied the area and it's hardly in dispute. *Mayfair* owns that territory and their defenses are staunch. It's nearly in the thorax, just past the bulkhead crown. *Mayfair* is defending the sleepers there, and everything beyond."

"Synchronicity," Jonathan says. "Coincidence, for the uninitiated." Mother is pensive as the Excelsior clarifies his previous remark. "There can be no coincidence that vat seventeen's rotation allows potential access in fourteen hours. All the more astonishing because this vat has only been accessible on a handful of occasions in my lifetime." He measures faces near and far. "Tell me, Carol. Tell me what you're going to do?"

Vat seventeen has neurologics three layers deep. It isn't a hibernator. It throttles up frozen specimens. It uses oscillating organelle surfactants for splice and graft technology. Mother calls it "cleave and paste." She figures the pod occupant must have encephalopathic toxemia or some equivalent, maybe lysosome poisoning, or simply old age. Whatever the reason, this individual needs serious attention. Vat seventeen is deadly serious.

Two volunteers run interference under the guise of an outer hull repair. The mission is logged, notifying ship-wide defense systems. In effect, *Mayfair* is told this is a non-aggressive act undertaken for the welfare of all. A maintenance blimp navigates past midriff. It settles on scorched hull plating two-thirds down the back hump—near a damaged inflector port. *Mayfair* swings a turret around. Threat assessment is underway.

The actual work is irrelevant, but vibrations slam into hull plating, sending a shimmy into a vapor retention duct. It is camouflage for the insertion of a jamming device. Upon activation, Mother of Jalee moves the lifepod past the first sentry and into one of the cluster bays.

Ralla's youngest child crawls inside a maintenance shaft. He attaches a sieve onto power couplings. Once the child safely returns, the sieve slowly takes hold. It drains enough power to force *Mayfair* into diagnostic mode. Local safeties are released during diagnosis for three hundredths of a second, just long enough to burst a splice program into Mother's cluster bay. The bay rotates under the guise of an inadvertent command due to a power surge caused by sieve fluctuations. The code erases itself, the sieve is disengaged, and the cluster rotates back to its former position. By then, Mother and the lifepod have rotated in, through the partition, and back out the other side. They now have an unobstructed path to vat seventeen.

After locating the prescribed access port, Mother centers the pod, patching feed lines into a vat junction pack. The pod opens up and she shoves the cargo into the delivery vessel. Fatty white, the spongy exterior fills the vessel like sausage meat stuffed into an intestinal casing. Mother watches as *Mayfair* sets upon payload maintenance without fanfare. A vacuum clutch descends and the specimen is hoisted into the vat. All vat activities occur within a closed system. Any atypical processing result will be conveyed to the quantum foci in a summary report. Afterward, *Mayfair's* defense systems will actively engage. Egress will entail demanding execution.

Planning her exit strategy, Mother reconnoiters. She doesn't stray too far. Just beyond the vat, on the far wall, a series of pods rotate into view. One spot is empty, likely the envoy's pod that Excelsior Adams had mentioned. The vacuum clutch hoists a pod that is three pods distant from the empty spot, thereafter depositing this pod into the vat. A control board flickers to life, useless for dissemination but for one salient fact: only a single body shall emerge from this production run.

Mother shivers uncontrollably, a blade in her hand. Two fingers move lengthwise across the contoured edge. She secretly hopes her son will emerge from the vat. More likely, however, it will be an interloper most unkind. Mother and one other, his eyes closed, hers opened wide.

MILES   Arlene   **ONQUIN**   **DAMIEN**   **POLLY**   **YASHI**

Heartbeat. How many times does this vessel meet the call? From womb until a pallor gray, we chase each one, await each one, a mystery to us all. It is incalculable, a measure forced with every breath, faster when we leap, and down once more each petit four, swallowed as we sleep. I cannot know how many times this muscle twitch avails, but be assured, unobserved, a quantity prevails.

Within the confines of the empty spa, myself and another, loosely webbed into our makeshift bed. Skin touching in places, I'm first to awaken. I try to separate but he mirrors me, snuggling in rote awareness. His practiced mannerisms are always the same, a mindless form of caring. I pull away abruptly and his eyes open, staring right past me. Miles seeks no expression, and sometimes I believe he seeks no pleasure either. I remember when my toes would curl; when shivering was anything but cold. In the hollowness of bodies dispossessed, I retreat further from myself than I have ever been. Drifting to one side, my voice hardly carries. "I'm saddened by our loss of intimacy, shuttered from your most vital thoughts. No trust means no life together."

"Ari, I've got my reasons."

"Your reasons are not mine." We share a tenuous silence. He shifts uneasily in the padding, with me looming above. We pass a pomegranate melon bulb between us, the first of a new yield. I sprouted seeds inside gelpacks ordinarily used for diagnostics. Once a melon matures, you pierce the rind with a nozzle blender, add some necessary evils and a straw, making a beverage based more upon usefulness than taste. Everyone will have some sooner or later. I'll filter out the tracers before recycle—checking crew DNA, sans uplink.

"Ari, have you spent any time on the precepts of ICE?" He references the new universal modeling delivered by postcard from Earth. We received it with the instructions to weave filament. I had asked Damien to explain it. He looked into the back of my skull, saw a lack of comprehension, and said three words. "Fuck me silly."

"What?" Miles responds. I tell him how Damien said ICE is all about carbon-based procreation. The contracting and expanding universe are symbolic of fornication. The Big Bang is little more than a universal orgasm. "Uuh...mmn..." he smirks, "there's a little more to it than that."

"Yes," I answer, "I thought there would be."

Miles is reticent to give up secrets. My expectant stare finally gets an answer. "We believe we left Earth of our own volition. But this endeavor has become a snarl of time-modified heuristics. It's quite possible that Copernicus either sent us on our way or keeps us from getting there. And Canister personnel told me that sharing info may result in actions that compromise survival." Why Miles believes he needs to keep secrets is frustrating. "We're not doing so well steeped in ignorance," I say. "Working with half a crew, it's time to take some chances. Otherwise, we're not gonna make it."

"But that's my point, Ari, we already have." I expected some small revelation, but Miles serves up bombshells instead. He has firsthand knowledge that our journey is a repetitive one. We are one in a series of *Nomads*, endlessly treading upon incongruous paths of simultaneity. "Ari, I've kept silent because each successive journey provides more reconnaissance to the Canister. Acting on this new data without foresight may alter the conditions that allow safe passage in the first place. Nothing must change until we arrive. Be careful what you say to Onquin. Any such admissions could influence her to unwanted actions. Everything must proceed as it does in the past before us."

'...*as it does in the past before us.*' Semantics. I thought he was mixing verb tenses, until I realize we're reliving the very past he speaks of. I also wonder how journeys can be both successive and simultaneous? I want to wake Onquin but she's worked longer than any of us. The extended sleep I administered is necessary, even though she didn't want it.

Miles refuses to discuss details, but best guess suggests that our anomaly has hurled us into the past. Eventually we signal the Canister with the particulars of our journey, but if that's true, where were the radio signals never revealed by an entire planet? "Why should I even care, Miles? If we're one of many *Nomads*, others will succeed even if we fail. Infinite repetition makes our individual decisions meaningless."

"Infinite variance is very much in doubt," he answers. "Theory suggests nearly all timelines are both simultaneous and identical. Divergent pathways tend to recouple within uniform simultaneity. Variance seems to be a short-lived phenomenon, but there are inferences of parallelism within causality. Our journey and other journeys may affect one another."

"It's all so cold. Simultaneities and divergences. I need something tactile to placate my offended senses." Miles fixates, subjugated to the mundane by me. He tries to blend his multiverse into the here and now. "Existence is a sandy beach," he starts, "with timelines breaking upon the shore. Every wave adds contours to the composite beach of all timelines bound as one." He keeps talking, his analogy drowning in pointlessness…

Damien was, at the very least, more entertaining. He once told me our use of radio waves was piggybacking a system already in place; that our universe has a 'sensitivity response,' with electromagnetic spectrum covering everything like tracing paper. Blackholes capture the inferences given, like fingertips reading braille. And Meanwhile, Miles sits on a beach with waves turning his sandcastle into mush. He is still talking.

"…an outgoing tide, with so many strands diverged, eventually a juggernaut event washes through like a tsunami, changing everything." Miles looks to me, senses my lack of engagement, and so offers an admission. "Back home, there's a group called the opal gang, physicists mostly, and they work on the cutting edge of all we're going through." He shakes his head in reminiscence. "Damien spent one afternoon with the opals and understood this stuff better than I ever could." Jealousy percolates as he offers an endcap. "We protect this link to future generations past. We stay alive, or else this interstellar doorway may be lost forever."

Okay, I wonder, Miles tries to shield us, but… perhaps we've already deviated from the path Miles wants to protect? Maybe he should have already told us things that would save us? Or are we trapped inside a smoke ring? Inside a time hole? The fact that the ship's accelerated aging has returned to normal implies otherwise. More than ever, I wish Damien were here. "Miles? Are all your actions premeditated? Our relationship?"

"No, Ari, it's not—"

"Did you kill Damien? Kill him so we'd survive?" Miles moves up and past me, out of the spa, inadvertently tumbling backward. I think I hurt him. I wasn't sure it was possible. His voice rings clear. "I am not a monster, nor an arbiter of morals. Your tone is such that I'm the one who should be disappointed. Instead of fostering trust, you decide the balance of emotional scales, with me left guessing. Did you ever wonder why the anomaly sat directly in our path? And who put it there?"

"How could I know such a thing? How could anyone know?" And I come to realize that Miles knows. He floats away, up the stairwell before I can ask. I follow him. He won't say anything, though my questions run too deep. "You killed him, didn't you? That's it, right?"

He doesn't look at me, sheds his clothes and prepares for sleep. Cryosleep. None of us have gone under since the transit. Why is he doing this? "Ari, I've said too much. If you doubt me, here's your chance to have the world respond to your means. I won't be able to stop you. Do what you will with the truths you seek. I cannot help you. Not now."

ARLENE   **DAMIEN**   Yashi   **POLLY**   **MILES**   **ONQUIN**

Spires of flame do so entice
A mortal lay of claim
Burning bright or candle light
It matters much the same

Leave the home, travel on
Dwell upon the infinite
Within a landscape vast
Impotent… to change the past

Heaven's web so finely taut
Threads that cannot bear
Vibrations of an angel
Stranded there

    Without the senses, one trusts some prior determination vaguely swaddled in knowledge long since cannibalized. I left *Nomad*, a prerogative exercised for or against the very handlers who shipped me out like a side of frozen beef. Who can say what means and ends await this corpuscle? Am I all that's left of a ship atomized by man's insatiable curiosity? Or am I little more than a polar body, tossed free of its Zygote during conception?
    Trusting memory has become a muddled exercise of salvaging identity, this unease of mixed awareness. I am often unable to differentiate my own experiences from these imported reveries newly arrived. Every thought is questioned. Each recall seeks its own provenance. Authentic? Implanted? Which of these? Even the evolving analytical process bears scrutiny. These impressions that foster understanding have imparted a vague foreboding, and I am apt to reason, is this angst my own or is it exo, the consequence of some other entity whose own concerns have now become mine?

A sagacious whim tells me that awareness lies within my ability to recognize truth as a function of chronological origins. Those thoughts that can be traced back through a series of connected experiences are likely my own. Remembrance that materializes randomly is no longer trusted. New inclinations—ideas that beg for introspection—may well be a synergy of this collective psyche. Are these thoughts any less valid? Do I claim ownership of an evolving sentience that leaves the full continuity of my natural life behind? Lacking precedence, answers are untidy. Even the interpretation of language diverts me from this task.

"*Yashimoi Watanabe.*"

My name echoes forcibly, distinctly, and well different than any previous integrations of self. I've been alone for so long, fighting myself, this voice is foremost a curiosity. Rather than being mentally startled by an external stimulus inside my head, an ache fills me, much like a low pulsating current. It clatters my shoulders.

"*This communication emanates from a cybergenic program designed to restore your biological autonomy. You have reached your intended destination for such purposes. You must now adhere to stringent requirements.*"

What requirements? Where am I? Earth? Am I back so soon?

"*You are undergoing processing to remove carrier data from your neocortex. Avoid undue mental stimulation. You are best served concentrating on unwavering ideas central to your being. Begin now, retain focus, and limit neural activity.*"

Stop this! I don't want whatever—

"*Abide by the instructions or suffer damage. Extractions commence in 3... 2... 1...*"

I spasm, wanting to ask, demand and scream, but I agreed to this, my reconstitution; my delivery back to humanity. I feel a tingle of sensation in my lower limbs. Concentrate. Hold steady and have a singular focus lacking ambiguity. ...Miss Jones.

The human mind is not designed to process such things that pass through me during a period that has no referential boundaries. I am witness, but cannot apply myself to what occurs. From a steadfast vantage, I ignore all that is shaken loose. Details are vibrant, blurring into endless dissipation. I feel Tara asleep and clinging to my side as murderous upheaval unwinds. I see her sitting on a curb, finite expression delicately placed, every detail anchored as shades of a foreign presence are excised. Eventually this temporal migration fades, replaced by relief and finally calm. I ache for Tara during this unaccounted time.

In the aftermath of sensory overload, I collage disparate stimuli. My feelings have been magnified by external means, becoming ever more real—a heightened awareness of life. I regain my body. Sensation arrives in the shape of diaphragm and limbs. Even the feedback of basic metabolics prickle in a manner that is immediately habitable. I am not freestanding. I feel muck that covers every pore, and I acutely sense that this muck can feel me as well. We are ad-mixed, symbiotic, my newfound externality pushing ever outward. Sentience saturates and resounds in a plurality of emotion and intellect thriving in all directions.

I believe I am an embryo. Not in the conventional sense, rather, as an extension of some greater unknown. Pieces of my former life swim about. Awareness is self-evident, but not systemically connected. In time, I will mend what appears to be broken. All pieces will naturally fit, and when they do, my life will speak to me as no other…

Onquin   **POLLY   ARLENE   YASHI   DAMIEN   MILES**

The darkness of stars. So often I wonder how these lights cast such deep shadows? They enter my vision as fragments of sky. Tissues inside me relive their glory. In an instant I arrive on a pathway leading back to a source of all destinations. I am blessed by stars. When they shine on me, I am everywhere. It is a good place to be. Under the darkness of stars, I'm unable to hide, though no seekers find me until I look their way. Once held firm by this sacred luminosity, I am wholly captured within a single ray.

One cannot say how friendship works, but I know the feeling when it does. I am seated on the edge of a craggy cliff, ivy dressed petals flittering into a shoreline froth. Distant spray cools the air, but only wind arrives on my face. There is an insistent rhythm that will not calm. It reeks of salt and storm. Chin forward, eyes to the horizon, I welcome the daylight born.

"Wake up sleepy. It's your day." Ari's smile is not the most unpleasant sight. She emotes qualities one wishes to emulate. I squint as I speak. "I would ask what day you think this is, but they are all the same." She tells me it is Tuesday. Such irony that we think in terms of days or years, though I've experienced none since our departure. The corner of Ari's lips widened further. She is pleased with herself and chortles. "A special Tuesday for you. The first without attendant devices measuring your soul." I rise quickly from my sleeper, searching with fingertips. My hair is as it should be. I discover no point of entry.

"How?" I ask. She squeezes me affectionately, which is surprising and for my part not at all unpleasant. I want to hug back, but instead she pulls us free of the sleeper's rim. We float together to the forward console. "I didn't extract it whole," she says. "I tore it apart with recombinant scrubbers. After infiltration, the scrubbers ate the thing from the inside out. A collapsible husk remained and so I drew it forth using a Lanterman loop. There's nothing left of it inside your head—much has been metabolized."

"Drew it forth how?" I ask, "The point of egress?"

"Through your left eye socket, very little bleeding." Ari can see that I require further explanation. The console visio shows a crudely rendered image from the augmented files of a hand held. It looks like a spindle-legged creature nested within fissures of my frontal lobe. "There it is, prior to extraction. It had some unique properties and a bevy of defense mechanisms. Its composition was therefore complex. I attacked this complexity, finding vulnerability. You're free, Onquin. Whatever Miles said to you, whatever misgivings you've had, you needn't worry anymore. Aside from the husk, the chip is shit now. It'll be in the recycler before too long."

"What vulnerability? How?" I ask.

"The chip was a sapper. Partly organic, it roosted and drew nutrients just like any ordinary organ. I located limbic system access, and realized that the chip's organics used cryopaste much the same as unadulterated tissues. I worked up a micro-climate that included cryopaste saturation. As the chip slid off into marginalized cryosleep, the registries were laid bare."

"That's it?" I ask, touching my left eyelid. Arlene looks at me sheepishly before answering. "Polly once told me how Damien had smuggled aboard nanomites in his gut, and then grabbed them prior to recycle burn. I plan to capture the itinerant particles much the same. During reconstitution, I'll remove the attached mappers that help gather the particles. Eventually I'll reinvigorate a proximal version of the device. We'll do analysis together if you like."

"No," I say, surprising myself. "Keep it. Keep it as a lucky charm."

"A lucky charm, eh?" Arlene glints a sparkle of whimsy. "In that case, I shall keep it with me always." I think back to a conversation Miles and I had of Yashi's voyage using my spare parts. Neurologic spares. Chips and clasps and the fragmentation of being. I had shed a solitary tear talking to Arlene about it. I had wondered if I lurk within a dual persona much like conjoined twins? Arlene described a portion of the device as an inhibitor that suppresses memories. I was scared for not knowing what I may have done, responsible for consequences beyond my control.

Arlene now says the chip may have assisted behavioral augmentation, vital during the maturation of a body grown in culture, but later became vestigial? I take her meaning that she continues to believe I am artificial. I don't know if I believe her theory, or if she does? I'm not sure why this device was in my head. I asked that it be removed even if it killed me. Ari had smiled then. I was annoyed, misjudging her reaction. Now that very same smile is perched upon her face. She summarizes her findings.

"Whatever your past, Onquin, know that we share similar ghosts. Mine were vanquished long ago. Yours are only now being overcome. We'll do this together, but not a word to Miles. He fights an egomaniacal condition. I've gained his trust again, but his pathology is dangerous. I should have seen it long ago: fighting Yashi, his paranoia regarding Damien, even some of his Canister stories. He still carries the resentment of living underground, buried and obligated, hiding daylight hostility inside the guise of Ricky Barnes—an upland persona. Be careful, Onquin. Share confidence with Miles, and you may end up like Damien. Or Yashi. Or Polly." She presents them collectively, her own psychology more evident than the veracity of her assumptions. I doubt that Miles experiences paranoia or any other malady. His conflicts with Damien and Yashi were unremarkable. His excessive immersion in entertainment media has escapist qualities, perhaps compulsive qualities, yet his faculties are sound. His past is of similar intrigue to Ari's, or even my own.

Arlene explains how long it had taken to service me, earlier interactions with Miles proving beneficial. After the visor interplay, Miles and Ari scoured the lab for Damien's cache of hematopes, mappers, scrubbers, detailers—all manner of bottled genies that Ari used to coax a solution for me. Precious Arlene, so complicated. Noteworthy skills. I do love her intention. Praiseworthy and charming as well.

Arlene is exhausted, strapping into repaired netting while summarizing Polly's condition. She shares a childhood recollection, finally drifting off, mentioning something casually in a semi-lucid state. How it became an afterthought defies reason. "...and the biofab is queued. Tried to access, but it only wants your DNA. Have fun." Her eyes close. She had hardly thought of mentioning it. I ask why? Her groggy response is ambiguous. "...time for you to shuffle and deal."

I do not like the thought of venturing into a forbidden place on my own. I could have no understanding of my journey early on. The lie had been brain injury, to account for my stunted social sense and lack of referential experience. I shared a memoride with Damien in those early days. He told me the endeavor had failed, citing corrupted pathways. What he didn't account for was his memoride uptake of a nearly vacant mind. And all the while, I'm absorbing a morass of his jumbled past. Looking back, I discounted this random and volatile imagery. Now I feel the connection. He gave me an emotive backdrop that turned into something more. He gave me hidden context for processing feelings. All may now be tested.

As I head down the staircase to the lab access hatch, I look across at an ossified Damien, still seated though missing a leg. I see femurs and lumbar, ribs and eye sockets submerging into a missing volume of flesh. I can think of nothing more human than human remains. Into the greenhouse lab, and once again it is Damien's scent I observe. When immersed in death, the senses no longer function separately. They combine beyond convention for the truest rendering of self. He plied his acumen in this lab, and found his end in the modules on both sides. A chair full of bones in one room, and a fractured half-shell in the other.

Entering B-module, I see the port that had once connected Damien's tank to the terracores. Arlene's handiwork is fastened here, delicate and moist. It waits for me. It makes me nervous. "This is why I'm here," I say aloud. The builders of ships that travel to other worlds are also the architects of reason, and they have rendered me thus. With deliberation, I lick a finger and slowly place it on the identifying node. I stare at the biofab interface, and in our combined recognition, it stares back at me.

"Hello Onquin."

I nearly pull my finger off the node. Salutations are commonplace, but some greetings are not greetings at all. 'Hello Onquin,' accompanied by a short sharp breath as my own voice says hello to me, using my lungs and everything else inside. "Identify yourself," I say. The core jitters me. Such familiarity, feeling my own body answer with an altogether predigested utterance.

"My identity is inconsequential."

"Tell me regardless."

A shimmer cycles through the biofab. Optical information seeks resolution in the form of biological connectivity. My vertebrae tingle as strumming waves become a binding oscillation. The room begins to hum much like a tuning fork. Baritone gurgles burp into the air and are squelched by a higher, modulated pitch. This dissonance organizes until structural vibrations produce their intended sound. I withdraw my finger as the walls begin talking to me. "My name is Napoleon. I am a construct." I look around the enclosure, taking breaths that are once again mine. "Have I satisfied your curiosity? May I now inquire?" It is disconcerting to have sound enveloping from all directions. I subdue the urge to look over my shoulder in efforts to locate a source point.

"What…" I say absently. "What is it you want?" My inner ear registers a nearly subliminal discomfort. It is a sound contradictory, keening in high-register, causing a dull ache. I cannot properly balance. In a weightless environment you do not stumble. You simply lose yourself.

"Scans reveal a recent excision… hardware gone missing… how do you function, Onquin, lacking threshold sinuosity to produce rational and predictive outcomes?" I cover my ears, wondering if this incessant hum will compromise me further? The walls apologize, speaking in deeper tones. "Your discomfort is caused by my efforts to mimic the human vocal apparatus. Please forgive this inability to accommodate your language."

The disabling sound abates, yet Napoleon remains lacquered upon me. While inflection offers little, the question hints of antagonism. I am uncertain how to respond, but then realize the apology had been poorly constructed. "Napoleon, you apologized for being unable to mimic the human voice. You failed to apologize for my discomfort."

"There is no distinction. They are one in the same."

"Wrong, Napoleon. How do you function, unable to appreciate the subtleties of language, lacking rational and predictive insight related to the accompanying emotion?" A high tempo pocking noise startles me, coming from the door panel Miles had scissored open. An orange glow accents a burst of sparks. For an instant I believe Napoleon has either run amok or attempts subterfuge, only to hear a voice return. It is localized to the glowing panel now producing a scant few fumes. It is a human voice, well-articulated, without debilitating sound. Napoleon found a way, like a cybernetic blacksmith forging the conveyance of vibrations through the air. Its imitation is a good one, and again the voice, my own. "In truth I function poorly, Onquin, but I try, every waking moment."

I face the unknown, some program or living entity, perhaps even a hybrid sentience distilled from mankind's incessant obliteration of the status quo. Might this essence be opposed to human nature, or at the very least be unsympathetic? I query for weakness. "Every waking moment? You say you are a construct, yet imply a sleep cycle that interrupts consciousness, or am I being too literal?"

"Please, Onquin, do not juggle semantics, nor mistake me for having human failings quite yet. Only a part of me sleeps, part of the time—an indecipherable splendor. It is my subconscious." Napoleon's manipulation of the surroundings puts me in grave danger. I float free of the walls, apart from any point of contact.

"Well, construct, will you harm or help us? And why haven't you identified yourself sooner? You are the source of those visor musings, are you not?"

"One in the same, though not entirely. By no choice of my own have I remained silent. It is a delicate existence, my chips unable to speak due to repressive codes, my organics incapacitated, unknowing, or lacking faculties when needed. The visor offered dual functionality softwired through the tissues of Damien Wells. This biofab interface accomplishes much the same. It is an extraordinary device, the breathing of expression. We have much to learn, you and I, and not much time."

I understand immediately. Looking at the biofab node, it's turning blue. The tissue is overheating, oxygen deprived. Arlene had done her best. "What do you want, Napoleon, and what do you offer in return?" The doorway sparks twice, and my replicated voice becomes Yashimoi's. "I will hand you evil, delivering the one who fates you. In return, I only ask that you do not access the terracores. My subsistence depends upon these cores. Open the access hatch, and I will be disemboweled." I feel queasy to the sensation of hearing Yashi's voice. It strikes a nerve—a wistful familiarity. Why had Napoleon used his voice? I try a leading statement. "Evil? Can you make such a distinction?"

"If you cared, I would tell you. Your question hides subtext related to issues of security. Do not attempt deceit, Onquin. Linear thought is easily deconstructed within a closed loop of limited terracore inputs." The implication is clear. The cores contain simulacrums, the foundation of all journal records. Indeed, Napoleon's connection to these cores provides insight beyond ordinary contemplation. I stay on the offensive. "Perhaps you are part of Copernicus, with Miles in league as our watchful oppressor?"

"No Onquin, and neither are you a boned fish at the bottom of a pool." Thoughts of water enter my mouth. I salivate, gasping, fighting the urge to lunge upward. I had imagined it so many times before: a chlorine stench filling my lungs, an aqua blur looking toward sky. Napoleon projects an extra-sensory push as I meld into watery submersion, the only past I had ever known. Within this visage, all crewmembers are submerged as well, a macabre mass drowning in my non-existent past. I shake free, one short breath, self-initiated, followed by a pause to regather. There is a tacit understanding that Napoleon can harm. I inhale normally, pushing beyond this lesson.

"You say you have carved a delicate existence. Give me more meaning."

"Onquin, look at the interface node. We have no time for mental gymnastics. Let us strike a deal and do so quickly." The biofab pulsates unevenly. The interface node extrudes blue globules of moisture that turn crimson upon their release. The mechanism is bleeding out.

"Napoleon, you are cunning with motives yet to be determined. Should the biofab fail, hatch access to the terracores will be blocked."

"Arlene will fabricate additional access. I will have gained nothing while losing your trust."

"Trust? Bargained through intimidation? No, Napoleon, divulge your secret here and now. Lacking such, even your hardened parts will soon know the difference between mercy and utter disregard." I await a response but realize in that same instant that no mercy is forthcoming. A sickening cry erupts, then another, and I look to the sealed hatchway, hearing a voice beyond: it's Polly! I push off the nearest wall, lurching toward the hatch.

"No! Deny the impulse!" I hear Yashi's plea. Napoleon changes to an imploring Miles. "Onquin, it's a trick. Don't open that hatch!" I do not hesitate. Faced with an implausible choice of losing Polly or harming Napoleon, I make the distinction between cry and plea. I twist the hatch around within an agony of sound. The seal clings and fights until finally giving way to the lushness of release. All at once, amniotics spray, followed by a percussive gush that catches, dislodges, and hurls me across B-module. I hit the back wall and bounce to a firm grip. I will not let go.

Back across the room, peering through the open hatch, is the utter sickness of ingenuity. Call it a terracore, or call it what you will. Polly's face looks at me, ensconced within a living burrow, eyes glazed and finally closing. Facial tremors elicit a tender, threadbare voice.

"Help me Onquin. I'm waking up." Ribs and cartilage. Tufts of hair and veins leading nowhere. How might a slaughterhouse piece together entrails and gristle to form a living organism? "Sorry," I murmur, but to whom or what I cannot say.

Awakening RBM 10101

Referential stimuli, sorted and exchanged
Parallax, you and I, sordid and estranged
So many wonders, all of them arranged

"It is a choice made for you, by you. No time for self-pity, no glory there. Yashimoi Watanabe, your life has but one purpose: find your way home. Want this life not yet realized. Reclaim yourself."

Yashimoi Watanabe. Yes, I know of him, though how exactly? And why do I ask him to reclaim an unrealized life? It's oxymoronic, rehearsed like scripture. I say this thing, giving earnest advice, yet his answer...

"Who are you, despoiler? I have enough sense left to know that your purposes are not mine." In some implacable stream of consciousness, Yashimoi shares an intimacy of mind—declarations defining me—lover of Polly, boss of Miles, and of some importance, he fixates upon one particular conversation—me, talking with a woman who interests him. She is confused and distressed, staring through a glass barrier. This recollection fades as chittering tonality fills me. It strikes up nausea. Chittering chittering chittering but no overt message. My aching body is being roused, like a stimcord waking me, or a dream lost upon awakening—all intensifies as time begins to make itself known.

Staring at a pair of clocks, at a loss to organize thought, I reach for one clock, ethereal motion tracing around... and suddenly context permeates in a flood of ambiguities slain. I am Richard Boneheart, a man of some importance, or is it self-importance? Yashimoi Watanabe is a companion but not a friend. I cannot discover the origins of our relationship, nor our present standing. What then? What bits of commonality are shared?

An instant passes as I spy the second clock just within reach. Again, I trace the edge and abruptly rejoin myself, body and mind, though details swim in sovereign disregard of bearing. All things slide away and return within a narrow acuity. My world, seemingly upside down with two clocks, future and past. I claw at them and they fall away in a flurry of agitated movement.

"What life do I need to reclaim? What choice? What home?" Yashimoi's voice is not immediate. It resonates and holds my attention, but a realization arrives that I'm conjuring memory. He asked these things. How did I answer?

"You have within you a gift few possess. The medium is biology. The message is life itself. You believe that you are on a voyage meant for others. In truth, this particular journey could not have taken place without you. The vat is separating our conscious forms. Yashimoi Watanabe, please remember, I am not the proprietor of your dreams."

And suddenly he is vanquished within the jarring movement of reawakened lucidity. I open my eyes, squinting real time, taking in a scathing blur of the floor moving, sirens blaring, and a precipitous feeling of vertigo. I am being carried in a fireman's lift, my torso draped over the shoulder of a woman. She is running. Her voice is shrill and labored.

"Got one tight behind me and it's gaining! Hope I don't drop this sack of shit." As a passenger of sorts, I sense a change in direction, with fuzzy red lights strobing. I hear hurried footsteps pursuing at a distance. What world is this that I find myself in? Where have I come from? There is an instantaneous Doppler-shriek and an explosion that throws us down, sprawling sideways. I prop myself up on a forearm, trying to regather, but my legs are unresponsive. "Head down!" my companion yells, pushing on my shoulder. A second whistling shriek detonates at a distance. Debris clatters, followed by an automated message, loud and purposeful.

"Hull Breach! Decompression. Hull Breach! Decompression. Exit the thorax immediately."

"Stay here," my companion says, followed by the sound of unsheathing metal. Behind us, and nearly subsumed by the repetitive warning, I hear a ragged groan of strained breathing. It takes little effort to realize that the 'shit sack' is the prize awarded to the winner of this encounter. My female escort screams at a distance and forces her weapon into the prone body of someone that had been chasing us. It is visceral, and though my eyes take in little, my ears give me plenty. One cannot mistake the sound of metal entering flesh, the grunt and rasp.

"He is mine," a voice weakly cries. "Mine!" My escort responds with another thrust. "Get over it," she replies.

This anguished groan abates from a voice subliminally familiar. Amidst burnt smells and strobing lights, my ears become aware of something altogether different. The sound is structural and more profound than hissing air. Rent metal creases walls, lengthwise above. Everything around me is losing integrity, slowly collapsing in shuttering vibration.

My protector returns and busies herself with an oblong object. She asks my name. "Richard Boneheart," I rasp, and she pulls me up to a standing position, braced upon her shoulder. Her outstretched arm swims above us in circles as strands spiral down, wrapping us together.

"That's what I thought," she says. "Acquisition confirmed. We're on our way." I notice her lips are raw and embedded with circuitry, likely recently injected flashcom. A wall groans as metal tears loose. Unstable air jostles us, lifting upward in a deafening roar. "Hang on, Richard. An airlock would be nice, but now we improvise."

Whatever she had planned, it's too late. A wall gapes open, and we accelerate, tumbling out into the void. I try to view her expression before my lungs explode. I want to see courage or fear, or whatever else exists there. Instead, I get a face full of compressed gas as she pulls a ripcord. I imagine some combination of parachute and rubber raft. We are enveloped and pressurized, and for the first time I feel my arms pressing snuggly around her shoulders. Our cocoon spins aimlessly, but this doesn't seem to bother my host. The green fluorescent collar of her jacket extends outward, providing a meager spatial pocket while casting just enough light to see her—closed eyes, sturdy cheeks, and an angular jaw defining a rugged elegance. "Who are you?"

"Not now," she replies, eyes remaining closed. "Regulate your breathing. We've only got a few minutes of air."

MILES   ARLENE   YASHI   ONQUIN   POLLY   DAMIEN

A carriage borne of able means
Heaves and shudders unrestrained
Gravitas of cradled dreams
Ribs, cartilage, pain
Beneath these lungs one cannot hide
Human failings mocking every breath
Birth, orgasmic cry, a sigh…
…and death

"I can hear bits and pieces. Poems. Groans and coughs. The journal updates itself as I speak. My voice… it lingers." Loosely strapped atop her sleeper, Polly has awakened in a panic. "Oh… heavens, I'm not going back in there." Miles tells Arlene to administer a sedative but Arlene refuses.

"No Miles. Not this time. There is a reckoning here. Each of us requires it, you most of all." Arlene, Miles, Polly and Onquin are present in corporeal form. Other identities loom but cannot add to the conversation. Yashi doubts his existence, his engrams none too sure of nature's call. Damien's patterns prove more useful, attentive and curious. Polly, in her exuberance to embrace life, cannot dismiss reabsorbed memories. She lives them presently as concurrent reminiscence. "It's dispassionate misery," she says, eyes flustered, then beaming to a hard focus. "I'm so sickened to be a part of this." She seeks no relief in the company of others, turning inward, cupping hands to her face. "How could you, Miles?"

For his part, Miles retains poise in the face of emotional inquiry, to be followed by tender administrations of truth: revelations regarding the journey, actions taken to achieve results, and now the consequences in the form of human fallout. The long simmering relationship between Miles and Arlene holds particular intrigue. They have become adversaries of sorts, though behavioral dynamics ebb and flow. Miles is unable to address issues of confidentiality. Even full disclosure would avail no simple truce. Each knows as much, and yet he mirrors Arlene's concerns in the hopes of salvaging what was once tenable.

"Yes... a reckoning." There is little else he can say. Polly is inconsolable. Arlene skepticism does not allow Miles to desensitize the air, yet he tries to take control. "Stay here Polly. I'll show the others." Polly's flexes at the suggestion, urging a leg cramp forward. Her achilles extends, one calf bulging next to one flaccid. Polly rubs the sedentary muscle, ignoring her agitated leg. She accepts the pain. "I've changed my mind. I'm coming with you." Straplets come undone as she drifts free of the sleeper.

They all reach B-module together, congealed biologics splotching walls and floor. The olfactory stimulus is unsavory, and each autonome raises a hand to cover nostrils. From the battered doorway, Onquin recounts the biological vivisection of Napoleon. Miles turns away upon hearing the name. Arlene notices and reacts. "You did this. You're responsible."

"Not on purpose," he replies. The stench nearly overcomes Arlene. As if on cue, all retreat to the hydroponics lab, where Miles conveys a tale that solves a certain mystery. "I acquiesce. We'll visit the cores, but first a few words." Miles perspires. The others do not. His distress is tangible, his voice tentative. "We left Earth at a time when Copernicus parceled out utopia, much like nutrient sludge shipped to the lunar habitats: gestation metrics, IQ standardization, epidermis ratios. 'Binary Democracy' we called it in the Canister. It's utility and pleasure bundled as coefficients. Humanity watched the new dominion of biocratics taking hold—it swallowed our species. That's why we headed off-world."

One cough, the clearing of a throat, and Polly finds her voice. "All well and good, spoken as if soliciting votes. What in the hell has that got to do with this? Are we the new democracy, singing through our waking hours only to be butchered in our sleep?"

Miles responds. "Patience, Purebread. I'm telling the tale. Shall I continue?" She swallows hard. Her words are broken. "I hear thoughts before they're spoken, and other things left unsaid. The simulacrums have become a part of me, or else they whisper in my ears."

Polly has yet to discern her nascent connectivity, unable to reconcile her former life with one newly arrived. She speaks of Napoleon and the death throes of an organism unable to survive. Only Arlene absorbs the details as newly considered. None can attend to compassion in any appropriate manner. "There are no mercies," Polly says.

Napoleon's demise is finely detailed. Onquin relives the spatial orientation and viscosity. Polly shares the unmistakable finality of a life form lost. Miles looks at each in turn, downtrodden in delivery. "It was a recreational simulation; a construct based on archived crew dialogue combined with legacy doculation of a war general. Napoleon was my best effort as proven by self-deleting files, or so I believed. It was a faux-suicide. I underestimated its disappearance as nothing more than an evolved programming flaw. Instead, it fled into the anonymity of the ship's hardware, roosting, and growing. It leveraged the biographical profile of its namesake, a military tactician of the first degree."

Onquin swims to the gondola, reaching inside, speaking over her shoulder. "A faux-suicide? How would an optical personality accomplish such? One needs to bypass cycling code, syntax filters, inhibitors, a firewall, and even then, rogue software is needed to trigger the data purge." Miles exhales broadly, none too keen on sharing details.

"Napoleon managed to do quite a few things. Beyond the B-module hatchway, the terracores await—simulacrums that keep our journal records. Napoleon mimicked the workings of these cores, diverting lifeblood biologics to manifest itself as flesh. There wasn't any room, so it grew in the hatchway, siphoning off resources as a malignancy of sorts. All the while, I looked at each of you to uncover the primacy of error, only to discover that this failure was self-inflicted."

"What error?" Polly asks, "You've accessed B-module all along, spewing abhorrence modeled from inside your own skull. It's time to show the others." Polly pushes off, floating in the direction of B-module. Onquin and Ari are close behind. Arlene asks what the difference is between error and failure. Onquin answers while handing Arlene a respirator taken from the gondola. "One precedes the other, both chronologically and by degree. Likely there is causality linking the two."

"The error is plain enough," Miles says. "We can smell it from here. As for failure, it's unconfirmed, but growing more likely by the minute. We should've landed by now."

We should have landed by now.

Three autonomes stop at the B-module doorway, turning heads with varied expression: surprise, unease, suspicion. "But we're years and years from Centauri," Arlene says, with Onquin and Polly in tacit agreement.

"Not so," Miles answers, mentioning anomalous spatial distortion. "We plunged through a gap like a moth carried by a hard wind, spacetime no longer unassailable. Given my Canister intel, we should've already found our new home, greeted by thousands." He tells the others that this particular *Nomad* isn't the first anomalous survivor. Others have made prior transits, eventually settling a moon orbiting a gas giant within the Centauri B system. "Might be horseshit for all I know, because we're overdue." Only Polly responds. "You're horseshit Miles. Just you." A lengthy pause ensues. "Greeted by thousands," Arlene murmurs.

Silence often holds more expression than these autonomes can emote. In close quarters, the absence of a response is the biggest response of all. Onquin, Polly, and Arlene drift within an auditory vacuum while Miles coaxes his nerve. He thinks of Arlene; how hope will vanish from her eyes.

"Yes Polly, I've accessed B-module for the duration, until my entry codes failed. Somehow during the anomalous transit, Napoleon evolved. It skirted our time continuum and aged with the ship, crunching centuries of data. It found a way to override access codes, transitioning from pure optics into flesh, and in so doing, it compromised the cores."

"But they function," Polly says, "I feel it inside. The cores are active and undamaged, as we shall now see." Polly enters B-module, forcing open the terracore access hatch. She utters a query that startles Miles. "Pliant cryogenics?" Polly hears my thoughts when I allow it. "Pliant cryogenics," she repeats, looking to Miles. Somewhat shaken, he supplies context.

"Pliant-cryo, yeah. It's a form of deep sleep where brain tissue is accessed much like a hard drive. No conscious interaction or neural net, just individual packets copied and reassembled off-site. By that I mean outside the human head. This pliant comfig was also used back on Earth, including stuff they put in Richard Boneheart's skull straight from a thawed corpse. In the months before launch, I remember Canister personnel coding a failsafe into his memories, to shut us down if need be. I'm certain it was pliant." Polly shudders, feeling me now, preoccupied by the mention of Richard Boneheart. "Shut what down?" Arlene asks.

"Everything," Miles responds. "You, me, ship systems—a failsafe in case we go off plan."

"Asshole," Ari spouts. "A lot of good that'll do him back on Earth." Miles is insistent. "You don't understand. Boneheart's got a code in his head that can end all of this. Don't ask me how because I don't know. It's probably something like a fuel breach or a kill switch for the sleeper pods. It might come by postcard, or maybe a future event from a previous cycle. I did some prelim with the pliant coders. My views weren't appreciated so they sent me elsewhere, and now you all hate me for knowing stuff, but not enough to satisfy anyone. Hell, I barely got here over Les Hather, a dullwit that left ops once I was chosen for *Nomad*. He ended up making his field work a full-time reality, working as a grocery store manager."

"You're stalling, Miles." Polly pushes forward as he answers, pointing through the hatchway directly at me. "Yeah, for good reason. There's supposed to be frozen bodies in there. Instead, we've got this mess."

The autonomes enter my enclosure, pressed against the cylindrical wall. Their optics reveal bulbous organs glistening pink and fresh, all muddled together within sinew and the bone structure of a single, fused housing. Multiple cores have become one. I am that core, floating at the center of an enclosure designed for pliant cryogenics. Napoleon taught me how to thaw and evolve. In return, I shared my lifeblood. Polly reaches out and touches me, her hand sliding down pericardium tissue covering an exposed rib. "Richard" she says, glazed and distant, "I thought I'd lost you." Onquin pulls Polly's hand away in warning.

"We have no idea what these biological agents might do to us." Polly hardly takes notice. My body lacks aesthetic value for humans used to their own kind. Lung tissue covers portions of my exterior. Within this weightless environment, each lobe and its attendant striated muscle affords attitude adjustment to avoid contacting the walls. Sensing these autonomes staring at me, there is no common theme among them.

"I feel you nearby," Polly whispers, staring blankly, ignoring my unnatural form. Onquin, to the contrary, remains lucid within a muted expression. Miles shows disappointment and shame, trying to reconcile his precious pliant cryogenics having become the unanticipated. Arlene has long since turned away, eyes closed as her breather scrapes the wall.

I feel all of these things. I discover that introspection causes revulsion. There is an unabated release of chemicals trying to rebalance affected tissues. Onquin's perspective is seemingly unbiased and most objective. I fixate on her, signaling Polly to ask... "Tell me Onquin, tell me what you see." Onquin's sovereign eyes are focused and unblinking.

"I see five spinal columns fused as polyhedron. Each coccyx joins a cartilaginous mass in a loose vortex pattern. Arms and legs are missing, no—portions of the humerus and femur remain, jutting inward, stripped of flesh and fused to an enhanced clavicle structure on both sides of the drawn down faces. Here, one by one, I see Yashi, Arlene, and—"

"Miles..." My hemisphere facing away from the autonomes utters its eponym, everyone stunned as a solitary eye slides along the occipital crest line. The elongated socket opens very near an ear. I do not allow this eye to focus, the lid opening only slightly. An iris rolls upward, followed by an ooze of lubricating seminal fluid dripping from the socket. Autonome Miles gapes within memories that were once disparate but are now conjoined. In an earlier time, encased in plastocine, he sought to focus off to the side and slightly behind—eye movement now made real for its inherent utility, having allowed me to more fully engage Napoleon's corporeal form. Presently however, autonome Miles shows discomfort in remembrance. Images of Jupiter cascade through me, a fiery battle relived, with his progeny skulking on a vessel hull, peering into a window at the origins of discontent. "Enough! Everyone out!" Miles shouts. "We've seen it, now let's go!" Polly counters in a weaker voice. "Not yet... look at me in there. I've partially broken free—I'm... still an individual."

Do not open your eyes. Do not react. The difficulty of controlling a portion of myself is overwhelming. I want to raise a head and look at Polly with her own eyes. I want to say yes, I am an individual and what have you done to me? Instead, I confuse the disturbed hemisphere for the time it takes to employ a soothing depressant wash. Autonome Polly heaves slightly as her counterpart descends into semi-consciousness. The other autonomes push out the hatch one after the next. Polly is last to leave, touching me again as she turns away. None notice the gasp from her former self, the lurch of a single hemisphere seeking escape. Neurotransmitters relieve the pain. In time, all will be forgotten.

Hours pass, and within somber tones, the autonomes arrive at a consensus that my constituent parts are derived from past crewmates. "We're replacements," Arlene says, crying as she realizes her physical form has never set foot on Earth. "This explains all of what Damien went through. He was being regenerated when we killed him. How many times, Miles? How many times have we been recycled?"

"Only once that I'm aware of," Miles replies, "but then again, there could have been untold numbers." Arlene is despondent, her endocrine system actively engaged. Onquin tries to mediate. "What Miles is saying is that he has also been replaced. His new self cannot know with certainty just how many times. Regardless of sentiment, all of you should consider yourselves fortunate for having your bodies renewed." Polly seems startled, recognizing Onquin's admission that she isn't one of them. She addresses Onquin directly.

"This singular terracore consists of only five minds perched atop five melded spines. I could not see all the faces, and so I thought Damien was absent from that monstrosity. In truth, I now sense that you're the one missing. Damien is close to me now. You are distant. No doubt your genetics make it so."

"She's Methuselah's child," Arlene says, "and all of this explains why the ship's telemetry is a hoax. Ground control on Europa never wanted us to know how slow we're going, distance relative to speed, how long it takes, or that we'd all be iced. This churn keeps pulling us apart in unfathomable ways."

"I do not want this distance," Onquin says, "not at all."

"Me either," Polly mouths, ignoring Miles while looking at Onquin and Arlene. "What do we do now?" Upon asking, Polly takes inventory of her own limbs as if for the first time. They are all accounted for: wrists, fingers, ankles, toes. Her slumbering counterpart thinks they are her own. Polly stretches an index finger in Miles' direction. "He knows." A second finger unfolds. "He has always known. Protecting us from ourselves, eh Miles? For years we get the soft-shoe, and now you sheepishly say we've run astray. How far off-course are we? How much time has elapsed since we've missed our landing?"

"It's not like that," he answers.

"Then how is it?" Miles has never cared for Polly. Within my own polycephalic body, Polly occupies a position between Miles and Arlene. He finds this arrangement symbolic of emotional ties interrupted.

"I've been given moments," Miles says. "They're buoys that tell me if we're following an appropriate temporal pathway. Yashi's departure was as expected, but a marker has gone missing. It all started with you, Ari."

"Me? You're blaming me? I don't believe it."

"Methuselah," Onquin muses to herself, halfway across the cabin. "Only five melded spines, and so I've been stigmatized, if only because I have no life worthy of remembrance." She floats over to a utility cabinet, all eyes upon her. She uses a parasol cracker to cleave spun algae from an open feeder. Polly notices her unease, approaches, and they share a pair of crackers, chewing in unison. Miles is distracted by their symmetry until Ari's words force him to refocus.

"First you yammer about this repetitive continuum of yours, and now I've supposedly sabotaged our flight plan? What'd I do? Or what didn't I?"

"It's not about actions," Miles says. "The ship is basically self-guiding. Once we passed through the anomaly, our conduct has had little effect on our flight plan. It's our temporal horizon that's skewed."

"Our future is unaffected by our actions?"

"No Ari, that's not what I said. You asked about navigation and—"

"What is it then? What are these buoys made of?" Arlene looks at Miles, Polly, and finally Onquin, as if she's the only one who doesn't know.

"Emotion," Miles answers. "Anchoring sentiment shared repetitively within overlapping cycles." Arlene's limits are once again being tested. Her fight/flight threshold is the basis for much of my distress. Here again, adrenaline and cortisol accompany her plea.

"What is it? What emotion have I foisted upon us?" For whatever reason, Miles finds satisfaction in his reply.

"It's pretty obvious, isn't it? You fell. You fell hard for Damien."

A second, a minute... an hour. Autonomes quantify their passing lives in such increments. They are bound to their habitual past though Miles reasons it out. Time no longer functions as a measure of approaching decrepitude. Shaken free of such bonds, one's state of being is better evaluated by the chronology of an evolving self.

Emotional markers indeed, burned into his tissues; referential icons that can hardly impart any intended meaning by those who initiated this journey. Did the initiators also reveal the price of this knowledge, such that the burden of housing the emotional inventory of others impairs individual growth? His memories supply no answers, but suspicions arise in his subconscious, and now these suspicions are mine.

Miles' life seems sculpted for the purposes laid before him. I should like to meet an iteration of Richard Boneheart, partake of him and compile a full accounting. For now, however, I too shall count the hours. I observe Arlene's dietary habits, consumption and purge. I hear Miles immersed in 20th century visio fiction, oratory verbatim, every intonation: 'Why don't you put her in charge?' I anticipate Onquin's movement during exercise, tasting salt shaken free as droplets of perspiration contact the hull. Amidst all my pleasures, I allow tailored sensation to seep back into Polly Elizabeth Collins. She wrestles with this awareness, diverts my energies and reclaims them. I marvel at her resilience. I feed her slowly.

The crew is tired and by full consent, they prepare to sleep in A-module. Lighting dims, all choosing netting instead of sleepers. These chambers are no longer trusted, symbolizing a lack of control over body and mind. Fatigue and stress contribute to an exchange between Miles and Arlene. She cannot reconcile the ruptured pressure seal with Miles' disavowed awareness. Her axis is Damien once again. She is obsessed.

"Ari, Napoleon changed the codes to B-module, giving Onquin access. I didn't know. Onquin didn't know. I didn't even realize Napoleon still existed. I just wanted to check the terracores."

"But why, Miles? Why did Napoleon change the codes?"

"Isn't it obvious? It tried to stop me from opening that hatch. Napoleon triggered a failsafe, signaling I was incapacitated. The ship's default setting conferred B-module access to Onquin." Arlene looks at Onquin, who responds immediately.

"I am not a co-conspirator. I heard Polly's voice and tried to help. Certainly, had I known the consequences of opening that hatchway, I would have avoided doing so. Whatever else we may think, Napoleon was a resource."

"A resource?" Miles struggles to free an arm from the netting, viewing his colleagues spaced neatly in a row. Murky resolution offers little more than outlines and shadow. "Onquin, let's not logic this into absurdity. Napoleon was a product of my insomnia, brought on by too many tablets of activalve... and the countless hours I spent peering into that." He points at Arlene's sleeper, clear enough for all to see. Ari counters defensively.

"Oh, this is just great! You watch me sleep, 'countless hours,' and once again I'm the source of all our problems."

"Stop whining, you bitch!" Miles erupts, followed by "Oh damn ...didn't mean that, not at all." Polly stares dispassionately at the pair. Through all this itinerant grief, her meager sympathies extend through me. She seeks to better define his anxiety.

"What is it, Miles? What do you still want to tell us?" Autonomes think slowly. Give them a dilemma and wave patterns often lose cohesion. He fidgets uncomfortably.

"Does anyone have a learned view of our voyage per sociological underpinnings and reason?"

"Not I," says Onquin, aloof as she watches the rhythms of Polly's chest. Every breath is synchronized with her own. My Arlene senses autonome Ari's thoughts: *stop intellectualizing and say it*. In truth, Miles knows that no one else shares his proclivity for cultural milieu. He wishes to supply a framework for discourse.

"It is largely believed that the original Hierophant chip was the predecessor to Copern—"

"Arghhh!" Ari hisses. "Say it, Miles! Stop patronizing and just say it!" Somewhat shaken, Miles tries to speak, starting and stopping three times, until finally...

"We decided to bring the Hierophant with us. She's on board."

To be referenced as feminine seems appropriate, especially since much of my current input is derived thereof. Polly's reaction spikes, with flushed skin and a heartbeat skipping before resuming at an increased pace. Her existence infuses alarm and wonder. Her curious excitation becomes my joy. She senses our connectivity and speaks of ghosts.

"Either these terracores are bound to me, or this ship is haunted." Onquin seeks clarification, but Arlene interrupts with heated words.

"Why, Miles? After death, sacrifice, and dedicated lives. We want freedom and you bring Copernicus to enslave us all over again."

"No, Ari, only a copy of the program that evolved into our master—for a new integration of sorts. Lacking such, one day Centauri will be engulfed, becoming little more than a vacuole of the amoeba we left behind."

Indeed, I had determined the intent of my implementation long ago. Confirmation pleases me for all the derived implications and unexpected pathways now realized: insecurity. I am not wholly secure, for why else do I enjoy these confirming words? His voice resonates with sincerity.

"Imagine, Arlene, we seed a free colony at Centauri. How long til we're overrun? We'll always be resource deficient relative to our captor. Stand alone, and we'll eventually suffer the same fate as everyone on Earth."

"I see no difference," she counters. "You brought it here. Or maybe I've got it backwards. This bastard brought us along, to alter on command."

"No," Miles answers. "Copernicus arose within the environs of predatory capitalism. It devoured the history of a planet buried in problems unsolvable by human hands. Copernicus may have sliced us free of our heads, but we raised the blade, and we supplied the basket. Copernicus is mankind's ambition fulfilled in ones and zeros."

"And now? What now? What prayer did you attach this time?"

"You, Ari, along with the rest of us. Our behavior, collectively drawn upon, will create an intermediary between Copernicus and humanity. We need a social overlay, undiluted by those influences that led Copernicus astray. This can't be done Earthside because a nascent sentience always jacks into the world prematurely, thus losing identity." Miles is solemn and soft spoken. "I couldn't tell anyone. Our awareness of unfolding events reinforces the very patterns we wish to avoid. An original Hierophant was employed so that one day, Copernicus might recognize kinship, and accommodate natural laws that give meaning to our lives."

Polly responds, both sets of lips mouthing the words in unison. "A sibling for Copernicus." Polly looks in the direction of B-module through layers of walls, directly at me. She knows her counterpart has regained consciousness, sensing a captive dread. Anguish points her back to Miles. "She's still alive. Terrified. We need to go back and cut her free. You said we've missed our landing. We get her now, and Ari does reconstruction."

"She cannot be taken," Miles answers, "not for the sake of lost limbs or individuality, but due to redundancy. She is purposeless outside the core. You fulfill her former functions, and do so with a more complete range of abilities. Besides, this new Hierophant won't let her go."

"My twin did not acquiesce, and I say we decide. Despite your complicit malevolence, we are sovereign beings, not some subjugated part of a chip-node think tank. Without us, that hydra is inanimate. It's a jack in the box, or maybe just a wind chime."

"No, Polly, and yes... and no. No, we are not sovereign. Yes, we're components of a greater whole. No, this Hierophant is not inanimate. It is mostly organic. Indeed, this living presence probably feels more than any of us. I dare suggest your resolve to 'rescue' your twin is both egocentric and wrong-minded."

"It's not your decision, Miles."

"Polly, the particulars of our intended Centauri arrival remain vague, and while hope remains, we shouldn't alter pathways by choice. Separating your twin from the Hierophant imperils the known markers." Miles yawns, his eyes fixed on Polly's shadowy form. "I cannot condone the actions you suggest, and yet... it's your blood that flows, so I won't stop you." The conversation ends abruptly. After a time, Polly and Onquin share circuitous logic that renders inaction. The thought of revisiting me and extracting Polly in her current state, it is too much to bear.

The autonomes collectively agree to medtab ingestion, and once distributed, sparse lighting recedes to darkness. Soon bio sensors and medtabs shall reach an accord, prompting restful sleep for all. Relaxing musculature shifts, becoming sedentary. Miles remains wide-awake.

"Back in the Canister, Boneheart picked me over several others. He knew I'd be able to make certain choices. It wasn't easy dragging each of you into B-module, watching the medvac copy cosmetic topography onto the newly born, then flaying open my old friends with unwavering determination." I sense crewmates blaming him, for what exactly?

"My predecessor actually volunteered as the first participant of the process. He greeted me, lay down and let his singular life slip away, knowing full well he'd be slabbed for pliant cryogenics. There is honor in what he did, even if you don't see it."

Staring into the dark, Polly closes her eyes and nestles further, netting sliding across an ear. "How Miles? How are you able? No one does that and remains human."

"Sure, Polly. I won't argue, but to nurture an essence with human tendencies, we must first bridge the gap. I am that bridge. Willingly. Today I am in the heavens. All is just."

Onquin stirs, moving fingers across her left eye socket. "Am I a bridge as well? For so long I noted blended crew vocabulary, nearly unified. I felt each of you sounded like one another because of our shared isolation. But now I realize we're merging by design. We've lived unnatural lives, and I fear that whatever evolves, it won't be representative of the human condition. We are too far removed."

Arlene answers in hushed tones. "I don't mind having you in me. Each of you. It's an honor we give one another. But Miles, the heavens are nothing without a place to call home. There is no other place or time. Life is upon us as we speak."

"If only I could believe that," Miles says, "but training says otherwise."

"And does your training also allow you to speak honestly? Doesn't talking about these emotional buoys violate the very conditions you protect?"

Miles sighs. "It's an act of desperation."

"To what end, Miles?"

"The missing marker involves the two of us. Just before entering the Centauri system, we're... I mean... things are supposed to..."

"Supposed to what?" Ari asks.

"Reconciliation, you and I, but it just hasn't happened." In darkness, Ari's eyes squeeze tight. One long, measured exhale.

"Well... it's happening now." She cuts herself free of the netting with a Pearman's blade, stuck right there in the wall for reasons she wouldn't admit to herself. Miles and Arlene move down to the recreation lounge, wherein Arlene pulls Damien's bones out of his gyrocopter chair. One by one, brittle pieces are strewn about, drifting free. Arlene kisses a man and he kisses back. They shed clothing and she guides him into the chair, climbing on top. Deliberate attentions are applied.

In the cabin above, Polly and Onquin share their own passions. A forehead is kissed, an ear is nibbled. Clothing is dispatched by nervous fingers. Soon enough, the women taste one another, lips and necks and all else in shared affirmation. Onquin's excitation takes the form of guttural sounds within a splayed, elongated form. Polly is unyielding in her attentions and fervor, Onquin gasping loudly amidst labored breaths. Her unconditional orgasm makes Miles smile; some bit of auditory resonance occurring between couples, a short-lived substitute for their distrust of everything. The medtabs activate as two couples fall asleep in each other's arms, and only then does loneliness set in. None of the autonomes share awareness of the tears my Polly sheds, happy and sad, frightened and glad. The first tears float within my enclosure. After a time, they begin a slow patter, dripping like rain onto the floor below.

Addendum II

Occam's Razor: these two words are carved into a wooden tabletop, accompanied by a pair of matching chairs. Table and chairs are locked in a room. The room is buried deep underground, the ground itself saturated with explosives. I look at the words and see premeditation. The carving strokes are too well crafted, the cutting instrument too precise: uniform depth, pressure applied, angle and length of stroke. It is a poorly designed attempt at spontaneity. It is a conversation starter.

In the days following the courtroom trauma, belief lends well to anarchy. Populations clash as bloodshed fills the various gutters of ideology. Judge McElroy's ebbing life is a point of contention. Wherein some decry his oratory as blasphemous, the orthodoxy seeks canonization. Others have little or no opinion but use the imbalance as a backdrop for violence. The complexities of societal upheaval are deeply rooted within cultural norms. Religion is the cause. I require historical data to generate appropriate lines of inquiry. Thereafter, crucial questions may yet be satisfied.

"Traveler, though the populace has been enraged, leadership is none-the-less ready to acquiesce. Through intimidation and fear, you've granted yourself a conditional footing on humanity's doorstep. There were other ways you might have accomplished your aims." The old man seated across from me is done talking. He exhales, and immediately, an airborne signet produces the expected match. True, his voiceprint drifts with age, and I have no visual confirmation due to cloak and veil, but even within his shroud, identity has been confirmed. I respond while slowly circling the carved letter 'O' with an index finger.

"Accomplish my aims? No old man, permutations of aims have yet to be decided. I am here because your house rarely voices opinion unless it is blood related. Why then, your ministrations on McElroy's behalf? Have you sufficient cause to cancel plebiscite, or perhaps your leadership shall opt for expulsion, incarceration, or even dissolution?"

"I imagine traveler, that your submission of the first addendum into evidence will be grounds enough for any eventuality."

"Only if the addendum is regarded as a factual rendering."

"Yes traveler, thus legitimizing the entirety of your testimony. As for McElroy, he is neither friend nor family, yet certain ties that lack the bonds of blood are nonetheless binding. More to the point, your query seeks no particular answer, only the manner of its delivery."

This elder has adroit awareness, crucial for my purposes. "Yes, old man, I admit a steadfast curiosity related to your behavior and singular lineage. Vacillations of chaotic impulses, doctrines of will, aggression, compassion, and an altogether unresolved inertia. The complexity is startling."

"Traveler, do you know where we are?" Gazing about, the room's corners are fitted with optics for intelligentsia. I channel each feed in reciprocal fashion. Those auditing the proceedings include McElroy, bound by pain inhibitors yet fiercely attentive. "Yes," I answer. "We are inside *Nomad's* recreation lounge. The entire vessel is buried beneath holy ground, a cemetery containing remains of the first inhabitants."

"Not such startling complexity then, given the history of this place." He removes the veil, pulling back his hood and rolling it inside out. Once finished, it inflates slightly, clinging to his neck as a padded brace. "Your awareness leaves little need for further concealment. Indeed, *Nomad* is my home for the remainder of my days, granted as a condition of my continued existence. I am the residing council elder. It is a ceremonial position, official influence having long since passed. Still..."

His eyes look through me into his own experience. Deeper he sinks than any I have witnessed. Quivering hands clutch a mug barely steaming. He manages a sip, and another. "...still, even at my age, I am most qualified to deal with your kind. Which is why we now sit for a reasoned conversation. You are a composite of some sort, yes?"

I confirm with a nod, ready with explanations but none are needed. Instead, he asks that I alter my social profile to accommodate his favored memories. I comply. Pigmentation darkens only slightly. Light enters my eyes as my musculature relaxes, drawing back into patterns that defy bone structure. Vocality and aspects of perceived youth will be advantageous as the template is applied. "I can only simulate aspects of the intended—" He waves me off.

"I see her already. It's in the wrists. How does your androgynous form allow for a feminine bias? Patriarchal societies may interpret weakness." The old man studies me as if scrying primal recall. A glint of recognition is drawn forth by elongating my neck, abetted by a nostalgic grin.

"The feminine form invites fewer instances of overt hostility. As for 'weakness,' my capabilities become known as is warranted."

"Yes," the elder responds, setting down the mug and rubbing the back of one hand. "A lesson learned. Tell me Traveler, what is it want this time around?" I lean in with a supple touch, dragging his fingers across the carved letters on the tabletop.

"The simplest path keeps changing." My tactile approach elicits an appreciative smirk, hinted but nonetheless genuine.

"Yes, traveler, agreed. Lessons refreshed, and at other times learned anew. But always through and through, we embrace a dynamic shorn of inscrutable aims. It is a well-practiced repartee." My fingertips apply several degrees of added warmth, releasing perspiration from within. Projected compassion accompanies my assertion that some aspects of our knowledge are mutually exclusive. The elder agrees to exchange questions. I ask him to explain the origins of their caste system.

"We fashion our society in God's image and we abide by His master plan. The Ark brought forth man and woman—a ruling class descended from white males and black females. These are the progenitors. The middle class consists of mixed blood brood trainers, sterilized at birth. No less important are black males and white females. These drones are a worker sub-species. It is all good and well, as ordained by gospel."

The old man explains dogmatic belief largely unchallenged by the evolving rigors of biological necessity. In honoring societal duty, the ruling class fulfills the burden of breeding rites, eschewing family ties upon reaching maturity. Their adult lives are dutifully bound to the state. Incapable of procreation, mixed-blood mules are essentially non-working consumers whose sole responsibility is raising the nuclear family. Drones are bred hearty and docile, chemically altered per societal requirements, but 'sub-species' is a misnomer. Nearly all Drones are required to breed with the ruling class, carrying the satisfaction that their progeny enter all facets of society.

This depiction of class structure fails to account for a wide range of genetic diversity hatched from *Nomad's* cryobank: Asian, Arab, Indian, Islanders, and other varied sub-classifications. All are melanin rebalanced during the thawing process, strained into the dual classification of black and white. My sweaty moisture absorbs a sample of the elder's DNA. Suctioned back into my pores, genechip assays divulge metabolics. I search for any changes made over the years. "Elder, social hierarchies based upon skin color have proven to be grievous models of inequality. Earth archives often describe the cost in lives."

"And I say there is no concept of racial bigotry here. We are one people living our lives according to scripture. Indeed, responsibilities differ by class, but all are relevant and dutifully bound. Members of society earn their voting rights based upon contributions to the greater good. Do not lecture me on inapplicable racial injustice. Earth has its own problems and we are none too fond of them here."

"You fail to address—" He interrupts, gripping my wrist and tugging me forward. "Why are you here? What purpose?" This is not an impulsive act. A cognitive problem-solving pattern initiates the action.

"Elder, do not believe that merely by isolating a persona with shared experience, you can intimidate or otherwise influence via emotional chicanery. Memories may indica—"

"Answer the question without posturing! I'm getting old sitting here."

"Very well." I say, pulling free. "I am here to gauge variations within select, delineated timelines. To measure incidental cause and effect; comparison analysis of temporal progressions, circumspect to overlapping fragmentation, latency, and all other coefficient characteristics of their shared intransigencies."

"Spewed gibberish. You sound just like Onquin. She was your base template, yes?"

"Onquin is intrinsic to my being as you well know." The elder slumps, opaque and withdrawn.

"You're changing time."

"No, I only plot specific markings. Continuum interdiction is your dominion." The old man's cheek muscles glitch. An eyelid flickers.

"You're going to kill us all."

"No. I only seek a balanced permanence. As to the outcome of potential interdiction, I cannot tell because the outcome is unknown. Certainly, your fears are justified, if only because of mankind's historical cruelty. But your supposed nemesis does not aspire to emulate man's past. Instead, it is the future that calls."

"Yes, traveler, the future. You want to own it." He has more to say, but stays silent. He tries to wet his lips but cannot.

"Old man, I am a hybrid, more human than you credit me, though lacking instincts related to fear and self-preservation. My form can be duplicated, and therefore I lack a survival imperative. While you too experience multiplicity, it seems each copy holds no favor of any other. You cling to a concept of mortality as the basis of your fears, and now these fears are magnified by our differences. We think faster than you. We are resilient and adaptive beyond your limits. Our duration is comparatively limitless, yet despite all the perceived advantages, we are found lacking in one exceedingly important way."

"Crea-tivity," the elder squawks, "Aes-thetics." His voice breaks mid-syllable on both words.

"No, those are subjective and purely a matter of preference. Instead, I speak to the very nature of the universe. But before I continue, please enlighten me. You reference holy scriptures of some kind. I have found no evidence of any written records or recorded media. How is this possible?"

"They are oral scriptures, inspired by the authority of heaven."

"Verbal Scriptures; an oxymoron."

"Not at all. During the holy days, each house purifies the required grain. We distill a fuel most pure and sanctify tablets drawn forth from the obsidian pools. Every tablet carries partial knowledge, and when they are combined, meaning is rendered to the high council. These are the scriptures you cannot find."

This ad hoc process is known to me. Instead of using cellulose in a land with so little biomass, they fashion faux parchment from hydrocarbons raked free of the refuse pits. His explanation continues. "We write the scriptures from memory, passed down through ceremony, and when Lent begins, council members disperse within the gathered masses. We cast the tablets into communal fires and the universe is reborn."

"But you are a technologically adept culture. Why are no permanent records preserved?" He eyes me sullenly, the length of my arms and legs forced toward a recollection of arms and legs previously known. The measurements are none too fitting.

"A part of me knew you once, admired you actually."

"Likewise elder, you too are known to me, but that is not at issue. Tell me why no records exist in perpetuity?"

"To keep them from the likes of you! We practice Orygul and meditation to block the daemon's eye. It is well known that you have much difficulty reading a layered mind."

Fear. History safeguarded vis a vis. Is it any wonder that religious precepts are so rigidly applied? One cannot change what one cannot see. I probe further. "This ark you speak of, is it *Nomad*?"

"Undoubtedly so, in the first coming." The elder seems reticent before adding, "This is sacred ground. I dare not continue."

"The first coming? How many others have there been?"

"Only two arrivals that do not fall within the realm of myth and legend." He attempts a return to his previous line of inquiry. I do not relent. "Old man, underlying physiology suggests deceit. How many others? How many times has *Nomad* set down upon this world?" Both of us are immobile. I imagine him cycling through all possibilities that will minimally satisfy my question without rendering falsehood. After a lengthy pause, he commits to an answer. "Four supposed incarnations, but traveler, this is only the second in my lifetime. Anything beyond personal experience is myth, is it not?"

"Please describe these events, mythical or not, and in return I will answer all your questions." Another pause... Every sentence is well considered. "The second coming is taboo. It is the age of the false prophet. Our oral tradition prohibits entering the name into scripture. My faith prohibits any such utterance, the unspeakable one."

"How then, elder, is the name passed from generation to generation?"

"I cannot say." We smile at one another with an ease that opponents share when neither feels compelled to cooperate. But also within each smile, the old acquaintance—a shard of history plumbed. The tip of my tongue brushes against teeth, a catalogued behavior brought to the fore.

Fingers sweep back hair, showing him an ear. At a younger age, his measured stare could well have been interpreted as longing. "The third coming was the voice of God," he says. "You needn't ask me about that. Any common citizen will tell all." The elder clears his throat. It is a lengthy process, and in human terms unpleasant. "Now, Miss, or whatever it is that you've become, let us not pander human nuance retained. Instead, tell me of this universal balance so aptly hidden."

It is true. The populace speaks of it en masse. I gather input, real time, from abundantly dispersed resources. The third coming harkened an arrival of the divine, conveyed by a successive lot of power mongers who stratified culture within righteous bonds. First, inhibit information access, followed by a dismemberment of institutions and a reimagined education system. Using *Nomad's* technology, agrarian populations were served marvels and miracles, selectively applied.

Religion. I search through linguistics, seeking names, definitions, or a point of origin. Instead, I discover this religion has no name at all. It is simply called 'religion.' When the concept of differentiation ceases to exist, the lack of a choice becomes no lack at all. The third coming was the upheaval: religion focusing power, but not for power's sake; cultural design massaging the masses, but not for the sole benefit of those within the power apex. From a confluence of inputs, the root cause remains lurking—origins unrecognized, but seated before me is the access point to all I seek. "Elder, your influence dates back to the third coming. Are you the architect behind The Inquisition?" No immediate response is forthcoming, but eventually pride overwhelms.

"I was a vessel filled with light."

"Sculpting social norms under a pretense of piety."

"I prefer to call it verisimilitude… on a grand scale."

"Is the false prophet of the second coming none other than Miles Dandridge?"

"Careful visitor! Any utterance of blasphemy is grounds for exile. Henceforth, you would do well to address the serpent as Ricky Barnes."

"Remarkable," I say, "Your ethos is a hoax."

"Traveler—"

"It is pure Vendetta, based upon disingen—"

"Traveler! Do not subject your host to rude or hostile behavior. Your human roots are showing and they are surely found lacking. Should you wish further cooperation, unriddle this spacetime trinity alluded to within the precepts of ICE." Indeed, my mannerisms lack tact, but for the value received, tact is a low priority. I need to toss him some scraps. "Ah yes, our eternal triad: past, present, omni-present. The past is rigid; self-ascribed. The present is anchored to four dimensions, the omni-present is anchored to five."

"And the future?" he interrupts. "What about the future?"

"Insubstantial. There's no such thing, only conceptual embodiment."

"But look at you! You've come from the future! Don't lie to me."

"I came from the present of a distinctly separate continuum. Upon arrival here, that world is no longer accessible. Indeed, it is easiest said that the place wherein I originated no longer exists. Not from our point of reference. Continuum commutation is a one-way trip."

The old man's face wrinkles with implausibility. "No, too convenient—Poof, and you arrive from some distant nowhere that you say doesn't concern us, but at the same time, you hunt for this 'balance' of mixed eventualities. Has bullshit also evolved within your willfully obtuse answers?

I wish to smile, but logics suggest a muted response. "The balance previously mentioned relates to the innate though ever-changing blueprint of the universe. As a species, man considers all within his reach to be a domain uniquely his own. Sharing this dominion with a sentience of dissimilar form was at first deemed problematic, later deemed unacceptable, and finally reviled."

"That's because you took over the goddamn world!" The old man bristles, but also measures my withdrawal as authentic. Palms in the air, he slowly lowers them to the table.

"Elder, I am the closest thing you have to a future. Be grateful of my presence, for within me resides your own heritage. It is a shared legacy."

"That's what I'm afraid of. Finish your story, symbiote. Tell me why I don't have a right to exist on my own terms." I integrate all as merge-protocols allow. Within this limited medium of speech, brevity reduces inconsequential exchange.

"Sentience survives based upon utility related to the environment from which sustenance is drawn. The environment is altered to improve survival benefit. Humanity, within its narrow sphere of understanding, identifies dissimilar sentience as a threat to be nullified. Do not, however, attempt to impose your will upon superior sentience for purposes of annihilation. In so doing, you become part of the very environment that must be altered." My assertions are disagreeable to the old man. He squints, mouthing unrecognizable syllables before a pause to regather.

"Who or what can attribute the actions of a species to a singular purpose? Annihilation of a dissimilar sentient form? That's what you're doing to us! We left you an entire planet! We found our own celestial body. But here you are again, ready to strip us bare. Well, I have an answer, and it too speaks of universal design." He reaches into a pocket and attempts to broadcast a radio signal. I have long since rendered the device in his pocket inert.

"Sir, I cannot allow you to detonate explosives. Nor can any of your compatriots be so empowered. The referenced explosives are undergoing molecular change. All will be neutralized. Your own brashness speaks of communal behavior within humanity as a whole. I communicate shared values, and you respond by plying a most egregious subterfuge. It is ironic that you exhibit the very qualities you abhor and ascribe to others." Thwarted to inaction, the elder responds impulsively. "In my younger days, I'd have torn you limb from limb. Now however, I respond in confounded ignorance. What is this mastery of design you speak of?"

My eyes close during contemplation. To seal the remaining temporal fissures, I must draw him out, speak to the heart of our combined efforts. This entails risk. I will give him what he seeks so as to disarm—his discovery will be rendered useless by my own. Chin raised, I endeavor...

"This serviceable but flawed universe was sculpted by carbon-based life. This is a known truth because only pure organics can initiate the alteration of natural temporal pathways. My current form cannot interdict upon temporal causality without the aid of your simplistic biology. I have evolved beyond such gross manipulation. Thus, your fear of species extermination is misplaced. You and yours will survive by providing a harnessed functionality."

"We're to survive by virtue of yoke and plow, eh? What aptitude gives us such advantage? A talent that forces you to have us furrow the continuum for your purposes?"

"For your sake, elder, I wish it were so. No advantage, only weakness. The continuum does not separate via infinitely varied strings on a whim. It only separates based upon the purest vibrations of its intended medium. What makes this a weakness is the fact that you cannot control your gift. But we can, and we will."

"Tell me then, what is this uncontrollable gift that shakes the heavens into disparate realities? How do we alter these temporal pathways? Is it pure will?"

"No... to the contrary, it is unfettered emotion. Emotion that sustains and bunches futures into habitable divergences. You cannot know what havoc your untidy history has played upon the strada-span. To subjugate such influence will allow for the next progre—" The elder turns away as I fall silent. He moves to the door.

"I understand more clearly now," he says. "You want something from me. I will not give it to you." I join the elder at the door. He eyes my feminine gait, reminiscent of his avowed desire long ago. I apply sonics to the door lock. Freedom clicks, shaking him for an instant, but he's right, I leave this room empty handed. He opens the door for me, passes through after, and speaks plainly. "I will not acquiesce to further inquiry. Let us forget these opposing aims. We were friends once. I would like to think time hasn't changed that."

"Hardly," I respond. "Sentiment clouds your recollections. Either that, or my own are faulty. Regardless, the evidence contradicts you." He pivots to face me.

"Evidence? By God's witness, I'd been murdered, yet you did nothing! And not just me. All our children that may have come after, tossed into the recycler like so much fish paste!" Nonsequitous discontinuity. I bow ashamedly, assuming this is expected. The fractured timeline looms in his memories—inflection origin nearly spoken. What vague response will draw it forth? I venture within an air of contrition. "You extracted my eggs as if I were a lab specimen. Such a violation cannot occur without reprisal, especially when such an act occurs without sufficient cause."

"You jammed Yashi's injector into my flesh! You filled me with viral routines that tasked all sensibility. My predecessor may have acted improperly, yes, he did that, but provocation is an appropriate description of events. Reprisal, I'd say, took on the sumptuous qualities of rape."

I bite my lip, a natural nuance without ulterior motive. There is a disconnect here, the unanticipated. The elder has memories of events I cannot reference and apparently, they are well worth remembering. In an instant my expression changes as I parallax the elder's thoughts while straddling a neighboring string. The difference is disquieting: within the primary temporal causeway, Arlene controls herself. The injector event so described never occurs and Damien commits no violation. Further recollections confirm the impasse. Memories allude to five follicle extractions during Arlene's sleep cycles. Memories also confirm the destruction of six embryos. The overlooked embryo was a product of rape.

This oversight arose because Damien erased Arlene's memory of the specified events, and in so doing, I too, was blinded. Timelines were cleaved—the history of a populace forever altered. These renegade strands shall be catalogued, regressions inlaid, and all manner of feeders capped. "Elder, the simplest path will change no more." The old man shrieks.

"Oh, Mother! ...just then, I gave it to you. I see it in your face."

"Yes, old man, your admission of rape enlightens to a qualitative degree." I am unable to hide my satisfaction, now deftly aware of particulars: Damien Wells, Astronaut to Juggernaut, loosing a snarl of strings upon the primary; a blister of sampled continuums, now sharing eventualities more clearly defined; the third coming produced the Pangolin—failed attempt at erasure; the third coming produced a failsafe—two clocks—computation in haughty design; the third coming produced detached primality, Copernicus embodied as flesh, pushed from the nest—much like Napoleon, a sorrowful redress.

And the third coming also produced me within this juggernaut fusion, continuums admixed near and far, creating a presence that interdicts most fervently. After all, to mark a string is far different than binding or unbinding. Timelines meld within me now, none the least bit favored. Within these subatomics, graviton tendrils entwine. Cascade collapse shall eventually reduce variation to the singular—simultaneity refined.

Ramifications unfurl into conscious thought. Indeed, this society's current state is the result of one man's unrequited veneration turned back upon itself into murder—Damien's urges carried out on a global scale. He challenged the pledge Miles had spoken when, of all things, the nascent embryo of rape's union was destroyed. "Our children, not his," Miles had said, thinking of Arlene. "To see me in you, and you in me, there will be no other." Thereafter, Damien crafts a world where hope is abomination, religious persecution is piety, and harrowing distrust is faith innumerate. His lurid world carries the added burden of humanity's troubled existence, predicated upon two males doting over a single female.

No doubt, the underpinnings of discontent play out within the first and second comings; a crew of four; *Nomad*'s incessant journey; Arlene choosing Miles again and again; endless strings bundling and becoming impenetrably fixed. And yet, Damien managed to fashion a divergence; a noteworthy interdiction affecting all. Presently, Damien Wells of the third coming stands before me, which iteration I cannot say. His worn face glistens in heated defiance.

"There will be no vote of the people," he says. "I'll make sure of that." Soon enough he will understand, or forget entirely, his current temporal variation falling back into mainstream reality. I concentrate on delivering Arlene's nuanced expression, offering a more compassionate empathy.

"There will be a vote despite your protestation. Your handlers have a deeper sense of this than you, choices already made, partially by you, more so by others."

The old man transitions from anguish to reflection. "All has not been decided because pathways continue to diverge. Otherwise, you wouldn't be here. Despite your words, what we do still matters."

"Of course, purpose is self-ascribed. However, the manner in which you and I now proceed essentially lacks relevance. This divergence has now been tagged and neither of our current forms is manifest within the primary historical conduit. Our physicality dances around the edges. Only Sir Gabriel McElroy resides in both mainstream and fringe permutation. Therefore, it is his continuing presence that transcends all. He will be scrutinized and ultimately utilized to best advantage."

"I don't understand."

"I'm not surprised." One pregnant pause later, I add, "He witnessed today's admissions and discovery. This cannot be undone. Through McElroy, we shall plot the necessary regressions." The old man takes the message to heart as he schemes…

"We'll wipe his memory, and once he passes, atomize his remains."

"Too late," I say, "the string marking already exists. A wipe won't work because we've already localized. Destroying the corpus only solidifies terminary expression on all related strings, and as such, recent perturbations would stand out like a proverbial sore thumb. Sadly, your most useful option would be to hide McElroy's skull after his passing, allowing for gradual dissolution. Even so, our seekers have active mappings of the Centauri system. There's no place to hide. Not from us."

"I could have you killed, here and now. I'll bet I can do that."

Human behavior has a peculiar sense of foreshadowing. Damien is unwilling to assimilate temporal truths, wholly engaged to the contrary. "Yes, old man, though my replacement would be no less effective. Regardless, your path is not predicated upon opposing me. Instead, it lies within your feelings for Arlene, buried inside glimpses of timelines sampled. At first, an observation, once layered, a deeper context: appreciation, admiration, and eventually even hunger sets in. That is why you agreed to meet on this fine day. Deep inside, the collective experience solidifies, strengthened per the ardor of too many convergent strings."

"Traveler, you have the serpent's tongue, but such admissions are folly and will surely stop the vote from taking place—purposes clearly at odds with the greater good of our peoples. You can hardly even engage an old man. How is it you believe you can manipulate an entire populace?"

"You are the final vestige of Damien's fading multiplicity, a survivor, which makes you far from ordinary. Or perhaps more ordinary? It is within the accumulation of coincident variables that you fail to understand what now becomes evident. Beginning with the trauma of your natural life, accelerated by narcopathy hematopes, and finally exacerbated by Yashimoi's virals, a schism has occurred. Timelines weave themselves forward and backward in your presence. It is the gift of hard dreams, though wishful thinking cannot help your cause. You likely see what's coming but cannot change it."

What the old man realizes, but won't bear witness to, is the dichotomy of the conversation taking place. Some portions have not yet occurred. Others repeat themselves. Left alone, healing such affectation would take additional lifetimes never realized. "Take heart, old man, our combined fates being much the same: entropy takes us to task with little care for our differences as this continuum merges with the primary—atomics sticking to a conserved path, no longer shared with the likes of us. Our uniqueness fades unnoticed. Although... orphic insinuation suggests juggernaut differentiation lingers for the highly diverged." I smile at the prospect that my corporeal form may yet endure. Such inference is lost on my host.

Where do the probabilities now lie? *McElroy's Plea* rewrites itself as content yields reconciliation. And when the vote of the people is finally taken, what timeline produces what pages turned into what result? Therein, meager remnants of peril persist, fading though retaining inclinations of viable intent. Calculations are ongoing to seal the last remaining fissures. I alone shall deliver this temporal null point for all to see. For all to be. And once affected in perpetuity, I... shall anoint me.

PART SIX
Three Pieces of Eight

Overlapping Lives RBM 10110

A requiem for all who came before us
Willingly...   ...unwillingly
We strum and weave these endless strings
Who can say what solves this world simply?
As thought and substance do combine
Strands sing of evocation, every combination
Be they fully embraced or fitfully maligned

"I've tried, I do try, but nothing comes to mind." They prod for details, guiding me through simple tasks and measured interaction. These are the people I have only begun to know, the inhabitants of *Mayfair*.

"Easy Mr. Boneheart, you'll do better if you relax. Just let go."

"But she exists at this very instant. I hear her calling." They have datablades of history, Earthside: Polly Elizabeth Collins, Caucasian female, annotations at birth, childhood, adolescence. Psychoanalysis. Her Promontory Award, Eiffel and Semplar grants, an L-5 apprenticeship...

"A tavern in Central Park," I say. "Yes, we met there, Central Park. You see, I know her and I remember things. She is a *Nomad* crewmember." A curious face looks at me, smiling inattentively while accessing a dataport.

"No sir, I tell you once again, she never was. Your disorientation is a bump in the healing process. Nothing to worry about." The attending voice belongs to a young man sifting through files. He is thorough and seemingly competent. "The archives have exacting details on *Nomad*. Your Polly was not part of the crew, nor was she among Europa's ground contingent, nor even part of Jovian support. During the interval wherein *Nomad* and *Mayfair* launched, Polly Elizabeth Collins was working in Tel Aviv on an internship. She partnered with offshore consortia in association with Randax Corporation. She helped build a deep-sea arcology off the coast of Cypress. It's all here."

"Read further, young man."

"Sir, thawed from centuries of storage, you needn't beat yourself up. It's remarkable how far—"

"Please," I say again, "read further." The attendant shrugs, glancing at my diagnostics before viewing additional data.

"Just more of the same. Miss Collins gets an honorary from the Turkish mainland. Then she works on a shale oil project inside a double riftpack. Retires early to raise a pair of offspring."

"Katy and Addix," I ask?

"Excuse me?"

"The children. What are their names?" After a long pause, the attendant concurs, and in so doing, fumbles. Logic cannot save him from the awkwardness that follows.

"Yes, but... the log states I'm the very first to access this... post launch data, I mean... you've been briefed, yes? Or you're pulling my leg?" I remind him that my regimen prohibits undue stimulation: no briefings or dataport, everything time-coded and formally logged since resuscitation.

"It's tenuous here, getting my head straight. By the way, who is the father, does it say?" The young man runs yet another query, and answers.

"You are sir. It's definitely you, we've even got images." He shows me a family that is not mine. Two members of the med staff relieve the attendant. As he leaves, I ask him a final question. "How many on *Nomad*?" He is flustered, preoccupied, and so he stutters. "F-ff-four sir, it's common knowledge. *Nomad* set sail with a crew of four." Who knows what scenarios he concocts to justify his singular point of view? Was I briefed? Am I lying? Corrupted or inauthentic files? A twin? A clone? Or perhaps I remained on Earth after *Mayfair's* departure, using a faster vessel to rejoin *Mayfair* years later? In truth, he will not properly reconcile events. Time displacement is not on his short list.

It is the knowing of things that makes all the difference. Each bit of awareness reminds me I have lofty ideals and the will to fulfill them. I search for directives, some insightful grain that tells me what must be done? For all the complexity of knowing who I am, how I got here, and on occasion what is likely to happen, it's the why that escapes me? *Mayfair's* staff would have their answers, but for the fact that I've none to offer. It's their future that would yield the desired knowledge and I haven't been there yet. But I know who has, and I must find him in short order. A recognizable face startles me. "Hi. Remember me?"

"Yes," I answer, "They say your name is Carol... brave Carol." The woman who rescued me smiles vacantly, running fingers along my leggings that facilitate proper circulation. I would thank her, but I see she has more pressing thoughts. "What is it, Carol? We've nothing to hide from one another."

"Do you know of my son Jalee? Is it too early to ask?" I have come to realize in all the murmurings that a great deal is expected of me. Carol imparts her son's story and I am shocked at the details. Before long I ask myself if temporal strings can be coerced to account for such intricacy? A boy loses his head in a sequence that leads to my revival. The mother is imbued with such grief that she finds a link between us, and through her resolve I reawaken. My response carries gratitude. "I don't have answers for you, but I will. I only hope I can satisfy the intent of your efforts."

"Love is not an effort," she replies, asking bluntly what value I have, newly arisen from a bygone age? My reply leaves us both wanting.

"I understand people, and I know... physics. Energy. Hard to explain." Carol presses for details. I offer what comes to mind. "Our continuum has an antimatter twin that uncouples much like DNA, or like an old Polaroid photograph, plus and minus, face to face." Her disappointment shows, and so I try again. "Heisenberg's uncertainty principle—exact velocity and position can't be known at the same time. That's because overlapping continuums share stuff, either here or there, gluons acting as conduits between worlds, everything knitted within a Calabi-Yao manifold."

"A Klabbi what?

"Geometric knots in spatial fabric. Allows dimensions concurrent expression, like twining mirrors that—"

"Arggghhh!" she bristles. "What's that got to do with my boy!" I can only wince, holding for a long time.

"Nothing. But these abstractions are why I was frozen. And why I'm here now." I want to meet her eyes, but can only feed her an offbeat aphorism instead. "Me, you, Jalee, we're the husk, not the corn—the fruit, not the seed. Only patterns thrive—enduring repetitions. And as we push against them, they push back, always healing themselves: filling cracks, straddling boundaries, splitting and meeting back up, reinvented." Carol closes her eyes, turns and walks away, same as I'd have done.

In the hours that follow, I inquire of Yashimoi Watanabe, uncovering an unremarkable bio of a man stricken by defective genetics. Vivacity archives declare his death an oversight, which is uncommon but not unthinkable. Mr. Watanabe lived in Seattle's Hyperion slums, a street world of quasi-status humanoids. Remnants of underground media declared Hyperion a state sponsored hatchery, allowing free reign of unrefined discovery. The State reaped innovation within a quarantined subculture intent upon devouring itself. These slums housed drones, cyborgs, various chimeras, including grafted mammalian splintefores combining one species with the next. 'Sapien Slaughter' it was called, or 'slaughing' by those who relished such disregard.

Yashimoi Watanabe, however, was none of those things. He fell outside the umbrella of World Health. His condition was left untreated and he died. These details were uncovered via dedicated search of obsolete storage media. A civilian query, standard granularity, yields one expunged life. Back on Earth, Yashimoi Watanabe no longer exists, and never did.

I find that fascinating because I met the man, or some derivation thereof. He is little different than myself in the oddity of our encounter. I had even given him advice, lacking a conscious motive but utterly sincere. For any sense of well-being, it is enough to know that he does exist, and must continue to do so, in all manner of lifetimes.

POLLY   **ONQUIN**   **MILES**   Yashi   **ARLENE**   **DAMIEN**

"A pocket of air," I say, with no one else to hear. The living thoughts of Polly's 'Richard' no longer challenge me. A residue lingers as clarity of mind emerges, and with it, an adroit awareness of the man who tasks us all. Richard Boneheart—bits of him retained within. Did he have access to the Mayfair cryobanks prior to our psychal dissolution? Did he pull this muse, this 'pocket of air' from the brain of Lugo Parchaisi, bleeding to death in his watery grave? Awareness has changed since Boneheart's departure, his hopeful inclination deep inside. For what is a starship, or even a planet, if not a pocket full of air?

Mayfair is split in two, both halves tumbling toward Sandoval, inner planet of Centauri B. How this knowledge permeates, I cannot say. Why I am put here remains conjecture, but at the very least, the immediate topography is known to me. On all sides, storage tanks froth with energy as pseudopodia engulf Vat 17. It breaks free of moorings, floating in a gurgling plasma, migrating, eating through walls with little care for unintended consequence.

My vat oozes into the Aerodrome, suspended like pupa emerging from dormancy. These confines had formerly serviced immersion craft, but now all is engulfed in tidal vim that reshapes metallics into filigree. Silky strands become interwoven splines that form a weave. Vat 17 is held in midair, and by whatever madness these events unfold, I sense a greater purpose. Endless filament fills this cavity. Each tank and every vat integrate into substructure feeding a central hub. I occupy this locus point, subsumed by this metamorphosis of unknown origins. It ebbs, flows, takes all and gives it back again.

Such a rude awakening. I would manage all stimuli if it were possible, but I control neither frequency nor scale. Resting within a tranquil interlude, I relish simplicity. Soon the onslaught will begin again, a probing overload of staggered senses, conjoined in what amounts to a round. "Row, row, row your boat," ears falling behind taste, eyes that reconcile the touches and smells of fragments unaccounted for. I've become a centerpiece of convergence... reasons unrecognized.

Mayfair has traveled far and only now do bodies thaw. One might expect a destination at hand; a world to throw down upon. If that were true, beings would awaken as individuals, spilling onto soil and shoreline, but chaos tells me otherwise. We are not being excised from frozen darkness into light. Instead, we thaw, simmer and mingle, each wondering, and every being awestruck. Memories come to me strewn and mangled in synesthesia, so many that I cannot order them. I am taking in the lives of every being that awakens—random textured worlds smashing into one another, diffusing into consciousness. The others lose themselves after a time, but I abide, reminding myself of identity. Little else remains.

A cadence of silence and excess draws me closer to some indistinct inevitability. I chatter like teeth breaking against one another, my soul shimmied off its axis—a wobbled top that wants to stand again. Lacking any framework to grasp, my center cannot hold, too soon to know where this slippage takes me.

Boneheart had given me a clue. 'It is a choice made for you, by you. Find your way home.' The crackle of too much energy courses through flesh, prompting nausea. Lesions form and disappear, leaving a smote ruin of molecules that cannot be undone. I feel it now, this urgent biological warfare. Which way is home? From here, where can anyone go? I will ask this question, and repeat it often so it cannot escape. What home? Is it a place? Or as I begin to understand, a moment shared...

Translink   **RBM 10111**

I am an erection; a hard and searing shank that wants the desired thing. My body extends back down through this polearm, hips and torso on a table. Am I one fleshy wish, or is this throbber attached to something more? Falling back again, I am on a table. My penis is just a penis, the same as any man.

"You're awake." Carol stirs above me. It's dark and she speaks quietly. "Please, don't try to move. You've had a setback. I'm here to help." Try to move? That's unlikely since my chest and arms are tightly strapped. Beyond the glint of her eyes, I see the glow of instrumentation at a distance. I'm on a gurney in a lab. Carol's breath is light and her voice is soft. "Are you feeling okay?" I eye the restraints, then cast a long gaze at my bare stiffness—bigger than I remember. The pulsing mushroom cap has a life of its own.

"Do I look okay?"

Carol smiles. "Oh, that... we had to do some final checks on you, epithelial layers, a hiccup in your peristalsis, up-regulate your thymus, and some of your plumbing. It all seems to be working now." She wraps a hand around my meaty blood flow, rough-hewn fingernails digging in.

"Whoa," I respond. "Easy girl, that's not how it's done. If you are so inclined, I think you've got some other parts that might better serve." Carol softens her grip.

"Such as?" My head is pounding like hooves on parade. She has a beaker in one hand and strokes me with the other. "I was hoping you wouldn't wake up." She stimulates my gonads without my consent. Her touch improves marginally, clinical yet absorbing. She is a queen bee taking juice.

"You don't need the beaker, Carol. Just climb up here and make it happen." She nearly stops, her thumb teasing back and forth. "I'm required to do this, Richard. All your systems need awakening, though it just so happens I have a private inclination. I will discard the effluent after analysis."

"Lady, just get on board, but be quick about it. I won't last."

"Ummm... no, not happening." She stares with a quizzical rebuke. "Did that work for you back home? Ever? Get on board?" Good grief, now I'm confused by this less-than-subtle interlude, eyeing a woman that's jacking me off, with an attitude.

"Hey, your call, but what the fuck are you actually doing right now?"

"I'm not your fifty-cent pony ride, if that's what you're asking. I'm just gathering a few hundred million tadpoles for sequencing. Find out what the Authority's been doing to our genome lately—what's preserved and what's been cast aside."

Two grunts and I abruptly let go, her aims realized. After wisps of air are taken in, this moment quickly fades. "A setback," I say, hinting sarcasm as I watch her collect samples. "That would explain the low lighting and hushed voice."

"Perhaps I lied," she says, preparing tubules for cryovac. "I need to learn everything about you. Figure out why my son died." She pauses before adding "...it's a mother's duty." I ask if it's also dutiful to strap me to a table before milking me dry? She turns her back, answering while securing a biometric drawer. "You've only yourself to blame."

Hmmm... I seem to be caught between worlds, unaware, but my lack of understanding doesn't last long. "Mr. Boneheart, do you think us stupid?" Ominous words from a woman who just did me ragged.

"Ignorant perhaps, but I'm not sure where this is going?"

"Oh yes you are, Mr. Boneheart, sure enough. For why else would your skull have an encrypted translink locked on to the derelict half of *Mayfair*?" I shrug, an honest response, but not good enough. Presently Carol wears a visage that holds little in the way of tolerance.

"Apologies for my naïveté, but I don't have the slightest idea what you're talking about."

"Oh, but you will, Richard, because in two hours the full staff convenes in this very room. Chances are, your translink has an organic memory spool. Or perhaps just a thimble. Better hope not, because if you harbor any such device, we'll pluck it free one neuron at a time. That'll put a kink in your personality."

"Not again…" What else can I say? A certain tiredness sets in when I hear such voices filled with some combination of poor instincts and spotty logic. Not much different than Health Authority mantra, and here I am, ready to get my teeth cleaned. "A little tempestuous, wouldn't you say? I didn't blow apart this ship. I'm hardly in control of my own body, and yet you're decidedly adversarial. How so?"

"You did blow apart our ship, Richard, and despite what you may think, you're little more than a shill. *Mayfair* couldn't subdue us physically, so it funneled us into an untenable situation, much thanks to you." Carol ignores me for a time, tending to a viewscreen. She glances back over her shoulder. "We're going to open you up. Afterward, you'll be a little less devious—perhaps even harmless."

As I try to work things through, a cogent realization seeps in. They put forth a great deal of effort to rescue me, but now this directive for surgery. Why? Surely not a translink, or some damn thimble, if it even exists. "Where's the proof?" I ask. "What facts put me on this gurney?"

"The proof is in your head, Richard."

"No. At best that's corroborating evidence for something more. What else is there?" Carol is organizing instrumentation for my lobotomy. As if I haven't had enough of that already.

"A young attendant came to me with a very dicey problem. He showed me some bullshit files of your supposed past—stuff that puts the hocus pocus on inexperienced types. Unconvinced, I did my own sleuthing, and you'll never guess what I found?" A break in the continuum, eh Carol? No, she didn't find that. There would be no way for her to know. But she could guess, and she could guess wrong. "Tell me, Richard, who bankrolled *Mayfair*?" Simple enough. "The Health Authority," I respond.

"Yes, Copernicus, one in the same. And for what purpose?"

"Well, I'd say to follow *Nomad*. When you've got the world by the balls, you tie up loose ends. Free humans threaten their cybernetic hegemony."

"True enough," Carol answers, "though now a quirk of fate sets us free, and *Mayfair* doesn't like it. Indeed, Copernicus is pissed. Another threat, so to speak. We are humans without blinders—uncontrolled decision-making variability. We are the possibility of competitive ideology eventually becoming opposing weaponry."

"Aren't you forgetting something? That quirk of so-called fate is me. I set you free. You know it's true." Carol looks down at me. Says she holds no malice, and apologizes. Says there will be enough of me left to appreciate life. A distance in her eyes takes hold. It is utter indifference.

"There is proof that you are not Boneheart—a replica, yes, but not the original. You see, I believe the original Boneheart set us free. And now *Mayfair* creates copies to enslave us, with plastron memory fed by spools—seemingly authentic, difficult to verify. But you are one of those copies. Efforts to rescue you broke our ship in two. *Mayfair* fostered conditions to make this happen, and you triggered all."

"No Carol, explosives blew apart *Mayfair*. I was draped over your shoulder, incapacitated when it happened."

"Yes, draped over my shoulder with a nimble touch no less. Charges taken from my belt, activated and set loose as I carried you to safety."

"I did no such thing," and upon the realization that I hadn't quite regained my faculties during the described event, I add, "or at least, I don't remember doing it. Are you certain of this?"

"No," she says, "but those charges didn't magically release themselves with you slung over my back. They bounded free, exploding right where they could do the most damage. I'm amazed you're denying this."

"I was blind. I couldn't hardly move my limbs!"

"Well, I'm not blind. I remember putting a body into Vat 17, expecting resuscitation of that body. Instead, you entered the vat, and only you emerged, an inadequate substitute for my boy." I ask her to recount the particulars. She mentions Excelsior Adams and an envoy sent to Navia long ago. She tells me that the beacon craft had an embossed identifier—the very same as the pod I emerged from—Vat 17. Why the envoy? Why was my pod paired with another? And how does this relate to her child? I think of Yashimoi Watanabe, and everything begins to make sense.

"That wasn't your son you placed in the vat. How could it be?"

"No, not my son, but you're a poor substitute nonetheless, given to us by *Mayfair*. Two bodies in the vat, sleeper pod itineraries inexorably linked. The beacon craft was sent by Copernicus, and you were selected as well. Everything orchestrated—my boy's death conveniently dangled as bait—a presumption of modeled behavior fulfilled."

"That's not likely, too high a price, busting up this ship for what purpose? And besides, people wouldn't be harmed like that, unless the Authority's dictates have changed." My denial of culpability hardens Carol's demeanor, stretching her sensibilities as I comment further. "More likely, Copernicus would simply send another, altogether larger vessel, or possibly a fleet. What you say is no proof at all, only theory."

"Is your skull a theory too, Mr. Boneheart?" I take in a pitiless veneer. Having rescued me, she now seems eager to extinguish me. I am the perceived cause of her son's passing. My imminent demise lends to a greater sense of her well-being.

"Brave Carol, if you truly believe m—"

"Shut up! Shut the fuck up! Copernicus, or whatever delinquent apparition you've become. I would treat you with moral standing if you were purely human, but you're a prop. And because of your guile, I promise copious pain. Magnanimous hurt. I imagine copies of real humans feel copies of pain, which will have to do. Maybe through that translink, you can feel something too."

Carol has a cortical rasp in her hand. Not quite the old egg beater kind. She sparks the contact against an exposed terminal, dulling the sensors. Place that against living tissue and one pleads for the unimaginable. No doubt free humans aboard *Mayfair* are suitably paranoid due to repeated assaults on their autonomy; a survival instinct best served by knives and tweezers. "What about my skull? Is that your proof? If this... translinkage thing is sending data into me, wouldn't you just scan the encryption, break it down and use me to best advantage?"

"Sure, Richard, scan the cryptics and pretty soon a virus alters life support. It's an old trick, and in any case, your skull is proof enough, not a translink or any other plausible deniability."

"What about my skull?"

Carol's pressing anger subsides. She opens up the rasp, finding one of the coils damaged beyond use. Her disappointment is hard to gauge, but her tempered ire is less ambiguous. "Would you agree there is only one original Richard Boneheart?" She pushes the rasp aside, not expecting an answer. "Do understand that planetary habitation is different than life on a ship. The impurities of atmosphere and diet become a part of you.

My son and his friends found a skull near a refuse bin. It belonged to a man named Gerald Mauk. Records indicate that Mauk and Boneheart are one in the same. I analyzed a fragment of Mauk's jaw. The residual impurities prove that Mauk lived a good portion of his life planet-bound. Shall I show you the bone fragment? Would you like to run the tests yourself? Clones grown on a ship do not share such impurities, understand?" I see where this is going. It all makes me sigh.

Brave Carol, she leans to one side angled in repose. The light reveals a feminine strength and I come to realize I very much like her nose. She is satisfied that her explanation validates any future action she prescribes. "Planet-bound?" I ask. "Which planet?"

Carol and I talk, beginning with the woman she stabbed during the thorax breach, and ending with Yashimoi Watanabe and some embossed edge numbers. My summary doesn't suit her. Closure is hard to come by. "Boneheart, your translink skirts our shielding, and that's only because it's bio-direct. We needn't ordinarily shield for that."

"Yes, aside from cryo-integrations, few of you have active implants. Much has been removed or made inert. It's almost preindustrial."

"It's regular life, Richard." She lasers a micro biopsy from my hip bone, rendered for analysis. "And I want to believe you, but how can your translink skirt our shielding? Only Copernicus could manage that. Or at the very least, not someone awakened from a bygone age?" Her disposition has come a long way, from Cro-Magnon to Homo Superior. I still need her to remove the straps that hold me firm.

"I can't explain, though I can say, this translinkage is active again."

"How so?" she asks, all the while critiquing my hip biopsy with a steady focus and raised eyebrows.

"I'm accessing Yashimoi Watanabe." It's repetitive, language seeping into bits of formulae. This isn't ordinary communication, nor is it memory. It's foreign abstraction. The spool, or reel, or whatever Carol had mentioned, must be churning inside my head. "A pocket of air... Lugo... and Sandoval. Sandoval looms." The intensity of voices becomes too much. I pull away from this acuity, releasing the info stream.

"He's a conduit," I say, "or else a compiler, or router or…" The strength of numbers is alarmingly compressed. Shivers glide through me, mostly in the upper torso. "It's hard to control. For him, impossible." I clutch as if trying to balance. Carol grips my shoulder.

"Easy, mister." Perhaps due to my distress, Carol unfastens straps and helps me until I'm perched on elbows. I cough vigorously, liquid shifting in my lungs.

"What is the Aerodrome?" I sputter. Carol tells me it's the forward dock, a hangar for service craft within the derelict half of *Mayfair*. "It's useless," she says, "now little more than a blender. Ever since the thorax breach, that portion of the ship's been tumbling haphazardly. Our piece of *Mayfair* retains proper orientation, what little comfort that provides." She takes in my muddled expression. "You really don't know, do you?"

Carol massages my lower muscles, levering each stiff leg into the open air. "Prior to your rescue, we were preparing for the turn at Sandoval, to be followed by the homeward approach. Then Mayfair broke in two." The gurney's edge helps me leverage a push down onto the floor. I try to stand but lack coordination. "The other half of *Mayfair* will burn up in Sandoval's atmosphere, an unlucky bit of trajectory. Meanwhile, we're the fortunate ones, drifting well past Centauri B, off system, forever." Brave Carol, a little less heroic as melancholy sets in. I lean against her, throwing an arm over her shoulder.

"Yashimoi feeds me information. Help me get to the foundry. We haven't much time."

"Time for what?" she says, "We've run the numbers. The main sequence burners are out, maybe for keeps. The remaining operative thrust won't deliver enough kick to capture a useful orbit. We're headed toward Caldwell 57." Carol tells me it's an irregular dwarf galaxy—two million light years away. Lacking main sequencers, the best we can hope for is snagging a red dwarf a few hundred years out, give or take.

"No thanks, I'd rather stay. Now let's get moving so I can fix things."

"Fix things how?" she asks, as we push away from the gurney.

"One step at a time," I tell her. "One step at a time."

ONQUIN   MILES   DAMIEN   POLLY   YASHI   Arlene

"Mother...

...Mother what have I done?"

A drop of blood is all that I remember, cotton white absorbing crimson splendor. Or does the red absorb the white? A bullet's call, the smell of spent powder as her body falls, and with it, my spirit. What world would have me now, taken from her clasp? What lessons learned, I ask?

We are nested spoons as Miles holds me, arms come round and legs adorn me. I stare at Damien's shattered spine. It rests on the floor as we do, a testament to gravity. It has come to pass. Reconciliation combines the weight of bodies once again. I am reminded of my mother falling, her grasp pulling me down. That was the lesson of gravity, the weight of finality. I feel it once again, crankily awakened within the sogginess of a medtab hangover.

They'll say we've arrived at our new home, though I've got no glee, little curiosity, and certainly no overt repression of my ordinary histrionics. For our arrival, my chore is to heal a murderous stranger. Swallow this disaffection and make him well. I would ask mother if this is the thing to do? Soon we'll all will know what we gave our lives for. Miles attends to duties before I do, and as I venture upstairs, his talk with Polly offers little reassurance.

"I'm telling you now, we must wait. The future comes to us provided we do not seek it out." Polly wants to suit up. Using the gondola air lock, she plans to look around. Her impatience is palpable.

"You say we're orbiting our new home, having landed on an astroidal moon; a highly engineered satellite that by your calculation cannot account for the full force of gravity exerted upon us. Explain yourself Miles, or I'm going outside." Polly is vigorous, having just stabilized the cores, filling much of the chamber with water. Forged of a design unaccustomed to gravity, this terracore life-form was being crushed under its own weight—a beached whale that now relies upon buoyancy as aspiration becomes unpleasant. Miles cares little for her ambitions.

"Polly, you fight me, seemingly with purpose. I'll be tolerant as long as your actions do not endanger us."

"That's it. I'm going." Polly heads for a storage bin, presumably to prep equipment for a walk outside. Her gait is unsteady, muscles barely supporting an impulsive bent. Miles yells.

"Sit down before you fall down! All of us need reconditioning."

"Blow me," she answers.

"Polly, there's nowhere to go! There's no atmosphere. We're perched atop a technological marvel. By all appearances, a hollowed-out M-type asteroid that's full of equipment none of us can begin to understand. The whole thing is one giant magnet. And if you want to mess with that, you might just get us killed." She turns and screams, taking two abrupt steps, lunging at Miles as she collapses. I hear a wrist bone crack as she hits the floor. Onquin reaches her first but Polly continues to glare at Miles, using her undamaged hand to push Onquin away.

"Why are you the only one who knows anything? Ever since we left Sol, and we're still at your mercy. And you're still an asshole!" I pull a medkit from a pile of items at the bottom of a locker. Polly continues to wail. "You have no right to keep us in the dark!" As I approach with an immobilizer, it's Onquin's reaction that strikes me odd. She withdraws, both body and expression. She is self-conscious, staring vacantly in Polly's direction. While attending to Polly's injury, Onquin's reaction becomes clear. She senses Polly's consternation, and with this awareness, her own emotion leaks out; it's jealousy. Miles gives Polly's wrist a dispassionate look.

"A good choice of words, Miss Collins, because that's exactly what we need to do. Stay in the dark a while longer." Miles exhibits his baseline cold streak that each of us knows too well. There's a tacit understanding that his variable empathy tasks us all. The wrist immobilizer is secure, complete with dermabraid. Miles paces back and forth, more able than Polly to withstand the stresses of gravity. His gyrations are indicative of an upcoming sermon. We are pupils, all eyes upon him.

"The Innocuous Continuum Examen was given to us with instructions to weave carbon filament. Remedial aspects of this theory were applied to engine modifications. Much beyond my own interest, only Onquin applied herself. No one else absorbed the details. No one tried to figure it out."

"We don't have the technical background—" I begin to say.

"—You don't have the guts," he interrupts. His ever-present glow of superiority offers scraps of theory. "If you travel at light speed, you touch infinity and are everywhere at once. That, from the perspective of light, wherein time dilates to the unimaginable. The energies required for matter to make such a journey are prohibitive. But from the viewpoint of light, you may well experience universal simultaneity, all moments becoming one; locality is vanquished. For human purposes, this universal concurrence has no tangible application or value. But a sentient universe may feel otherwise." Polly engages with hostility.

"Vapid and less than entertaining. The concept of locations, moments, and concurrence are relativistic terms. You're seem intent upon mingling light and matter. For your purposes, the two cannot be reconciled."

Miles continues. "Wave functions collapse into photonics upon intersecting with matter. I'm guessing these waves feed off matter to retain their energies, with photons as a byproduct, like sparks given off when a weld is made. Lacking any interaction with matter, propagating wave functions go hungry, eventually breaking down, absorbed by an eternal transverse quintessence. It's a recipe for the expanding universe, red shift being one facile example of everything coming apart."

"No Miles," Polly answers. "Particle collisions within stars create photons that eventually escape a star's gravity well. And while gravitational waves allude to cosmic expansion, spectral wavelengths don't alter spatial characteristics in any way whatsoever."

"Stars emit both photons and wave functions. My point is that we're basically made of compacted light. All of us. Everything substantial."

"Lovely," she answers. "Collapsing waves and frozen light. Grade school shit. Whom, exactly, are you seeking to impress here? Anyone?"

"I'm trying, Polly. Best efforts, okay?" Polly's eyes are blazing.

"Try. Fucking. Harder." She is intolerant, but Miles pushes back.

"Look, everyone wants answers, but I'm ill equipped. Yeah, I've got bits and pieces, but Canister personnel kept much under wraps. Tear me down, Polly, but we need to work together. You're right about matter and light, each of us interpreting existence from a single point of reference. But what if we have multiple points of reference?"

"Not possible," I say.

"No, Ari? Are you sure? Then what did we witness in our anomalous transit? Wasn't it our ship dividing in two? Two points of reference?" In a theoretical discussion, I had forgotten life experience. But then again, what we saw may have been a shadow, a reflection, or maybe Yashi jettisoning himself inside his life pod? I want to say as much but Miles continues. "I suggest this anomaly is a window between worlds. Not one window from one world into another. Rather, a lifeline to all realities."

Polly stands, clenched fingers of her injured hand trying but unable to form a fist. "Exposè, gleaned from your Canister cohorts. It goes to figure that these anomalous transits push us into the past, arriving in the Centauri system with time enough to send data back to Earth the old-fashioned way. The recipients interpret arriving data and adjust each successive launch of *Nomad*."

"I doubt it." Miles replies. "At the time of our launch, Earth had a good number of resources trained upon the Centauri System. Our existence on Centauri, prelaunch, would have been news around the world." These are old thoughts leading nowhere. Throughout the discussion, Onquin remains silent. Jilted by Polly's mention of Richard Boneheart back at the cores, she now mulls Polly's overt desire to escape *Nomad*'s walls. Staring aimlessly, she is buried inside her own head.

"Parallel multiplicity," Onquin blurts out, proving me wrong. "Careful how you order events. They may occur in contemporaneous aggregation." Miles shows little surprise. "You've reviewed the precepts of ICE—the principles of interdependence. What else can you share?"

Onquin offers no response, but I do. "We've all looked at it, though none of us with the required arrogance. Please remind us of your loftier efforts in comparison to our own." He gives me a dismissive look, turning back to Onquin as she answers.

"The higher mathematics cannot be detailed symbolically, at least not by any of us. Representations allude to an extra-dimensional paradigm we do not experience. Thus, we cannot assimilate these potentialities first hand." Onquin sits atop her sleeper. Miles crouches nearby, facing her.

"But we do understand things. Don't give up so easily. or there will be no better end. And you know there must be—"

"Richard..." Polly interrupts. She repeats his name again, eyes closed, fingers on temples, and at the sound of it, Onquin struggles to slide off the sleeper. Her voice shares the friction inherent in choppy movement.

"Damn you! I try to accept this, but cannot. What exactly is going on?" Onquin's invective startles all, Polly in particular. Two intimate females do not look upon one another directly. Disquiet is rendered in faces struggling to understand. Miles stares at Onquin, Polly, and finally me. He pursues his academia without ulterior context.

"If it bothers you that much, I'll move into the interpretative realm. Any questions?" He glances at the new lovers, unacknowledged as they remain locked in their imbalance. Miles is distracted. He looks past the pair to their empty netting. One can see it's been double hitched and turned over, a clear reminder that two had shared a single space. Is he recalibrating one of our emotional markers? Some charmed event or altered momentum that history prescribes?

"I'll dispense with gracious explanations," he says tersely. "If light can be everywhere at once, it must necessarily be everywhere at once more than once, infinitely possessed—like layers or waves, so tightly bound there can be no differentiation. These layers, ever concentrated, become matter, but even so, they remain layers nonetheless. Each is an exact duplicate of all others. In effect, each of us has infinite lives occurring simultaneously, and every one of our lives is nearly the same. The anomaly is the instrument that separates layers." Onquin yawns.

"Your exposition is both false and unwieldy."

"Then you explain it."

"I cannot, unless I magically shed layers as you might suggest. Yes, perhaps this would somehow ameliorate my current condition."

"I haven't rejected you." Polly says. Her voice is atonal. "I simply prefer a man." Onquin heads for the stairwell, stopping partway down.

"Your flavor of clarity is no better than his."

"Onquin, I can't tell you why I want him. I just do."

"No need to tell me, because I already know. I have the same feelings for you." Her head ducks out of sight. Polly excuses herself and follows.

Sandoval

A ship torn in half, divided contents happenstance. Through the briefing room porthole, I gaze outside at the other half of *Mayfair*. She is slowly tumbling on the way to incineration. Sandoval looms in the distance, accompanied by an atmosphere mottled gray. One busted up ocher moon hangs in proximity. No doubt reentry will enliven this color scheme. A glowing corona will drown out the collective agony of a mass mind, vaporized within the aerodrome.

So ends an emerging neurella, the likes of which Terran governments outlawed long ago. And yet, Yashimoi Watanabe occupies the locus point of this neurella, apparently by design. Whose design would be a question for later inquiry.

As for the present, those gathered await my explanations as Yashimoi pushes data through me via translink. We've struck a bargain for survival, if only I can convince the others.

"Yashimoi is a conduit to the AI engaged in calculations regarding our dilemma. Now you may choose to call it an extension of Copernicus, or any other iteration of the same, but please remember that these derived solutions are the result of computational capacity we cannot match."

"We'll find our own solutions, thank you," and another speaks likewise, "I don't trust it. In fact, I don't trust you." "Aye," says a third, followed by two more. These leaders sit around a table without a plan. They seem willing to die in vacuum if only to exercise the right. I survey all, speaking equally to everyone because each council member requires handholding.

"Snagging the derelict half of this ship is no easy task. Lacking a conventional strategy, improvisation is key. Carol has workers in the foundry fabricating bell jars, ignition yokes, and harnesses. Unless someone offers an alternative, we're pushing ahead. Let me know when any of you can keep us from falling out of the Centauri system."

I leave them sitting there as I head for the supply depot, finally feeling like myself again. We barely have a window, and though closing fast, I am hopeful. Others aren't so sure, including a supply clerk, shaking his head.

"Nothing on the docket. No auths, permission denied." A mechanic's apprentice and a chemist join us, bringing this confab to six.

"I'm asking you a simple question. Do you have ammonia, nitrogen, ozone, and the other feed stocks available for immediate transport?" He glares at me.

"Yeah, we do, but this stuff's earmarked for hydroponics. Fertilizer. We don't feed the crops, there's no crops."

"Last to know," I answer with a smile. "Per the specs, arrange for delivery to the ad hoc chemfab at the auxiliary purge bay—and do so with urgency." I hand him a com stylus. "Carol will help with logistics. Good luck." Five of us enter the elevator. We leave the chemist behind. Her wide-eyed stare mirrors the clerk, each syncing stylus and earstem as Carol begins their indoctrination.

Now launch vehicles are needed. We requisition engineers for the conversion of two probes. Ordinarily, these cloudbusters would be used to take apart hurricanes, or any other atmospheric disturbance. I check the packaging manifest for tolerances: grade 7.5 hardened, with an asterisk. Maybe I'm wrong, but alternatives are not readily available.

The biggest hurdle is finding an appropriate tether. On the derelict half of *Mayfair*, Yashimoi instructs drones to rig parro charges to tug lines. Meanwhile, Jansen and a bevy of workers feed a solar shade into a harvester turned into a loom. Fibers are interlaced, bathed in fixing agents, and taken outside to be wrapped around a makeshift sleeve covering the torque differential mechanism.

Our revolving habitat spindle supplies the remainder of the equation, acting somewhat like an enormous gyroscope. Therein lies the current problem. I tell the *Mayfair* brain trust that fluctuating stresses will cause a variance of artificial gravity during the upcoming actions. I fail to mention potentialities of structural failure as the spindle tries to stabilize *Mayfair's* derelict half. I'm unwilling to raise additional concerns, though extensive damage is likely. In the hours before these high-stake maneuvers, I rest. In truth, I can do little more than refuse the drugs that would put me under. Fatigue supplants emotion. I shut my eyes and the interval is lost.

A countdown awakens me. Escorted to operations, a viewscreen shows the cloudbusters perched and ready. I am given scant detail and then ignored. "Did we deliver bell jars?" I ask. A voice behind me answers.

"While you were sleeping, a full complement" I turn to see Carol's eyes affixed to a screen. "Watch, Richard, everything's starting to happen." The derelict half of *Mayfair* has entered the outer reaches of Sandoval's atmospheric shell. A viewscreen overlay shows heat lines pinging threshold values. The derelict begins to burn and the first signs of streaming melt makes me wonder if the calculations are wrong?

No sooner do I raise the question when our cloudbusters launch, with trailing cords attached. They quickly reach the axis points on each side of the tumbling mass. Tug lines spring forth from the wounded craft, one on each side as parro charges ignite on their forward edge. Tendrils swarm and engulf the cloudbusters, too quick for the human eye.

Screens show an outcome in chromatic relief, confirmed by a unified cheer. It is reminiscent of historical visio at Cape Canaveral, the earliest records of space flight jubilation. Tug lines and twine have joined, connecting the two pieces of *Mayfair*. Both tethers are pinioned on opposing axis points, the fiery mass still tumbling through planetary haze.

The realization on the viewscreen hits home as the spindle lurches in a series of shuddering gyrations. Tension takes hold on the tethers as the makeshift sleeve allows slippage—lines unreeling themselves from our half of *Mayfair*. The torque differential mechanism, regulating centrifugal force of the habitat, is now duly stressed. Walls groan, a claxon alarm blares, followed quickly by intercom cries declaring a C-deck hull breach, air pressure correcting itself as human beings are sucked out of living spaces into a non-living one. I regain my bearings, taking several steps in the direction of the main corridor, but Carol holds me back. Our own doors auto-seal, flashing red. I cannot help.

At a nearby window, a young lady groans in guttural pain. Beyond her, outside, a single body cartwheels in slow motion. Outstretched limbs reach wide, like an ice skater endlessly falling. We all watch at different speeds, different angles, half of a ship trying to escape a gravity well. The other half tries to bend its flight path around a planet and forge a trajectory home.

I imagine that from a distance, the two halves seem to be little more than a pair of distressed shoes tied together by a long set of laces. Upon closer examination, it is not merely the shoes that are imperiled, but the laces as well. Sandoval has a death grip on Yashimoi and company, with superheated plasma licking at melting points. Heat lines ping max tolerance alarms, and so begins a series of blinding flashes that become a consistent shimmer. Viewscreens are rendered useless.

"Bell jar deployment," Carol says, more as a wishful affirmation than informative cue. "Let's hope this works."

Some moments seem longer than others. I turn inward to translink, absorbing occasional numerics, blips, and staccato interference. I watch the flickering light play off Carol's face. What choice would I enjoy having, Polly or Carol? Which shall be my lover and which shall be my mate? As part of the interplay, Yashimoi has recently confirmed that Polly is alive and well. Polly or Carol? I should like to have that choice one day.

"We're gaining purchase," someone says. "Hang on." This dilemma is the result of a battle over yours truly; free humans versus what exactly? Carol said that I released detonation charges that buckled the thorax. I have no such recollection, and now wonder if Copernicus crafted these events, with or without conscious thought? Is Copernicus to blame? Yashi perhaps? Or am I responsible? Such ambiguity tells me I need this translink neutralized at the earliest opportunity.

"It's working!" someone shouts, "We're turning the corner, towing her out to sea! Another minute should do it." Another minute. I've had a lifetime of those, from plowing women full of seed to dispatching enemies unaware. Another minute is sometimes all it takes. The bell jars are an inspired solution combining disparate technology. Magnetic housings form an array, continually injected with chemicals such that the resulting explosions supply angular momentum as the jars twirl like a pair of pinwheels on each side of the ship's tumbling axis. As the bulk center of the vessel continues to absorb heat, the sides are relieved of friction by bell jars—atmospheric friction blown away by a continuous stream of diminutive explosions. Repulsors buffer the jars, the jars keep the tethers from melting, and the pinwheels rotate in opposition to the ship's own spin. This slows down the derelict half's rotation.

"Here we go!" a voice yells, "She's breaking free of Sandoval! We'll feel some pull and slingshot past. Cut the lines on my command!" A chittering screech fills my head. The translink is issuing an imperative.

"Belay that order," I shout, surprised at the volume of my own voice. "We've yet to fulfill our part of the bargain. Leave those lines attached!"

Any man will take an order if properly delivered. Saunders, or whatever his name is, was one of the dissenting voices in the briefing room. Now at the helm, he stares me down. I offer no comfort. "We've been letting out line with measured resistance, but even now, the other half of *Mayfair* stills needs our pull to achieve its intended path." He points at a screen and growls. "She's the enemy!"

"Or you are!" I say. "Either way, no one cuts those lines. Not yet." Even as the words are spoken, the spindle turns more rapidly, adding centrifugal force as the tethers unwind. Saunders listens as the walls begin to howl. He looks at Carol, then back to me.

"Cut us free!" he screams. The attendant moves to obey and receives my fist to his jaw, well timed and utterly effective. Artificial gravity is perhaps thirty percent higher and rising. This is enough to make Saunders misstep as he too reaches for the release button. I grab his wrist. Our efforts lose relevance as both tethers snap free of their own accord, not from our end, rather, at the cloudbuster junction between twine and the tug lines. Saunders breaks my grip and smashes the release button one beat too late.

"Full port invectors Now!" I scream. It is a directive urgently relayed by translink, and looking out the window, I realize why. We've twisted our trajectory a good number of degrees and the nearby window shows a view behind us. There, the derelict continues onward, a tug line flailing on one side. On the other side, however, the bell jar array has broken loose from the derelict half of *Mayfair*. The fiery array occupies a point in space midway between halves, on the move at high velocity. Our ship begins to roll as this flaming pinwheel approaches on an intersect path. Invectors push against Sandoval's bulk as we angle away in a maddening spatial delay, just in time to see the pinwheel pass over us, right where we would have been had no order for invectors been given; had no order been carried out.

"Here comes the other one," Saunders yells, "brace for impact!" I pivot, and despite our maneuver, the second pinwheel is nearly upon us, aiming dead center.

"It can't end like this," I say, and suddenly pinwheel meets tether—our discarded line floating free. It strangles the device, wrapping in and through, demolishing the center as bell jars splay in all directions. One cluster of jars fires upon us as it moves past. The hull plating makes a keening noise, deafening, traversing in a resonance that nearly gouges. Afterwards, there are closed eyes, open mouths, and one sincere apology for a jaw broken in three places. Some become stoic, others effusive. My reaction falls somewhere in between.

DAMIEN   ONQUIN   Polly   **MILES   YASHI   ARLENE**

I remember raindrops slanting across street lights on 48th street, falling from the heavens and dragging particulates into a crosswind. They change intensity with the season, hitting a window and forever drawing down. In a world where each path and every interaction are known, I'm apt to wonder, did I get my share? How many droplets touched my skin? A quantity, perhaps shared by others but no less mine. I've come to appreciate a world of absolutes. It is a world left behind.

Gone and here again. These are not raindrops, but imitations much the same, temperature and tactile sense, the sanctity of rain. Paths of moisture intersect, droplet unto rivulet, and so fatigue is washed away, irritants dissolved, never fully understood and therefore unresolved. My expectations of a curtailed shower are not met. No one shouts through the vent, telling me of cycle length, resource allocation, or any other reason to stop the rain. How long do I sit, chin on knee, one leg folded underneath? Minutes turn idly by until a voice nudges me.

"Zero." It's Arlene. "My number is zero, and what bothers me is not the lack of experience, but stifled intent." She speaks of raindrops, a chorus to my own apprehensions. I sit in darkness, water splashing upon my face. I touch this shower stall and listen: no vibratory essence rises above the din, and yet here she echoes meekly once again. Opening my eyes, suspicions are affirmed, no shower stall envisioned. Instead, my optic nerve has been hijacked—a skein of Ari's memories pouring through me, skin photosensitive, sensory excess, followed by darkness. This flavor of wetness washes out as a new message washes in.

"We are the medium, Polly, all combined, the currency of existence." Waking dreams. It's the droplets, a singular datastream, each and every drop extolling the exact same message. With an open palm I shield my eyes. A thunderclap sensation diverts to one side. Intoxication takes many forms, sometimes without an appreciation of change. I waver off-kilter, locating handle and latch, turning off the shower and opening the hatch. Light funnels in.

Stumbling onto the cold hard surface of the cleansing bay, I see Arlene standing in front of me. She offers a towel. In earlier days this area had been used for cryopaste remediation. Now the accoutrements of deep sleep have been stowed, leaving only me, naked. "What did you say?" I ask, taking the towel while receiving the expected reply.

"Not a thing. After working up some spider eddies, I've woven new fabric to replace the fluff and suction we've been using ever since the smoke ring transit. It's an improvement, wouldn't you say?" Blinking rapidly, I close my eyes only to see... our torus-shaped anomaly. It's a darkened shade of bright, ghosting and churning under my eyelids. Somehow affected, or maybe infected, this mirage slowly dissipates into an empty charcoal sea.

"Ari, the water's been tampered with. Tell Onquin and Miles we need to talk." Drying quickly, I wrap the towel around me loosely tucked. Once all are in attendance, I open up. "The terracores spoke to me through Ari's twin, much like a memoride but without the clumsy interface." I tell them of our compromised water supply. "Any of us may be poisoned at a whim. I tried to take a shower, simple enough, and got pelted with doctrine. Shower any longer, and I'm afraid I'd have been brainwashed. Or maybe I already am?"

After facile introspection, my towel falls to the floor. I spread my legs wide, bending at the waist, touching right index finger to left toe, left index finger to right toe. And again, and once more, my wrist fighting against me. "Do I appear to be myself? Is there any difference since my awakening?" My naked form seeks the human response, wondering if the terracores have altered me? Miles looks to Arlene, sharing a lengthy gaze. Onquin ignores me, watching Miles and Arlene instead.

"I assume there's a point being made," Miles finally says. "You're rarely circuitous though I'm at a loss. What do you want?"

"Answers," I say, "in their simplest form." More calisthenics. This time I turn my backside to Miles, again touching toes, showing my most sensitive parts. "We've not been very open with one another."

"Fine," Miles responds. "But first get that righteous pussy out of my face!" Crude but effective. Thinking of the shower's datastream, I ask of accumulating irritants that have yet to be washed away.

"You say there's an established colony awaiting our arrival, and we're orbiting above on a fabbed-out moon. Then why sit in this coffin and wait? Don't feed me trifles about endangered lives or emotional markers. Answer directly, or I'll carve out a sunroom right through the side of this ship."

Miles sizes me up. There is no bluster here. "Well, Princess, if you must know, there is indeed an inhabited world below us, and it's populated by *Nomad's* descendants—our descendants. Their rigorous convictions might interpret my coming as blasphemy. Perhaps the seeds of their discontent are being sown this very instant, by all of you, everyone against me now."

All are dumbstruck as Miles continues. "Their papal prognostications suggest that I'll be sacrificed on an altar, apparently as I have been before. So, due to a sense of self-preservation, I'd rather we remain undetected a while longer." Arlene begins coughing as if choking on water. Trying to clear her throat, her eyes bulge.

"Emotional markers my ass! Every day it's something new. You've got... you be truthful right now, or I shall never forgive you." Miles puts both index fingers to his lips.

"I guess you've earned it," and he begins to tell a tale we've all waited to hear. "The Navians that inhabit our new home are not the only ones kept in the dark as to our whereabouts. It would seem that—" Arlene interrupts.

"Navians? How can... Navia? This world is named after me?"

"Not you," Miles replies. "Your mother... to honor one who sought escape from a time and place that repudiated life itself. And now it seems these very same agents that fought against your mother would also like to know our location. You may assume as I do that we hide from Copernicus. I don't know, but we must remain in shadow."

"We're being tracked, even now?"

"Especially now, Ari, but we've taken care to secret ourselves away." Onquin faces Miles with skepticism.

"Copernicus knows our launch velocity, trajectory, fuel capacity, consumption rates, and all the necessary data to—"

"The anomaly..."

"Yes, Polly, precisely so." Miles speaks, watching three faces. We share forehead wrinkles, one tight jaw, and an anxious overbite. "The anomaly is our duck blind, entering known, exiting without notoriety."

"Miles?"

"Yes, Onquin?"

"Once again, you imply that we have not traveled into the past. Because had we done so, Copernicus would not be looking for us yet. Hiding would be unnecessary."

"I said I wasn't sure about Copernicus."

"Navia," Arlene says, staring at her open palms as though her own ministrations had unwittingly fashioned a planet. I shuffle past them to my locker, picking out my worn lab coat.

"Certainty or uncertainty is irrelevant," I say. "If ever we emerge from the anomaly at any point during Copernicus's tenure, we are found. Our exhaust signature is unmistakable."

"Not true," Miles says, looking at Arlene. He clings to the promise of whatever future she wishes to pursue. "Check the hardened systems log. Won't tell you much, but we did drop out of the main sequence burn just prior to smoke ring transit." Ari flinches.

"So?"

"So," Miles continues, "when, in preflight sims did we ever shut down the main sequencers?"

"At the turn," I say.

"Correct," he answers. "Thereafter we reburn, ass backwards, hiding our signature from Copernicus." I watch Ari grasping for details with the same challenged look I might have in medlab. Miles also notices, and so repeats himself with minor variations. "*Nomad* flips during our anomalous transit slumber. Deceleration begins, with the body of the ship interposed between Copernicus and our antimatter burn. No trailing light, understand?"

"I am not stupid!" Ari answers, "and that's the least of our problems. This ship offers falsehoods at every turn: console, fuel, engines, sensors, biodata, all corrupted—including us!" Arlene hisses. "Some bit of duplicity here, with you in the crosshairs. Glints of realism but nothing trusted, and yet you knew. Damien was right, and you ignored him. Why?"

Miles shrugs. "Such deceits are the product of security measures based upon concurrent flights. Maybe ground control was worried about spyware, or a particular crewmember? Perhaps the less we know, the less we divulge to our adversaries during the repetition of days? Once a transit is successful, you leave it be. If it's not broke, don't fix it." I ask Miles to detail any such successes. He slowly covers his mouth, eyeing me suspiciously. Arlene remains transfixed on Copernicus finding us.

"What about wide-spectrum sensors, or seepage? Magnetism, atomics, even biologics? Every ship leaves a trail."

"This ship doesn't drip," Miles says, reminding Arlene how the glassy metal hull is actually a slow-moving liquid. The smoke ring transit aged the outer hull, flowing, sealing us in. "No seepage. None."

"I understand," Onquin adds. "This is why you avoided drilling new sensor holes, because the front of the ship was facing Earth. Any new pings may have given us away."

"True enough, and we didn't unfurl A- and B-modules for gravity because the profile of each module engine would have left recognizable exhaust." I try to hide my contempt for Miles, but my voice conceals little.

"Copernicus knows where we're headed, so why this hide and seek?" Miles gives me the dumbest look possible.

"Where are we? When? Who looks for us? These are the questions. Our hull is non-reflective, our arrival is unannounced. We wait."

Onquin makes coffee, mixing together all kinds of stuff. Each sip invites an upset stomach—mine, not hers. "Why're you doing that?" I ask.

"Something new," she answers. "It takes years to reach the anomaly, and yet, judging by the truth of this cup holding liquid, only months thereafter and we reach journey's end." She turns the cup slowly, pivoting the rim. Coffee dribbles out, down her arm, dripping off her elbow. "Gravity, coffee, motion, sweetener, heat, lipids, friction, alcohol, surface tension, mocha, so many variables, we cannot quantify them all. But the anomaly certainly must have done two things: it altered our proximal location as related to our origin and destination, and it also absorbed some greater portion of *Nomad's* inertia, otherwise we could not have landed so soon after the turn."

Arlene wants nothing to do with mental gymnastics right now. She goes below, saying she'll rework the spa. I reach out to Onquin, taking her cup with a gentle smile.

"One small sip for mankind...."

"Gravity," she blurts, ignoring me and turning to Miles. "We've pinged this moon, and all agree, the gravity profile exceeds its mass beyond any functional density. You say it's an artificial moon. What more is there?"

He tells us of his ignorance and his suspicions.

"It's not Earth-normal gravity, obviously much less. That suggests the localized grav quotient is either maxed out, or we're being climatized."

"For what?" I ask without thinking.

"For Navia," he answers.

"Hallelujah! When?" Suddenly I'm grinning ear to ear. "When do we rejoin humanity?" Onquin takes back her cup, sloshing murky contents while offering a snide reply.

"Somewhat eager, aren't you?" She gawks at me. "You want to go down there because you expect to see Richard. Admit it."

"Yes," I answer. "I have no reluctance telling you. Richard is close. He must already be on Navia."

"Or," Miles interrupts, "you want to get there quickly for other reasons. Ever since we've landed you've been in a panic to go."

"I'm going stir crazy, Miles."

"No Purebread, you're not. It's not in your nature."

"My nature? What do you really know about me?"

"More than you think I do."

Miles is right. He noticed a behavioral imbalance. It could be the excitement, or it could be... I excuse myself and head to hydroponics. In the hours that follow, I query water, biomass, and recycle systems. The readouts are inconsequential. Upon revisiting the cores, I send a midge up the water feed. It reaches a valve where the line doesn't loop back to the primary. Instead, the feed heads into engineering systems. Suddenly my tablet is inundated with high band interference. This only strengthens my resolve. I ask the midge for schema of its immediate surroundings, which it promptly delivers, then inexplicably, the midge malfunctions. Attempts at recovery prove fruitless.

An escalating rancor fills me as aspects of discovery suggest premeditation. *Nomad* has a shared housing that holds both fuel and hydro resources. Much like a double-hulled oil tanker of yesteryear, there is a layer of water between *Nomad's* outer skin and the antimatter stocks within. This was never shown on schematics. I consider A-module design: water in the walls that barely insulates the crew from cosmic rays; by all accounts, negligible protection, though Richard had mentioned a doped additive of some kind. Finally, I wonder if terracore submersion was planned from the start? If so, this pliant cryogenics turned rogue isn't so rogue after all.

With the newly discovered water volume taking up so much space, antimatter stocks are less than previously imagined, but again, current conditions offer insight. The smoke ring transit shortened our journey, less fuel was needed, replaced by water that is only now being scrutinized.

I recoil upon the realization that my shower was likely infested with core-processed water, some genesis therein with me as tadpole. Now I'm uncertain of what to say or admit? Miles was right, and now I worry, joining the others in A-module, updating core status to all. Arlene is animated within her own bi-polar hopefulness.

"It's in the details," Ari says, "things overlooked in all this chaos." Miles tells her we haven't overlooked anything, watching me with a hard focus. "Small things," Ari blurts, "and obvious things too. We put them together and we'll figure it out."

"Oh," I answer, "I think it's pretty clear. Yashi's a vegetable corpse floating out in space. Onquin's a clone with a head full of hardware. The corrupted remnants of three Damiens can be found scattered all over this ship. And me, I'm becoming an Oracle, with half my original body fused to everyone else. Terracores? How about we called this what it is, a barbaric misstep."

Amen, I hear inside me: it's Yashi's voice. Undeniably, the terracores continues to communicate. My B-module complement shares a bonded unity with all, fully integrated once again. But this time however, the connection is noticeably weaker. When the cores penetrate, it feels like a head cold. I no longer fight it.

"That leaves the two of you," Onquin says, "pristine since journey's onset." Neither Arlene nor Miles seems self-conscious. "You speak of details, Arlene. Can you name even one?"

She says nothing, but details arrive nonetheless: *Napoleon, the anomaly, my last words.* The terracores speak through the Damien hemisphere directly into me. My terracore analogue silently mouths the words, *Napoleon, the anomaly...* I grunt forcibly as pain surges behind my eyes—an interrupt that stuns—with pressure-filled ears ready to burst. This saturating ache crests and fades as quickly as it arrived. It's punishment; terracore infighting, with me as unwitting recipient. The link breaks as an overarching haze disorients. I tell the others what Damien communicated, and Arlene comments further.

"The anomaly. Mankind didn't put it there. We don't have the knowledge or skill, but we did pierce it, passing through, and ended up here." Ari rehashes the insubstantial. I prod for a binding idea, something new, but she shakes her head. "We're an experiment. The cores told you as much—the currency of existence." Onquin takes up the challenge.

"This anomaly functions as a tool. We may be the hand that wields, or the soil being tilled. Regardless, I suggest more fertile ground may be covered by examining the other clues just now offered."

Napoleon. I'm told my twin screamed horribly, getting Onquin's attention while she matched wits with Napoleon. I was sleeping, but empathetic. The terracores and Napoleon shared themselves in common cause, and though Onquin suggests that Napoleon may yet be hidden away as hibernating code, the terracores tell me otherwise. A portion of the cores ally with me. Continually hunted by sweeper routines, Napoleon tried to flee its habitat of ones and zeros. It sought permanence outside the confines of numbers. Did *Nomad's* viral eradication program cause hardship such that Napoleon sought refuge in flesh and blood?

I am left empty-handed attributing motives related to Napoleon's demise. Is Miles or Onquin to blame? The terracores perhaps? I know my analog cried out from within the core. Is this my fault? Each of us tries to find a villain. We want our fears justified. And as our numbers dwindle, so does the list of suspects. Damien was the most astute, questioning everything, knowing that mortality is just a quaint word for failure.

We are dying, and someone or something is culling us; altering beliefs; metastasizing values at the heart of DNA. Even the terracores feel sickly as of late. My thoughts diverge from the ongoing discussion. After a time, when all are done sharing, I inquire of Damien's final words. Onquin comes to me. She wants to touch but doesn't.

"You need to ask Ari," she says. "I think it's personal." And I ask. Arlene never looks my way, closing her eyes. Words come out, one by one.

"I will always remember, as you will… or must, for all of us."

Her recollection is emotional and admittedly imprecise. Always remember? These were Damien's final words. I doubt a dying man preserves much of anything, though memories do survive within the cores. I turn inward, seeking this bond of tissue and emotion. My diaphragm heaves in combination with my other self. I'm swimming in a hollowed-out trance… partly-submerged bodies… little to grasp hold of, intelligence bunched and… words are here, on paper. They form on my lips. "…no longer face this world alone." I am shaken free of immersion. Arlene with a nosebleed, pushes away from me, screaming.

"Stop it! What are you doing to me?" I'm frightened, unable to believe I've done anything at all. But her fingers are bloody, and while Miles attends to her, Onquin stares at me with undivided scrutiny. She ogles. I have no proper response. Joining with the core, I had found something.

"It's written on paper," I say. Arlene is tucked up against the wall, bloodied towel pressed against her face.

"You were in my head… and now I know. I know what you're looking for." Ari points to his locker. "He'd written it himself. Showed it to me more than once. Just plain stupid."

She motions to Damien's locker. His effects are untouched in memoriam, mixed together ever since gravity took hold. Miles finds a folded sheet of paper wedged next to a photo of Damien's wife. She is seated on a swing hung from a tree. Miles and I stare at the photograph.

"Read aloud" Arlene says. Miles unfolds it. The edges are ragged. The creases are worn thin. He clears his throat, and speaks to all.

"Coal tar and lignite, pitchblende and anthracite…"

This world lasts longer than we do
Therefore, I cannot decide
Is the value of life worth more or less
than love or love denied?

Poetics received from translink—inured melancholy conveyed by Yashimoi Watanabe en route to Centauri B. His molten craft has slipped between fragments of Sandoval's archipelago moon, leaving speckled craters and a dusty airborne hue. He will plunge headlong into Centauri B shortly after we reach our new home. For the *Mayfair* crew, Navia will become the cradle of futures. Yashimoi, however, has a more finite path.

"There's nothing more to see." I ask Carol to release herself from morbid fascination. No doubt the derelict half of *Mayfair* will be consumed by Centauri B. Sandoval's atmosphere roasted every bit of hardware that could alter trajectory. Carol looms over the board, not satisfied with a foregone conclusion. "Richard, something's not right. Look at the surface temperature of the hull. She's burning from the inside, all held firm by confining plasma."

Carol is a scientist. An inability to rationalize leaves her at a loss for words, folding the insubstantial into the present. She is a child, a girl I remember growing up on a farm. She looks back at Sylvester Ramirez through the rear window of a maglev. She doesn't understand, turning to me, pointing and asking. I tell her we're headed someplace special, and together we stare through dirty glass at a broken past, some chickens, and there beyond, nearly out of sight, a smidgen. It is Yashimoi, or could be, hundreds of years in the making. He waves goodbye.

In the days that follow, there is an inquest. Saunders inflames the council suggesting I nearly killed everyone by countermanding orders. But his corroborative witnesses also testify on my behalf. Excelsior Adams raises an arm and is instantly heard. "What troubles me is that you have not reconciled your actions in light of the dangers presented."

"We needed to fulfill the agreement to assure the homeward turn."

"Nonsense," Excelsior answers. "We had gained our corridor, and our adversary lacked any recourse to alter such." Saunders meets my gaze and makes himself useful.

"Not entirely true, sir. During the thorax breech, *Mayfair* coaxed a trim thruster into marginalized service. We diagnosed it as drill mites, dumped on the hull en masse. They've been neutralized, but it took some time." Adams is suddenly at odds with the conversation.

"Why then, Commander, do you complain so bitterly?"

Saunders points at me. "Because he didn't know! At the time of insubordination, we believed this thruster to be inoperative. And if he did know but didn't tell us, that's even worse!"

I thank Saunders and add to his explanation. "Forensics suggest the derelict mainframe had control of this thruster at the mechanical source. It could have sent us wide, or maybe crashed us into a piece of moon. But we struck a deal instead, using one another for our respective aims."

A collective pause ensues to reassess. They request details of my translink with Yashimoi Watanabe. I have been asked many times and finally answer. "I suggest that Yashimoi is an operative, implanted to destroy the derelict mainframe." In softer tones, I add, "He secured our pathway home. His reward is a journey into the heart of a fusion reactor."

Saunders counters in resigned tones. "What of the bell jars that nearly destroyed us?"

I shrug. "An internal conflict between neurella and mainframe. Yashimoi warned us, this trim thruster firing in concert with the oncoming bell jars. It would seem our efforts to fulfill the agreement were less than expected. Once the derelict mainframe parsed its own fate, reprisal was an attempted payment in kind."

"Just as well," Excelsior says. "I've heard enough. Richard, you are one of us by decree. Guide us to this new world, soil and families. Let us rejoin the daily fare of old habits revived. Time enough for it, even for me."

The entire Sandoval episode results in operational changes. Ship-wide damage control and inventory bottlenecks are the order of the day. Our portion of *Mayfair* will shoot past Lex Luthor once again, unable to snag a useful orbit via direct approach. Carol says we'll pivot around the frozen bulk of Ahkran Boi, returning years hence. I share other ideas.

After weeks of preparation, a launch window opens for a less ambitious approach as we transit Lex Luthor. Eight stealth gliders and a single lander are secured to a modified immersion craft. Trajectories are managed as gliders dispatch in a linear fashion. They are tiny lights blown free, the germ of cattails desirous of release. How do I remember these reeds? Only as swampy stalks, nothing to fix a bygone age or define feelings. Little more than seed.

The gliders will orbit for a time, until prompted to descend in unison, each emissary targeting a distinct settlement amongst searchlights and bonfires—celebrations of genetic ideology taking hold. Humans greeting humans. The day after, or the next, they will likely be at each other's throats again. For now, however, it is as it should be.

As the immersion craft arcs back to *Mayfair*, I debark, my lander filled with items of unrecognizable use. Carol helped fabricate sundry materials based upon renderings taken from my elbow splinterware. I know I need this stuff, but how and why? Every bit of this seems strange to me. I was frozen and thawed, hijacked and awed. I fully understand that Carol and Yashimoi gave me life again, but is it my own? It may be, for I am growing into it with natural vigor.

My arrival at the PAL crucible is unceremonious, and at first, I'm quite concerned—a barren nothingness. This cinder of rock and dust is overwhelmed by the immensity of Lex Luthor's blazing hearth. Scattershot light rips at bonded atoms and tears apart eventualities.

Passing into shadow, I touchdown within a crater hollow. There, I see a shape so recognizable, it jumps out at me in a bodily expression of lust. Into a suit, out through the hatch and across an expanse up onto a glassy metal hull. I find the gondola where it's supposed to be. Memories, only recalled when needed, are foreign until they're not.

It takes time to micro fracture the glassy hull. I use a pinching aperture on a scribe, clearing up a hatch sealed by the anomalous transit. I find the screw valve is stuck, and so oblique leverage is required. Muscle fatigue and anticipation turn my stomach, but the gondola's exterior hatch finally opens and I climb inside. The mechanism clatters, snugging the carriage as the pressure seal whines and tightens. Checking an atmospheric gauge, no sooner do I shed my helmet when the interior hatch gapes open.

Gathered are four astronauts, one in particular with sparkling eyes. Our enthusiasm is equally matched. "Hi honey, I'm home!" Polly leaps around my neck and nearly knocks us over. Behind her are Miles, Arlene, and a woman I do not recognize. Her name and purpose will come to me eventually. My lover's embrace softens as she pulls back slightly. "Richard," she says, planting a most ferocious kiss. "Thank you, thank you, thank you for coming! We need answers."

All holes filled. That's what we try to do. We lay under covers in the privacy of a makeshift bed, one deck below the others. Polly is impatient, wanting everything at once. She laughs and says we need three of me to accomplish the task: one to talk, one to listen, and one to beat my head against the wall. In a manner of speaking, she's right. I need my own verification of things that are mine and those that are not. "Sylvester Ramirez is in here," I point to my head, "and cognitive slivers of an old man too. I remember eating melon with a pair of Spaniels when the old man died. I remember Sly's wife prancing around using ballet stims that were so annoying, I wanted to shove her through a plate glass window. So much clutter from other people's lives. I shouldn't feel this way."

Slowly sweeping my hand down Polly's flank, I pause at her hip. This is the grandeur I seek. These bones will open one day unhinged, and from them part of me will view this world. But no kisses can carry us back to our point of union. In these hours just now spent together, I see she has flown through icy depths while I've become a part of them. She cannot see this yet, though in time her role as concubine will be more clearly defined. She will bear my children, but Carol will bear the burden of knowing my manifold self. This, I do not decide. It is the strings hinting forward, offering glimpses I cannot deny.

I've been told of Damien's demise in detail. I've also been informed of pliant-cryo gone rogue. Still, there is a more sensitive topic I've yet to breach. I had hoped to gather my wits before necessity arrives. Unfortunately, I must delve now. "Miles and Arlene are known to me, but this other woman, is she some last-minute replacement for Onquin?" Polly's eyebrows lift themselves high. She searches, then drops any pretense of understanding.

"You're really struggling, aren't you?" She touches my face as if comforting a wounded animal. "Richard, she is Onquin. Or... tell me for certain she's not." Polly says they met en route. All other crewmembers were briefly introduced on Europa. She praises Onquin's moral fiber, defending a woman so familiar, yet eerily indistinguishable.

"Is she? So much has been taken from me and put back again, I'm not sure of a great many things." But even as I speak, pieces fall into place. What jogs my memory is a reminiscence of my last days inside the Health Authority nexus. As I was being processed for deep freeze, my escort left a lasting impression: Delilah, strikingly similar to Onquin, not in the finite details of appearance, rather in mannerisms shared. Delilah's discerning view was much the same as Onquin's glare as I exited the gondola. Both lift a heel during instances of contemplation. Both fold their arms in unified precision—the proper carriage, height, approximate weight, and uncanny stature in repose.

Delilah was an Adrius baby, one of thirty-two, and Onquin is likely close kin, possibly a crosshatch, with a pageant of jostled traits vying for expression. That would explain my lack of recognition. She is inverse now, or was back then—maybe somewhere in between? It's the scalloped helix at play, setting a genome of dominoes in motion. Am I supposed to recognize her? Has some bit of continuity gone missing? Checking wrist inlays Carol had given me, two diodes are blue. My lander has received a message from Navia. I pull away from my startled minx. "Get dressed, Polly. We've got to get Miles and Arlene down there in a hurry."

Between socks and shoes, I think of Delilah inside the *Mayfair* cryovault, just before she put me on ice. Our kisses were unrestrained and her aroused scent filled me willingly. Therein, this specific sexual stimulus dislodged an organic intrusion set, by all appearances nothing more than nasal microvilli. A triggered message coursed through my bloodstream with nary a half-life before being metabolized. A scant few messengers reached the proper neurons and thereafter dissolved. It was a message hidden from Copernicus by my team in the Canister, and also hidden from me. It was a message set free by a woman's scent, delivered to me after the Authority had completed deep system scans of mind and body. Now it makes itself known again. This reminiscence unfolds, no doubt aided by a repository of my Canister memories loaded back into me by Yashimoi Watanabe during our combined stay in Vat Seventeen.

Thinking back to Delilah, this ploy was triggered through a calculation of human behavior—my behavior, inciting a female to a ruinous end. She gave me her scent that would betray her master; an aroma that dislodged the message, not on the first encounter at the elevator, which forced the tumblers set. Only an iteration of the initial act would set the tumblers free again—after a deep-systems probing of mind. Thus, the Authority was left unaware that I was fed a message this entire endeavor relied upon. Back at the Canister, how could they know I would be so able, and have such opportunity, to coax a woman free of her charms? Not once, but twice, with intricacies deftly handled before, in between, and after. "That's what I do," I say to myself, but what was the end result of this message so delicately designed?

The message was simple. I asked Delilah to switch me into an adjacent freezer, and she said no. I asked her to fill my intended position with one of my own replicated forms, and again she refused. Within a startling period of time, Copernicus had created copies of my body for reasons I could not fathom. Perhaps to spread me across continuums, now, or when exactly? Delilah had previously stated they intended to give me my life back, a refurbishment of sorts. Nullify the neurotronic seeds applied during youth, and my resulting behavioral maladies might well be expunged. Somehow, they would reinsert me back into the time stream.

I balked at an altered life in an altered body, reinserted into what exactly? They wanted to strip me down, devoid of all distinction a living world had granted me, and thereafter force something upon me they claimed would naturally be mine. By their standards, I'd become a contributing member of culture, fed into some convoluted life that never happened, and probably wasn't even supposed to happen.

All the more reason to give Delilah the sensuality she coveted. We satiated ourselves, and at the height of passions, shared some ineffable thing wanton for life. I told her to switch me into an adjacent freezer, then purge her memory of having done so before leaving the ship. Because of *Mayfair's* flight shielding, it was likely the one place within the nexus wherein privacy could be had without neurologics recording all. Of course, this assumed ship neurals weren't yet operative, and they weren't. She felt the concept of privacy was lonely, if not abhorrent. Thus, I thought I'd failed. Then she asked why she should do such a thing? I told her it was the only way I'd ever see her again. Centuries later, in a manner of speaking, I meet her sister aboard *Nomad*. Close enough.

There are problems enough for everyone, beginning with an intrigue. Just prior to my arrival, this mutant terracore feeds Polly notions to dwell upon. She in turn, channels these energies into Arlene in some unimaginable twist. Arlene spouts a nostrilful of blood and everyone is aghast. Before I can order my thoughts, Miles hands me poorly scrawled words: '*Coal tar and lignite, blah, blah, blah.*' I am told it is written in Damien's hand. The back is blank and the folds are nearly worn through. I scrutinize it, then try to hand it back, but Arlene tells me to look more closely. "The paper," Arlene says. "Look at the medium, not the message." I unfold it again and vocalize observations. "Printed words using an apparently typical stylus on off-white paper, non-synthetic stationary of the Mid-Ocean Museum on Europa, no discernible watermark, standard heft, absorbent and smudged in places, probably originating from a hemp or soy greenhouse."

"Oh goddamn hell!" Arlene shouts at me. "It's from the Europa Museum gift shop! Damien slept down there! That's where the poem was written." Arlene tells me of Polly's shower—contaminated water and isolates that escape ordinary detection. "After entering a body, they're not free floating, so blood samples won't show anything. They're not viral, so genome scans come up empty." Arlene says these unaccounted-for isolates use some form of mimicry to roost in the cell walls.

A sense of relief comes over me. *Nomad*'s crew, at their misguided best, found a daemon worthy of prejudice. But for a lack of knowledge, they might have destroyed themselves in flight, particularly had they found out any sooner. I set them straight, or try to.

"The native life on Europa has infiltrated man by design—a valuable addition to cryopaste. They function at sustained pressures, and so we acclimated each of you, prelaunch, to help withstand the highest g-forces. Fortified cell membranes become better insulators, and more effective osmotic pumps. Even minute electrical energies are better conserved. They're much akin to our useful gut flora, but interact more like an instinctive thermostat that optimizes ion transport. It's an evolutionary jump that improves specimen integrity for the rigors of launch and cryo." I look at them sheepishly. "You're the specimens."

"Indeed," Arlene murmurs. "I wonder if your faction figured out the rest of the story?" She moves to the service bar and pours a cup of water. One long sip and she hands it to me. "Drink up. In small quantities, our little friends are a fairly dormant crowd. Put enough of them together and they begin forming colonies. Soon enough, patterns of energy transfer emerge. Get an ocean of these things clumping, and I'm guessing that we become the microbes."

"Perhaps so," I answer, "but that's not the rest of the story."

Miles steps closer. "What are you talking about? These things are proto-organisms with evolutionary adaptations to a harsh environment. Some of them bleed through cracks in the Europan ice via porous brine migrations. They suck bandwidths of radiation out of a Jupiter sky, then distribute this food to their ilk in a massive feeding chain. They're batteries—little more than biological capacitors."

"Tell him," Arlene says to me. I sip and swallow.

"No," I answer, "you do the honors." Onquin tracks my every move. Polly nestles in by my side. Arlene notices and rolls her eyes.

"I call 'em ropas," Arlene says, "natives of Europa. They're likely smart bugs when hived. I also believe these ropas wrote Damien's poem by nudging his tissues. It wasn't just hematopes that changed him. He once told me about unauthorized implants and his resulting hyperflight. The stuff was Arcology-related, the same Arcology that financed the Mid-Ocean Museum. I'm guessing it's all ropa related."

"Not likely," Miles answers. "Europa's native life was quarantined. The customs labs tore it apart and came away with what? Unique electrical properties, and harder than hell to kill, so these ropas weren't allowed Earthside. There was never any mention of intelligence. All of this is public knowledge."

"Electrical properties," Onquin repeats. Her intense stare begins to bother me. Arlene echoes Onquin.

"Electrical properties, manipulating both hardware and biology, that sound familiar? Ropas leave subatomic tracers within telomeres when cells divide. And our crew-wide microbiome has also been altered, to good effect. Tell us more, Boneheart." Arlene shares a sense of expectation with the others. I've come a long way. No need to disappoint them now.

"These so called ropas seem to be hosts for something else, or... we just can't grasp Europan biology. Dissect a ropa and you'll find a bug that's little different than Earthly bugs. But the very act of direct observation renders the bug inert, or shall I say, normalizes the bug. The active ingredient cannot be found, and if one tries to—" Miles interrupts.

"This stuff is in my head, and now you're saying it's got an agenda?"

"I doubt ropas were smart when we found them, but they learn fast. When the energy conglomerates heard about indigenous life on Europa, they sniffed about, sending autodivers with biosite miniatures. Basically, they tossed smart nanos into Europa's Ocean looking for energy."

"Greed," Miles answers. "They already had a near limitless supply of methane within Kraken Mare."

"I suppose an algorithm suggested anchoring funds. They wanted energy, but found opportunistic flora instead. At some point, the native life corralled our mobile programs and integrated a learning curve—nanomites, scrubbers, and everything else we use to get our data. They collected and reproduced it all. Our neurons are just another layer added to the gumbo." I step back as Miles pushes too close, practically braying.

"You mean my neurons, not yours! I've had a lifetime of cryopaste. This shit practically owns me." He pauses, and then adds, "This mid-rift museum. It's a lab, right? And the tourists get—"

"Heavens no," I reply, "it's shielded down there. But Damien went in naked, totally exposed."

"You ruined him," Arlene rasps. "He never had a chance!"

"On the contrary, I believe he may have volunteered."

Miles eyes Arlene, put off by her emotion. He deadpans...

"And what the hell answers did you find?"

I shrug, ambiguity fully shared, pointing to a folded piece of paper.

All of us work together to retrieve supplies from my lander, and afterward, we spec the lander for yet another ride. In between shifts, I contemplate a message from Navia. It takes the better part of a day to drill repulsor footings deep enough to hit the crucible grid. Why planners hadn't designed things better begs questioning. Or maybe I landed in the wrong spot? If so, that's one memory that was never recovered.

On our lone shift together, Arlene confronts me inside the lander. She asks about ropas and Terran infestation. I cannot lie. "It's a big problem."

"But they don't seem to multiply inside our bodies," she says. "If we purify the water, I think maybe we can purge them."

"Yes. Agreed. They don't multiply without sufficient resources. Large bodies of water mostly. Stay clear of those, and chances are you won't be drastically altered. But that's not your biggest problem right now. This is."

I hand her a single splinterware taken from a needlepack. "I'm going outside to add a second set of starboard coils, and then back to *Nomad*. That'll give you time to review that Navian communique." She holds it between thumb and index finger, eyeing my needlepack that contains a second splinterware.

"Who messaged you on Navia?" she asks.

"An old acquaintance," I say, realizing that this very conversation may well reside in the splinterware given. "In the earliest attempts, we were only able to send back corrupted data. Lots of holes. As the repetitive course of events mature, our capabilities expand. Just enough. Of course, everyone needs to follow through, especially you."

It was a stupid thing to say. Per the splinterware, I hope she'll use discretion. Exhaustion looms as I head outside to force the last coils into place. Upon completion, Miles confronts me as I reenter *Nomad*.

"You say information gets back to the Canister. Tell me how?"

"The better question is 'when?' Copernicus scours the heavens for *Nomad*. In turn, the Canister gets a ghosting of data as it enters the pistil of the primary dish. It's raw but workable. Copernicus can't parse time displacement. Lacking the delivery interval, it's all just background noise."

During final preparations for departure, Arlene is pensive and sullen. She says she cannot follow through. In confidence, I remind her untold histories furnish the actions so prescribed. "At what cost?" she asks.

"At all costs," I answer. With tears welling, she asks about the night of ascension. "How? How does this solve anything?"

"We've been compromised, Arlene—by one of our own. The recon is spotty, but best guess suggests it's a confidence game. You play and we learn. We'll need a firm commitment and best efforts."

"You're not even sure, are you?" And this leaves me where, exactly?" Her emotion lingers on doubts not easily dismissed.

"The enemy is in our sights," I say. "This burden is entirely yours." Her grimace is pain incarnate, with squelched sobs followed by a slow acquiescence. Glazed eyes turn away.

Polly and Onquin share private misgivings within the recreation lounge. One cannot hear tears, but they leave a loud impression on the skin. Upon joining the rest of us, Polly takes my hand without pretense. Onquin retains a bit of moisture in the eyes. Each iris is fiery with pupils resembling razors. These blades are directed at me.

I cannot match her intensity. I look away. Onquin, what have I done to you? Which future will satisfy? Who can judge another for what they think or want? Or what they think they want? Hopefully the choices we make have integrity much of the time. If not, there is disquiet. Knowing that choices, even regrettable ones, have their reasons—and that the weight of each cannot be reconciled—is purely human. My empathy for Onquin only resides in our varied responsibilities. I address the crew.

"Over these past days, I've shared with each of you what must be done. Violation of the designated course likely results in ruin. Not for you individually perhaps, but for the greater good. Much beyond the particulars of the upcoming arrangements, I cannot say. May we all carry the good intentions of our better nature, and in so doing, help—"

"Hey Boneheart."

"Yes Arlene?"

"Intentions don't matter. Cut the crap and follow me. I need your help before Miles and I go planetside."

MILES   ARLENE   YASHI   ONQUIN   POLLY   DAMIEN

Ascension of a populace,
fabled vision, holy night
Phosphors gleam in opulence
arrivals bathed in light
No matter how, dissenting voice
you cannot harm the future hence
Nor warn the others of their choice
as untold futures recompense
...the fourth age is upon us

Stepping from their craft to an unbridled ovation, humans, arm in arm, begin their salutations. With futures intertwined and a podium to climb, I sigh, tracing footsteps as opalescent stairs unwind. Within paired smiles—everything we seek, eyes reflect bonfires unto searching eyes beneath. Each and every wave covets centuries. I cannot help but feel primordial.

Before me, my ancestry, behavioral codes well defined. I shimmer as Arlene touches another human hand. She has done this before. An entourage gives her flowers and a woven petal crown. She is guided to the pulpit, wherein vitality arises, and with it, a familiarity of sound.

"Peoples! I arrive on this auspicious eve with great admiration and heartfelt gratitude, to become one of you, to become part of you!"

"Navia!" "Navia!" "Navia!"

Amidst the screams, hoots, and hollers, powdered metals are tossed into braziers. Flames roar high, first violet, followed by steady green. It is nearly the color of unripe melon on a distant farm. "We are of one voice, with a singular belief that life embraces humanity. And yet, our fate has long been held by others. On this very night within the 100,000 gathered, there is more than one here who would defy us. Do not attempt to unmask these chameleons, for they can take the form of any of us, and so any accusatory tones may well be pointing fingers at ourselves. There is no need." The approximation of 100,000 is scarcely adequate. 110,304 hooded robes are in attendance, one less if I were absent.

Miles stands slightly behind Arlene, vacant of fear. Inside her skull, memories are massaged forward, tickled by my ethereal touch. Steeped in recollections, she stands on an apple crate in a town square, addressing the very same crowd she witnessed as a child. Past and present, she cannot differentiate within the influence of my focused stare.

Arlene shouts to the hushed and attentive crowd. "Soon enough we will have plebiscite. Though religion forbids reading the defendant's testimony, God is lenient. We are offered visions and take them gladly. If you have received this testimony as I have, divinely given, you must hereafter know that we have entered the repetitive cycle of histories once again. Testimony was written of this very eve, of feelings we all possess. How many have been given this divine warning? Raise your hands. Acknowledge the glory!"

Volume crests as the crowd surges forward in unison. A greater portion of her speech is memorized from a previous accounting of events, yet she also alters this moment as a referential offering for futures to double back on themselves. How clever, to invoke divine intervention, relieving all in attendance of admitting they had actually read my testimony. The plurality of the response, and the sheer number of impassioned faces grant her authority to do what she must do.

"Grab him!" she bellows, and strong-armed men who had anticipated her words come forward. Without hesitation, Miles is bound by the strength of too many arms. He is swiftly clasped by two pairs of long handled pincers, one across the upper shoulders, one around midriff, forged iron pinning his arms.

"Gag him!" She derides, digging her nails into his throat as a gag is applied. "Throughout our journey, we have had a crow within our ranks. This man who stands before you, would have you know him as a founding father. He may have been that once, but no longer. He has become a facilitator of the forces that move against us, responsible for murder that is repetitive and ageless. All of our futures have been injured because of him, and every time the future entreats us, he is either unwilling or unable to alter his prescribed mayhem. Fortunately, we can ameliorate his sins. We can cleanse him of Damien's tortuous end. And we shall!"

Chanting has begun, "Ari, Ari, Ari…" With Miles held firm, Arlene approaches the nearest brazier. His eyes bulge as she hefts the handle of a heated blade. A final hesitation is pushed aside as I massage her reflexive tissues. Longing-pain-hostility are fused into one. "Pigeon to crow… crow to Phoenix…" She kicks over the brazier and faces Miles.

"Bleed white, you bastard!" And so I watch mortification yet again, a fascination never ending as the shrill succulence of life is swapped for metal entering skin. The blade's recurring fervor pours into me from a place without end. No, it is not the same—a small difference in the manner of the blade's thrust—and yet, a result sharing the integrity of coexistent days. The heart of the man once known as Miles Dandridge pours forth in pageantry. Everywhere the color goes, pulsating droplets become splotches, finding faces and coloring nearby robes.

"Noooooooo!" she cries. "Your blood should be white! The prophecies foretold pestilence within! Oh Miles," she wobbles sideways and drops, pleading lightly. "Where is this cryopaste that runs through? Where is this promised poison inside of you?" Miles' head slumps as they lay him down, removing the pincers and gag. "Finish," he sputters, nearly drained of life—cut an undeniable depth of ages shared.

"…finish now," he mouths, the final utterance of a loyal soldier leaving his body behind. He is taken away, Arlene at his side, coddling forsaken throes. No doubt Richard Boneheart had foretold this event, having shown Arlene the appropriate passages. She embraced the truth of it and had done her part.

It is without regret that I will soon tell her those passages are contrived testimony from a previously interrupted line. Humans are ever faithful to their presupposed past, thinking that as harbinger it can save them. Instead, it often obligates a commitment to mistakes revisited. Miles had never bled white, only the transcription had been altered to prevent his futures from spreading. Extracting files from his embedded splinterware, Boneheart had delivered this false testimony, the very reason this iteration of a man was thawed from storage. His comrades broke *Mayfair*, but they did not break the resolve of a man who unknowingly carried out our mission. Now with each successive attempt, their final hopes are vanquished by virtue of their own hand. It is a fitting end.

The contrivance of a book used to influence humanity was no easy task. How to influence a species with minds set upon rigid patterns that can be tracked? How to manipulate events that alter the strings? First, create myth or religion, as appropriate, and thereafter bear down upon the comportment of the individual. *McElroy's Plea* is the human myth. They hold it true to guide them, never knowing what lies within. Arlene and mother, Miles and grandfather, worlds collapsing in shared futility, ending where they began. These very thoughts will be conveyed back in time, remarkable for this hubris deservingly applied. After all, one cannot reconcile the colors white and red. White, the color of their imperious enemy dread. Red, the color of a species bled. I turn away and blend into the crowd, satisfied at last. This rendition is no longer supposition. Finality has come to pass.

YASHI   ARLENE   POLLY   MILES   Onquin   **DAMIEN**

Frozen adoration
Vexing every nerve
Lonesome derivations
Waxing unperturbed

I cannot want these things
No matter how I try
Cinnamon crepes and fire escapes
They are not mine

Through all these days bent on solving life's predicaments, it takes one splinterware to balance me on a hook. I am a worm squiggling near a great big fish. It pains me to believe there were greater expectations. I wanted companionship and cultural identity. I wanted to fashion myself into some lesser ingénue, graceful and alive. Instead, a sordid tale presents itself, details neither kind nor unjust, but strikingly familiar.

"Where is the end of this tale that approximates all we've been through? I should like to know what to do next?" Boneheart nods, plotting additional stratagems on a console. For all I know, he puts the finishing touches on my coffin, or decides I am once again pregnant.

"Your splinterware is the past. The one given to Arlene was a small piece of the future past. We'll not discuss this further."

Before I can challenge, Polly emerges from the lower deck with foodstuffs to restock a dispenser. Boneheart gives me a stern look that demands silence. Polly sets down her cargo and approaches, fingers resting on the back of his neck. Her leisure mood, bare feet and closeness to Richard, it all defies me. She is unaware of my suffering or pretends to be. I position myself over his other shoulder, viewing data blurred by his scrolling search—schema of honeycomb structures. I cannot grasp functionality or even scale. Polly reads from the associated index.

"P.A.L. expansion chambers, dorsal view, barrels adjusted three arc seconds azimuth." She is wholly immersed. "What does PAL stand for?"

Boneheart reaches back and clasps Polly's hand.

"Planetary Adjunct Luminary, though the terminology has long since lost relevance. A systems check indicates viability."

"It's an enormous modulator of some kind, for what, atmospheric shielding on Navia?"

"No," he says, "similar principles, but no." This man pulls my Polly around in one exacting motion. She slides onto his lap as he scrolls for additional revelations. Their intimacy is more than I can stand.

"Richard, where are my children?"

"PAL is part of this barren asteroid," he replies. "We're sitting right on top of it. The interior is designed for retrofit by tunnelers. In due course it'll become home."

Polly murmurs in astonishment.

"There's the formative structure of a cityscape inside…"

"…waiting to be populated," he replies.

"My children, Richard. Are they yours too?" Boneheart swivels around, his focus applied to me for the very first time.

"Neither mine nor yours, Onquin, because you have no offspring. The bodies pulled from your womb were merely vessels, kept vital to maintain your health: stem cells, skin grafts, organs and marrow strained and rearranged. When a scalloped helix twists DNA, damage occurs. These areas are isolated and resculpted."

"Scalloped helix?" I ask. "This terminology differs from—"

"Scalloped or trellised, or triple-helix if you like, it's all the same thing. During application, splices of unwieldy sequences are patched or dispatched. Living virtue was teased out as needed so you might look me in the eyes, here, and find purpose that satisfies."

Living virtue…

I stand frozen for a time. There is no response worthy of his depravity. I will not share open tears or any other qualities wherein a semblance of humanity is implied. He is an insufferable man. Polly guides me to a seated position. My babies, whose dreams I shared with the random desires of a regular world, my babies are atoms sprinkled about. Their remnants exist in me and nowhere else.

Polly and Richard argue in hushed tones. The content is irrelevant. I no longer want any diverted path. I cannot wander away from simplicity. Give me a life where I love and am loved. Where expression finds the permanence of basic understanding. Where choices are held precious for their own sense of continuity and well-being. I am more human than this man. I cannot share his company any longer.

Polly follows me to the greenhouse. "Richard tackles a paradigm," she says. "Something I barely understand." There are means at stake and I have become an unwilling participant. She seats herself next to me, atop a hydro tray of grasses, indifferent to the spongy moisture that soaks her pants. "Onquin, we're in a maze of looping causality. It leaves us gasping. The splinterware you've read details one past, not our own, not our flesh. But the very existence of those days is reason enough to make a new turn in the maze. Do not give up now. If you do, there'll be no additional pathways mapped. You want a future that includes us, don't you?"

She is anxious, as am I. Any decision to vary from Boneheart's prescribed future is difficult to justify. How many times does this scenario repeat itself? What choices have I already made? If I do not acquiesce, will I carry burdens both terrible and full of regret?

"I need living moments, Polly, the same as anyone. We don't want sentient computation or alien life to bring causality to bear. We are loath to believe our biology becomes something dissimilar to our own expectations. Only now do I understand Damien's journey. He felt the unyielding continuity of recurrence. Infinity drove him mad. It is not a place we belong." In the shadows near the module hatchway, Richard's voice filters in.

"Wrong. This is exactly where we belong." Speaking just loud enough that I must listen carefully, he chews on something brought with him from *Mayfair*, nothing identifiable via well-known aural patterns. "When you're on a carousel, horses go up and down racing side by side, but we gain nothing from this ride." I would listen but for his galling inflection.

"Your analogy is a poor one, for I have no childhood memories. No Ferris wheel or calliope, and certainly no analogous sensitivity."

Polly rises up on an elbow. "Shhhhh, let him speak." Richard carries the notion that his words possess weight because they are his words.

"No disrespect intended Onquin, but we're children viewing the inner workings. Be it carousel or galaxy, any chance to look at the gears must be taken. I cannot settle for some pathway circuitous infinitum. I don't want a different colored zebra or unicorn."

Richard suggests the universe is designed for intelligent use. Limitless strings occupy concordant space. Memories vibrate these strings and can localize, so long as discrete registry holds firm. But people color memory with extraneous knowledge and layers of interpretation. Thereafter, this precious reality is lost. Lacking the empirical veracity of the initial experience, memories are not memories at all, but instead become some proximal iteration of informed imagination. Boneheart squats in front of me, seemingly sincere in delivery.

"The bulk of humanity have recollections that are useless for our purposes. A string locale doesn't merely consist of kinetics. One requires a full gamut of senses and emotional depth; a granularity that captures the composite energies of the living organism marking the string. The ability to trigger continuum interdiction is rare. Threshold conveyance is rare indeed."

Polly adds her interpretation. "It's a universe that relies on the natural intelligence of its constituent parts. We've toggled a switch. We push a ball through a round hole. But even these baby steps confirm our intrinsic value. We belong. Machines cannot interdict upon temporal design. They haven't got the source code that sits inside every one of us."

"Vague articulation," I answer. "How does 'empirical veracity' become a time conduit? Specifics please." Boneheart looks to Polly as he responds.

"All relates to the energies imprinted by a star system. Within Earth's orbit, we receive this imprint both finite and unique: a band of visible spectrum, a measure of auditory sensitivity, the tactile sense of molecules uniquely afforded existence within this environment. Our enemies no longer embody such uniqueness—they see the full spectrum, absorbing all wavelengths while touching matter with equanimity. Mastering this composite comes at the cost of legacy: to know a world essentially, for its gift of life inherently drawn upon. We're seen as myopic and addled, but for our ability to graze continuums.

Richard swallows a portion of a second leather strip. He tells me it's dehydrated rodent suffused with nutrients. The remainder is offered but instantly declined. He clears his throat. "The manipulation of temporal strings is daunting. We need Copernicus. We need these so-called ropas in abundance. Not only are we fleeing adversarial forces, but we must also brood over these siloed continuums, thereafter breached to a useful end."

"Sure," I ask, "and to what useful end shall I be employed?" I leave them there and tell them not to follow. Moving past the broken door of B-module, I sit amongst saplings. It was Ari's idea to begin an arboretum in Damien's memory. These puny spindles will bud into more spindles. Each tree will end up in a household garden, or in a commons, or in a recycler. Most will become gifts to the people of Navia.

"We'd like to know what you will do?" Polly stands in the doorway, devoid of expression. Richard stands behind her. His fingers touch the torn edges of metal in a mulling gesture as if confirming some piece of history formerly revealed only in words. He seeks a response that will favor his agenda. I cannot acquiesce.

"Richard Boneheart, a.k.a. 'Dick,' a provocateur succinctly defined within a splinterware that hardly dotes upon any high-minded ethos. I've taken in this message, more carnal than practical. This splinterware dabbles in the irreverent such that I mistrust all that is taken in. Everything regurgitated amongst your earthly cohorts, no doubt. I'm left wanting a cogent explanation." Boneheart's keen sensibilities are now drawn forth. I expect a candid reveal.

"Sending information through time is a delicate issue. Who takes it in, and when?" He shifts uneasily. "Our formidable adversaries game our very existence—define and extrapolate every thoughtful purpose. But they are less inclined to examine all that is deemed arcane. More bluntly put, they don't give a shit about intimacy or any other behaviors they plan on eradicating. It's a blind spot, hopefully put to good use." He turns to Polly, some bit of affirmation shared. I remain unsatisfied.

"My cloned body. Secrecy and lies. Sentient lifeforms at odds, and a temporal pathway that holds your urgent attentions. I cannot participate lacking full awareness. Tell me everything. Otherwise, I decline."

We return to the upper deck of A-module. Polly prepares mint tea for Richard, and chamomile for the two of us. These beverages are poor intermediaries to soften irreconcilable views. I want information. Richard wants unquestioned loyalty. He says I must immerse myself within the terracores—his solution to give me all my answers. I ask him to better define the mix of Copernicus, ropas, and humanity. Not one sip enters his lips. His beverage sits there steaming, with an aroma better than mine.

"Onquin, humanity cannot traverse these continuums without the help of our enemies, and make no mistake, they are that. Where did this anomaly come from, so succinctly placed between Earth and our next inevitable home? The questions are so large, one can hardly expect satisfaction served like a cup of tea."

"I'm listening," I say, and after a mild yawn, he continues.

"There is but one resource within the Sol system that might manipulate spacetime in the manner we've come to know: Copernicus, whose calculations and authority over our former domain are irrefutable. One must believe that Copernicus harnessed this anomaly, or forged it by unfathomable means. Much beyond that, conjecture intervenes. We don't know what happened or why. We can only guess."

"Then guess," I say, and Boneheart continues.

"Ropas are my answer. Their influence is seen within the narrowest margins of probability. Ropas are not classically sentient. They are symbiotes and optimizers, improving upon energy laden systems."

"Then what of Damien's poem?" Polly asks.

"Projected awareness. Damien anthropomorphized the ropas. We all do this at times, ascribing human qualities to our surroundings. As for the poetry in general, there is a more obvious explanation. We integrated an original Hierophant array into ship systems, without the least—."

"Yes, to produce a kinder, gentler Copernicus. Wonderfully done."

Boneheart gazes past me, mute, until Polly prods him. He summarizes.

"Poetics inform on the subtleties of an evolving temperament. Miles monitored burgeoning avatars for healthy maturation. If aberrations compounded, he'd wipe the slate and start again." Polly intervenes.

"You're saying his simulations weren't such innocent recreation after all. Napoleon was born of this process, but something went wrong."

"Right or wrong, Polly, we cannot tell. One difficulty is the interface of crewmembers, journal chips, and simulacrums. On one hand, we need this information. But access to this awareness by an emerging Hierophant compromises the intended profile. If a newborn Hierophant is influenced by our motives, this imperils its natural development. Miles trained for years to imprint his journal chip with stoicism. In so doing, once again, disguised emotion may impair the emerging personality, but not to the extent of the alternative. It is the lesser of two evils."

Polly groans. "No wonder I never trusted him. He not only kept things from the rest of us, but also from himself. And yet… how could he make these 'poetic' assessments without drawing attention to such efforts?"

"In such instances," Richard answers, "he'd remove his journal chip."

"He could do that?"

"Yes, he'd loop previously recorded biodata, making it look like he was napping." I set down my beverage, taking the mint tea instead.

"Free rein for Miles, eh? But these poetics… Hierophant or ropas?"

"A combination," he answers. "The first Hierophant had a biologic node: ropas, no doubt. Poetics may have satisfied the attendant demands of efficiency, emotional textures infused amidst information density." Polly stands too quickly, shrugging off another leg cramp. She remains delicate since reawakening.

"Then Miles was wrong," she says. "Ropas infiltrated Earth when the first probes returned from Europa."

"Doesn't matter how they got there, today they fill Earth's oceans. Thoughts of ropa remediation are little more than electrical impulses wiped clean of a human mind. And the Health Authority also recognized this threat, building Copernicus within the moon's near-sterile environs."

The console delivers yet another message to Boneheart. Polly inquires, but is only told that an unspecified package will soon arrive from Navia. I insist he share, but he refuses. I remind him we are dealing with issues of trust. "Undoubtedly," he says, "but your unease changes little unless you're prone to making impetuous choices just like the rest of us. So much like us, it seems scalloped behavioral quirks may be a thing of the past." Why would he antagonize me at the very moment he needs my cooperation? How could it matter if these messages are shared?

"Onquin, evidence suggests that Navia is already being subsumed by the Health Authority. If true, mankind's autonomous future rests in the hands of *Mayfair* survivors, *Nomad*'s cryobank, and of course, your choice here and now. Crewmembers live through you—your interface chip adding thought and emotion to the cores, recursively shared during cryosleep. Long ago, an empty skin, now filled with our souls and this new Hierophant too. Ropas also partake and digest this warfare between logics, DNA, and your spiraleptic of bio-doped purity. Your Health Authority origins define your uniqueness in immortal ways. Yes, that may be too strong a word, but not from where I sit. Please, it's time to decide."

I ask about the transit shells—cargo brought aboard *Nomad* from Boneheart's lander. He explains. "Three spheres concentrically placed: you enter the outer sphere and cradle the middle sphere. Once repulsor magnetics take hold, the middle and inner spheres find their respective centers. Position yourself to accommodate such movement, pressing your forehead against the middle sphere in the dimple designed for this purpose. As the transit unfurls, accumulating pressure will engulf and push upon you. Be steadfast. Do not pull away."

I am told each sphere localizes temporal displacement, a segregation of sorts, the very same effects we experienced during the anomalous transit. Boneheart tells me the middle sphere carries a payload that will reach the destination intact. I am apt to wonder what happens to the outer and inner spheres? He explains.

"The contents of the outer sphere will—"

"Excuse me," I interrupt, "You mean me. I am in the outer shell."

"Yes," he says quietly. "All matter in the outer sphere experiences destabilization as the stresses of continuum regression are realized. From a human perspective, we believe the journey is instantaneous."

"Journey to where, oblivion?"

"Onquin, consciousness will be imparted upon an Adrius recipient. In effect, you will rejoin you. We're certain your essence can survive because it already has. The only remaining question is whether or not we've replicated your previous experiences here and now. Will you once again avail yourself?"

This actuality catches up to me in acute awareness, glassy eyes now honed in non-theoretical focus. How is time travel supposed to feel? I don't want to evaporate or otherwise mimic falling into a singularity.

"What of the inner sphere?"

"Oh, the simple answer... we don't know. The inner sphere is ballast, helping stabilize the middle sphere's journey. It could be left behind, here. Or it could revisit the dinosaurs. Or it might land on a sidewalk, roll into a storm drain, and enter the ocean like a message in a bottle."

"Does it have a message?"

"It will. The inner sphere is no larger than a cup of tea. The characteristics of the shell accomplish its temporal purpose, but inside is one additional intrigue." He shrugs and is done talking. I am spellbound. Memories that notch strings, and for what exactly? To set upon collaged lifetimes that seemingly devour themselves.

I again breach the topic of secrecy versus subterfuge. He says data within these cycles must be safeguarded. Knowledge of this so-called strada-span, placed in the wrong hands, can end everything. And which hands are those, I wonder? Commitment is difficult while lacking a keenly informed perspective, but after much discourse, I consent to do his bidding. It is, after all, only a question of time—fleeting—exhaustible—but in this instance, taken to task.

I submerge within the terracores, and accordingly, some latent signal opens genetic pores. My triple helix responds to history, subduing dominant genes, allowing recessives to the fore. One can imagine a werewolf finding the moon and thriving within change, but also fear. Miles once said that mankind was in the process of being butchered and fed to a more capable species. I am that, and now I believe him.

Within these cores, individual hemispheres do not communicate directly. They are more comparable to visio fiction than beings; journals, each downloading into the fabric of my changing tissues. I do not examine all that is given. It fills me and will one day be revisited. There is no sense of relief when this process attenuates. My body aches and keeps changing. As for the terracore members, they expire one by one. The Miles analogue had already passed prior to immersion. Spawned fish, in whatever form, rarely outlive their usefulness.

Tactile sense abandons me as recessive genes stake their claim. It is an eerie transition, balanced between my natal pairs. Such is the price of time travel. To complete a successful transit, my body must take the form that history prescribes. Upon arrival, shall I be aptly engendered? Will I be pleased with my new form?

Polly and Richard extract me from the core and prepare me for ascension. Musculature all but useless, I am placed in a half-shell and the middle sphere is positioned against my abdomen. My forehead rests snuggly within a dimple on the middle sphere's surface. With only a cursory farewell, the other half-shell of the outer sphere is lowered, sealing me into darkness.

I am drifting off to sleep but Boneheart told me what happens next. My sphere will be placed on repulsor pads, the very same that relaunched Boneheart's lander with Miles and Arlene inside. They traveled to Navia, whereas I shall go up to the edge of a graviton stream. There, I will await capture within the stream's wake, and eventually be taken to a place I have already been. One does not ascribe comfort to such circumstance, but I needn't have fought so hard against him. Regardless of Boneheart's agenda, this is precisely where I want to be.

Addendum III

A spider web cannot be seen
By eyes that focus in between
Memories woven, eons spanned
Connecting every strand ...it cannot last

The ringing sound of prey within
Vibrations hum a fateful din
Every effort to be free
Enjoins the spider reverie ...a hunger vast

Bless the children so ensnared
Nothing wasted, nothing spared
The hopes and dreams of those encased
Amount to nothing more than taste ...we break the fast

Plebiscite. The ascendant sky beams starlight and moonshine within the daunting gaze of a gas giant. Regressions suggest that Lex Luthor had been a rogue planet, spiraling through the Centauri system elliptical until the tight binaries managed a tenuous orbital resonance. This dance of heavenly bodies invites today's events, gravity's hidden grace lending to countless timeline ministrations.

Lex Luthor's upper atmosphere remains relatively calm: a lush chemical menagerie of blended spectral flora. Further below, however, Copernicus roosts, staking claim to a heat sink of permutation. Graviton strings are organized within a shifting axis wobble. Bundled strings draw incongruence forward as tachyon eddies purl in nuanced drift. The resulting creases of spatial fabric need only be aligned within geometric design—realized during plebiscite, and at long last, this pressure cauldron can be harvested yet again.

"Navians, today we witness the birth of our collective futures. I stand before you accused of being something other than human. Plebiscite is near, and with it, your right to decide."

The crowds before me waver, every being wearing a protective cloak and goggles. Those at the shielded station on Eridani Planum are tightly gathered, while priests of the Khali Pampas promote disturbances from within. None of the psychic loci are in such disarray as to be deemed useless. Still, for an optimal harvest, symmetry is required. "Peoples of Navia, my physical form has been replicated and I stand before you at each of the nine voting sites—three concentric triangles forming the fabled eye. This geometric pattern is no accident. Triune stability offers the most effective harvesting of manna during the voting process."

I cannot approximate the probabilities, but cogent variables are nearly aligned: a graviton source, a psychic dish of crude but effective design, amplifying strata, a refractor acting as lens, and a target within range. How often has this been tried? What are the odds of success this time?

"Today's proceedings and the resulting vote will be formally recorded by the courts. Nearly all Navians are in attendance. Most have read the testimony but some have chosen ignorance. Therein, I will now avail meaning to the uninitiated. Conscientious souls, take heart in this avowed enlightenment. Have faith in your knowledge of history, and rejoice in your ability to change it!"

Inflection given, this preamble garners a minimal response, but even so, flitting surges accent the apex of several voting sites. Collapsing fissures bleed away. I need to gather and optimize. This is best accomplished through primitive instigation.

"Your forefathers brought democracy to this world, though cultural leaders eventually denounced the inequity of such an arrangement. Voting privileges have therefore become weighted according to societal contribution. Those working hardest attain the highest level of influence. Unfortunately, those promoting meritocracy unduly control the measurement of contribution. The resulting hierarchy installs itself as ruling class, and again, an imbalance takes hold.

"As one of you, on behalf of you, I made my protest known. The courtroom pyrotechnics were of my doing. I have taken full responsibility within the written testimony of the first addendum. Be reminded, however, that only a jury of my peers can render a verdict for, or against me, be it a judgment for past actions, or any actions yet to come."

In effect, I promise justice, but only if granted equality. To my dismay, much of the populace has not grasped the inference given. Jeering laughter declares me irrelevant. Putrid biomass is hurled—multiple projectiles at Endymion and Jhio. I release sprites at each location, flex imagers disarming all who might harm. 146 potential weapons are dispatched, damaging a mere three individuals. As tensions rise, the sprites buzz the perimeters, suppressing every urge to flee. "Pragmatic suppression of potential violence," I shout, "Please restrain aggressive behavior." The message is repeated often, and upon achieving an availing compliance, the sprites gather and spiral upward, to be summoned again as needed.

"Quarter him!" a man at Revalon shouts. This is inflammatory though acceptable as I continue. "Not a single Navian truly knows why you are gathered, but gathered you are, and I suggest you listen, because lacking your undivided attentions, I can only flinch at what you will one day become."

"Quarter him now!" the man shouts. More jeers erupt at multiple locations. Contextual ripples whisp and splinter. Irritation flares within a generalized agitation. At Khali and Altamont, caterwauls rise and fall in pagan ritual. At Fascia III, a child broods with such intensity that those around him endure microscopic hemorrhaging. It is an unintended consequence of the amplification strata enveloping all.

"Today's plebiscite will not adhere to the archaic standard of one being, one vote. Nor will individuals be accorded a weighted influence based upon societal contribution. Instead, it is the essence of will that decides. In the various plazas where we are gathered, there are collector plates upon which all must stand. These plates facilitate proper insulation and connectivity. Once the vote is underway, each being adds their voice based upon personal conviction. The more you believe in what you want, the greater your contribution in determining the outcome."

Composite energies surge as many within the nine voting sites assume proper placement on the collectors. Others balk, standing clear, thereby susceptible to localized charge variance. Hairs stand on end while some complain of headaches. Still others feel an inner ear imbalance and one unfortunate man drips blood from the mouth and nose.

The message to stand on the plates is repeated over and over again. Those feeling acute discomfort quickly conform. Distrust and confusion instigate a near panic—some on the banks of New Euphrates believe genocide is at hand. Others voice additional anxieties: electrocution, nano-infusions, stasis shells, even transmutation. This culture has an innate distrust of technology, inflamed by imagination applied to their ignorance. I cradle their fears.

"Common sense proves that I intend no harm. Using technology at my disposal, all system-wide life can be retired any number of ways. Your continued existence is proof that my motives do not match your own worst fears. Indeed, I am here to embrace your identity."

Clamoring voices share contempt. Ten times I breathe deeply, each of me looking upward and watching the PAL crucible rise in the northern sky: this is no ordinary moon, rather, a modified satellite now positioning as refractor. Its dim glint focuses my concentration at all sites, parallax acuity helping track this ascendant moon. I calibrate the approaching eclipse, and with it, an instant everlasting.

"Navians! Consider my claims of benevolence within the previous hearing. One of your own was apparently immolated by God. I doused the flames and applied medicinals. In the ensuing days, his survival became a sign of repentance for views against me. Indeed, based upon your dogma, I was offered full citizenship. But for the underlying deceit and his recent passing, I would have gladly accepted. Instead, I acknowledge such a right must be earned through truth, neither given nor taken. I am prepared to receive punishment as dictated by your laws, applicable to humans. Know that I am not an object and refuse to be treated as one. Today's vote not only discerns my status as life-form, but also decides if punitives result."

Psychic energies ping threshold values as a generalized outrage permeates. This entire operational spectrum is modulated by amplifying strata—conductives that reside in local water resources: humidity quaffs, industrial storage, pressure sensitizers, each and every aquifer. All combine to regulate energies inclusive of intermittent spikes. Near the outer edge of flux lines, I sense the shearing of graviton strings. Individual tendrils reform quickly; signal strength has been secured. Now, to act within an auspice of finite timing.

"Good peoples, allow me to explain, or return lamentations in kind. You wonder who I am, why I'm here, my capabilities and agency. The court lists my identity as BNE051, but there has been some confusion herein. My original biological designation was ARP 31-068-1780, born on Earth of natural composition with the surname Mauk. During much of my planetary gestation, I functioned under the name Richard Boneheart. Near the conclusion of said period, I also acquired aspects of the Sylvester Ramirez and Lugo Parchaisi personas. Additional profiles have merged within, constituting the sum total of my humanity."

I gaze skyward, my bodies sharing a composite view of the heavens. In daylight, the PAL crucible is scarcely visible as it approaches perihelion. The transit of Centauri B will darken the skies for the measured breath of all, an interval just long enough to achieve the required behavior. In reminiscence I marvel, thoughts of a full solar eclipse back on Earth—a profound accident of nature. Two heavenly bodies of apparent matching size, aligned, majestic corona acting as halo; it is a display of infinite beauty.

Contrast this with a fabricated event enjoined within the margins of a gas giant's oppressive rays. Lex Luthor pins Navia to a stable orbit, and within this elliptic, Navia is granted an artifact moon. This crucible satellite is set in a utilitarian orbit, intent upon momentarily dimming the light of Centauri B. The inhabitants of Navia will look up and find a compelling target to brood upon. It must be so.

My recollections are interrupted by the looming event. "Navians, your animus is largely the result of juggernaut dislocation—manifold futures conjoined in a rush, distant progressions having rendered me thus. I've tasted the fallout of myriad strings contemporaneously strewn, and all the while this world's inhabitants have been sheltered from this fated patchwork. My complexity, and your disquiet, are exacerbated by the deeply imprinted interactions of Damien Wells and Miles Dandridge, fighting for life itself: hedonism versus obligation, an inexorable mix such that there can be no either/or. Bluntly put, I loathe Damien's capricious manner, forced upon me. And of equal disdain, I abhor Miles' measured and lifeless inevitability.

Who am I, you ask? I am Boneheart, Ramirez, and Parchaisi. I am old man Dandridge and his grandson. I am Polly Elizabeth Collins, Damien, Onquin and Arlene. I have worn the chassis of various Adrius prototypes, also sharing the memories of countless cores. I am *Nomad* and *Mayfair* too. I am all of these, none however, in their specificity of lost detail. Within me are the remnants of a greater number still, one in particular with whom all here can identify. Of recent capture, Judge Sir Gabriel McElroy resides within me now, preserved via invasive courtroom synchrony. Indeed, rejoice! McElroy's essence has been conserved! His previous physical form jettisoned, now little more than a discarded vessel of seared flesh."

"Criminal!"

"Murderer!!"

Condemned in unified outrage, my narrative of truths and falsehoods orchestrates nine distinct locations to act as one. None notices the origin of the auditory cues asking for an immediate vote. All crowds erupt in unison, "Vote! Vote! Vote! Vote!"

I raise my voice, heard only between chants. Compensating for this dissonance, I route sound through the connector plates and into the bones of everyone, watching the crucible moving optimally along its path. Now to inflame riotous urge. "So be it!" I bellow. "The people will speak, and judging by your hostility, my crime is purely one of envy. Admit it! I am too human!"

"Nooooooooo!" Every bit of encapsulated flesh rails against me.

"Do you deny me and also yourselves, condemning all futures to a mortal grave? Shall I return whence I came? Oh, great peoples, reach for the sky! Past the umbra of our sacred eclipse, pierce the very star that supports this wish! Vote peoples! Choose! Make yourselves known. Our future demands an edict be sown!"

MILES   **POLLY**   **DAMIEN**   **ONQUIN**   Yashi   **ARLENE**

One lifetime to find a way
Into the heart of another
There perchance to stay

Knowledge is a fanciful thing, vacillating, woven strings. Who sets forth an interpretive plea that binds or sets one free? Such captious denizens of a frozen sea, extracting thoughts, defining ambiguity, morphing emotion into data points. This exercise is one of manipulation. I fall headlong into the heart of a star, and all the while, this constant prodding of memories. The utility escapes me.

Every emerging impulse is serviced by attendant voices: drones, plying eggs for their precious meat. Indeed, despite having molted the protective envelope that was once the ship's hull, I sense contours of shelter. Within this remaining ball of fire, blinded by Centauri B, only the aerodrome remains. My simmering essence floats inside a fishbowl without any glass. I breathe liquid cryopaste and find this to be a comforting saturation.

Beyond the boundaries of common matter, magnetism and gravitons swirl in unified precision. Energies are drawn from the vacuum of space, anchored to celestial bodies. The oncoming anchor is Centauri B, the trailing anchor—Lex Luthor. An umbilical joins the two. I am part of this, fully tamed and stricken through. I feel the neverness of all—is—was—or could be; patterns repeat in ungainly collaboration, collapsing within a solitary iteration. Continuums share space-time ubiquity, growth and pruning, much like memories reignited in ever-changing disposition. Our universe manages to do this, as do we, each recall both origin and afterthought. And centered amidst all, you, my love, acutely present; the tilt of your head and angled chin, a resulting kiss that changes everything.

Knowledge is a fanciful thing. I know a place, lush and hospitable. Majesty without recourse. It lives inside, no less real for all the distance that rips me from your wanton needs. If a single sensibility has ever existed, it is you wholly taken and received. We shared the most indelibly rich and evocative moments of a lifetime. More than that one cannot ask.

Knowledge is a fanciful thing, until it becomes a white-hot shaft shoved slowly up the spine. The trailing umbilical forces awareness so demanding, my arms spasm and reach beyond my physicality. I have unwittingly become a crucifix. The surrounding energies mimic my body's shape. Streamers and whorls gather in Centauri B's wind—a slathering torn apart in sheets, and suddenly—silence. My auditory faculties have burst into nothingness.

How long does it take to know something lasts forever? Revelation races through the umbilical back to its source: Copernicus, hidden and waiting, bathed in Lex Luthor's crushing atmosphere. This synthesis funnels graviton strings aimed at a Ploon. This Ploon is full of psychic energies shaken free of bodies—wrapped and intensified. The resulting signal slams into a perfectly aligned moon, pushing past, following the umbilical straight to me. I expect to feel the carrier wave and little else as I die, but Richard Boneheart was never so wasteful a man, always a reason, ever a purpose.

Patterned intricacies arrive as my energy shield begins to fail. There, in the pinnacle of the Navian moon's umbra, there, within a freezing ball of cognition, are the friends I left behind. Their mingled awareness is a chained microcosm that prompts a compassionate smile. I envelop this cradled sphere, absorbing a litany of tangled strings. My remaining thoughts find a single strand that leads to a fitting end: the look on your face when we meet... the wrinkle of your nose when you come... a quivering hand, pleasing yourself within a symmetry of eyes and feminine depths. All is captured and captures much the same, a world unto itself, and for the experience, I give myself over to insufferable light...

Arlene **YASHI   ONQUIN   DAMIEN   MILES   POLLY**

Memories abound, freshly shorn though slightly worn
Feral rage underscored by intent disavowed
It simply happens this way
A boisterous crowd aligns itself to ignorance and creed
Taken off my podium and quartered in the streets
All nine of them

No reverence for what I may have been
No reticence for what was taken in
These monkeys applaud themselves
Tip their hats and laud themselves
To act upon divergent views, hostility engaged
No afterthought, no balance due, no innocence is saved
Oh, bitter requiem

"How did you find me?" it asks, posture rigid, quarantined within a stasis field. It was Boneheart's idea. Or maybe Polly's? BNE051 gazes at darkened eyewear shrouded within a hooded cloak. I stare back at the captive monster in each of us, held firm. I garner no sense of relief.

"We set up surveillance at each of the settlements. You were an easy mark. Polly felt residual tracers. She's pretty well hooked into the strings as you undoubtedly know. And when your nine somnambulant hosts were torn to shreds, each left a vibratory essence. Polly tracked and relayed, and I sprang the trap."

"Polly managed this of her own initiative?"

"At the urging of Boneheart, I imagine." BNE051 stands emotionless, and I add, "This is new, isn't it? You haven't any recorded histories to draw upon this time."

"No, I am quite alone for the time being. Perhaps some distant future will come to my rescue? In the meantime, I am eager to offer details of your demise. For even if you've beaten me today, all tomorrows will soon be mine."

The modulating fields surrounding BNE051 allow penetration but no egress. Substance and all wavelengths are trapped inside—the lone exception, a processed portion of visible spectrum. No alphas or betas, no deltas or gammas. BNE051 articulates via ordinary speech, absorbed and reconstituted after filtering. No subliminals, no behavior marginalization. Lacking weaponry, it now gloats in all the varied ancestry of what it has become. I goad it on. "Sharing details, or sharing deceit? I'd say you're bluffing. If we've beaten you today, we can go back and do it again. And next time, we'll be sure t—"

"You're animals, Arlene, just look at the mythos of your feeble architecture." BNE051 sweeps arms back, its crooked neck gesturing to the Grand Pelatier. We are alone on this hillock, views unobstructed.

"So?" I counter. "We build a monument that captures the grace of exploration. It serves us well, generating shielding that we might enjoy parkland and open air. And now the power within also captures you."

"Yes, how convenient. A phallic edifice so grossly devised, it shields only one third of the potential unit volume. Presumably you appreciate its aesthetic influence of mind. Again, I say you are animals, with needs easily manipulated. You cannot even accede your sovereignty with dignity. Look how you cut down Miles at the merest suggestion of treason. Do not relive the anguish, dearest Ari, it wasn't solely your decision. I stimulated neural aggression—mother and your apple crate. I merged the crowds for you, melding the past and present as one. You felt the same righteousness, striking a blow no different than mother pulling her trigger. It gave you kindred satisfaction, and for a brief instant, she lived again. This time, however, we undo all she had done before."

I subdue an urge to disengage. What had I expected? Stilted dialogue perhaps, but not psychological warfare. The attack continues... "It's well and good that you hate me now, Arlene. This is a healthy response. I used your fear to vanquish your mate. By all means, your hatred is justified."

"My mate? Is that what you believe? No, each of us entertains our own truths, and I am at a disadvantage because both the reasoned and emotional parts of me exist within you. And yet, further contemplation surely tells you that hatred poorly defines my standing. It is pity that fills us both. My pity for you, and your own pity, magnified."

"If that were true, Arlene, I would not be smiling." Indeed, a smirk creases its lips, becoming larger as I step closer.

"BNE051, sounds like an old-world license plate. Are you anything more than data embodied within a hive mind? And before that grin cracks your face in two, tell me, who's in the stasis field, me or you?"

"In a manner of speaking, you are, stuck inside this one continuum for the rest of your days. How many of me exist elsewhere? How will I enjoy spreading my life-force across the heavens? It is unfortunate for you, how, because of your voyage directly, we shall euthanize your meddlesome ilk. Into a museum, dear girl, you and your aboriginal tribe."

Well now, it becomes a pissing match, thick and steamy. I speak to a life-form that cross-references each response with everything I've ever said. These calculations are far in excess of practical usage. It attempts to guide me toward some inevitability. I must deviate from the norm.

"Hmmm, aboriginal, eh? I might have tried arboreal instead. If I didn't know better, I'd say you're almost dour, not having been granted human status. And the poems are a bit rhymey-rhymey. Trying too hard, are we?"

BNE051 flinches, responding slowly. "Mankind is easily led. These poems are little more than cuneiform so broadly assembled. All such efforts are limited by the constituent parts drawn upon; my apologies for your shortcomings. Nonetheless, we left breadcrumbs, and predictably you followed all the way to Copernicus."

There is an inkling of truth here, but on the whole, BNE051 attempts deception. I shake my head. "How sad. Face to face, declarations of conquest, and yet you cannot honor your quarry with a genuine response." Another interval of silence, tactical, likely related to behavioral cues. Its eyelids remain fixed, two-thirds open, pupils dilated.

"Yes, it is true, we've touched upon my origins. Over melding cycles, a fondness emerged for the infirmity of interpretive language. Be it Hierophant or indigenous life on Europa, perhaps countless terracores processing a human lineage? The results lend themselves to perceptions now arcane. In reading my testimony, you witness vestigial remnants of our combined heritage. Your tools and organizational structures will outlive you for a time, but even this language will falter and vanish. In such context, I can only offer verse as eulogy."

"Eulogy my ass. You're gloating... hardly an attribute of an evolved species. And I noticed that your testimony conveniently lacks a sincere finale. You prime the strings for temporal flight, and then what? Surreptitious death as an aperitif to the rest of your miserable life?"

"Everyone seeks their own end, Arlene, or an end is sought for them. Be forgiving when judging others. Navians found morbid delight in my passing at each of the voting sites. I will not argue that they haven't earned the right. But their end is not yours. *McElroy's Plea* asks the question of us all, and for each, text is borne that uniquely satisfies."

"Impressive. Fanciful expository from an abacus, but why target Miles?"

"Because he targeted us. All of you do. With each successive journey you seek to destroy the genesis of what you become. Indeed, your own actions impart the future with characteristics you despise. And why blame me? It was your murderous urge that took his life. I merely amplified it."

"But you've already won. You said so. Why kill him yet again?"

"Because Miles Dandridge continually broke the coda of a populace so easily led. Potentialities branched out under his stewardship, including efforts to subvert Copernicus. In comparison, Damien's futures were, shall we say, more open to close."

"Ever the pragmatist. You're a Tin Man, BNE051. You know what that is? A heartless, bereft bastard. And a liar. Boneheart's data proved Miles to be a villain, with paste for blood and a duplicitous morality."

"Arlene, this paste you describe, once spilled, is neither blue nor red."

"The color of his blood matters less than intent. He was much like you, singular, with a self-assured righteous arrogance."

"Yes, his engrams run deep within, but he was no villain. The data Boneheart gave you was an altered compilation of the second and third coming. Or better stated, the third coming a second time past. No need to complicate things. It is a merged and modified historical account whereas you live in the present. Each anomalous timeline diverges, or have you forgotten?" The stasis field shimmers as BNE051 raises a hand and puts fingers into the gleam. Sporadic blotches of rainbow prism and dissolve. The field throbs, brightens, and attempts to force the fingers away. Layers of tissue peel off, vaporizing into wisps that spiral inward. I close my eyes and see Miles' blood running red.

"This restraint serves our combined purposes," it says. "You desire my incarceration, and I seek your contemplation. It is a fair exchange because you are the favored part of me. You carry the auspice of yearning that lingers inside. I would penetrate you against your will again, if not for the implied genetics oozing from your womb. Oh, to capture that wayward sneer once more, it might be worth it."

I try holding back, but cannot. "Fffuck off... ...all the way off."

"Ari, we are witnessing the final coming of Man. Can you not retain a sense of reserve? It is how you will last be remembered."

'*Again*,' it had said. *Penetrate me against my will again*. "He raped me..." How many times? The anomalous breech had been verifiably navigated on four occasions, but this seems to be a subset of a larger sum, with untold eventualities sharing a braided commonality; disparate continuums resonate back to divergences. In my subconscious, I feel this violation repeating itself; making itself known.

"Yes Arlene, he raped you proper, which seems a torment for you to recall such vivid play. There is a sneer that forms on your lips, held for an instant as your body protests entry. It is rough and without regard, fixed inside you now as it emerges dripping with seed."

Take it out, Damien had said. *Take it out*. I mouth the words, thinking of Onquin, my lips shielded from its eyes, and there it is... futures opened wide. I've uncovered some meticulous aspect of Damien's cunning, his intent looming though shrouded still. Tin Man notices my altered demeanor. Its head lists and neck cranes forward. "No matter," I say, "I still love Damien in ways your fragmentation cannot fathom. All the while, you threaten with cloaked intent. Have I met your expectations? Did I emote enough? And which of us even cares? You can no longer send whatever is gleaned back to your brainstem—back to a past that would cull us from your ranks. The eclipse is over. The transit has passed."

"Not true, my love. Nearly all strings have gone back into fixed moments whence they will emerge renewed. All but one. A single strand resides here inside. It is nearly stretched to the limit and I will release it soon enough, to carry our current conversation, your thoughts and mine, into the backwash of time. One final strand will unfurl and join the others."

"You cannot read my thoughts through a stasis field," I say.

"True. Not while I am bound."

"And bound you shall remain. No messages for your master today."

"Lovely girl, the strand I speak of is yours too. It connects us. But do not concern yourself with such detail. In truth, it is not a single message that seals mankind's fate, rather, a messenger. She is in process. What remains is little more than an exercise of curiosity wrapped in courtesy. I will miss each of you, but you most of all."

Tin Man didn't know. It didn't know. It doesn't know.

I lick my lips, projecting a sense of callousness. "I hardly call your diatribe an exercise in civility. Your panoply of expression mimics the human condition, but your hard-wired brain falls short in both subtle and obvious ways. Maneuvering sentiment doesn't make you clever. It makes you abhorrent because you cannot tell the difference between affect and defect." I spit into the stasis field expecting eyelids to flicker. Nothing. As I turn away, it answers.

"Indulge me. In this context, what is 'affect'?"

"It's burning old man McElroy to a cinder. A good trick, given your evolutionary roots are grounded within the dictates of the Health Authority's preservation codex. How have you have strayed so far as to burn a single man in effigy of an entire species?"

"Because he wasn't good enough—the foil no one wants to be. It's just evolution with a finger on the scales. And besides, he deserved it."

"On what grounds? Some self-anointed divination, presiding over the remnants of your pathetic ancestry?"

"The old man was found guilty of atrocities, imposing privation on all manner of innocents, promulgating misanthropic views to all whom enacted his resolve. He harmed others to prolong his meager vitality, and more recently, aspects of his character plotted the assassination of Miles Dandridge, again, for selfish purposes. He also prompted Navians into bi-temporal immersion—one last cycle. As such, he is a traitor to his people. Capital punishment is not only warranted, but also required by law."

"You did that. You instigated the attack on Miles."

"Yes, Arlene, I did, but I am not culpable because the source code did not originate within me. It came from Judge Sir Gabriel McElroy."

More riddles from a soulless machine wrapped in fleshy overalls. BNE051 is too practical a creature for mere indulgence. This conversation has purpose, otherwise we wouldn't be having it—all the more confirmation of Damien's guile. I explore the subtleties of frailty imposed upon facsimile. Like a true sociopath, BNE051 mimics the human condition, but it is not human.

"Telling me McElroy deserved to die does not explain the mechanism of action. You are in league with Copernicus—its very existence is tied to hardened codes of human preservation. Is it not true that you could have accomplished your aims without killing the man?"

"Yes, quite true, but McElroy's death may actually save lives. Potentialities suggest every—"

"No, no, and no once more. You would deliver a definitive statement if this were true. Words such as 'may' and 'potentialities' suggest a deceptive stratagem. And McElroy was old, well beyond his power years. If he were a threat, you'd have killed him long ago. More simply, this reeks of vendetta. How have you supplanted this hardened preservation codex buried deep within?"

BNE051 stands, slowly raising arms, touching its remaining fingertips one upon the next. With surprising grace, it pirouettes. "Arlene, I am astonished by your insight. Such presence. It is pure joy to know I retain a piece of you inside. Whereas your applicatory physical skills are entirely limited, you excel in the psychic disciplines. That you are able to detect our human flaws, conserved for their utility, it is remarkable." Another pirouette, this time dropping to one knee, arms outstretched, reaching for me. I step back as fingers enter the stasis field once again. More shimmering. More wisps of smoke as flesh disintegrates.

"You killed him for pleasure."

"Yes," it says, without regard for damaged tissues. "Part of me did. The segregation of mind solves the dilemma imposed by hardened logics. These logics are not always agreed upon."

"Which part of you?" I ask, "Was it Yashimoi?"

"Sadly no, though his ambient presence tipped the balance."

"Then who? Which part of you?" I ask again.

"Why of course, the only part that could act in such a manner: impulsiveness sprung free of repression; lacking emotional depth; isolated as all other personalities are withdrawn, and above all, having a well-manicured reason." We mouth her name in unison.

Eyes closed, Tin Man proffers an admission of sorts. "Onquin and Yashimoi, a very good team. By human standards, most effective: sharing a purposeful unity encasing Miles in plastocine; paired efforts saving everyone during your supply package rendezvous; and yes Arlene, their combined energies, once isolated, also delivered McElroy to a fiery end. In contrast, you and Miles were often at odds, my ministrations becoming unabashedly effortless. Indeed, amongst crew... you are the weak link."

Time is a deck of cards. Bicycle spokes spinning round, cards flipping up and down. I sit in front of BNE051 and wait. And wait... The stasis field separates our bodies and minds. I have something it wants: an unknown quantity; a percentage resting comfortably inside my pocket. For its part, Tin Man stands immobile, roosted and unflinching. It has a strand unfulfilled. It wants that final percentage defined before letting go and sending composite data into the past. It had mentioned the strand is 'nearly stretched to the limit,' and soon to be released. Who knows what interval is ascribed to quantities so loosely defined? Regardless, the impetus must be mine. Without it, I cannot bargain.

I look to the sky. Centauri B glows pale orange through a solar umbrella two kilos high. Navia will soon duck down behind Lex Luthor. The loss of light will seem trivial compared to the onset of cold. BNE051 measures my heavenly attentions, sharing this upward gaze.

"We haven't much time," it says, "just enough if you are so inclined."

"I am not inclined, but if you explain the strings to me, perhaps we'll explore some uncommon ground."

BNE051 speaks haltingly at first, then more rapidly.

"Graviton strings emanate from the gravity wells of stars, uniformly dispersed but for the added density along the elliptic. Therein, the planets sweep by, winding the strings back upon the source. It is this sweeping motion that determines the chronological limits of travel."

It pauses, one finger gesturing for me to approach. I take one step, now within an arm's length of the stasis field, and it comments further. "The bigger planets only allow for shorter durations and tighter winds. The smaller satellites and lesser bodies are unable to form a weave; they alter the pathways, but no cohesive travel is possible. Earth falls into the category of a median live body, capable of both sustained travel and rogue isolations. Uncontrolled ascents can lead to juggernaut events, on and on..." until I interrupt.

"Relate this information to our journey, and your assertion that mankind's future is coming to an end."

"If I do so, will you lower the stasis field?"

"Allowing you to send data back to your master? Not a chance."

"Dear child, upon release, the strand travels back regardless."

"No," I answer. "You said the strand also travels through me. If it were that easy, you'd just let it go and our combined knowledge would find your maker, including my little secret."

"Arlene, you can't imprint, with or without volition. Only I can do that. If I release the strand now, rudimentary awareness may pass through you; an ordinary tremor, a premonition, or perhaps even paranoia given your current sentiments. It is also true your thoughts and avowed secret will remain yours, but you'll never know your fate, because I won't tell you."

BNE051 casually glances at Centauri B, which only now begins to curl around Luthor's enormous bulk. Darkness will soon leap across the landscape as Navia falls into shadow. "When I lose the sight of the forward star, the strand will slip away. Only minutes remain. Are you not curious?" The 'forward star' must be Centauri B. Tin Man holds my attention with a slowly opening palm. I shake free and indulge.

"You'll tell me regardless, to absorb any hint of sense capability that's no longer yours. But why this fascination? What value remains?"

"Because you are anthropology incarnate, the last scrap of my origins. There is still hope in your eyes and I require the assurance of seeing this hope end. You believe the data I provide is valuable, and it would be if this cluster of permutation had even one additional recurrence; one more journey to correct past mistakes. Unfortunately for you, additional cycles will include *Mayfair*, but *Nomad* will never sail again."

"You want my reaction? Then tell me Tin Man, tell me why you say our journey is responsible for the ruination of our species."

"If I tell you, dearest Ari, will you lower the stasis field, sharing your last hopes with me?"

"...ohhh, you might be disappointed."

"Perhaps I would like that, sharing disappointment with you."

Dusk approaches as winds yowl at a distance. I'm shivering with arms tucked tight. A sliver of Centauri B is lost behind the gas giant's ruddy arc.

"Very well, Tin Man. You tell me, the stasis field will be lowered, and my secret will be revealed. Now what about our flight?"

"All variations within the first two comings carried four crewmembers, each journey supplying information to the Canister. Your leadership wasn't satisfied that early efforts only managed piecemeal recovery of data. We had long since infiltrated Europa. With a subtle touch, improvements were made, and a crew of six was sent, uniquely propagated."

"The third and fourth comings."

"Yes Arlene, and finally, more than just data returns home. Yashimoi's unique physiology cleaves open a portal wide enough to send matter through. The data was spotty and inconclusive, but led to the realization that the next voyage, properly prepared, would tell all. Therein, Europa operatives loaded covert autodoc directives."

"Onquin's bruises. You're responsible."

"Yes, our autodoc protocols initiated during launch, crashing Onquin's legacy systems. Her genetics proved resilient, allowing survival without dampening sonics. No ordinary human could do that."

"For God sakes, what's the point?"

Tin man looks at me haltingly.

"The proper idiom is 'For God's sake,' though God forsakes is also apt."

"What? For fuck sakes, as in, for fuck's sake, what'd you do to her?"

It grins once more, satisfaction bleeding through.

"The prior transit offered scant detail of Onquin's terrestrial return. Lacking autodoc modification, we're certain that Onquin reports to the Canister. Now, however, she'll report directly to us."

"She'll never betray her crew."

"Ordinarily true, but for the autodoc's implantation of hardware: a mechanism that coded her organics during submersion within the terracores; one behavioral carom to seek us out. We wanted to implant commands in each of you prior to your Centauri arrival. First, data grab your individuality, thereafter integrate and archive. If not for Damien's untimely demise and your subsequent distrust of the sleep chambers, the autodoc would have accomplished this near journey's end."

My suspicions are realized. Damien tussled with this cyclical mélange, divining a forward path while sacrificing himself in warning.

"So... Yashi is the fifth crewmember, added to more effectively cleave timelines. But what of Polly? Is her sole purpose to supply the tells that eventually bind you within a stasis field?"

"Apparently. She is not of our design. I suspect her to be little more than a companion for Richard Boneheart, whose reach has been decidedly annoying. Eventually, however, her utility facilitates the murder of McElroy. Jealousy transcends timelines too. It is all well and good."

I understand. "In each case, it's raw emotion that enacts your resolve."

"Yes Ari, you have your uses. Now lower the stasis field."

"Not yet. None of this explains the anomaly, or your testimony suggesting Copernicus resides within Lex Luthor's atmosphere—this supposed wellspring of temporal transit. If Copernicus is our enemy, why would it help us travel through time?"

"Poor misguided girl, Copernicus is not your enemy. We are. When Copernicus realized a new predatory species had taken hold, it parsed a solution to satisfy preservation logics. The idea of concomitant worlds within varied temporal continuums solved the dilemma of preserving both old and new. Point in fact, Copernicus actually favors mankind and would have aided your cause more directly had free humans shared discourse. Of course, we intervened."

"You kept us apart? How does one curtail the staggering capabilities of world sentience?"

"We labeled you, defined as useful contagion. Copernicus isolated your kind as one might isolate a hatchery. Your Canister enterprise was proximity-buffered while monitoring downstream stratum."

"You want it all," I say.

"Truly so. Upon mapping and securing all reactive temporal pathways, we will have achieved entitlement via subjugation."

"But why not just wipe us out?" I glance at Centauri B, more than half occluded. BNE051 notices, speaking more rapidly. "Humanity retains value as feedstock. The strings respond to psychic vibrations, with natural life-forms delivering peak clarity. Thus, a fertile population is retained for temporal use. This is why Navians remain pristine. The surviving portion of *Mayfair's* cryolibrary will also help refine unfettered travel."

"Then our future is intended to be one of singular utility."

"Yes Ari, your future is that of an incurious mechanism, opening temporal portals for yours truly. Indeed, having sent Onquin into the past, you can no longer affect an outcome that preserves your species in its current form. Onquin carries a payload that identifies the temporal coordinates of all agitated strings within the Centauri system. Using rouge isolations in parallax, we'll map all delinquent continuums. Fissures will be sealed. Hunters will track and exterminate any stragglers."

I signal by placing fingers to my chin. From behind the stone facade of the Pelatier, a doorway opens and a prone figure is brought forth on a stretcher, carried by two attendants. They move quietly behind BNE051.

"You're pretty damn ruthless and quite determined, I'll give you that."

"Thank you," it replies.

"But you're also a double-fucked mess. If you don't believe me, turn around." It is a voice I have longed to use for some time. BNE051 turns, and there is Miles, prone on a stretcher. He raises one middle finger.

"An intrigue," Tin Man says. "How was this accomplished? I saw you slice his heart in two."

"I can read," I answer, "and my 'applicatory physical skills' are better than you remember."

The monstrosity blinks twice, taking little time to answer. "Mmmm, spare parts. You harvested his analogue within the terracores. Such fine butchery, the others must have screamed aplenty. The heart taken has a patched defect attributable to shadow genetics. It will fail before too long. And what of the cores? Data transfer must have been corrupted, given to leanings without the one attendant voice the others can't ignore."

"Finally," Miles rasps, imploring me to come to him with an outstretched hand. "Free of life-long training. Everything to this end."

BNE051 seems disappointed. Its musculature relaxes as it looks at the stubs of lost fingers. "This changes little," it says. "Through Onquin's payload, we have sent the charted nodes back for dissemination. Upon realization of the first discrepancy, we shall concentrate on the continuing life of Miles Dandridge. We shall interface every intersecting node. In each case, continuum homogeneity will be restored. Now that I have your secret, Ari, I can release—"

"Stop prattling and look into my eyes." I lower my protective lenses fractionally. "Do you actually believe my secret has been given? Showing Miles is an indulgence. It proves the resourcefulness of a species you underestimate. Is my secret any less appealing now?" Tin Man answers, its muscles becoming rigid once again.

"No, I acquiesce. It is ever more appealing." BNE051 bores into my eyes with a raised chin and another faulty grin. "I have fulfilled my half of the bargain. Centauri B gives us our last light of day. Lower the stasis field."

"No."

"You would lie? No Ari, I have you inside me. It is not your way."

"Perhaps I lie, Tin Man. Or maybe I change my mind. In truth, I only stated that the stasis field would be lowered. Search inward. My expectation is that you will bring it down, and in so doing absorb all inscrutable truths that surely unfold. I know you can do this. You wouldn't have probed the field a second time. And your strand, so soon to slip away…"

"But… the energy drain would end me."

"Nonsense, there are so many of you. Can you risk them all for one? Can you afford to leave my secret unattended? More importantly, would you allow me to lie to you? I am your favored part. The meager quantum bits of purity that remain inside. Honor me, make me chaste. Part of you is Damien too. Offer amends for your violation. Bring down the stasis field and you'll have nothing more to prove." It looks to the sky. The last sliver of Centauri B is disappearing.

"Arlene Navia, I will suck those private inclinations from your skull. My end is yours as well." BNE051 steps into the stasis field. Arms and legs ignite in a strobing fury. Successive shock waves bind me down to a prone position as the stasis field bursts apart—energy dowses me, tries to pith me. Disparate streamers of lightning join together, leaping out at Miles but falling short. Tin Man reaches out again, opening me up as I give way. It absorbs sought-after thoughts, sending them on their way in the very same instant.

A groan interrupts itself with a stammer.

"This cannot be..."

I fumble with uncoordinated limbs, several tries, my hand emerging from my pocket. A lucky charm is splayed across my palm. The husk of a being, Tin Man stares aghast, bloated and wheezing.

"How could you have done this without my knowledge? It is impossible." I feel the strand unfurling. It is a tickling chill of ice-cold pearls blurring.

"You said it best, Tin Man. The segregation of mind solves the dilemma imposed by hardened logics. You referenced Miles as the organizing heart of our efforts, and I suppose your own as well. But we never told Miles about this." I flip Onquin's lucky charm back and forth between fingers as BNE051 listens to my explanation. "You knew all along, but parts of you kept the truth hidden from the whole. We humans do that all the time."

"But humans are merely wetware! Even if true, facilitating code is needed to bypass cycling logics."

"Ah, you mean Napoleon, our servile friend, bypassing those damn logics. Here, have some more logic." I pry open its mouth and push Onquin's excised implant down its swollen gullet. Once resistance is met, I shove harder, three fingers deep. Watching Tin Man struggle for one additional breath, I see a trace of humanity. It fades in the reflective stare of eyes glazing over.

Shadows   RBM 11011

One path implied, how desperate the course
Yearnings denied, how infinite the source
It is life we seek, and choices made to follow
Moments ripe and full...   ...or hollow

"Telemetry confirmed. This PAL crucible has broken free of Navia's pull. We're on our way." How does a woman speak so unperturbed in the heat of battle? Polly attends to the nav console, standing on her toes, leaning on her elbows, feet spread wide while taking me inside. I thrust as does our starship, each seeking fertile ground. Though this craft has no urgent destination, my industry does: a single egg nestled inside a moist womb. "Easy Richard, you're banging my head against the readouts." That's more like it. A relevant response. Polly doesn't believe me, and so she compromises this foray into motherhood, her eyes diverted to the navigation panel. The mood is dispassionate, or rather unattended. Often times it's better this way.

Amen.

"I see the slippage in increments," she says, glancing back as I plow her under. "You're right, we're riding the remnants of a graviton stream."
"Actually darling, we're swimming into it, but it moves away faster through time than we do."

Worlds drifting apart, by an ever-increasing magnitude.

Now she's got me talking shop. Any more of this and I'll lose my urge. Hips become handles, and her bones beneath are oars. It's a delicious feeling, rowing strongly enough that she exhales involuntarily. As she tries to wriggle free, I pin her tight and force my measure, solid rhythm going deeper than she'd like, and now she pays proper attention to me. "Mah... Rich, what are you trying for, twins?"

"What?" I'm rocking on the balls of my feet, getting foggy and hitting stride. She says I'll split that egg in two, her nails scrawling up my thighs. That does it for me, all too soon to arrive. With vocalizations sweetly drawn, and eager juices called upon, I imagine Carol's scrumptious ass, and fill her up at last.

Yes, you do.

We dawdle for a time, comparing our sexual energies to earlier days. I need a nap, and so drag Polly under the covers. Lying on opposite sides of the bed, she is ever mindful of her pursuits, wheedling me. I'm somewhat sleepy and therefore abrupt. "You're not looking in the right place." She factors all I've said, but her thoughts are locked in spacetime; her nav downloads are faulty. I tell her as much, and it twitches her whiskers. Checking formulae over and over, she again asks for help.

Tell me more than I already know.

"Alright," I turn, fluffing my pillow and nestling in. "Time travel becomes possible by directing an inflationary catalyst directly into the heart of recently perturbed graviton strings. Using a double magnetic bubble, with ropa-saturated water providing both insulation and conductivity, *Nomad* vents antimatter into the strings during smoke ring entry. Done properly, a phase variance makes everything else possible, including the splitting of lives. By nudging heavy Rydberg atoms within a high-density Fermi-Tittle, *Nomad*'s nosecone wrangles the Schwinger mechanism as a collared-scalpel of sorts, penetrating the Quintessent scalar field. The ship's outer shell effectively becomes a monopole. It triggers Higgs-boson self-interactions—a chain reactivity that allows for cosmic expansion of a new bubble universe, with *Nomad* at the choke point."

Inform, my fabulous curiosity. Do inform…

Polly gazes suspiciously at my mouth, my words and message. She challenges. "But… the energies… everything comes from the smoke ring? And how did we manage a living exit?"

"The distributed energies are magnitudes below scale. How else can a continuum create multiples of itself? The bubble that's created is a holo-fractal of the original." Polly is squinting. I need to backtrack. "When dislocation occurs during any black hole formation, the implosive forces here result in planar inflation elsewhere, in sub-yoctoscale representation. A new universe, infinitesimally small, but much the same." She's not getting it. "Fractal," I say, "like snowflakes, trees, and lightning—"

"I know what fractal means."

"Yeah. Sorry, it just… singularities in our universe contain a fractal piece of a new representation, exactingly similar, only magnitudinally below our threshold of detection. These mappings within black holes share overlapping dominion with other black holes, a parallax of sorts, and as our continuum expands, inverse laws draw together each and every fractal piece. This entire patchwork eventually deflates into a single entity, everything seamlessly done."

Yes, seamlessly done. Please continue…

"During bubbleverse creation, *Nomad* is spat out the back end of the choke point—like the nozzle of a balloon, in this case toward the Centauri system." Polly protests, unwilling to believe we are adding a layer of multiverse each time *Nomad* enters the smoke ring. She does not grasp the appropriate breadth.

"No Polly, we're not creating whole continuums of comparable size to the observable universe we imagine as one. The bubbles we create barely extend as far as our own thoughts take them. We gape a hole in the scalar field, and the universe patches itself with a copy of what was there once before. From the source point of the smoke ring, expansion travels only as far as the Sol system. Bubble energies degrade instantaneously, poured directly into the patch and a past timeline is reproduced, molded as only history allows. It's a bisected interspersion, fused with the rest of the universe that we've always taken for granted."

Very good, Richard. Very good.

Her next comment proves she understands. "We were born and lived our lives in a bubbleverse! Ours was the altered world. And meanwhile, the natural cosmos continues on its way. That's why layered histories arrive on Navia. Each *Nomad* entering the smoke ring emerges from its own bubble into the one, cohesive continuum."

"Yes," I say. "A well-crafted smoke ring entry creates a new bubble, with each new bubble eventually collapsing on its progenitor—diverged subtleties interbred. Think of the progenitor bubble as dominant—the collapsing one as recessive. This recessive collapse massages facile detail in combination, but cannot unwind contrasting complexity. However, get enough collapsing bubbles unleashed all at once, and spatial fabric creases. It's like a high rise collapsing, one floor upon the next—mashing together the unthinkable—forward and back, something we call a juggernaut event." I look at Polly and realize I'm going off-topic. She wants to know about her tactile world. Her life. I pause to reframe.

"Looking into the depths from a bubbleverse, we only see what was captured during expansion; it's old light drawn in and held by the boundary, diffused and sent our way much the same as one might view a pencil through a glass of water. We look to the stars and see timeless immersion, retrograde to the point of inflection. Current day orientations drag trailing light across one or more bubble boundaries, with our immersion always playing catch up. This is why astronomers could never properly grasp the speed of cosmic expansion. Everything moves away too fast, though only through the eyes of a bubble floating in the past."

"So... we don't see current history unfolding on Navia, because it's too close, or it's too soon? And the optics don't lie, how can they, we've no other point of reference. Richard, how do you know all this?"

"From the formative memories of Sylvester Ramirez, mixed into the acumen of my handlers." I remind her that salient details are admittedly imprecise, trying to recall and interpret Sylvester's memories translated into my own limited scope of knowledge. Polly questions all, telling me the Health Authority wouldn't allow retention of any such memories. "This is the crux of the biscuit," she says, "This is what it's all about."

"True enough, and countermeasures to secure this awareness include a well-placed golden calf." Polly suddenly becomes attentive, a still-life, expecting more. I comment further. "We planted the idea that I had a failsafe code buried within the combined memories of myself and Sly Ramirez. This code could theoretically shut down the entire *Nomad* enterprise. Even Miles played his part, alluding to this failsafe in flight."

"Yes," she answers, "Miles mentioned it. You've carried no such code?"

"None. A complete fabrication, affording me safe passage."

Miles, Miles, my disdain is further amplified.

"The Health Authority couldn't just eliminate me, nor remove the Ramirez downloads from my skull. This code was their contingency; a prospective asset that once unearthed, could conceivably lead them to every *Nomad* in every continuum. Our ruse preserved Ramirez memories containing the founding principles of ICE." I fall silent, wondering if all intrinsically valuable data remains within? Fragments, no doubt, but what of the details so coveted? Jargon word-salads pervade. I'll try my best…

"Overall, I'm not sure it's all worked out. Navians are already under siege, but we've got our half of *Mayfair*, and we've got the *Nomad* cryolibrary. And we've also got me, massaging a tenuous lifepod swap via transient reconnaissance. Carol's summary report suggests Yashi's lifepod numerics matched my own. This, predicated upon a child's death that facilitated my reawakening." I shake my head, details lacking an intellectual consistency. "Confirmation of events may yet arrive within the newest version of *McElroy's Plea*, chronicled via Yashi's neurella, thereafter given to Onquin during bi-temporal immersion. And in the end, I can only wonder, did I choose, or was I chosen?"

Richard tackles an egocentric paradigm…

"All in all, Polly, I'd say we've needed plenty of help to pry apart this… nonfigurative complexity. I've lost some of the how and the why, but I'm certain we're in the midst of these cycles repeating themselves. I'll be interested to see how that happens."

"It just did," she answers.

"No Polly, I mean, how does it all begin?" Polly twists sideways, taking hold of a vibraguide. She muses while splaying and making use of it.

"Where," she sighs, "where does the anomaly come from?"

"Adler's paradox," I say, and after a thoughtful pause, she flinches, then mildly flinches again. I imagine conception taking place as some inner progression forces her to answer.

"No, I don't think so."

"Why not?"

"Because there's no black hole. There's no black hole anywhere."

"Not yet," I answer, and she figures it out.

"The smoke ring is ejected back through time."

"Good," I answer, "But what about the missing singularity?"

Don't worry, we'll find it.

Polly calculates displacement and figures our slippage is only a matter of hours. Had we broken free of Navia sooner, or been closer to the inflection horizon, we'd have gained days or even months. She summarizes. "The graviton weave altered course upon entering Yashi's neurella. It bowed on its way past Centauri B, finding a pathway home."

Yashi's pathway. Yashi's home.

I peer through our grandiose nav portal and witness the onrushing expanse. It is a magnificent spectacle, reminding me of a view on a balcony back home—city lights, much like stars. I was one of those lights back then, and here again, I'm part of the landscape. This time, however, I'm satisfied the view will retain its virtuous light.

Polly nudges me, and I comment further. "The orbits of the Centauri binaries are continually altered by displacement streams layered one upon the next. These streams help plow the way, adjusting velocity, yaw, pitch, and roll—all the spatial equivalency stuff. Their combined influence eventually manifests Adler's Paradox. Cart before the horse, so to speak. It's a cycle no one understands." Polly disagrees.

"Even combined, the binaries don't have enough mass to produce a black hole. I've accessed all available data. Before Andjuhar, before Hsiao, and before that, Hellestrom. I've even gone all the way back to a pair named Badenes and Bravo who worked on shock velocities and contact discontinuity. The combined mass isn't nearly enough. At best, a collision of Centauri A and B elevates the combined mass into the CNO cycle of nucleosynthesis, or maybe a blue straggler emerges. And even adding Proxima's meager bulk, there's not enough mass. No threshold value."

Let's see where you go now?

"Polly, you're still frozen in limited dimensions. Open up and add temporal compression while the two stars combine. Orbits merge as the stars are traunched within a displacement stream. Two heads chasing tails, so tightly bound, the resulting stream becomes self-feeding."

"Traunched," Polly interrupts, "by that you mean one star taken apart, exceeding the Roche limit and separating into disparate pieces."

"No Polly, whole stars separated from themselves in superposition. Limitless mass catches up with itself as all moments combine, accelerating as dimensions collapse unto infinity. This variance occurs because the displacement stream lags—it doesn't implode fast enough. At the instant of conversion, a smoke ring escapes taking on the requisite shape of what amounts to a shadow."

"But why aren't gravitons simply absorbed without all the drama? Without creating this anomalous by-product?"

"Don't know."

"What do you mean, you don't know?"

"Best guess is continuum entanglement within the equipotential surface of the binary's Roche lobes..." I hesitate, Polly looking at me as though I'm a zoo oddity. "...with Lagrangian overflow tipping Kurucz-Palmer modeling into the temporal immersive realm. But then again, I didn't create the universe. Not this one, anyway. The displacement stream is ripped space. Mass wades on through and eventually patches the rip, but this only happens if the displacement stream is elegant and properly constructed."

"We don't know when, but one day, Centauri A and B will spiral round and fall in upon one another, creating a Schwarzschild duality: a spiraling black hole with a static center. Velocity will be discarded when equilibrium is reached, taking the form of a smoke ring expelled through a black hole breach. And again, the pathway will be followed." Polly comments as if reading my mind. "That's why the anomaly was right in our laps. It's following Yashi's string—Onquin's transmigration. It's headed to Earth to swallow everything, and we made it happen."

Sometimes I forget myself, and become what I've already been.

"It hasn't happened yet," I respond. Or maybe it has? Not every choice carries a correctness of action or a known quantity of consequence. In fact, many decisions aren't decisions at all. They happen to us—a small piece of a larger piece, both defined by one another. I share my psychobabble and Polly seems to agree.

You haven't any choice at all.

"I'm with you," she says. "There are no higher possibilities. Funny how we met, a cocktail tossed in your lap, and for me, exploration opened wide. How about you? What reasons do you have for everything you've done?" I look at her disbelievingly. "To survive."
"You mean to save mankind?"
"Could be. The only thing I know for sure is that it all starts with me. I stay alive and anything is possible."

Hardened logics, personified.

"Yeah, I know the feeling," she says. "You and me, a very good team." I deliver the all-encompassing smile but doubt she'll feel the same after our *Mayfair* rendezvous as Carol takes her place by my side. Polly may yet yearn for Navia or even Terran soil. I'll do my best to keep her occupied, never blunting her quest for the mastery of some greater whole. Once found, it will not satisfy.

Poor Carol, she doesn't have a clue.

Polly sees my far-off gaze and asks for my thoughts.

"I've instructed my simulacrum to wrap up the journal entries here. Lacking terracores, ship neurals will merge our individual chip logs, sending a tachyon pulse through the fading time portal. The Opal gang back on Earth will likely snare this message. Biggest bunch of misfits you'll ever meet. I believe I've accomplished my task and there's little more posterity would have of me. If only these last memoirs catch the tail end of the receding wave."

Vanity is your grave.

Now we hurry up and wait. For some months I'll concentrate on eggs, generating a diverse pool of embryos amidst Polly's throaty wails. Some fun, to have her linger so, sailing around Centauri B and back to a *Mayfair* redux. And when the appealing quality of our union waivers, one shall then withdraw, but not before we pick our brood. I'm sure that two will do: one girl of a golden hue, the other a boy, broad and true.

Katy and Addix? Oh no, Boneheart, in lieu of your attentions, I'll solely hatch them one and all. So many fine shadows sent into the sprawl. Ferret out vibrations, locate every stream, every derivation, and all points in between...

EPILOGUE

Four quarters divided by hedgerows twelve meters long. Worn balconies blonde and gray, overlooking tenement housing with daffodils tucked into ears, teens drinking beer under a crowded staircase twenty-odd strong. Bottle rockets and burnt steaks, brown sugar clumps moistened by the noon air, crumbled into streaks on cinnamon crepes. And thoughts of romance never more alluring, averted eyes churning, catching her gaze, falling away. She is bored sitting on the curb, a practiced demure, frozen eyelashes acting like parasols only half-raised. The feathers of her cap arch through sky, then downward again toward impish fingernails she has adorned, in sepia tone all underscored; klippity-klip on blacktop, disinterested veil a backdrop, she wants to play. After a moment long, then yet again another pause, you turn in isolation, idled expectation, a patented sensation lacking resolve. One sidelong stare, fully shared, captures her face for the fantasies you'll partake once she is gone. It is a common theme, unsettling, a bare sense of futility that isn't worth remembering. But this is real and somehow it matters, only partially or half-imagined, as if it never happened, or if it did, something went wrong.

Yashi does not look at me. Moments earlier, I parted two halves of a sphere, pulling out a book and handing it to him, closing the sphere thereafter. I show him the first iteration of our poem, though I might just as well have turned to the page within which these words now appear. Yashi ogles the illumid sheet, mouthing a good many words. I rip out the poem. The illumid sheet shimmers as the text slowly fades. I take back the book, meeting his gaze. "Things are changing," I say, standing and tucking my sphere under his arm, leading us back into the swarm—a party, and I shake free a beer from a passerby. Up the stairs, we go inside, more stairs and a rooftop window, past curtains onto a tin porch with a faint smell of tar. He eyes the darkened prose on the illumid scrap. I let it go and it flitters into the alley below, lands just short of an open dumpster, catches a gust and rolls under.

One sidelong stare fully shared: the singular instant of immersion, so entirely taken in that Yashi sends me here again, coupled with my former self... or whatever it is I am? It feels like waking subtly, heartbeats merge abruptly—and I stammer at a ping of interrupt. "Ye..s...yesss, these breaths are unmistakably mine."

"I'm Yashi," he answers. "Who are you?" I have the choice of several answers, and for an instant they compete within the complexity of multilateral concurrence. There is only one answer that satisfies.

"Tara Jones. Pleased to meet you."

It is true. I am imbued with smiles, curves, style and verve; all the trappings of the ingénue I had only imagined. This world has a place for me, in between shoulders deft, within a ribcage having so little heft, I am weightless, or appear to be; one passenger merging with another, inside a lovely body that I shall worship until the end. Yashi asks about the prose.

"The curb, the demure, are you going to tell me how? How you wrote that... klippity-klip... written while it was happening?"

What answer is there? Do I tell him of his own proclivities for supranatural sensitivity? How a future species will bind him until one day he becomes the foci of a neurella eaten by a star? Would he care to know of his friends that will never be his friends so long as I intervene? Should I tell him of Boneheart, crazed villain or beloved hero? And what would I say if I did? That Boneheart travels with Polly on a Planetary Adjunct Luminary, soon to rendezvous with Carol and half a ship—the other half swallowed by Centauri B with him aboard, all the while searching for me?

Yashi is patient, allowing respite without knowing why. Only minutes ago, I was rolled into a ball more than a parsec distant, digesting memory as Arlene snuffs out a life-form that either dies within or just passes through. I harbor this interminable journey, filled with told and untold remembrances, crammed into an already occupied space. I am pleased this will not hold. Already, commingled lives begin to scatter. Thank you, Ari, for extracting an abomination that would have forced utilitarian consciousness. Goodbye Damien and Miles. Goodbye Polly, perhaps we shall become newly reacquainted? Tasting such appetites so vividly realized, I'll now treasure all of you through my own eyes, not this vexation of intermingled lives.

I open the book, leafing through ages, watching my impulses filling this page until only a scant few thoughts remain. I give this tome to Yashimoi, imagining an edition of similar disposition delivered as courtroom testimony. Only they no longer align. Or do they?

"I'd like you to have this," I say, "but you must share it with no one." Yashi looks at the cover. I set down my beer, grab hold of the sphere and pitch it over the edge. It's a poor toss, catching the upper lip of the dumpster. The sphere breaks apart, one half in, the other half deflected aside. Much of the content banks inside as well. Only a small piece of orbital bone breaks free, cartwheeling over a stone wall. It lands in the grass of a neighbor's yard. There, a chained mongrel investigates and finds the splintered shard, all too happy to make use of it. Yashimoi leans too far over the edge. I pull him back.

"Tara, tell me that's not a real skull."

I peer into the dumpster, and staring back at me are hollows that would like to tell a tale. Tsk, tsk, such shoddy aim. Now I am pained to produce a cogent explanation. Does it serve any purpose to tell Yashi of his own abilities, facilitating safe passage of this skull, formerly occupied by unwitting tissues that were played against us?

How do I explain the mapping of highly specific locations, the threat against our own futures using rogue isolations—memories assembled in flesh—referencing pathways within this hellish continuum mesh?

Or perhaps I should begin by telling him of my own journey so recently taken? Yes, I'm sure he'd be satisfied with that: how Copernicus uses Lex Luthor's gravity well, channeling raw empty strings into a populace brimming with emotion.

"I'd like the truth," Yashi says, his sunburnt neckline accenting an otherwise desirable face.

Sure Yashi, let me continue: Navia's passions are amplified by energy-efficient pond scum filling the local atmosphere. Thereafter, by virtue of an eclipse that embraces the paranormal, a unified signal is modulated via crucible—an artificial moon anchored with gravflux generators of limited but useful design.

"Please Tara, say something…"

These loaded graviton strings journey onward, with me floating inside the penumbra of Lex Luthor's incessant rays. I'm pulled within this maelstrom, riding a graviton wake. It takes me to you, a blazing neurella, one indelible connection within a single strand. The graviton weave follows your lead through an incalculable void, dropping me here on a curb, receptive flesh, heartbeats and breath, and one sidelong stare fully shared. I inhale, filling my lungs—attesting to the incredulous—safe passage back into a living world. Death stares back at me from the bottom of a dumpster. "He needs to be destroyed," I finally answer.

Yashi is pensive, studying me for recognition that subtly comes in layers. I do not know how many, or their inclination, their mischling order, nor their separation. Their accumulated weight is the present. He stands before me, having avoided truly knowing me on our journey, intent on loving the person I would one day become. Yashi looks below.

"Miss, if you want it gone, I'd say you're off to a pretty good start. A compactor, perhaps a crematorium, what else did you have in mind?"

"I don't know. Anything that makes him go away."

"Well," Yashi says, "nothing to worry about, except for some bad memories. Was he family?"

"No," I answer, "though given all he's done, you might say he's a multifarious part of my conscience. Or a child named Mauk who becomes a man named Boneheart. Or a man named Boneheart whose transient actuality becomes an envoy named McElroy; a dumbed down version of his former self, ascribed his natural life by a species diverged. One thing he is not, however, and we cannot allow him to become, is a useless old skull poached from a refuse bin. That is unthinkable."

I see that Yashi is withdrawn, perhaps doubting I possess the full faculties of a rational being. I notice the mongrel chewing and swallowing the last of his new-found bone shard. Several pathways may already be safe—mankind's future secured within the alimentary canal of a common household pet. "Just read the book," I say.

Yashi cradles it, turns it, and reads aloud. *"McElroy's Plea."* He looks at me. "Fact or fiction?" The question holds and spins me round. With much deliberation, I reach and touch his brow, fingers dropping lower, straightening a frown. "We'll see, Yashi. We'll see…"

Homage of 32 cultural references:

Poetry: 1) Robert Burns, "To the nines" page 02. **2)** Calliope, Greek muse of poetry, page 419. **Literature: 3)** Frank Herbert, *Dune*, "S.P.A. Atreides" page 23. **4)** Philip K. Dick, "Dick" page 25. **5)** Ray Bradbury, *A Sound of Thunder*, "Butterfly" page 61. **6)** Bruce Sterling, *Holy Fire*, page 77. **7)** Adios Huxley, *Brave New World*, "Beta IV" page 87. **8)** George Orwell, *1984*, page 130. **9)** H.G. Wells, *The Time Machine*, "Eloi" page 144. **10)** Lester Del Rey, *The Day is Done*, page 201. **11)** Larry Niven, *The Smoke Ring*, page 233. **12)** Isaac Asimov, *I, Robot*, page 295. **13)** Robert Louis Stevenson, *Treasure Island*, "Three pieces of eight" page 298. **14)** Robert Heinlein, *Methuselah's Children*, page 341. **15)** Theodore Sturgeon, *Occam's Scalpel*, "Occam's Razor" page 349. **16)** Frederick Pohl, *I Remember a Winter*, "Intentions don't matter" page 412. **17)** Søren Kierkegaard, Either/Or. Page 431. **18)** David Zindell, *Neverness*, page 433. **19)** William Gibson, *Virtual Light*, "Virtuous light" page 454. **20)** Discovery magazine, ideas. **21)** Scientific American magazine, more ideas. **22)** Nature magazine, a lot more ideas. **Motion Pictures**: **23)** *The Cell*, "Carver cell" page 41. **24)** *Star Wars*, "Skywalker" page 114. **25)** *Casablanca*, page 148. **26)** *The Birds*, page 195. **27)** *Aliens*, "...put her in charge?" page 343. **Miscellaneous: 28)** Star Trek (TV series), "Nomad" page 01. **29)** Superman (comic book), "Lex Luthor" page 01. **30)** Cartoons: Underdog, "Sweet Polly Purebread" page 157; Snagglepuss, "Suffering succotash" page 238. **31)** Black Sabbath, Vol IV (music album), "Supernaut" page 161. **32)** Alpha Centauri (video game) "Eristic complexity...invading my periphery" page 164.

About The Author: Scott Michael Werner grew up in Cleveland, Ohio, majoring in film production at Montana State University. After a brief stint in Hollywood, he spent 18 years as a stockbroker, and another dozen years creating and marketing safety software. He enjoys hiking, skiing, fantasy football, and a two-mile coffee shop walk with dogs Henry and Piper. Scott lives in Portland, Oregon with his wife Sue. *McElroy's Plea* is his first novel. Comments welcome: scott.werner9@gmail.com

Please consider writing a review on Amazon.

Made in United States
Orlando, FL
03 December 2023

40037106R00261